IRISH EYES

THE IRELAND SERIES
BOOK 3

SUE LANGFORD

ISBN: 978-1-998531-00-4

To the spice lovers, the smut lovers and the ones who are really here for the story...we know you want this

"I was just thinking about my own natural way of one-night stands; always wanting to be more attached to something. I'm not very good at detaching myself."
— Sampha

SUE LANGFORD

Chapter 1

Yet another business dinner. Ronan hated them. Hell. He wasn't a fan of the company events, even if he was running it. He would've rather been at home with a beautiful lass doing anything else. The one problem – he had no lass and being home alone was worse. At least he was away at a fancy hotel. He left the party and made his way down to the hotel bar, opting to get a drink away from everyone. He grabbed a seat at the bar and saw her. She was gorgeous and in a dress that could kill. Talking to her was his next feat. He ordered a drink and ordered her another round.

Ronan Kelly, the billionaire, the man. Every girl in town wanted him, and every woman wished she had him. He was almost 6 foot 4, sandy blond hair, blue eyes, muscles and tattoos. From the outside, women thought he was the good guy. The one that they could swoon over. The one that everyone thought was a romantic but was actually the one man that nobody wanted to mess with. The one that had the money, the power and the life that women could only dream of. He'd met his share of girls after him for his money, and he'd never fallen for a single one. Even one-night stands knew better than to try and get anything out of him. The difference was, all it would've taken was one woman who wanted him and not his money. One who valued picnics and small gestures along with the big ones. He hadn't found one yet.

"And you are," the woman asked.

"Ronan. And you," he asked.

"Kathryn Ryan," the woman said.

"Nice to meet you."

"You too. So, tell me about you Ronan."

"Do we really have to," he asked.

"Drink," Kathryn asked. He nodded and they both chatted over martinis. After a few drinks, he asked her if she wanted to come up to his room. "Ronan."

"We can talk away from all of the mess down here," he said.

"Just for a drink," Kathryn said.

"It's quieter," Ronan said as he paid the tab for them and walked over to the elevator with her.

"Maybe we should just sit and talk," Kathryn said.

"We're both single. What's the problem," Ronan asked.

"I don't normally go to hotel rooms with guys I meet."

"It's a suite to be honest. Lots of space to just talk," Ronan said. The minute the elevator door closed, he looked at her. "What," Kathryn asked.

He took a deep breath. "Something I need to do. Don't be mad."

She looked at him and he leaned in and kissed her, pinning her against the wall of the elevator. "Mm," she said as her arms slid around him. The minute the elevator door

2

opened, he slid his hand in hers and walked her to the presidential suite.

"This is…" He leaned her against the door and kissed her again, swiped the key card and walked her straight to the sofa. "Ronan," she said.

"What?"

"I don't normally do this," Kathryn said as he leaned her onto the sofa and slid into her arms, not breaking the kiss for even a second.

"You're so damn sexy," Ronan said as she slid her arms around his neck.

"Ahh," she said as she came up for air. When she slid his jacket off, he knew. Another one-night stand, but this time she was sexy as hell. She undid the buttons of his shirt as he undid the zipper of her skirt.

"Tell me what you want," Ronan asked.

"Take the pants off." He picked her up, wrapped her legs around his hips, sliding the hem of the skirt up and carried her to the bed, leaning her onto it. He needed more room if he was really gonna go through with it. He slid her skirt off and saw the lace panties. She was more than sexy. Way more. He peeled them off, slid her shirt off then went for the lace bra.

"You're overdressed," Kathryn said. He slid his dress pants off and his boxers, revealing the tattoos and the muscles underneath. "Oh," she said as he leaned back into her arms and kissed her.

"Oh what," he asked as he leaned into her arms.

"Condom," she said. He grabbed one from his pants pocket, slid it on and kissed her again. "Ronan," she said as he kissed her neck, and his stubble tickled where the kisses laid. He nibbled at each breast until she was almost moaning.

"Oh, I'm not done yet," he said. He kissed down her torso as her stomach trembled and licked at her wetness. She tasted so good he almost couldn't stop himself when her body orgasmed just from the licking. Two fingers slid inside her and he kept going, pleasuring himself as he dined on her.

"Ronan."

"Yes."

"Come here," she said as he worked his way up her torso and kissed her. He slid deep inside her as her legs wrapped around him. "Oh my god."

"This what you wanted?"

"Ronan." He slid in and out over and over, going deeper and harder until her body throbbed around him. He kept going, flipping her to her stomach and went deeper, harder, faster until she was moaning his name again. He finally found his release and fell onto the bed beside her. "Shit," she said.

"Again," he asked.

"My legs are still shaking," Kathryn said.

4

"Is that a good thing," he teased. She turned to face him and kissed him. "I'll take that as a yes."

"How long are you here for?"

"Just tonight," Ronan said.

"We need to make the most of it then," she said as she kissed him again. He slid the condom off, flushed it and came back into the bedroom.

"Come here," Kathryn said. He leaned into her arms and Kathryn's arms slid around him.

"You sure you're good," Ronan asked. She nodded and kissed him again as she leaned him onto his back. "And what are you up to?"

"My turn," she said as she slid on top of him.

"Condom," he said. When he felt her slide her hand down his length, his breath almost hitched. "You..." She kissed him and her hand slid up and down again and again until he grabbed hold of her hands and slid deep inside her.

"Ronan," she said as her breath hitched and she moaned.

"That what you wanted?"

"Mm. Yes. Hell yes." He kept going in and out over and over until her body was tightening around him, then went deeper and faster. Harder. "Aah. Ronan, come here," she said as he leaned in tight to her and kept going. "Don't stop." He kissed her and her body tightened around him again as she found her release.

"Please," he asked.

"Please what?" He devoured her lips and pulled her legs tight around his ribs and went that much deeper as she moaned his name. He climaxed and kissed her again. "Shit," she said.

"Damn. You sure you're okay," Ronan asked.

"Better than okay," Kathryn replied as she kissed him again.

He kissed her, got up and threw the condom out then came back into the bedroom, seeing her curled up in the bed. "What," Kathryn asked.

"I have to head out. Stay and get some rest."

"Ronan."

"I have to get back down to the business event downstairs."

"Are you coming back up here?"

"Not sure. I'll be in touch."

"Without my phone number?"

"Let's just call it what it was." She grabbed note paper from the bedside table and wrote her phone number down and handed it to him.

"Next time you're here, call me." He nodded and got re-dressed.

"I have to go back down to the business event or I'd stay,"

he said.

"So, you ducked out of your event to meet me?" He nodded. "Tell me that we can do this again."

"We can. I'll call you," Ronan said. She nodded and got up as her sexy naked body walked towards him. "What," he asked.

Kathryn stood on her tiptoes and kissed him. "I mean it," she said.

"I know. We'll talk."

"Okay," Kathryn said as she kissed him again and went into the bathroom. By the time she came out, any trace of him was gone.

Ronan made his way down to the event, went in and found an excuse to leave, heading home. He walked into his flat, grabbed a drink and went and showered. He could get used to having a woman around, especially if she was like the lass he'd just been with. She was smart, sexy, hot and tasted way too good to walk away. He'd done it though. Walked away from the sexiest woman he'd ever met.

Kathryn got home and her legs were still shaky. Whoever Ronan was, she hoped that she'd see him again. The sex was insane. It was better than she'd had in years. The fact that she'd been working her tail off at work and helping with the foundation meant barely any time for a relationship. She was almost 5 foot 9 but always had a thing for the tall guys like Ronan. Even his name was sexy. She was fit and had long legs that attracted everyone, but she'd been single too long. Way too long for her liking. Her short dark hair and crystal blue eyes were enough to turn heads, but every time she met someone, Galway girl was always joked about. Fine. She was from Galway and had the dark hair and blue eyes just like in the song, but she wasn't a tramp by any means. If anything, she'd spent too long looking for the wrong guys and not paying attention to the good ones.

The fact that Kathryn had met the sexy, tattooed, muscular Ronan had her stunned and she wanted more. Part of her wondered if she'd see him again, but the other said not to bother hoping for that phone call. She went back to work the next morning and got pulled into the boss's office.

"What's up," Kathryn asked.

"A position came available that would give you some responsibility with the hospital foundation. Are you interested in it?"

"Depends on what I have to do."

"You'd be doing the admin for the hospital foundation. It also means being at the events that we have like the one this weekend. Would you be interested?"

Kathryn nodded. Her boss showed her the contract for the position with the pay bump and the responsibilities. "This works for me. When would I start?"

"This weekend. There's an event on the books and I need to get you in the meeting with the foundation this week." Kathryn nodded, signed the paperwork and got to work.

She looked through the file that she got and started reading through the papers, getting whatever information that she could before the meeting. "The man who runs the foundation isn't at the meeting. He hasn't been anyway," her boss said.

"I guess I'll meet him at the event then," Kathryn asked. Her boss nodded and she headed back to her office to get the rest of her work done.

"So, what was the meeting about," her friend Moira asked. "They asked me to do admin for the foundation. Now I have double the work."

"Girl, you know that you'll be amazing. You always are. I heard there was a really hot looking man on the foundation board. I can't remember his name, but supposedly, he's single and really sexy," Moira said.

"That's the last thing I need. I can't just run off and date some guy on the foundation. Besides. Most of them are probably married anyway."

"Not this one. He's single. The most eligible bachelor of the group. You'd probably like him," Moira joked.

"I guess we'll see when I go to the event this weekend."

"Do you want me to come as your plus one? I could scope out the hot guys for you," Moira asked.

"I'm good. It's work. A glass of wine, small talk then I can head home."

"You sure?" Kathryn nodded. "Then we're going dress shopping," Moira said as she headed off to get some work done.

Kathryn went through the paperwork for the foundation and looked up the list of people on the board. There were photos of everyone but one person. She looked at the name and shook her head.

"Shit," she said quietly.

"Is there a problem, her boss asked.

"No sir. Just realizing a typo on a form," she said as she shook her head. If it was the same person that she'd met in the bar the night prior, she'd be working for him. She looked at the name again and hoped it wasn't. She took a deep breath and got back to work, finishing up the paperwork for the hospital and the foundation. Before she headed out that day, she asked one simple question to her boss.

"Do we have the name for the head of the foundation so I know," Kathryn asked.

"Mr. Kelly. He's been donating to the hospital for years. They have him as the head of the foundation along with Dr. Pierce. I believe they're friends," her boss said.

"Do we know his first name?"

"Starts with an R."

Kathryn shook her head. "I guess I'll meet him on the

weekend at the event," Kathryn said.

"You will. There's a company card coming for you since you'll need dresses for the events. Sort of a clothing allowance," her boss said.

"How fancy," she asked.

"Cocktail dresses mostly." Kathryn nodded and headed out.

"Sir," Ronan's assistant said.

"Who did they hire to take over admin for the foundation," Ronan asked.

"Her name is Miss Ryan. Kate or something like that sir."

"Kathryn?"

"Yes sir." He shook his head. He'd been part of the hospital foundation for years. He'd been one of the main people to donate to the hospital and planned to be in future, but now his stupid one-night stands were messing up foundation business. He went through the employee list for the foundation and didn't see her name or photo. He could only hope. Why he'd picked her out of anyone else he didn't know.

"When is the holiday event," Ronan asked.

"Saturday. The Hilton."

"Can you get me my suite?"

"Yes sir."

"I also need to see a photo of the new admin for the foundation."

"Yes sir." He leaned back in his desk chair and pulled out the note paper where she'd written her phone number.

"There's no damn way that you are doing this. No way that you're the one," he said to himself staring at the phone number. When his assistant knocked a few minutes later, she handed him the information. One look at the photo and he saw her. The same girl. The same one that he'd seen at the bar the previous weekend. The one that he'd been with in the hotel suite. Of all people, why her? He shook his head and almost called her but stopped himself. That wasn't how things were supposed to go. She wasn't the one with the upper hand. She was the one waiting on him. That's the way he wanted it.

He spent the rest of the week getting work done, avoiding making a phone call to her and staring at her phone number. Finally, the night came. The night of the event that was gonna either be really awkward, or just as insane as that one night with her. Finally, he bit the bullet and made the call. The one he knew he shouldn't. When it went to voicemail, he hung up and ignored it, determined to let it go.

Kathryn saw the missed call from a number she didn't recognize. There was no way she was calling whoever it was back. How someone got her private number she didn't know. There was only one....one person she'd given that number to outside of girlfriends, and there was no way that the one-night stand would call. He'd probably disappeared into the sunset by that time. That is unless he was the guy that she couldn't get any info on for the foundation event. The guy who she guessed really was the guy from the bar that night. She tried her best to brush it off, but she had a feeling. Ronan was the mystery man. If he was, she was stuck working with him whether she liked it or not. She attempted to work until she could fully get her mind off of it, but when her boss came in with a note to the foundation board, she shook her head.

"Shouldn't I be the one that's writing all of these up?"

"Mr. Kelly wrote it himself. He said that he wants everyone there early on Friday. He wants to talk to everyone."

Kathryn shook her head. "I have work. I barely have enough time to change and make it there."

"They need you there by 7. If you have to duck out early, so be it," her boss said. She nodded and took a deep breath. Being face to face with him again wasn't something she was looking forward to. She'd given…. then it hit her. She looked at her cell at that phone number that she didn't recognize.

She returned the call, blocking her phone number. "Ronan Kelly's office," his assistant said.

"It's Kathryn Ryan. I believe he was trying to reach me."

"One moment Miss Ryan." She went and attempted to get a little privacy then heard his voice.

"Miss Ryan."

"So, it is you," she said.

"I called earlier. I wanted to speak with you."

"About what," Kathryn said.

"Since you're part of the hospital foundation now, I thought we should probably talk about what happened the other night."

"The one where you vanished and didn't call? That one?"

"Can we meet up to talk," Ronan asked.

"You realize that I have a job right? I work…"

"I know. I'll meet you at 8. Same bar."

"So that you can take advantage again?"

"So that we can discuss what we're gonna do. I don't want the awkwardness at the event. We're supposed to be a team."

"Team? You do that until my legs are freaking shaking and vanish and you're talking about a team?"

"Talk."

"Fine, but if you…"

"8pm. I'll meet you there."

"As long as we don't end up back in bed."

Kathryn took a deep breath and went home to get ready.

She had 3 hours. Three until she was face to face with him again. She went through the traffic and went home, going through dress after dress, outfit after outfit until she found something that would make him drool if nothing else. When she found just the right dress, she slid it on, did her hair and put on a little perfume.

Then headed over to the bar, getting something quick and easy for dinner and when he walked in, her heart almost jumped. He walked over and ordered a drink and turned to see her having a drink.

"Nice dress," he said walking over to her and sitting down beside her.

"Thanks," Kathryn said.

"So, now that we're actually gonna be working together..."

"And here I thought you were here to apologize for ghosting me after last weekend."

"I didn't realize that we were gonna end up in this predicament."

"So, now I'm a predicament?"

"The fact that I want us back where we were Saturday, yes."

"Meaning what," Kathryn asked as she sipped her drink.

"The sexy dress that would look damn good on the floor of..."

"Weren't we supposed to be discussing what we were

gonna do since we're going to be working together?"

"We were, but I'm thinking we should..."

"Ronan."

"Can we discuss this somewhere else?"

"No."

"Please."

"I know exactly what you're thinking, and the answer is no. You want to talk; we talk like professionals."

"And what did you want to discuss?"

"We can't exactly pretend like we don't know each other."

"And what did you want to do about that lass," Ronan asked.

"Keep things professional. The whole one-night stand thing isn't going beyond that," Kathryn said.

"And why is that? Seems to me you were sated and happy."

"Until you walked out. Used comes to mind."

"I honestly didn't think we would ever see each other again."

"And we did. Now what are you gonna do?"

"Come with me and I'll tell you," he teased.

"Not falling for that again," Kathryn said.

"Talk."

"Yeah, you said…" He kissed her, paid for their tabs and took her hand walking her to the elevator.

"Ronan, we're talking."

He nodded and they headed to his suite. "What," Kathryn said as he looked at her in the elevator. He walked towards her and kissed her as she felt electricity shoot to the tips of her toes. "Ronan, talking. Just talking." He kissed her again as the door opened. He took her hand and walked her down the hallway. "Ronan." He got to his suite, walked in and pulled her into his arms. "Talk."

"After."

"Ronan, I'm not a damn toy for you to play with. Talk or I'm leaving," she said as she sat down on the sofa.

"Tell me what you want then," he said as he sat on the sofa beside her.

"Respect. You not disappearing for days. Talking to me."

"I'm not the relationship type."

"And you think that you're gonna be able to do the one-night stand thing forever do you," Kathryn asked.

"Right now, yes."

"Ronan, you have…"

"What?"

"An ego so over-inflated that I'm surprised you can fit through the dang door."

"Seems like you liked that ego the other night."

"Before I knew who you were you mean."

"And the whole, 'I don't do this kind of thing' stuff," Ronan asked.

"I don't."

"Right."

"Ronan, you are so..."

He looked at her. "What?"

"Frustrating." She went to get up and he grabbed her hand, pulling her onto his lap. "That's your move is it," she asked.

"No. This is," Ronan said as he kissed her and pulled her tight against him. He slid the hem of her dress up her legs and barely let her up for air.

"Stop," she said.

"Why?"

"Because I'm not doing this again. You walking out after you're done."

"I was far from done."

"Meaning what," Kathryn asked. He stood up, picking her up with him and walked into the bedroom.

"Ronan."

"What?"

"I can't work with you if we're..." He kissed her again and undid the dress, seeing the overly sexy lingerie under it.

"If we're what," he asked.

"This," Kathryn replied as her dress slid to the floor.

"This could just be fun."

"Or maybe we don't..."

He kissed her again, picked her up and slid her heels off, and leaned her onto the bed. "Don't what," he asked as he slid his shirt off.

"This," she said as he pulled her legs around his waist.

"You want this right?" She caught herself inadvertently nodding and he leaned into her arms and pulled her legs around his waist.

"Then tell me what you want."

"More," Kathryn said as she covered her mouth. She couldn't even control her lips from saying the words.

"How much more," he asked.

"More than a one-night fling." She felt his hand slide under the barely there thong and start teasing. "Ronan."

"What?"

"I meant it."

"You're getting more alright," he teased as he kissed her again and peeled her sheer lacy thong right off.

"I meant..."

He kissed her again. "I know what you meant." He almost growled as he peeled her lace bra off and nibbled at each breast as his fingers teased and plunged in and out of her until her legs were shaking.

"Aah."

"This more?" She nodded and he went lower, licking and teasing as his fingers kept sliding in and out. One finger, then two, then her legs shook even more.

"Aah. Ronan, stop."

"Which part," he asked as he licked her wetness until he could see her shaking and heard her moaning.

"I get it," she said as her body stiffened around his fingers.

"Good." He undid his belt, slid his dress pants and boxers off and grabbed a condom from his pocket, sliding it on and kept teasing her.

"Ronan."

"Tell me you want me."

"Mm. Yes. Yes, I want you."

"How badly," he asked as he kept licking and nibbling and teasing.

"Yes."

"How badly?"

"Aching for..."

He slid deep inside her and kissed her. "That what you wanted?"

"Aahh," she said moaning.

"I'll take that as a yes," he said as he kissed her and slowly started sliding in and out until she was exploding around him not once, not twice, but three separate times. He kept going, harder than faster than even deeper until he found his release and she was crumbling in his arms.

"Don't move," she said.

"And why is that lass?"

"Don't."

"Sore?"

"More."

"You couldn't..." She kissed him and he shook his head.

"I'm getting up."

"No."

"Kathryn."

"Katie." He kissed her again and slid out of her as her legs tightened around him. "I'm getting up."

"No." He kissed her forehead, got up and came back into the bedroom a minute later naked.

When she looked him up and down her jaw almost dropped. Muscles. Tattoos. Bad boy attitude. All of it just made him sexier. The fact that he'd just slept with her, and she was aching for more blew her mind.

"What," he asked.

"Come here for a minute."

"What happened to I want to talk and nothing else," Ronan asked.

"Come here first."

He sat down on the bed beside her. "Talk."

"And if I said I wanted more than hotel rooms?"

"Meaning what? You want to be my girlfriend or something?"

"I said more than hotel rooms. Honestly, one-night stands are kind of ridiculous. Especially when they happen twice in a dang week."

"You're saying what," he asked.

"A real date. Not a hookup. Can you even do that?"

"Depends on where we're going."

"I have a plus one to the party on Saturday."

"And I don't think anyone would be happy with that situation right now."

"Tomorrow."

"Where?"

"Pick the pub."

He shook his head. "Determined to get more out of this?"

"You need someone at your side. What would the harm..."

"Not this weekend."

"What do you even do," Kathryn asked.

"Meaning?"

"Work."

"You're asking that right now," he asked as he sat naked beside her.

"Well?"

"I run a big corporation. A lot of small businesses and a few bigger ones. Why?"

"Like what," Kathryn asked.

"Two TV stations, film production, markets, clothing stores, electronics. Stuff like that."

"So, you own a big company that owns other ones?"

He nodded. "That's why the life doesn't really give me time for a relationship."

"If you wanted one it would. You'd find that time."

"While I appreciate the psych evaluation, no."

"Then why is this happening again Ronan?"

"I don't know why. You wanted to talk, and the moment is kind of over anyway."

"So, you're just gonna walk out again?"

"Depends on what you want," he asked as his hand slid across her lap.

"Meaning?"

"We're already here. Just tell me what you want."

"Tell me why you don't date."

"Because women are only after me for what they can get. They want my wallet, not me."

"And you think that's what I want."

He nodded. "There's nothing wrong with it, but that doesn't equal being my date for anything."

"You do realize that I could care less about the money, right?"

"Meaning what?"

"Meaning if I had that kind of money, I'd still be working the same job. I'm not looking to be a kept woman Ronan. I'm saying a damn date. Period."

"You want more than that."

"Then ask me what I want," Kathryn said as she slid a leg across his lap.

"Tell me," he said as his hand slid up her perfectly silky leg and he pulled the other around him, pulling her tight to him.

"I don't want the money or any of that. A date for the parties. Someone to curl up with in the bed that I know is too big for one. Someone who makes me forget a shit day and makes it better."

"Boyfriend." She nodded as he went to lean her back into the pillows. "To me, that means a lot more than that."

"Such as," she mewed as he kissed down her neck.

"Being there when I need you. Looking sexy as hell when we do go out. Never saying no in bed. Being my friend and everything else."

"What's so…"

He kissed her. The kiss deepened and her legs wrapped tighter around him as he slid to the bottom of the bed. "What…"

"Protection." He grabbed a condom from his pants and slid it on, pulling his boxers off.

"Tell me why you're so damn convinced that…" He kissed her and leaned into her arms, pulling her legs around his ribs so he could slide deep inside her.

"Aah."

"What," he asked as he kept going.

"Shit," she said as he slid deeper and harder into her over and over. "This what you wanted," Ronan asked as her body tightened around his over and over again.

"Ronan."

"What," he asked as he collapsed into her arms and kissed her.

"I can't even think," Kathryn said.

"Well, is that a bad thing," he teased as he leaned onto his back, and she slid on top of him.

"What," he asked.

"No more hotels."

"Meaning what," Ronan asked as he caught his breath.

"I can't walk away from you any more than you can avoid being with me."

"You can't be serious right now," Ronan said.

"Admit it."

"What makes you think that you're..."

"What," she asked.

"The only one?"

She kissed him and he shook his head. "Because I know you want me. I'm not playing games with you." He leaned her onto her back and shook his head.

"You think it's gonna be just like this?"

"Twice you made me feel like a random hookup. Now, it's not random. Now. This. You can't really think this is random now."

"I needed to get it out of my system."

"Then when you see me Saturday, rethink the whole getting it out of your system. I'm not gonna..."

He kissed her again. "Not gonna what? My suite is booked."

"Have fun sleeping alone," Kathryn said as she went to get up.

"Where are you going?"

"I'm not your girlfriend remember? Not so random hook-up. Isn't that what you called it."

Ronan got up, disposed of the condom and walked back into the bedroom, sliding his boxers back on. "So, you're just gonna take off?"

"Not so random hookup. I'm not doing this Ronan. You barely even know me, and we've already slept together more than once. That isn't bad enough?"

"Then stay." She shook her head. "Tell me what you want."

"More than a damn hotel hookup. That's what. You want to sleep with me without knowing me at all, and don't care if you ever do, fine. Leave it at that Ronan. A stupid hook up at a hotel suite. Twice. That's all it is to you, fine. When you decide to grow up, let me know," Kathryn said as she got re-dressed and walked out. He shook his head. How could she do that? To him of all people. He got re-dressed and headed out, heading home and thought about it all the way home.

To the big house, the empty life, the house where something had always been missing. He got inside and went and poured himself a drink. He needed it. The thing was, she was right. The first time he saw her, something attracted him. The second time, he was almost excited to see her. Fine. His life was alone and lonely, but he didn't need a woman messing up his life. He didn't need to lose everything over a woman he couldn't avoid. She was practically working for him. He wasn't gonna be able to avoid being around her and he knew it. He really had no choice when it came to her. Either avoid her and let her torture him or try to date for the first time in years. Dating was something he hadn't bothered to try. Nobody ever interested him. The fact was, Katie was the exact type he always liked. She had strong opinions, of which he wasn't exactly sure he liked, and she knew exactly what she wanted. He couldn't fault her for it. She was sexy, the short dark hair that he loved on her, the sexy physique. Hell, she was even smart as hell. She had to in order to have got that job doing admin. It wasn't an easy job, especially putting up with him. One way or another, he had to choose. When he finally did, he grabbed his phone and sent a text:

> *Fine. One date. Tomorrow. If it goes well, we'll discuss what's next. No promises that we aren't gonna end up in the hotel suite.*

He pressed send and shook his head. Was he really giving her a damn chance? The forever bachelor actually willing to date someone who wasn't hand-picked by a professional matchmaker. A random hook-up became a damn date? He was wishing he could take the text back, but when his phone buzzed with a reply, he shook his head:

> *Are you picking me up? By the way, no more hotel suites. A date that doesn't end up there. Dinner or something.*

He took a deep breath:

> *Fine. Send me the address. I'll come pick you up and we can go to dinner. We're still going to the party separately. Agreed?*

Kathryn: *Fine. When is the next party after this?*

Ronan: *A few weeks anyway I think. Monthly meeting is sooner.*

Kathryn: *After hours meeting?*

Ronan: *Yes. After we can go out or something*

Kathryn: *Maybe. May get sick of you by then.*

Ronan: *Or you won't be able to walk after.*

Chapter 2

Within a matter of seconds, his phone rang. "Kathryn."

"Katie. Kathryn is too formal."

"What can I do for you?"

"What do you mean I won't be able to walk?"

"You asked for it. You wanted to try and date. The man you know nothing about. You have no idea what I'm into, or what I do. All you know is two times in my hotel suite."

"Meaning?"

"I guess you'll have to learn that for yourself," Ronan said.

"Meaning?"

"You don't know me Katie."

"What are you into then?"

"Things you won't know until I'm ready for you to know."

"Ronan."

"What?"

"Whips?"

"No. Nothing that would intentionally leave a mark."

Hearing that was enough to make Kathryn get goosebumps. It could've meant a million things. She'd seen the movies.

She knew that some people were into things that she had no idea about. Nobody she'd been with was ever like Ronan. He was a lot more intense than the regular guys she'd dated where they thought 3 seconds was enough to turn a woman on. Ronan had her turned on that fast and teased her into multiple orgasms over and over again. He could've taught her exes a few things. Her body was still shaking from being with him.

"Meaning what," Kathryn asked.

"Could just show you instead."

"Ronan, just give me a hint."

"Anyone ever tie your hands?"

"No."

"With handcuffs?"

"No."

"Tie?"

"Ronan, no."

"Anyone ever kept going so long that you couldn't walk?"

"Last weekend."

"That was just the starter. When was the last time you played with…"

"Ronan."

"When?"

"A while ago."

"You may want to take back that whole dating thing. I don't know that you'd be able to handle what I like."

"Then tell me what it is."

"Better idea. I'll give you a hint tomorrow night."

"No more stupid…"

"Fine. Wear a dress."

"Meaning what?"

"A short one."

"And what were you planning on doing?"

"Dinner. Make your legs shake all the way to the car. Bring you back here and keep going until you can't walk."

"We have a party on Saturday."

"Might be able to walk in."

"And what else," she asked almost regretting asking."

"Something that will make you squirm all the way through the party."

"But…"

"But what? Changing your mind?"

"You trying to scare me into changing it?"

"Trying to prove a point. You aren't ready for me."

"Ronan, I don't scare that easily."

"Tying you to the bed with my belt."

"Doesn't scare me."

"Blindfolding you until you beg me to remove it. Not stopping when you beg me to stop."

"Ronan."

"As in saying you've had enough. That you can't take any more."

"You aren't scaring me Ronan. When was the last time you had an actual girlfriend?"

"I don't date."

"How long?"

"Long enough that I know I don't."

"5 years?"

"About that."

"You're just determined to push everything away aren't you," Katie said.

"You really want to do this," he asked.

"Yeah, I do, but you're scared."

"You know that you're scared. Just say it."

"You don't scare me Ronan. I scare you…"

She didn't. At least he'd never admit that she did. He took a deep breath.

"I don't date Katie. I haven't for a damn reason."

"Then it's a test. If we do, you're not as scared of it as I think that you are. If we don't, I know that the tough guy crap is a joke. That you are scared."

"So, you're daring me?"

"I'm saying that you're a scared overgrown…"

"You don't know what you're talking about."

"Then try it."

"Fine. That's what you want, you got it. After the party."

"What did you want to do after…"

"Hotel room. Negotiate," he said.

"Pass."

"Katie."

"No more hotel rooms Ronan. I meant it. I'm not gonna go to a hotel and have you ditch me."

"And if I didn't leave?"

"Then you'd vanish in the middle of the night. I'm not falling for it."

"Tell me what you want then."

"I want the relationship with it Ronan. Dating. All of that."

"And a hotel isn't enough now."

"You and your hotel suites in every damn hotel. I'm not a hooker Ronan. When are you gonna understand that there isn't a woman in the damn world who wants to be used like that."

Ronan shook his head. "Used? Funny. You were the one using me."

"Nice try Ronan. I know better." He took a deep breath. The regular things weren't gonna work on her.

"Fine. We're leaving the party early. Going to your place."

"And then what," she asked.

"You want to know what I'm really about? You get it in your place. Not mine. You really think that you're prepared..."

"Fine. Hotel, but no vanishing without me." He smirked. He'd won round 1. "And Ronan," she said.

"What?"

"Bring your worst. You still aren't gonna scare me off."

"Then you are gonna be at my mercy through the event. Whatever I say goes."

"Meaning?"

"If I make a request, you do it without question."

"Such as?"

"If I tell you to take your panties off, do it. If I say bend over, do it."

"And if I say no?"

"That's not an option. Not tomorrow night anyway."

"And that's how you think things are gonna be?"

"Yes."

"You get your way for one night Ronan. One. After I pass your so-called test, we try dating."

"If."

"Since I know that your little test is completely ridiculous, we're going out Sunday."

"Maybe," Ronan said as he took a deep breath and got turned on thinking about what he was gonna do to her.

"Ronan."

"What," he asked.

"Pub Sunday night."

"Fine, but only if you pass." He hung up with her and went home, ate dinner and was just getting comfortable in his joggers when he thought about her again. He was past being turned on every time he heard her voice let alone saw her. Now was no different.

Fine. The girl had him turned on without even trying. She had since the first time he'd tasted her. If he'd managed what he wanted, she would've been in his bed screaming his name by then. She would've been begging for more and he would've kept going until she was begging him to stop. Hell. She was sexy. She was just the right height, just sexy enough to turn a head or two. Just good enough for him to bring out the dirty girl in her. Hell. He was just getting more turned on. He could just picture what he'd do to her when he got her naked. Teasing her until her body was shaking. Tasting her. Shit. He shook his head and called her back.

"Ronan."

"What are you doing right now?"

"Why?"

"Come over here. Sweater and nothing else."

"Address." He texted it. "Come over here."

"See you in 20."

He pulled on boxers and jeans and went downstairs, trying to calm himself down until she got there. He grabbed condoms from his drawer, putting them on the counter by his bed and went and got himself a drink. She showed up a half hour later and the minute she stepped on his front porch, he opened the door.

"About time you got here."

"And why…" He kissed her, pulled her to him, slammed the door shut and locked it, pinning her against it. He undid her sweater and saw the lingerie under it.

"I said a sweater with nothing under it."

"You don't like it, take it off."

He picked her up, carrying her up the steps to his bedroom. He leaned her onto the bed, took the sweater fully off then kissed her, sliding the lacy bra off and nibbled at each of her breasts until she was moaning.

"Should've left the lingerie at home."

"Then you wouldn't have had all the fun of taking it off," she teased. The minute she went to wrap her arms around him, he tied her hands to the headboard.

"Already," she teased.

"You wanted to know what it'd be like, now you know." He nibbled until she was squirming beneath him.

"Ronan, stop."

"No." He kept going, working his way down her torso. He kissed just below her belly button as he felt her stomach trembling. "Do I make you nervous," he teased.

"Barely a hello even." He peeled the lacy panties off.

"Next time I see you, don't wear them."

"Why?"

"Because I said so."

"And I'm just supposed to do whatever you say?"

"Yes." He kissed her inner thigh, sliding her legs over his shoulders so he had full and complete access to her.

"Ronan."

He licked and her heels slid off. "What?"

"Can you undo..."

"No."

"It's not exactly comfortable."

"It's gonna be more intense when I'm inside you."

"Ronan." His fingers started teasing then sliding inside her deep until he could feel her body throbbing around them.

"And I haven't even started yet," he said as he kicked his jeans off, revealing him completely turned on.

"Ronan." He licked and nibbled and teased her even more until her legs were shaking around him.

"Tell me what you want," he said.

"Hands untied." He shook his head and grabbed the condom from the side table, sliding it on and kicking his boxers to the floor. "Ronan." He slid deep inside her and her body imploded around him.

"You wanted to know, now you'll know," he said.

"Aah."

"The things I have planned to do to you," he teased as he pounded into her over and over again until her body was shaking in his arms. He took his time, but every move got more and more intense.

"Shit."

"Too much," he teased.

"More," Katie said.

"I was hoping you'd say that," Ronan said as he kept going, harder and harder until she came all over again. He looked at her hands and she was holding onto the velvety rope around her hands.

"And you thought you could scare me," she said with a shaky voice as her body exploded around him again and he followed.

"This is just the easy part," he teased.

"So, what, all of that conversation had you all turned on?"

"Figured why not start now," he said as he got up and disposed of the condom then came back into the bedroom.

"Untie me."

He shook his head. "You disobeyed."

"I'm not your pet Ronan. You can't just think you can tell me what to do and I'm gonna do what you ask."

"Yeah, I can. You either do what you're told…"

"Or what?" He shook his head. He kissed her and grabbed the blindfold. "Ronan." He put the blindfold over her eyes and then teased even more.

He nibbled at each breast until he knew she was aching. Until he knew that one more flick of his tongue or nibble of her breast would make her explode. "Still think you can handle it," he teased.

"Aah. Please just take it off." He smirked and his fingers slid inside her, teasing her all over again until he was just as turned on. "Ronan, I can't take anymore."

"And you said that you could handle it."

"Ronan, please." He kept going until her legs were trembling around him.

"Which part do you want? Do you want me to lick you and taste you until you can't move or slide deep inside you all over again and make you come until you can't breathe?"

"Shit."

"One or two."

"Two." He grabbed a condom, sliding it on and slid deep inside her until her breath hitched and her hands were white knuckling the rope.

"More," he asked.

"Harder." He did and kept going until she was trembling in his arms.

"You're mine," he said.

"Aah." He slid deeper into her until her breath hitched again and her heart was pounding through her chest. He kept going with her exploding around him more than once when he finally exploded into her.

"Shit Ronan."

"Can't take anymore," he asked.

"Shit." Her body throbbed around him again and he smirked.

"What," he asked.

"I can't."

"So, you admit it."

"Untie them." He did and she slid the blindfold off too.

"I can't even move."

"So much for that whole I can handle it stuff," he teased.

"You didn't tell me that your intention was making sure I

couldn't walk."

"Still want that date?"

"Yes. You're taking me on a real date," Katie said.

"I don't know if you'll be able to make it to the party let alone a date."

"You're not funny."

She went to get up. "Where are you going?"

"Home."

"Says who?"

"Ronan, it's almost midnight."

"Then we're not done yet."

"I'm done."

"Didn't want to talk," he teased.

"I can barely even move."

"So, we aren't going on the date Sunday."

"We're still going. You can pick..."

"Then you'd need to give me your address."

"I will tomorrow."

"Then meet me in the suite before the party."

She shook her head. "I don't even have a damn dress yet. You can wait and meet me at the…"

"I'll send a car to pick you up."

"Ronan."

"Be ready by 5."

"Dress."

"Then you should probably get one."

"You aren't funny."

"Just remember what I said."

"About what?"

"Not funny."

"Does this mean we're going together," Kathryn asked.

"This means I'm sending a car to pick you up and bring you. So, when you get into the drinks at the party and can barely walk after we're in the hotel suite, you don't have to drive yourself home."

"You're hilarious."

"I dare you to get up and walk back downstairs." She kissed him and slid towards him. He got up.

"Where are you going Ronan?"

"You're heading home."

"Ronan."

"You got your way tonight. Now you can get some sleep and find a dress for tomorrow."

"You do realize that you...."

"What?"

"This is what you're doing right now? I thought we were gonna try and date."

"You have work in the morning and so do I Katie." She got dressed, slid her coat on and walked out without a word.

Ronan had a shower, slid his pajamas on and went to bed. He never did like having someone there with him when he was sleeping. He'd done that intentionally. He had his reasons. Fine. They were because of the one girl he let in. The one girl that managed to tear down the protective wall. It had been years, but he never forgot how it felt when she'd destroyed him with one sentence. All it took was her saying that she was leaving him and that he was a loser to make that wall pop up just that fast all over again. Nobody had managed to get close to him. Nobody since her. He'd never given anyone the chance.

He went to go to sleep and within a half hour, he got a scathing text:

> *I come all the way over there and you seriously treat me like that? I'm not a damn street walker that you can use and throw away Ronan. If this is how you're gonna treat me, forget tomorrow.*

46

He took a deep breath and called her. "What," Kathryn asked.

"Letting you come here was hard enough. I told you that I don't date."

"And? You treated me like a random hookup. We've already done this three damn times Ronan. Three. You can stop trying to scare me away. You don't want anything to do with me, fine. You don't want to date me? Fine. You treat me like that, you don't get another damn chance."

"I don't date."

"Ronan."

"I haven't dated in years alright."

"You treat women like that, and you'll never date again."

"Katie."

"Then say it Ronan. If we're gonna attempt to date, you aren't doing that again. Never."

"I'm sorry."

"Good first step."

"Couldn't have just…"

"I know you wanted to leave it at a hook-up, but I'm not doing it Ronan. You want to be with me, it's gonna take more than a damn hook-up in a random hotel suite."

"Did you at least get home safe?"

"Shaky but yes," Kathryn said with a smirk.

"I did kind of say..."

"You aren't funny. You do realize that you're gonna have to explain why you're so determined to get rid of me after we're together right?"

"I don't sleep with anyone. Nobody."

"What did the last girl do Ronan?"

"Doesn't matter."

"Made you scared to have someone sleep beside you. I'd say it does, or you wouldn't have asked me to leave."

"I still would've. You didn't have clothes for work, and you can't really show up naked."

"And if next time I bring an overnight bag?"

"Guest room."

"What's the problem with sleeping beside you."

"No."

"Why?"

"Because I said no."

"Who pissed you off so badly Ronan?"

"Meaning what?"

"Who broke your heart so badly that you were petrified of anything that was even close to a relationship?"

"Katie."

"Who?"

"Doesn't matter."

"It does if you're that scared to date."

"Are you always this damn pushy?"

"When I know that you're intentionally pushing me as far away as you can even when you said we'd try to date."

"I said date. I didn't say sleeping in my bed. I didn't say going by your rules."

"That worried that you'll like it," she asked.

"That convinced that you couldn't handle sleeping beside me. You'd wake up with me buried deep inside you and not able to move."

"Promises, promises."

"Go ahead and dare me. That hotel suite is for the entire night."

"Then bring an overnight bag. I dare you."

"So convinced Katie."

"You want to wake me up like that, fine."

"And if I woke you up with me between your legs?"

"Just keep teasing Ronan. You're so determined to be all seductive and hot. Do it."

"Fine. Be prepared tomorrow."

"That's all it took," Kathryn asked.

"You really think you can handle it, fine."

Ronan hung up with her and attempted to get some sleep. When he ended up tossing and turning, he looked at his phone and saw a message from Katie:

> *You really are grumpy. Maybe you need a human teddy bear. A naked one.*

He replied back:

> *And maybe you should sleep since you won't be tomorrow.*

Kathryn: *Yeah right. You'll be asleep before I am.*

Ronan: *Care to make a wager on that lass?*

Kathryn: *If I do, I'm at your mercy and you can do whatever you want. If you do, I get to take advantage of you.*

Ronan: *And if I make your legs shake so you can't walk?*

Kathryn: *Then you might win.*

Ronan: *I always win. Sleep.*

Kathryn: *I sent you a link to something.*

A link popped up on his phone to a toy.

Ronan: *And how naughty is this toy?*

He downloaded the app and saw her giving him access to it. When he saw it was active, he took it over and turned it on high.

His phone rang a minute later. "Not what I meant," Kathryn said.

"That would be tomorrow. You touch it, you forfeit."

"Just turn it down." He did and turned the other two parts of the rabbit toy on high.

"Ronan."

"I'm liking this."

"Then don't have them both on high." He found a way to tease and make her explode more than once. "Please stop."

"I'm not done yet," he said.

"Aah."

"Legs shaking yet?"

"Ronan." He bumped the speed up of the part that teased

instead of the part that thrusted into her.

"Shit."

"You sure you wanted to make that bet?"

"Ronan, stop."

He turned up the thrusting part. "Oh my god."

"Shaking yet?"

"Not fair."

"Kinda liking the control."

"I can revoke it."

"Right now, you can't."

"Ronan." He bumped it up even more.

"Aah. Please...turn...ahh." He flipped it all to low with one flick of his thumb.

"You aren't playing fair," she said while he heard her breath racing.

"I'm not done yet," he teased.

"No more." He flipped his thumb and turned it on slowly increasing the intensity then turned the other parts on slowly increasing the speed.

"Shit."

"You aren't gonna last tomorrow."

"And why is that," she said as he could almost hear her heart racing.

"Because it's only round 2."

"I'm turning it off."

"Nope."

"Shit," she said as he cranked it up all over again. "Ronan."

"If it were me, you'd have teeth marks on those breasts. You'd be wet just with that."

"Shit."

"Then I'd be the one making you explode with my tongue."

"Ronan, stop."

"Can't take anymore?"

"Aah...mmm. Please."

"Are you done?"

"Aah. Please stop. No more." He slowly eased it down but kept the thrusting going full blast.

"Ronan." He heard her moaning and then flipped it to off.

"You are seriously not fair."

"You gave me access. Nice toy. Bring it with you."

"Why?"

"And charge it. It'll be going for a while," he teased.

"Shit."

"Re-thinking that bet yet?"

"Yes."

"Good. Sleep." He hung up and realized how turned on he was. He imagined what he could do the next night and pleasured himself until he was finished then cleaned up and went to bed.

He got up the next morning, going for a workout then home to get showered and ready for work. When he saw a message on his phone, he smirked:

So a short dress?

He replied back with a yes and went and had a quick breakfast. He cleaned everything up and saw his housekeeper coming in. "Good morning," Ronan said.

"Good morning. I thought you would've been gone by now," his housekeeper said.

"Just heading out now. I put in a grocery order if you can bring it in for me around 10."

"Yes sir." He headed off to his office, grabbed his coffee and went into his desk, going through emails as he grabbed a seat.

"Sir, there were 5 messages after you left yesterday. They asked me to give you the messages," his assistant said.

"My suite was booked at the foundation event tonight, yes?"

His assistant nodded. "Yes sir. Were you needing anything else in the room for tonight?"

"Champagne."

"I'll get that ready for you. Did you need a dinner reservation?"

"The event is a dinner I believe."

"Did you need anything else?"

"Just the champagne." She nodded and left his office, closing the door behind her. Ronan got work done and spent most of the day going over paperwork and in and out of meetings until it hit 4pm and he got a message:

> *And what do you think?*

On his screen was a photo of Katie in a red dress that was short.

> *Better in black for the event tomorrow. Very sexy.*
> *Almost too much for the business event but get it*
> *anyway.*

When he got a reply back with another black dress that was sexy as hell and a lot better for the event, he smirked:

Perfect. Will look even better on the floor.

When his phone buzzed with a call a minute later, he answered. "Katie."

"So, about that whole hotel suite thing."

"What about it?"

"What if we skipped the hotel?"

"We're staying."

"My place."

"Katie."

"You stay at my place."

"Suite."

"Ronan, what's wrong with being somewhere other than a hotel?"

"Because I have plans."

"Meaning what Ronan?"

"Champagne. Suite."

"Because you want..."

"Either my place or the hotel suite, and the suite is faster."

"Trying to get it overwith?"

"I'll see you at the dinner."

"Ronan." He shut down and hung up.

It was as if every time he got close to having some kind of happiness, he intentionally sabotaged it. He was a dick to every single woman. The only difference this time was that she wasn't letting him shut down. She was breaking down the wall with a wrecking ball and destroying any way for him to put another wall up. She terrified him and turned him on with one swish of her hair. She confronted him with every fear, every worry, every uncomfortable moment that he tried to put between them. It had to be his way or nothing. That's the way it had always been, but now, she was getting her way.

Ronan spent the next hour going over papers, getting what he needed ready for the following week done. He went home, showered, put on his cologne and tux and headed to the hotel in the waiting SUV. He walked in, went into the bar and grabbed a drink and saw Katie sitting at the bar in the backless sexy black dress. Her silky leg was in full view and the stiletto heels were enough to make him almost trip over his feet. "Sir, what can I get you," the bartender asked.

"Double Jameson on the rocks."

Kathryn turned to face him. "About time you got here."

"Nice dress."

"Thanks. Figured you might like it."

He nodded and smirked. "Are you heading in or up," he whispered.

"Since we were supposed to be there 10 minutes ago, I'd say we're going to the dinner. They sat us beside each other," Kathryn said.

"Did you do the other thing I asked?"

"I have my bag at the front desk. About that other thing, I guess you'll find out." He shook his head, and they made their way to the banquet room for the dinner.

"Sir," the doorman said.

"Where are we sitting," Ronan asked.

"Up at the table at the front. Miss Ryan, you're seated beside Mr. Kelly."

"Thank you," Katie said as they headed up to the table. Ronan pulled out her chair for her and Katie smirked. "Ever the gentleman," she said.

"Until later," he replied in a whispered hush.

"Mr. Kelly. Thank you for taking the time to come," the treasurer said.

"You're welcome. Miss Ryan was just getting acquainted with the rest of the members," Ronan said as Katie shook her head.

"You're being formally introduced during the speech after the dinner. We're doing cocktails after," the treasurer said. Ronan nodded and took a deep breath. Cocktails before dinner. A lot of them, then skipping dinner was his norm. She wasn't about to let him drag her off before she was introduced.

"I see you met Mr. Ryan," Moira, the treasurer, said.

"Yes I did. We were both grabbing a drink at the bar," Katie replied.

"Come let me introduce you to the rest of the board." Katie went and chatted with some of the other people, then finally made her way back to her seat up at the front of the room by Ronan.

"Why are you sitting up here," she asked.

"I have to do a damn speech. Kinda hate doing them."

"You didn't tell me."

"Long story. Guess who's introducing you."

Katie smirked. "Then you want to duck out."

"Drinks then upstairs," he whispered. She nodded and the food came out. A quick dinner passed by then Ronan got up to do his speech. As soon as he was finished, everyone got up.

"Great speech handsome," Katie said.

"I hate speeches," he said.

"And here I thought it made you sexier," she teased as he shook his head, and Katie went and started chatting with people. Ronan went and got himself another drink and got her a refill, bringing it over to her and went and wandered and chatted with people. When he found a way to duck out of the entire event, Katie saw him.

She excused herself and walked down to the bar, seeing him ordering a drink. "Ronan."

"You ready to head out?"

"Depends."

"On what?"

"How much longer is the event going?"

"Until midnight at least. Why," Ronan asked.

"Half hour then we head off."

He shook his head. "I've had enough. I rallied up enough donations for one night. Here," he said as he handed her the key to the suite.

"Ronan."

"Either you're coming up with me or I'll meet you up there," he said.

"Come back in for a little while then we'll go." He shook his head.

"I'll meet..."

"Come. Half hour then we'll sneak out."

"Fine, but when you see me sneak out, I'll meet you by the elevators." She smirked and nodded. They went back in and made the rounds. When she saw Ronan sneak out 45 minutes later, she grabbed her purse and followed. She grabbed her bag from the front desk and followed him into the elevator as the door closed behind them.

"And you brought the bag with you."

"Where's yours?"

"My housekeeper dropped it off this afternoon. It's in the suite already."

"You're actually gonna stay the entire night. A whole new..."

He kissed her and pinned her to the wall of the elevator. "You were saying?"

"Whole new thing. Think you can handle one entire night in the same bed?"

"I have an early morning workout."

"If I have to wake up at 4am so you can go do a workout fine. You get up and leave and I'll never..."

"Never what?"

"You're never gonna live it down."

"5am."

"Then wake me up."

"You sure this is what you want?"

"Think that I'm changing my mind," Katie asked.

He nodded. "Something like that."

The elevator door opened, he grabbed her hand and her bag and walked her down the hall, opened the door and the minute they were through it, he had her pinned against the back of the door, locking it. He devoured her lips until she was undoing his shirt. He pulled the jacket off then the tie and the shirt.

"By the way, this dress should be illegal," he said.

"I thought you liked it."

"Next time, I'll show you how much I liked it."

"Meaning what?"

"You wear a dress like this next time, you're gonna beg to come up here."

"And why is that," she asked. He put her bag down, peeled off his shirt, throwing it on the chair and kissed her, sliding his hands down her curves. "What," she teased. She felt the zipper come undone and felt the dress slide down her body to the floor.

"And would you look at that. She even did what I asked," he teased as he picked her up and wrapped her legs around him with the heels still on. He pinned her hands against the door and devoured her lips all over again until she was pawing at him. He walked her to the bed and leaned her onto it.

"Take them off."

"Not yet," he teased.

"Ronan." He kissed from her neck to her breasts then nibbled and teased and licked until she was almost begging. He ignored it and kept going.

He worked his way down her stomach to her inner thigh. "Shit. Ronan."

"What," he asked as he licked at her wetness and kept going until her toes were curling in the heels.

"Ronan, please." He kept teasing until her legs were shaking.

"Please what," he asked as he continued and slid two fingers inside her as her body instantly throbbed around them as he teased, and her breath hitched.

"You were saying."

"Shit. Ronan please stop."

"No."

"Aah."

"Ronan." He just made everything even more intense until he felt her hand on his head.

"Come here," she asked.

"Nope."

"Ronan." He kissed his way back up her torso as his fingers

continued to tease until she exploded around them more than once.

"Still think that you…" She kissed him and he leaned into her arms as he wrapped his arms around her and pulled her legs around his hips.

"Tell me what you want."

"Take the pants off." He grabbed the condoms from his pocket, kicked the dress pants and his boxers to the floor and she tried to flip him onto his back.

"Not happening. You're at my mercy," he teased.

"Says who?"

"Don't make me grab my tie."

"Ronan." He kissed her again and she felt him grab her hands and hold them down.

"What," he teased.

"What about the…"

He kissed her again and slid deep inside her. "Shit."

"What?" She kissed him and he took his time going painstakingly slow and deep and hard.

"Ronan."

He smirked. "What?"

"Why are you teasing?"

"Because I can." He sped up and she tried to free her hands.

"Ronan." He kept going and kissed her until she was moaning into his mouth.

"Aah."

"Something you wanted," he said as he pinned her hands back down and kept going harder and faster until her body exploded around him.

"Shit," she said.

"That's what I thought," he teased.

"Ronan, please."

"Please what? Stop because your legs are shaking?"

"Because I can't breathe."

He kissed her again and her legs slid around his torso. He refused to move one inch, continuing to tease until her body was shaking in his arms.

"About that thing you said wouldn't happen."

"Aah." He kept going until his body gave in. She shook her head and looked at him as he leaned onto his back.

"Fine. You're gonna win about the whole make my legs shake thing."

"And just think. Next time you can wear the short dress and

I can tease you all the way through the dinner."

"Ronan."

"Did you think that it'd be that damn easy?"

"Meaning what," she teased. He got up. "Where are you going?"

He grabbed his tie. "Ronan, be serious."

"I am." He put the rest of the condoms on the bedside table along with the tie.

"What's all of that for?"

"You." She looked at him and he kissed her again then went into the bathroom and cleaned up a little.

"Ronan, seriously though."

"What?"

"Why me?"

"Why did you go to the bar that night?"

"Because I was having a shit day and needed a drink. I'd just broken it off with a guy I'd dated."

"And?"

"I was going for a drink. That's it."

"Then 3 or 4 later, you're in my hotel suite, in my bed."

"You're so damn determined to not have a damn relationship."

"And you're so convinced you can make me want you. You want that happening then you're at my damn mercy."

"Not exactly," Katie said.

"Katie, you're at my mercy like it or not."

"Meaning what?" He walked out of the bathroom, and she saw the tattoos and the tall man in front of her, lording over her.

"Meaning you're doing what I want you to." He grabbed the belt from his dress pants and tied her hands to the bed.

"Ronan."

"This what you want Katie? You want to turn me on until I'm addicted to you?"

"I just want you to stop pushing me out of your life. Fine. You're scared to date someone. Put up whatever wall you want, but it's not gonna change anything. You're an overgrown, tattooed, sexy scaredy cat."

"Might want to rethink that," he said as he grabbed his tie from the bedside table.

"Ronan, don't you dare..." He tied it around her eyes so she couldn't see anything. "Ronan."

"Trust me?"

"No."

"Good. Tell me what you want."

"Come here." He stood beside her and her head turned and slid around his length. "Mm."

"Katie." She took him deeper into her mouth and his hand slid to the wall behind her. "Shit," he said.

"And would you look at who's all turned on now," Kathryn said as she took a breath and kept going. She tried to wriggle a hand free, and he stopped her. He heard her make a noise in protest then pulled away from her. "What are you doing?" He kissed her, grabbing her throat.

"And you think that's gonna get what you want?"

"Ronan."

"Flip over."

"No." He flipped her over, so her backside was in close to him then grabbed a condom and licked and teased until her legs were shaking all over again.

"Ronan."

"What?"

"Still think..." He slid deep inside her and heard her breath hitch before she could finish the sentence.

"Still think what," he asked.

"Aah."

"That's what I thought."

"Ronan."

"What?"

"More." He started a little harder than deeper until her body was throbbing around him.

"Still think that you have the upper hand," he asked.

"Ronan." He kept going until he found his release and she'd climaxed more than once. He untied her hands, and she slid the blindfold off as he slid to his back.

"And," he asked.

"Me of all damn people," she teased as she looked at him.

"Still think that I can't handle more," he asked.

"I never said you couldn't handle this stuff Ronan. I said you couldn't handle a relationship that was more than just this."

"Why," Ronan asked.

"Because you vanish. You're better at disappearing and having a one-night thing instead of this."

"So, the fact that I'm staying tonight?"

"We'll see. You're still disappearing to go to the so-called gym."

"I do a workout every morning at 6. If you're awake, fine. You aren't, I'll wake you up if that's what you want."
"Ronan."

"What?"

"I don't know that I'm gonna be able to move if you do that again."

"My plan was to do that until you pass out from exhaustion."

"Not fair." He smirked and got up, cleaning up and throwing the condom away. He came back in and pulled his boxers on.

"Ronan, seriously though. Who caused the damn wall?"

"What wall," Ronan asked.

"The one you have up so you never have to live through a relationship again."

"Never gonna just let that go are you," he asked.

"Nope."

Chapter 3

"Why," Kathryn asked as she leaned against his shoulder.

"I don't do relationships Katie. Not when I'm being used."

"Like you aren't using me and every other woman you pull this on," Kathryn said as she turned his face so they were eye to eye.

"I don't like being used for my money Katie. I don't want to be used for my connections or my lifestyle. Like that wouldn't make you put up a few walls."

"Did I ever say that I wanted any of that?"

"Who knows."

"Ronan. If that's what I wanted, you would've known. I don't."

"Then what do you want," he asked as she curled the blankets up over her.

"A date that doesn't end in a hotel room or in your bed. Talk. Dance. Have dinner. Date stuff. How long has it been since you had a real date," Kathryn asked as Ronan started getting uncomfortable.

"Long enough to know better," Ronan said.

"A year?" He was silent. "Two? Three?"

"Five."

"Ronan."

"What? I make the decision. I know what I want."

"And just what might that be?"

"Someone who wants more than the money and the cars and the lifestyle."

"I want the real relationship Ronan. The dates. Going to a film. To a concert together. Going on trips for the day. Seeing stuff together. I never asked for anything."

"Yeah, you did."

"Meaning what," Kathryn asked.

"You want what everyone wants Katie. That's why you and I aren't dating."

"Then leave."

"Fine." He grabbed his tie, belt, condoms and tux.

"Tell me one thing that you think I want from you," she asked.

"The money."

"I have my own Ronan."

"You want the travel and the cars and..."

"Day trips to things together. I have my own car. You're the one that sent one to pick me up."

"You don't want to date me Katie. You just don't."

"Get over here."

"Make up your mind."

She got up with shaky legs and walked over to him. "What?"

"Picnic."

"What?"

"Go pick a nice day and have a picnic somewhere."

"You're serious?" The words were enough to knock him on his backside.

"What problem do you have with that now?"

"Picnic?"

"If you'd come to my place, I'd make you dinner. Ronan don't automatically assume that everyone is out to get you. I'm not. I'm just a regular person who happens to end up being in one of the same circles as you are. That's it. I don't care about the cars or the house or the restaurants or whatever."

"Picnic?"

"Why are you stuck on the damn picnic idea?" He kissed her, devouring her lips and deepening the kiss. When he picked her up and leaned her onto the bed, she pushed him away.

"Ronan."

"What?"

"What's going on in that head of yours," she asked. He put the condoms back on the bedside table. He was still stunned that one word could make him think differently. That one simple word could make him second-guess his hesitancy. It could tear a wall down completely with one word.

"That what you really want," he asked.

"It's called dating. Hanging out and watching a movie or a show together. Watching the fire in the fireplace. Having a glass of wine by the fire. It's the easy stuff Ronan." He kissed her, devouring her lips. "What," she asked.

"That's all you want?"

She nodded. "It's called dating Ronan." He kissed her again and her leg slid around his. "You're not disappearing?"

He kissed her again. "Promise me that it won't change."

"What won't? What I want?" He nodded. "Ronan."

"Promise me."

"This mean you're really giving it an actual chance?"

"Answer me."

"I promise." He leaned in and kissed her again and felt her hand on the edge of his boxers.

"Katie."

"What?"

"I know what you're doing."

"Good. Sort of good that you know," she teased.

When he felt her hand on him, making him even more turned on, he shook his head. "That what you're up to?"

She nodded. "Roll over." He shook his head.

"Ronan."

"Give me your hands."

She shook her head. "I get my way first."

He kissed her again and grabbed her hand, pinning it above her head. "Ronan, stop."

"Why?"

"Why can't I touch you?"

"Because this is what I want."

"And what I want?"

"You get what you want."

"And what's that?"

"Me."

"Ronan." He kissed her again and grabbed her other hand.

"Why are you so determined to not let me touch you?"

"Because I want you."

"Ronan."

"What?"

"Tell me."

"Because if you do, I'm not gonna be much good. You already have me turned on lass. What more do you want," he asked.

"To taste you."

He shook his head. "Haven't had enough of that yet?"

"Roll over." "No." She fought him, and he pinned her hands all over again.

"Ronan."

"What," he said.

"Let go."

"No." She got enough strength to flip him to his side then slid on top of him. "And what do you want Katie?"

"I get to enjoy this as much as you do," she teased as she kissed down his torso and her hand slid around him again, sliding up and down as she teased him as much as he'd teased her.

"Katie, please."

When she slid down his torso and took him in her mouth, he shook his head, and his breath hitched. "Please," he said.

"What," Kathryn asked as she took him deeper down her throat.

"Stop."

"Why?"

"Come here." She kept going and the minute she came up for air, he pulled her on top of him and kicked his boxers off. She handed him the condom and he slid it on then pulled her to him, sliding deep inside her. "Shit."

"Come here." She smirked and he flipped her onto her back and slid deep into her again.

"Ronan."

"Mine."

"What?"

"You heard me." She kissed him and he kept going, making it more and more intense until her body was almost trembling in his arms.

"More," he asked almost out of breath.

"Yes," she said almost moaning. He kept going harder, faster until she exploded around him, and he followed, collapsing into her arms as she turned to face him.

"Shit."

"What," Kathryn asked.

"Had to, didn't you?"

"Had to what?"

"I swear, you start..."

"The part that I wanted you?"

"Not playing fair with that."

"I bet. You do realize that if I did..."

He kissed her. "It's not a every time thing."

She kissed him. "And if it was?"

He shook his head, and her legs wrapped around him. "I have..."

She kissed him again and slid her arms around his neck. "What are you up to?"

"Making you stay right where you are. Feels good."

"Which part?"

"The part where you're still inside me." He shook his head and kissed her.

"I'm getting up." She shook her head. He slid out of her and got up, throwing the condom away.

"Had to," she teased. He walked back into the bedroom and laid down on the bed beside her, pulling up the covers so they were both covered.

"Tired," Ronan asked as he pulled her to him and her leg tangled around his.

"A little. What about you? Still determined to get out of here and disappear?"

"You want me to stay, I'll stay."

"Ronan."

He kissed her. "What?"

"You're seriously gonna stay?"

He nodded. "You asked."

She shook her head and kissed him. "You sure you want to stay?"

"Honestly, I'd rather sleep in my own bed, but if you're here then I'll stay."

"And if I got up and disappeared like you did the other night?"

"You'd be tied to the bed first."

"What's with you and that stuff anyway," Katie asked.

"What stuff?"

"Tying my hands, holding my hands so I can't move them.

That stuff."

"Something that I like."

"And what other things are you liking that would scare women off?"

"You really want the answer to that question?"

"Yes."

"Then we should probably go to my place."

"Ronan."

"You want to know, then you'll know."

"Just tell me."

"That's the simple, easy stuff."

"Meaning what?"

"A lot more where that came from. Real handcuffs, rope."

"Ronan."

"Toys."

"Meaning?"

"Enough to make you come in a million ways until you beg me to stop."

"Yeah. Not so sure I want to come near your house now."

"It's not like I'm gonna tie you up in a sex dungeon."

"Ronan."

"I'm not," he joked.

"Instead you'll tie me to your bed."

"With handcuffs."

"You see what I mean now."

"Or a tie." Kathryn went to get up and he pulled her back to him.

"What," he asked.

"Tell me why you don't like..."

He kissed her. "What?"

"Are you that worried about me doing something you don't like or something?"

"I like to be the one in control. That's all," he said.

"Then start enjoying just being with someone. You can't go tying my damn hands every time."

He kissed her. "And if I keep tying your hands intentionally so you can't move?"

"Then I get to tie your hands."

"Right."

"Did you think that I was kidding?"

"You're not going to Katie. I can snap anything you try to wrap around my wrists." She went to slide into his lap again and he pinned her to the bed.

"What," she asked.

"It's gonna be too much fun," he teased.

"What is?"

"You really want to do the whole dating thing, fine. So you know, I'm the one in control. That's how I want it. Can you handle that?"

"So long as I get to take that control once in a while."

He shook his head and kissed her. "Nope."

"And you're still here."

"I could leave if you want," he teased.

"And if I said that I wanted us to get out of here?"

"Then we're going to my place."

"Mine," she replied.

"Get dressed and we'll go to my place."

"Ronan."

"Get dressed." They got changed and headed downstairs, bags in hand. He checked out and walked outside to see the SUV waiting for him. "Come," he said as he took her bag and handed it to the driver. He slid in beside her and the driver put the bags in the back and took them to his place.

"And why can we not go to my place," Kathryn asked.

"Because I have plans for you."

"It's almost 1am."

"And I have plans."

"Sleep?"

"In bed."

"Ronan." They got to his place, and he took her hand, grabbing the bags and walked her inside.

"What," he asked seeing the look on her face.

"Tell me what you're up to." He locked up, took her hand and walked her upstairs to his bedroom.

"Ronan, we could just..." He kissed her, throwing the bags to the floor and pulling her to him. "What," she asked.

He leaned her onto the bed and kissed her. He kissed up her neck, undid the dress and slid it to the floor.

"Ronan."

He kissed her and wrapped her leg around his hip. She went to undo his shirt and he stopped her.

"What?" He kissed her again and then trailed the kisses down her chest.

"Ronan." He nibbled at each breast until her breath hitched. "Ronan, stop." He undid his shirt and threw it into the laundry.

"What," he asked as he kissed lower, making his way down to her inner thigh.

"Shit."

"What's wrong?"

"I can't even move." He had clamped her legs in just the right spot so he had complete control of what was about to happen. He let go of her legs and kissed her inner thigh.

"You alright," he asked.

"More."

"Which part?"

"Mm." He kept going, teasing with his tongue and his fingers until her body was almost trembling.

When he got up, she reached for him. "Stay there. Back in a minute."

"And what are you going to look for," she asked. When he came back in, she felt something wrap around her hands. "What's that?"

"Silk scarf." When he came around in front of her, he was naked.

"Ronan."

"What?"

"Come here." He kissed her and pulled her legs around him, leaning into her arms.

"Why are you so damn determined to not let me touch you?"

"Because if you do, I'll explode in a matter of damn seconds and I fully intend on taunting you all damn night."

"And just how are you intending on doing that?"

He slid deep inside her as her breath hitched. "Aah."

"That's how." He kissed her and kept going harder, faster, more and more intense until her body exploded around him not once, but twice. When he couldn't hold back, he crashed into her and didn't stop kissing her until he felt her arms slide around him.

"How did…"

"I don't know." When he looked, the scarf was on the floor without a knot in it.

"Now you're intentionally playing games."

"We don't exactly need…"

He kissed her. "Sneaky."

"I need sleep."

"And here I thought you wanted to keep going all night."

"And if I said I wanted sleep instead?"

"Then you're staying tomorrow for a while."

"Meaning I'm sleeping in your shirt."

"Meaning you're staying in here."

"No guest room?"

He kissed her again. "Sleep." He kissed her, getting up and disposing of the condom. When he came back in, she was out cold in his bed. He went and curled up in bed with her and nodded off not long later.

When Ronan woke up the next morning, Katie was curled up in his arms. He went to try and get up and she smirked.

"Gym."

"Not leaving."

"Get some sleep," he replied as he managed to get up. He changed into workout gear and went downstairs into his gym and started his workout. Maybe an hour later, he looked up after stretching out and she was standing in the doorway watching. He pumped weights, did pull ups, and walked towards her.

"And how long were you standing there," Ronan asked toweling off the sweat from his face and his chest.

"Long enough. I was wondering where you went."

"You don't remember me telling you?"

"Not really." He shook his head, kissed her and took her hand.

"What," she asked as he leaned her against the door. All it took was one kiss and her legs were wrapped around him.

"You sure you can," he teased.

"What are you saying," Katie asked.

"After last night."

She smirked. "I'm good I think," she teased as he walked back to the bedroom and pinned her onto the bed.

"Don't move them."

"Why," she asked.

"Don't make me get the tie out."

"Ronan." He slid his shirt off of her and kissed his way up her torso.

"What," he asked as he threw the shirt to the floor.

"What are you up to?"

"Making last night look like child's play." He pulled her legs around him and reached for a condom from the drawer.

"Ronan," she said.

"What?"

"What if I wanted to do something."

"Depends on what it is."

"No holding my hands down."

He kissed her. "And if I did it anyway?"

"Ronan."

"Fine, but no taunting me." She nodded. He kissed her again, devouring her lips until her toes were curling.

"Ronan." He kissed down her neck again, teasing just enough to make her want him.

"What," he asked as his kisses got harder when he reached her breasts again, nibbling and licking at the peaks.

"You can't keep teasing," she teased.

"I can and I will," he replied as he kissed her side.

"Ronan, come here." He shook his head and kissed her hip, then her inner thigh, then the other.

"Mm." He licked and teased her wetness until her legs were trembling.

"Don't move them," he said.

"I can't help it." He kept teasing then his fingers slid deep inside her and teased even more.

"Shit Ronan. Aah."

"Much better. That's what I was hoping for," he teased.

"Ronan." He kissed his way up her torso again and felt her legs wrap around him.

"I want..." He kissed her and slid deep inside her with one thrust. One deep, intense and throbbing thrust that had her body almost throbbing around him instantly.

He kept going, harder, faster and more intense until her nails were digging into his back. It almost felt too good. The feeling like she was digging deep into his back was almost addictive. A feeling he hadn't felt ever. He kept going even when her body was throbbing around him. Even when he didn't think he could hold back he held on until his body couldn't hold back anymore. She exploded around him and he came harder than he ever had. He looked at her as his heart rate calmed and his breathing calmed. She kissed him again and he held her in his arms.

"My legs are still shaking," she said with a smirk.

"Good. I kinda planned on that," he teased.

She kissed him and somehow, it's like the darkness lifted. The wall dissipated. He deepened the kiss, and he finally let her up for air as he leaned onto his back with her curling up beside him.

"You okay," Kathryn asked.

"I should probably get you home."

"Ronan."

"Breakfast first, then I'll take you home."

"That determined to get rid of me?"

"If I don't, I'm not gonna be getting out of bed," he teased.

"Is that a promise," Katie asked. He kissed her and got up.

"If I don't, you're not gonna be walking for a month lass. Second, I need food."

She smirked and got up, grabbed his shirt and slid it on. "Katie."

"You're complaining now?" He kissed her, pulled on joggers and a t-shirt and walked downstairs with her two steps behind him.

"I should probably charge my phone."

"Already charged it on the charging pad with mine."

"You grabbed it out of my purse?"

"It was in your coat pocket. I grabbed it when I woke up. I wanted to make sure it was charged up."

"Thank you."

"You're welcome. Now, omelet or scrambled," Ronan asked as he walked into the kitchen and grabbed the fry pan.

"Ronan."

"Yes lass."

"What are we doing now?"

"Meaning what," he asked as he made them both scrambled eggs, toast and bacon.

"Are we gonna try dating?"

"Is that what you want?"

"Yeah. I don't want this to just be messing around whenever we bump into each other. I want to have real dates. What do you want?"

"I want what happened last night."

"And?"

"Dating. Going on day trips, road trips, spending time together."

"And if we cool it on the stuff from last night?"

He shook his head. "No."

"Ronan, we can't spend the time we have together in bed and nothing else."

"But last night was fun, was it not," he asked.

"More than fun. I'm not exactly sure that I can really walk," she joked.

"And that little thing you did last night was part of the reason."

"See, if you hadn't got up and gone to do a workout, I could've done that to wake you up."

"And all I'm gonna say to that is this. Don't start something you can't finish. You can barely walk right now, and that could be a whole lot worse lass."

"Meaning what?"

"Meaning if you start that, you better be prepared to finish it my way."

"That could be interesting."

"Katie."

"What? All I said was that it could be interesting."

"Eat first," he said. He finished cooking breakfast and plated it for them both. "Coffee," he asked. She nodded and he handed her a mug of coffee and sat down with her, inhaling breakfast.

"Hungry," Kathryn asked.

"A bit. Honestly, I could probably eat mine and yours and still be hungry."

"Ronan."

"What?"

"If you're still hungry, then have something else." He kissed her.

"I'm still hungry alright," he teased.

"You are so bad." He got up, kissed her and went and

cleaned up. She finished her breakfast and brought the dishes over to him, sitting up on the countertop.

"I have a question," Ronan said.

"Go ahead and ask," Kathryn said.

"Why are you so determined to date me?"

"Because I haven't been with anyone like you. You're irresistible to me and I don't even know why. It's like I see you at the bar and I'm just attracted. I can't explain it."

"And you're sure it isn't the money or anything."

"I wouldn't have known about it if you hadn't told me."

"And it wasn't because of the fancy hotel suite?"

"I didn't notice anything other than you naked."

"Oh really," he said as he wrapped her legs around his hips.

"Yeah."

He kissed her and picked her up off the counter. "Where are we going?"

"Bed."

"Ronan."

"What?"

"Shower."

He shook his head.

"Why?"

"Because I want every inch of you shaking in bed."

"Ronan." He kissed her and within minutes, her back was against the soft sheets on the bed and the shirt she had on was gone and in a pile on the floor with his joggers and shirt. He kissed her again and she wouldn't let him move.

"What," Ronan asked.

"No more teasing."

He kissed her and went to get up. "Where are you going?"
"Have to grab something."

She shook her head, and he smirked. "Don't you dare pull out what I think you are," she teased.

He slid a blindfold over her eyes. "Ronan."

"Two options. Either you keep your hands where I put them, or I make sure you don't move."

"You aren't playing fair." He kissed her and slid the leather cuffs around her wrists and wrapped the end around the bed post. "Ronan." He smirked, then came back around to her, sliding between her legs and kissing his way from her toes up.

"You were saying," he teased.

"Not fair Ronan."

"Which part?" He got to the apex of her thighs and the teasing ramped up until her toes were curling and her body was almost trembling. He licked and kissed and teased until she was begging him to stop.

"Ronan, please." He kept going, letting his fingers slide deep inside her and tease even more.

"More," he teased.

"I can't," she said as he kissed her hip and slowly worked his way up to her lips, kissing and nibbling at each breast.

"Shit."

"Getting too intense for you," he teased.

"Getting there. I need you. Kiss me."

He kissed her breast again, nibbling as her legs wrapped around him.

"Now."

He smirked and kissed her, devouring her lips and deepening the kiss until he could tell she was trying to wriggle out of the restraints.

"Can't wiggle out of those, lass."

"Ronan." He kissed her again. "Take the blindfold off."

He grabbed a condom, sliding it on then slid deep inside her and her legs curled around his ribs. "It's staying on," Ronan said as he went deeper and harder. He kept going until she was moaning and begging. "It's staying," Ronan said.

"I want to see Ronan." He kissed her again and started going faster and harder until he slid her legs over his shoulders and kept going as she exploded not once, not twice, but three times when he gave in and found his release. He slid the blindfold off and kissed her.

"Hands," she asked. He smirked and undid them, then slid her hands out. "I'm still shaking," she said.

"Good. See what I mean about it being more intense?"

"I see that I'm lucky if I can walk back into my place," Kathryn said.

He kissed her. "And that wasn't even intense."

"Understatement."

"It only gets better," Ronan said as he leaned onto his back and she curled up in his arms, wrapping her leg around his.

"And what else do you have planned," she mewed as she kissed his neck.

"There's so many things I haven't showed you," he teased with a grin that could've made her toes curl all over again.

"Ronan."

"What?"

"I want more than just this. You know that right?"

He nodded. "I was gonna take you to dinner tonight if you can still walk."

"And where were we going?"

"Leave it at you need a dress. I'll pick you up around 6."

"Ronan, I don't have clothes like you think."

"Then we take you shopping."

She shook her head. "You don't have to do that."

"Pick out something nice to wear. It's not super dressy."

She nodded and he kissed her. "I can take you dress shopping if you're worried."

"I don't want you taking me dress shopping. I can pay for my own stuff."

"Never said you couldn't. I said I wanted to see all of this in a sexy dress."

She kissed him. "I probably should go home though." He kissed her again and picked her up. "What are you doing?"

"Shower." He sat her on the counter, got rid of the condom and flipped the hot water on.

He stepped in and reached out a hand for her. Kathryn slid from the counter and with shaky legs, walked over and stepped into the oversized shower with him. He kissed her and she watched the water trail down his body, passed the sexy tattoos, passed the muscles. She was almost drooling.

"You do realize that you have to be under the water to shower right," he teased.

"Just admiring the sexy man in front of me," Kathryn said.

"Good."

"Meaning what," she asked.

"Meaning go ahead and look."

"And if I said I wanted to do something more?"

"I'd say that you're lucky you could even walk. Don't start something you aren't gonna finish."

"And who said I wouldn't finish it?"

"Then you're gonna need some extra strength protection. I can't promise there isn't gonna be a moment where I don't pin you to the wall and screw you until you collapse."

"That could be arranged."

"Then tell me when it is." She kissed him and he shook his head.

"Don't you start."

"And if I said I was finishing what I started," she asked.

He shook his head again and washed his hair then rinsed it out and felt her hand on him. "Don't."

"Why?"

"Because you can't handle being pinned and fucked against the shower wall right now, and you will be if you start it."

"Like this," she said as she did it anyway.

"Hand off." She shook her head. He removed her hand and he pulled her under the water, washing her hair for her.

"Ronan."

"Shower. That can wait until later."

He rinsed off and stepped out, leaving her to shower on her own. He went and started getting ready when he felt her arms slide around his waist.

"What are you doing," he asked.

"Nothing."

"Yeah you are. I'm taking you home Katie. Remember?"

"Or."

He shook his head and turned to face her. "I have work to do lass. While I love that you're all determined to spend all day in bed, I have to get you home so I can clean up my work desk."

"Then I get to ask you something first."

"Which would be what?"

"I don't share. I don't want to know that you're sleeping with someone else."

"Staking your claim are you?"

She nodded. "And what do you think about that?"

"I think it's a little soon to be saying that."

"If we aren't gonna use anything then I'm not gonna share you."

"And now you understand why I was perfectly fine with..."

"Ronan."

"We can discuss it later."

"Not if I'm gonna be on something to prevent me from getting pregnant."

"And if I was with someone else?"

"Ronan."

"I didn't say it was happening now. I'm just saying if." She walked out of the bathroom and went and grabbed her bag, sliding on her blue jeans and a sweater. "Are you talking," Ronan asked.

"You want to go screw someone else, go ahead," Kathryn said.

"I said if."

"Then go ahead. Don't worry about dinner," she said.

"You're seriously saying this right now."

"I said I wasn't if you were with someone else. Period. I'm not running that chance."

"And if I agreed to nobody else?"

"Doesn't matter. I get it Ronan. Just keep..."

"I have no plans to be with anyone Katie. Nobody."

"Then we're using them until..."

"If it's just you?"

"Then we can talk about it when you decide to not..."

"Katie."

"What?"

"I didn't say I was gonna be with a bunch of other people. I said if."

"If there's anyone else, you don't have me."

"Katie."

"No. I'm not gonna play second to a random hookup Ronan. You want to keep playing around, fine. Call it what it was." She went to put her dress in her bag, and he stopped her. "What?"

"I never said I was going to. I asked what would happen if."

"Then make a choice Ronan. You either grow up and have a big boy relationship without screwing every woman that passes you, or you keep meeting random strangers and running away. You choose," Kathryn said as she brushed him off and put her things into her bag, grabbing her phone.

"You're not leaving."

"Looks like I am Ronan." She went to walk downstairs, and he grabbed her hand and walked her back into the bedroom.

"What?"

He kissed her. "Never said there would be someone else. I asked the question."

"Meaning what Ronan? What do you actually..."

He kissed her again, devouring her lips. "I have what I want right here."

"Then it's me and only me."

Ronan nodded and kissed her. "I'm good with that lass."

"Is it bad that right now I don't believe you?"

"So now I have to prove it?"

She looked at him. "If you want to..."

He kissed her again, picked her up and sat her on the bed. "I said if, not when. Hypothetical."

"And?"

"We're going out tonight Katie. End of discussion."

"You aren't gonna run off and pull another one-night thing?"

"I already have a date tonight."

"And?"

"Rather go out with her. Lot less work, plus it's a really good restaurant."

"You aren't funny," Katie said.

"I wasn't kidding."

"A lot less work?"

"Because I already pulled my best moves."

"Funny. Very..."

He kissed her and got dressed. "Come." He took her hand, walked her downstairs and took her home himself.

"Ronan, I mean it. If you want to go be with..."

"Stop."

"Why?"

"If I wanted to be with someone else right now, you wouldn't have been back at my place. Leave it at that. I'm not walking off and screwing someone else right now. I'm literally going into my office to get the last of my paperwork together."

"Then I'm not going to all the damn trouble of getting

something so we don't have to..."

"Katie, while I appreciate the whole stubborn woman thing you have going on, I'm not gonna mess around. If I'm giving this an actual try it's only you and me."

"You sure that's what you want Ronan?"

"Unless you changed your mind," he replied.

"I just don't want you to walk off and mess around with someone else while we're doing whatever this is," she said.

"You said you wanted to try and date. We are," Ronan said.

"This mean that people are gonna know what we're doing?"

"About us dating, possibly. We don't have another event for a month or so. Next one is a company cocktail party. Appetizers instead of actual food. Don't ask me why..."

"Ronan."

"What?"

"Turn left."

He drove her the rest of the way home and got her door for her. "I'll come get you at 6."

"You don't have to."

"Just put on something nice. I'll be back."

"Ronan."

He kissed her. "Go. Rest for a bit. Might need another overnight bag."

"Maybe," she replied. He shook his head and hopped back in the car and headed into the office.

He walked in and swore he saw a light on down the hall. He went into his office and sat down to go through the papers. "Who knew that you came in on the weekends," one of the assistants said as she knocked on his office door.

"Just getting paperwork together. What are you doing here on a weekend?"

"Liam needed a file from his office. I told him I'd get it and bring it in," she said as Ronan heard the door close.

"You can leave my door open," Ronan said. He wasn't even paying attention.

"Want some company," the assistant asked as he looked up and saw the white lace bra with the open blouse.

"If you value your job, you'll get dressed and leave before I have HR remove you from the employee list," Ronan said.

"Nobody has to know Mr. Kelly."

"Someone is gonna know. You might want to clean out your desk."

"You can't just fire me," she said.

"Camera in my office. Yeah I can."

"And I can say you told me to."

"And a microphone."

"You can't fire me."

"I can and I have." Ronan sent a message to HR with the situation and got a reply within a few minutes that they'd draw up the papers.

Ronan got back to work and had everything done that he needed to finish and headed home. When he got there, the house was back to being pristine. He went and changed into something dressier than jeans and a tee, and his phone buzzed. When he saw Katie's name, he got a smirk.

"Katie."

"You sure you really want me there tonight?"

"Bring the lingerie."

"Is that a yes?"

"I'll be there in an hour."

"Ronan."

"What?"

"Are you sure?"

"Sure that you won't be getting much sleep."

"I'll take that as a yes."

"Katie."

"What?"

"Don't start making demands. You get me all to yourself, but I'm telling you that you're gonna wish you didn't."

"And why is that Ronan? Because you have people lined up at your door to get into your bed?"

"Because it's not gonna be that easy."

"Meaning what," Katie asked.

"We can discuss it tonight."

"Then I'm leaving the lingerie at home."

"Probably won't need it anyway unless you wanted to see it on the floor."

"Ronan."

"I'll see you in an hour."

"Okay." They hung up and he finished getting ready, then ordered over some groceries they'd need for the morning.

He got everything put away, grabbed flowers and showed up to pick her up. When he rang the doorbell, she answered within seconds and saw the flowers. "And what are these for," Kathryn asked.

"We're going on a date."

"And?"

"When I go on a date, from what I remember, it involves flowers."

"Thank you, but you don't need to Ronan."

"Put the flowers in water and we'll go."

"Are you gonna tell me where we're going," Kathryn asked.

"Chef's table at a steak place. Are you ready," he asked. She handed him her bag and she locked up. He took her hand, got her door for her and put the bag in the back, then slid into the driver's seat and headed to the restaurant.

"Ronan."

"What?"

"You sure that you want to date me? Really?"

"You're the one that spent all that time trying to convince me that dating wouldn't be that bad. That you were worth it. That I had to at least try. What's wrong with dating now?"

"You sure you want to date me?"

"One minute you say you want to, the next you're asking why you. Which is it Katie?"

"You sure?"

"I'm willing to try this one-woman man thing. Up to you if you want to try it out."

"You think you can handle it?"

"Since I already turned another woman down today, yeah."

"Meaning what?"

"Long story. I told her I had a lass."

He got out of the car, got her door and walked her into the restaurant. "Mr. Kelly. Right this way," the host said walking them to the private table in the back.

"And we're all the way back here why," she asked.

"Best table in the house." She slid into the booth, and he slid in the other side. "What do you think," he asked.

"While I love that you're going way overboard, we could've gone to a pub."

"And this was a nice night out. A good dinner without hearing the Rocky Road to Dublin mid-meal. We can talk."

"So, now you wanna talk too. Wow. Big step up," she teased.

"Drink," the waitress asked.

"Double Jameson. Katie," he asked.

"White wine," she replied. The waitress headed off and got their drinks.

"I have dinner handled Ellie. Thank you," the chef said.

"What are you surprising me with," Ronan asked.

"I thought we'd start off with that fancy steak you liked last time you were here. The fancy roasties, the grilled vegetables then a fancy something for dessert. What do you think," the chef asked looking at Katie.

"Sounds amazing," she replied. The chef made their dinner, as the waitress brought over a salad for them both.

"And," Ronan asked.

"Nice restaurant you picked," she teased.

"Still mad?"

"I wasn't mad."

"You said you wanted all of this."

"Picnic Ronan."

"Comes with restaurants when it's too late for a park dinner."

"Ronan."

He looked at her. "You got all dressed up for me."

"Sweater dress Ronan. It's nothing fancy."

"Didn't have to be fancy. You look great."

They got through the salad then the chef came over with dinner. It was perfect. It was so good that Kathryn was almost silent all the way through it. "This is so good," she said.

"And now you know why we're here," Ronan said.

"Only the best restaurants?"

"Just the ones that are really good lass. Making a good impression," he teased.

She shook her head. "Ronan."

"What? You said you wanted a real date. This is one."

"Trying a little too hard."

"Just making sure that you know I wanted you here with me. You needed a good dinner," he teased.

She shook her head. "Thank you."

"Not done yet. He's making something for dessert."

"Still," Kathryn said as the waitress brought her a refill and brought Ronan a bottle of water.

"Not having another," she asked.

"Someone has to drive us to the house," he teased. She smirked and kissed him. "What," he asked.

"Would he be offended if we skipped dessert?"

She felt his hand on her leg. "Yeah. He's been raving about it," Ronan said as his hand slid up her inner thigh.

"Ronan."

"Happy we have a tablecloth."

"What are you doing?"

"Teasing," he whispered as he licked the edge of her ear.

"Ronan." When his finger reached the edge of her lace panties, she shook her head.

"All warm."

"And you're teasing intentionally."

"That's not even teasing yet."

"Ronan." His finger slid under the warm lace and teased just enough. "Stop."

"Nope."

"Mm."

"Did you sleep?" She shook her head. "You're gonna wish you did," he said as he smirked.

"And why is that?"

"Because you aren't getting any sleep tonight." The crazy part is that with one finger teasing her, he had her legs already shaking and was still acting like he wasn't doing a thing. He could say what he'd said with a completely straight face like it was part of conversation.

He ramped up the teasing and two fingers started teasing her as she gripped his arm. "Ronan, cut it out."

"Too much," he asked.

"Unless you want me in your lap right now, yes."

"So, if I did this," he said as one finger slid inside her.

"Not fair."

"Finish your wine," he teased.

"I would if you'd stop."

"Stop what?" She took a sip of her wine and she grabbed his arm.

"Please just stop. Not here." He kept going until he felt her body throbbing around that finger then slid in a second and kept going.

"Don't even think about it," Ronan whispered.

"Almost done that dessert," the chef said.

"Thank you," Ronan said as he felt her body give in.

"It's gonna be an adventure tonight," he whispered.

"Meaning what?"

"That's gonna be how it starts, and it's gonna keep going until you beg me to stop," he whispered.

"You do realize we're in a public place right," she whispered. He nodded and slid his hand away from her, licking his fingers. Hell. Even that was turning her on. "You are so bad," she teased quietly so nobody would hear. When the chef brought over the crème Brule, Ronan got a smile ear to ear.

"Tell me you didn't do the fancy one," Ronan asked. "One for each of you, and yes I did the one you liked. Special occasion. I finally got you to come down to the restaurant and you brought an actual date. Glad to see you took my advice," the chef said.

"Funny. Thank you for this tonight though."

"Most welcome my friend." The chef headed off and Ronan smirked.

"What is it," she asked.

"Taste it." She cracked the top and tasted the peach dessert and Kathryn got a smirk.

"This is amazing." The chef smirked and continued with work as they finished the dessert. As soon as they were done, and Kathryn finished her wine, Ronan paid, and they headed out.

Chapter 4

"You do realize you don't have to take me to the most expensive restaurant in town right?"

He smirked and got her door for her. "Yes, I did lass. This is my style. Get used to it," Ronan said.

"Still, we could've just had a picnic by the fireplace," Kathryn said.

"Next time."

"Why does that make me think that you're just saying that?"

"Because I like going out for dinner. Especially there," Ronan said.

"And why especially there," Kathryn asked.

"Because nobody interrupts us. We have a table away from everyone."

"That's the only reason?"

"That plus I got to tease you all the way through dinner."

"That wasn't exactly fair Ronan."

"Says who? You wore a sweater dress that was short lass. You were asking for that teasing."

"Really. You think so do you," she teased as he smirked and pulled down his street.

"If you knew what I wanted to do, you might not want to be at the house with me tonight."

"Ronan."

"Do me one favor."

"Anything."

"Take your heels off."

"Why?" He said nothing and pulled into the driveway and into the garage then parked the car and locked the doors, closing the garage door behind them and flipping the car off. "What," she asked. He reached across the console and undid her seatbelt.

"Did you bring any," he asked. When she pulled a condom from her purse, he grabbed it and pulled her onto his lap, sliding the seat back.

"What are you doing," Katie asked. He kissed her, devouring her lips and slid her coat off, almost tying her hands with it. "Ronan." His hand slid up her leg and went back to teasing her like he had at the restaurant. "You're not being fair," she said as he intensified it even more.

"Not being fair would be us having sex in the car." When she felt him fidgeting with something, she shook her head. "Here." He nodded and ripped the condom package open, sliding it on and into her within a matter of a minute or two. "Shit."

"What," he asked.

"I can't move my legs."

"That's how I like it," he whispered as he devoured her lips again and she slid up and down and almost moaned as he teased.

"Ronan."

"What?"

"I can't move."

"Then turn around." She shook her head. He turned her to face the window and slid deep inside her, guiding her up and down hard so she was almost moaning with every thrust.

"Harder," he teased. She kept going and he thrusted harder and deeper into her.

"Shit Ronan."

"Keep going." His fingers continued to tease as she kept going until he could feel her almost shaking in his arms.

"Keep going."

"Aah." He guided her deeper onto him until her body was throbbing around him and he couldn't hold back.

"Katie."

"Aah. Shit Ronan." He exploded into her as her body tightened around him.

"I don't know that I can move right now."

"Grab your heels,"

"Ronan."

"More when we get inside."

"I can't move." He kissed her neck.

"Up." She got up and he handed Kathryn her heels.

"My bag."

"I'll get it." He unlocked the door, and she got up. Ronan slid the condom off, throwing it into the garbage, then grabbed her bag, locked up the car and walked her inside.

"How am I supposed to walk after that," she teased.

"And you really thought that would be all that happens tonight," he teased.

"Meaning what," she asked.

"That's just the warmup."

"Meaning?"

"Couldn't wait."

"Ronan, you do realize that we can't..."

"And just this morning you were all worried I was gonna cheat."

"I want to know you aren't."

"If I was, I already would've. I'm giving this a chance like you said. Just know that if I want something, I find a way to get it even if it means doing it in the car with you on top."

"And it's gonna be more than just having sex on every damn surface of this house, right?"

"Figured we could start with the bedroom," he teased.

"We sorta already did." He kissed her, pulling her into his arms and devouring her lips until her arms were wrapped around him.

"My bag," she said. He handed it to her and picked her up, wrapping her legs around him and walked her upstairs. "Ronan." He kissed her again and sat her on the counter in the closet.

"What are you doing?" He peeled the wet, lace panties off and threw them into the laundry. "Ronan."

"What?" She shook her head.

"So, now I'm just your sex toy all night?"

"You did say something about every surface. Figured we'd start in here."

"Meaning what," she asked as he slid her dress off and he saw the sheer lace bra. He shook his head. "What Ronan?"

"Determined to tease until you get more."

She nodded. "Part of my plan."

"And what else happens in this mischievous plan of yours?"

"The counter, the floor, the bed, bathroom counter..."

He kissed her and shook his head, leaving the room. "What are you doing," she asked as he walked in a minute later.]

"Making sure that I have what we need."

"Meaning?" He slid out of the dress pants, and she saw how turned on he was all over again.

"Making sure I have..." She kissed him and went to slide off the counter.

"Where are you going," he asked.

"To take care of something."

"I have a better solution," he teased as he grabbed a tie, and tied her hands to the drawer.

"Ronan."

"What?"

"Untie them."

"Nope." He kissed his way up her inner thigh and her legs were almost shaking.

"Why," she asked.

"Because right now, you are at my mercy. Just the way I

want it."

"Meaning what?" He kissed her, deepening the kiss until she was covered in goosebumps. "Mm."

"Better," he teased as he slid the bra off and slid it over her hands.

"Determined not to let me move."

He nodded and kissed down her neck, nibbling at each breast until she was moaning. "Ronan, please."

"Tell me what you want."

"I need you inside me." His fingers teased instead, sliding deep inside her.

"Aah."

"More," he asked.

She nodded and he kept going, taunting even more. "Tell me."

"Mm. I can't." He licked her wetness and nibbled at her and her toes curled.

"All hot and wet and ready," he teased.

"You're teasing." His fingers kept going until he could feel her getting close. He kept going until she climaxed then slid deep inside her and kept going until she'd climaxed two more times. Hard, deep, fast then slow, then fast again until she was more than just moaning his name. She was almost screaming it. Finally, he found his release and crashed into her as he untied her hands. She almost crumbled. "I can't move," she said.

"Yeah you can lass. Your legs are just sore."

"And what else are you planning," she teased. He picked her up and carried her to the bed, leaning her onto it.

"I have a lot of plans for you tonight."

"Ronan."

"What," he asked as he walked into the bathroom and cleaned up, then came back into the bedroom and slid on a fresh pair of boxers.

"No movie night?"

"Fire in the fireplace and curl up by the fire?"

She nodded. "Rest. I'll be back in a minute."

"One thing first," she said.

"What?"

"Can you put my phone on the charger," she asked.

"I have one downstairs. You can put it on there." She motioned for him to come closer. "What?" She kissed him. It wasn't just a peck. It was a flat out, sexy, I want you kind of kiss.

"Fire coming up," he said as he broke the kiss and walked

downstairs. He hadn't gone that all out for a lass in years. He couldn't remember when he'd last had a curl up by the fire kind of night. He hadn't even made a fire for himself since he'd first moved in.

He got the fire going, grabbed the blankets from the sofa and heard her making her way down the steps. When she walked into the tv room, she was in his dress shirt he'd worn to dinner.

"Had to," he teased.

"Why," she asked as she slid onto his lap.

"Did you at…" She handed him a handful of condoms.

"These?"

He shook his head. "Phone charger is in the kitchen. Do you want a drink?"

"Wine?" He kissed her and Kathryn sat down and curled up by the fire, warming up her hands. He came back in a minute or two later, handing her a glass of wine, putting his drink on the table and grabbing her cell, putting it on the kitchen charger. He came back in and saw her curled up with her wine in hand. "You wanted a fire, you get a fire," he said.

"If I said I wanted us to talk more," she asked.

"Ask what you want to Katie."

"What do you do other than the foundation stuff?"

"I run a business that runs a lot of smaller businesses."

"Like the Irish Mr. Grey?"

"Something like that. I'm real though."

"I get that. I'm just saying. How many companies?"

"Publishing, music, construction, a grocery chain and a line of planes."

"Ronan."

"Trucking company is the one I had to get the paperwork finished to get."

"You really went to work?"

He nodded. "Did you think I was lying?"

"I didn't think you'd voluntarily go into work on a Saturday."

"The boss works harder than the employees. Without him there would be nothing."

"Still. You deserve a weekend to relax Ronan."

He kissed her. "I am."

"You..." He kissed her again, devouring her lips. "You have no idea do you," she asked.

"Meaning?"

"This. Dinner. The car. Upstairs. Now."

"What about it?"

"What would you do if I said that I wanted to go without it."

"Without what?"

"Them."

"I don't want you getting…"

"Ronan."

"What?"

"Promise me that you aren't gonna be with someone else."

"I won't if you won't."

"I mean it Ronan."

"I have no intention of being with anyone other than you."

"Then we…"

He kissed her. "You're on the pill?"

"Something like that. I can't unless I go off it." He pulled her on top of him.

"You're not lying to me." She shook her head. "I'm the only one." She nodded. He kissed her and kicked his boxers off. "Promise me." She nodded again and within a matter of seconds, was flat on her back on the blankets without his shirt on.

"What," she asked.

"Promise me that you aren't doing this to get..."

"Ronan, I'm not about to lie to you about that."

"Promise me."

She nodded. He kissed her again and he grabbed the shirt, tying her hands with the sleeve. "What are you doing?" He kissed her then trailed the kisses down her neck, her shoulder, her breasts. He nibbled and licked and kissed until her breath hitched and her toes were curling. "Ronan." He kissed down her stomach then licked at her inner thigh. "Aah."

"Tell me what you want," he said.

"You." He licked at her until her legs started shaking. "I'm gonna keep going until you say it," he teased as his fingers started teasing even more then slid inside her.

"Ronan."

"Say it." He kept licking and nibbling and kissing until her toes were curling.

"Mm. I want you inside me."

"I am."

"Ronan."

"Say it."

"I want you to fuck me right now."

"Katie."

"Ronan, please." He kept teasing until her body was trying to hold back.

"Let go," he teased.

"I want you."

"Oh, I know you do," he teased as he flipped her onto her stomach and slid deep inside her.

It almost felt too good. She was warm and wet and at his mercy. That's what he wanted. He took his time, sliding in and out until she was close again, then flipped her to her back and started the slow torture all over again.

"Ronan, please." He kissed her and pinned her hands to the floor. He slowly sped up until her body wrapped tight around him.

"Aah. Ronan, harder." He went harder and she crumbled around him.

"More," he asked. She kissed him and he kept going, harder and faster until she climaxed all over again. "That what you wanted," he asked as his body gave in and he found his release.

"Now, yes," she teased. He kissed her again and devoured her lips until their heart rates calmed.

"Untie them." He did and kissed her.

"This what you had in mind," he asked.

"This too," she said with a silly smirk.

He devoured her lips. "You wanted to curl up in the blankets by the fire?"

"And be with you."

"Well, what do you want now?"

"Talk."

"About what," he asked.

"Why did you start with the hospital foundation if you don't own anything to do with it?"

"There's a wing dedicated to me."

"From donating?" He nodded.

"Children's wing?"

"Yeah. When I started, they were raising money for it, and my donation put them over. It funded the wing. They asked if I wanted to be part of the foundation, so I did."

"But why?"

"Charity work. Something I can actually do. I never said that I liked being at the stupid dinners and the meetings but being at the fundraisers I could do."

"And how many times did you pick someone up and pull the hotel trick?"

"Enough. Nobody ever made it past one time."

"Until me."

He nodded. "And part of that was because I knew we were working together."

"And if we hadn't been working together?"

"You mean since I was thinking about you all week?"

"And here I thought you would've just found someone else to taunt and tie up."

"Saving that for you. Which reminds me."

"What," she asked. He pulled his boxers on and walked upstairs.

"Ronan."

He walked into the other guestroom he intentionally kept locked and grabbed the rope and the leather handcuffs from the cupboard and walked out, locking it behind him, and walked back downstairs. When he came back into the room, she was curled up in the blankets, leaning against the sofa. "And what did you have to disappear to get," she asked.

"Really want to know?"

"Part of me says no," she replied.

"Give me your hands."

She shook her head. "Wine first," she teased. He handed Kathryn her glass of wine and took a gulp of his drink.

"Ronan."

"What?"

"Why do you have a thing about tying my hands?"

"Because I know what you're capable of."

"Meaning what," she asked as she slid onto his lap.

"Don't start," he said.

She kissed him. "I'm not starting anything. I was looking for the TV remote."

"Behind you on the mantel."

She got up and grabbed it, handing it to him. "Pick a movie."

"And what are you doing," he asked.

"Waiting and having my wine." "

And if I said I'd rather watch you?"

She kissed him. "Movie." He went through his movie list and flipped on one he knew she probably hadn't seen. When he looked down, she had him in her mouth and was licking and turning him on.

"That's why," he said.

"Why what," Katie asked as her hand slid up and down and then she took him in her mouth again.

"Don't start if you aren't gonna finish," he said.

"Mm."

"Katie."

"What," she asked as she kept going, taking him deeper in her mouth.

"Shit." The look on her face said it all. She got her control. She got what she wanted.

"Come here," he said as she shook her head and kept going. "Now."

"What," she asked as he pulled her on top of him and slid deep inside her.

"Aah."

"That's why I tie those hands up. So you don't start something," he teased.

He thrusted into her again and pinned her to the floor. He wasn't taking his time this time. Now, it was urgent. It was hard and deep and almost forceful until she was moaning and crying out at the same time. When he came, it was like he'd been hit with lightning. He kept going until he was completely spent and she was crumbling around him all over again.

"Shit Ronan."

"You have to stop trying to taunt me," he teased.

"Trying? I succeeded," she joked.

He kissed her again. "No more."

"In the morning, I'll think about it."

"Then I may have to tie you to the bed before you go to sleep."

"You wouldn't."

"I have a much better way to wake you up," he teased.

"Oh really," she said.

"Besides that, you're lucky if you can even move in the morning."

"Promises, promises," Katie said. He kissed her and she shook her head. "What's with the rope?"

"I have plans." She peeked up at the tv screen and looked at him.

"What are we watching?"

"It's called Mine," he said.

She looked up at the screen, the male character taking control and making love to the female character, but it was intense. It was like they were on that screen. They were having sex in a car with her on top of him, ignoring the outside world.

"Ronan."

"What?"

"This where you're getting all your ideas from?"

"My publishing company published the book."

She shook her head. "Turn it off."

"Why?"

"Because I swear I thought you were gonna turn on something else."

"Oh, I have other options. The story of O, Fifty shades, Sex/Life. I have..." She kissed him and grabbed the remote, turning the tv off as the room went dark except for the glow of the fire. "What," he teased.

"Not watching something that's giving you dirty ideas."

"Kinda watched them all already lass."

"Oh, I bet you have Mr. Dirty Mind. You don't need any more ideas," she joked. He kissed her and grabbed his drink, taking another gulp.

"Oh I have a bunch more ideas," he teased as she got up.

"Where are you going?"

"Back in a minute," she said as she went upstairs for a quick minute. When she came back downstairs, she was still naked and he was back in his boxers.

"Everything okay," he asked.

She nodded. "I put my phone on the upstairs charger."

He shook his head, and she curled up in the blanket beside him. "Better movie?"

"Something not sex related. Girl movie," she said.

"And if I said the Notebook?"

"Here's a better idea. No movie."

"But, you said you wanted…"

"Fireplace works. We're never gonna make it through it anyway."

He kissed her. "And what else did you want to do lass?"

"Which airline did you buy?"

"Atlantic airways."

"What?"

"What's the problem?"

"That's the airline I took when I went to New York with my friends."

"I bought it a few years ago. Things changed when I got it."

"I know. It went from a semi decent flight to fancy," she said.

"A friend of mine owns a tour company and he started recommending it to his customers coming from over there."

"I still can't believe that."

"Can't believe what?"

"Who would've thought that going into that hotel bar meant this."

"Believe it or not, that's where my friend met his wife."

"What tour company?"

"Emerald Isle I think it's called." She shook her head.

"Ronan, are you being serious?"

He nodded. "They're a pretty good tour company," he said.

"They met in the same hotel we met in?"

He nodded. She shook her head. "What?"

"My friend said they made a great espresso martini." He smirked.

"Go figure," he joked.

"What?"

"His wife had her first Irish espresso martini there."

"Of course that's what would happen. The one with the Baileys in it?" He nodded. "It is really good," Katie said.

"And who would've guessed that's where I'd meet the one lass who convinced me to date."

"I did," she asked.

"Nobody has ever been in here with me," he replied as he kissed her shoulder.

"Ronan."

"What?"

"Why were you so dang convinced that you weren't the dating type?"

She took another sip of her wine, and he shook his head. "What?"

"Why were you so convinced?"

"Because I don't like putting effort into something that's pointless."

"And I'm not," she asked.

"Too stubborn to be pointless."

"Me? Stubborn?"

"Yeah. You. You're stubborn and determined as hell. I like it."

"And what else do you like," she teased as she slid onto his lap.

"You know what you want and are so damn determined to get it. Even if it means talking me into a date that I wasn't sure I wanted."

"And how do you feel about that date now?" He kissed her, devouring her lips and her hands slid around his neck.

"I think I'll do this again with you. Only you."

"Oh really," she teased. He peeled his boxers off.

"What," she asked.

"Come here." She kissed him and he pulled her on top of him as he slid deep into her.

"Ronan."

"What?"

"I um..."

He kissed her. "What," he teased as he slid her up and down and he pulled her close to him and kept going.

"Shit."

"That's what I thought you'd say," he teased as he flipped her onto her back and pinned her to the floor.

"Ronan."

"What?"

He kept going, harder. "Shit."

"That what you wanted?"

"Ronan, I can't."

"Can't what?"

"Aah." He kept going until he felt her body throbbing around him all over again.

"I'm not done with you."

"Ronan." He kept going until he couldn't stop himself and exploded into her.

"I don't think that I can even move."

"Good. Part of my sinister plan," he teased.

"Ronan."

"What?"

"Not that I don't love the messing around, but we have more than just mind-blowing sex right?"

"Working on it. We have all day tomorrow to do other stuff," he said as he rolled to his side.

"And what other stuff are we talking about," Kathryn asked.

"Walk. Go hang out and see a few sights we take for granted living here."

"Like where," she asked.

"Saint Patrick's cathedral."

She smirked. "The one-night guy goes to church on a Sunday?"

"Thought you'd want to go and see it."

"Ronan."

"Or we just go out for breakfast."

"You actually go to church?"

"Not every Sunday, but I go."

"Ronan."

"Disappear on Saturday nights. Head home and get up early. Sound familiar?"

"Gym?"

"And when I'm home on my own, I go to church."

She shook her head. "And you were all concerned that we weren't gonna get to know each other."

"Why am I thinking that there's so much more to you than just that," Katie asked.

"Because, short of us in bed, you don't know anything I don't want to tell about me."

"Meaning I should start asking more questions and making you answer them."

"This is really what you want to do? Spend all night talking instead of something a lot more fun than that?"

"Since I can barely move, yes."

"And here you thought you could keep up with me," he teased.

"Meaning what," she asked.

"You know exactly what I'm saying Katie."

He got up, cleaned up and slid his boxers on, then sat down on the sofa and finished his drink.

"I have another question."

Ronan rolled his eyes and put his glass down. "Go ahead," he said.

"Do you really think that messing around is enough in a relationship?"

"It's part of it. The only part that ever really worked for me," Ronan said as she looked up at him.

"And why was that? Because you knew that you could get that right no matter what?"

"Is that a compliment I hear?"

"I'll just say that it is. It was the first night we were together."

"That good?"

She nodded with a smirk, wrapped herself in the blanket and got up, curling up on the sofa with him. "That is a compliment."

"I didn't know that you gave compliments about that."

She shook her head. "You're ridiculous. You do know that right? How many one-night stands have you had?"

"Not about to start that conversation and see you running for the door. Leave it at enough that I wasn't alone much. I like my alone time at home, but I also like company when I can have it."

"And how many ladies have you invited here?"

"Three. You being one of them. The other two were years ago."

"And how long ago," she asked as he wrapped his arm around her and snuggled her to him.

"4 or 5 years ago for one. Four years ago for the other. Neither of them really worked."

"Why," she asked as she looked up at him.

"Because they found out about the money and the perks of dating me and made a mess of everything. They each lasted less than a month."

"Ronan."

"What?"

"What's the longest relationship you've had?"

"6 years."

"And what happened?"

"She slept with one of my friends."

"Seriously," she asked.

"Yeah. Wasn't a happy memory."

"So that's why you were so determined to have the time alone."

"Used to it. Nobody uses me for anything. That's what I wanted," he replied.

"And that's why you're so worried that I'm with you for bad reasons."

He kissed her. "No more talking," he said, determined to get onto a better topic.

"And why is that," Katie asked.

"Because I don't want to talk anymore."

"Ronan." He pulled her into his lap, and she straddled him.

"What do you want," she asked. He kissed her with a kiss that gave her goosebumps all over. His arms slid around her, and his hands rested on her backside.

"I'll give you a hint."

"Ronan." He kissed her again, devouring her lips and deepening the kiss until he felt her arms slide around his neck.

"And here I thought it was get to know each other time."

"It is. Getting to know every inch of you first though."

"You're in a mood tonight." He nodded and kissed her again until he knew her toes were curling. One hand slid between her legs. "Ronan."

"What?" He kissed her and the teasing started all over again.

"Shit."

"All turned on and nothin to do about it," he joked as he teased until her legs were shaking.

"Ronan, stop."

"Why?"

"Shit," she said as two fingers slid deep inside her and teased even more.

"More?"

She kissed him. "You're intentionally taunting me."

"Distractions are one of those things I'm just good at," he joked as he kissed her neck, and her hand slid down his torso.

"Don't start that."

"You started it already."

"Katie, don't."

"If you start, I'm starting." He grabbed her hand and pinned her hands behind her back with one hand and ramped up the teasing with the other.

"Shit. Ronan."

"What?"

"Aah."

"That's what I thought you were gonna say," he said as he kissed her, and he felt her almost trembling in his arms.

"Bed or sofa," he teased.

"Shit."

Her body exploded around his fingers, and he shook his head.

"Aah."

"I'll take that as the sofa."

He pinned her on the sofa and kissed from her mouth all the way to the apex of her thighs and teased even more.

"Ronan, stop."

"Why?"

"Because I can't take anymore."

"Tell me what you want."

"You." He kissed back up her body, nibbling and licking at

each breast until she was moaning, then kicked his boxers off.

"Tell me you want it." She kissed him and wrapped her legs around him.

"Now."

"Say the words."

"I want you. All of you."

He slid deep inside her and her breath hitched. "This what you want?" She nodded and went to wrap her arms around him when she felt him holding her hands down.

"Ronan."

"Don't move."

"Let go." He slid deeper into her over and over again, going harder and harder until she was almost moaning his name all over again.

"Say it," he said.

"Aah. Please Ronan."

"Please what," he asked.

"I want you." She moaned again and he felt her body tighten around him.

"More," he asked.

"Mm." He kissed her again and exploded into her before he

could even slow himself down.

"Aah." She held on tighter to him and wriggled her hands free. "Shit. I can't keep doing this," she teased.

"Good thing the fire is almost out then. We can get some sleep."

"Ronan."

"What?"

"I don't know that I can walk." He kissed her, got up and went and cleaned up, pulling his boxers on. When he came back into the tv room, she was curled up asleep on the sofa. He tamped out the fire, got himself a drink, took a long gulp and put it upstairs, then saw texts that had shown up on his phone:

> *Are you calling me back? Was gonna see if you wanted to meet up. Call me*

> *I need a hit of you. I'll meet you at our place. The suite.*

He deleted the texts, put the glass down and walked downstairs. He picked Kathryn up and carried her upstairs to bed, leaned her onto it and covered her up. He laid the blanket back on the bed, freshened up and slid into bed with her. Not even two minutes later, her head was on his shoulder and her arm was around him. Feeling her sexy body against his was almost turning him on. He kissed her forehead and heard his phone buzzing again. He ignored it and nodded off.

The next morning, Ronan went and did his workout and when he came back, she was still asleep in bed. He brought her up a mug of coffee and placed it on the bedside table, then checked over his texts:

> *I can't believe you stood me up. I was there waiting until 1am.*

He shook his head and deleted the messages then walked back downstairs and made breakfast. He was just plating the eggs when she walked downstairs. When he saw her come in the kitchen in his t-shirt and her shorts, he smirked. "At least you're more dressed."

"Thank you for the coffee," she said.

"Good morning."

"Morning. What did you make?"

"Scrambled and bacon." He handed her a plate and she put the plate and the coffee down on the table. "What?"

"Thank you."

"For what? Breakfast?"

She nodded and kissed him. "You realize that if you start something…"

"Just a thank you for actually giving the date stuff a chance."

"Feel any better?"

"Can't walk all that well. Did you carry me upstairs to bed?"

He nodded. "I wasn't about to leave you downstairs. How'd you sleep?"

"Good I think," she teased. He kissed her and sat down with her.

"Good. You were out cold when I brought you upstairs. The minute I laid down, you were curled up against me."

"I don't remember doing it."

He smirked. "I managed to get you to roll over and curled up with you. I swear, you were out damn cold."

"Someone tired me out," she joked. They had breakfast and he cleaned up as she hopped up on the counter and sat with him while he washed the dishes.

"Ronan."

"What?"

"Did you really want to go to church?"

He smirked. "Yeah, I do lass. Did you want to come with me or head home?" She got a grin and that gave him his answer. "We have to be there by 10."

"And what time is it," Katie asked.

"8."

"Then we have time for a shower."

"Go ahead. I'll be up there in a few minutes." She kissed him and slid her arms around his neck.

"I want you to come with me."

"I'll be there in a few. I just have to finish the dishes." She kissed him again.

"Fine, but you better hurry. I might steal all the hot water."

She walked upstairs, slid her shorts and his shirt off, then stepped into the shower. Having the warm water all to herself was nice, but she wanted him in there with her. She washed her hair with her eyes closed, massaging the shampoo into her hair when she felt kisses against her breasts, then a nibble. She rinsed her hair and opened her eyes to see Ronan with his arms around her, teasing and nibbling and licking each breast until it made her moan. "Ronan."

He smirked. "You were expecting someone else?"

"Aah." His hand slid down her torso.

"Tell me what you want," he asked.

"I'll give you a hint," she teased.

He shook his head. "Say it."

"From behind." He kissed her and turned her, so her face was against the cool tile of the bathroom wall.

"No teasing," he joked.

"Couldn't if I tried," she replied. His fingers slid over her wetness, teasing her until her legs were almost shaking. "Shit Ronan."

"What?"

"What happened to no teasing?" He kissed her neck, then down her back as one finger then two slid deep inside her.

"Aah."

"You complaining lass?"

She shook her head, and he kept going until her knees were shaking. "Ronan."

"What?"

"I want you."

"Not good enough," he teased as his body leaned against hers. She went to slide her hands free, and he stopped her. "Nope." She tried to turn to face him, and he leaned her against the tile wall.

"Ronan, please." He slid deep inside her and her breath hitched.

"Please what," he asked as he slid deeper in and out until he could feel her throbbing around him. "This what you wanted?" She moaned and he knew. He kept going harder and harder and faster until she crumbled in his arms.

"Aah."

"Still think it's a good idea to try and tease," he asked.

"You may have to carry me to church." He kissed her shoulder, slid under the stream of hot water and showered quickly, then looked at her as she sat down on the shower bench.

"You okay?"

She smirked. "So, yeah, you're carrying me."

"Driving."

"Can't move." He walked over to her and kissed her. "Finish showering then we're heading out."

He stepped out of the shower, wrapping himself in a warm towel then went and freshened up. "I mean it Ronan," she said.

He smirked. "I know you do." She rinsed her conditioner out, finished washing off then stepped out as he wrapped her up in the other warm towel.

"So bad."

"What did I do," he asked.

"You know what you did. You broke my legs."

"Funny," he teased as she shook her head and went and slid into her sweater dress to head to church with him. When he came out of his closet in a dress shirt and tie and his black dress pants, she smirked.

"This enough," she asked.

"Depends on what's under it."

"Clothes," she replied with a grin ear to ear.

"Are you attempting to tease lass?"

"Not attempting. Succeeding. Does this work for you?"

He nodded, attempting to keep his cool. He helped her with her jacket, she slid her boots on, and they headed to the church.

"Had to wear the high heels," he whispered as she teased him the entire way over.

"That was part of my plan. You started this Ronan."

"And how did I start this?"

"All the teasing all morning."

"Let's just keep that quiet."

"Maybe," she replied as the car stopped and he parked and came around to get her door. He helped her out, locked the car and walked into church with her, sitting down mid-way to the front.

"What happened to sitting near the back?"

"We're sitting up here. You wanted to come, we're doing this my way." They sat through the service and as soon as it was done, they headed out and went back to his place.

"So, now what did you want to do," Kathryn asked.

"You staying or heading home?"

"That's sorta up to you Ronan." He slid his suit jacket off and walked upstairs with her two steps behind him.

"Pub."

"And you're seriously going to the pub right now? We could just stay here and watch the game."

"Pub. Put on a skirt."

"You're hilarious," she said.

"You gonna come with me or not?"

"Not in a damn skirt in the pub."

"Jeans." She nodded. She went and changed into a sweater and jeans and saw him change into his jeans and a t-shirt.

"Ronan, why would I really wear a skirt to the pub?"

"Jeans will do."

"Meaning what," she asked.

"You'll see when we get there." She shook her head, and he kissed her, pinning her against the wall of the bedroom.

"Ronan."

"What?"

"Are we actually going or do you have something else planned?"

"Oh, I have plans lass. You wanted to know what dating me was like, and now you'll know."

"Meaning?"

"You want to know, or do you want me to show you?" She kissed him.

"I'm going home after the pub." He nodded and kissed her again. "Ronan, I get that you're all bossy and demanding and stuff, but you do know that dating is kinda more than just messing around, right?"

"You came to church."

"And we had dinner last night, but there has to be more than just us having sex."

He shook his head. "There is."

"Then prove it," Kathryn said knowing that she needed to say something before they left.

He took her hand. "What?"

"We're going over."

"Then let me pack my bag." She packed everything up then slid her shoes on and walked over to the pub with him.

"You really convinced that what happened upstairs and in the shower this morning is all this is?"

"Right now, sort of yes."

"Right now, it is."

"Ronan."

"You keep teasing and I'm gonna take full advantage."

"Meaning what," she asked.

"Meaning I know what lingerie you're intentionally wearing."

"And who says I'm wearing..."

He kissed her and pinned her against the wall outside the pub. "Don't start teasing lass. If you do, you're getting it."

"Meaning what?"

"Meaning I can take you anytime and anywhere."

"Says who Ronan? You?" He nodded. "Good luck with that," she said as she walked around him and headed inside. She found a quiet booth and sat down and within a few seconds, he was sitting beside her.

"Ronan."

"Pint or drink," he asked.

"I'd say a pint, but something tells me that you'd probably already have ordered me a drink." The waiter came over a few minutes later with an espresso martini and a pint of Guinness.

"Are you trying to get me tipsy?"

"Trying to make sure you enjoy the game."

"And which game are we playing?"

"Rugby," he said pointing up at the tv screen.

"Not what I thought you'd say," she replied.

He shook his head and took a gulp of his pint. "Hungry?"

"Not yet," she replied.

Chapter 5

Just as they were getting comfortable, another couple came in and walked straight over to Ronan. "About time you two got here," Ronan said.

"What's the score," his friend Kian asked.

"5 to 3. We're winning at least," Ronan said. "Kian, Mia, meet Katie."

"Nice to meet you," Mia said as she was beyond happy to have another girl to talk to.

"Oh, come on," Kian said as he and Ronan intently watched.

"So, how long have you two been dating," Mia asked as she got comfortable and watched the game along with them.

"A week or so," Ronan said answering her question with a reasonable answer that was complete shit.

"How long really," Mia teased.

"A few dates. Just talked him into dating," Katie said as Ronan's hand clamped down on her thigh.

"About time he did. We've been trying to set him up for years," Mia said.

Mia Snyder, one of Ronan's friends along with her boyfriend Kian Reeves had been friends with Ronan for years. Since high school. When Ronan's business took off, they were always right there to celebrate with him. Mia was almost 5 foot 9, Kian was 6 foot 2. Both had smiles ear to ear when they saw Katie with Ronan. Mia worked at a tour company that Ronan had an investing interest in, and Kian was the head of transport for the same company. The more Mia talked to Kathryn, the more she found a kindred spirit in her, and they became fast friends.

"Love, can you get me a pint," Mia asked as Kian and Ronan got up.

"So, how long have y'all actually been together," Katie asked.

"Almost 10 years. We just got engaged last week. Ronan was supposed to be at the party, but he had an event he had to be at. We even had an engagement party. I have no idea what was going on with Ronan."

"Foundation event for the hospital. I was there."

"Really," Mia asked.

"I just started doing some admin stuff for the foundation."

"So, that's who had him all distracted."

"Sort of," Katie replied as Ronan looked over at her. He motioned to ask if she needed a refill, and she pointed to the pint glass. He smirked and nodded then brought her over a pint of Guinness.

"You two having fun yet," Ronan asked.

"Just getting to know each other. You two having fun," Katie asked. Ronan nodded and sat down with her, determined not to have her divulge any more information he didn't want Mia to know. "So, you blew off the engagement party for a foundation party," Mia asked.

"Had to be there. Kinda the head of the thing," Ronan said.

"Such a party pooper. You think you'd actually be happy for us," Kian said.

"I am. I think you're insane to marry this crazy man, but I am," Ronan said.

"And what's wrong with me now," Kian asked.

"Insane. Workaholic. You are married to the damn job already. Cheating on it with Mia for years," Ronan joked.

"And who's dang fault is that? You invested in Emerald Isle. You're the one that added all the dang pressure. Hell. My boss even let up a little, but no. You have to be the cranky one. The one who's tried to one-up the workaholic."

"I'm running more than one company Kian. I'm the one that invested remember? I have more..."

Mia kicked Ronan under the table. "Then you're buying the drinks," Mia said determined to get the guys to stop trying to outdo each other.

"Have you two been like this forever," Katie asked.

"We grew up like brothers almost," Ronan said.

"So, you've both been all competitive for years then," Katie asked. Ronan nodded.

"We're not that competitive," Kian said. Mia shook her head and started laughing, lightening the mood completely.

"What," Ronan asked.

"I swear, if the two of you had a damn foot race, you'd be trying to trip each other up the entire time. You two are worse than you were in high school," Mia joked.

"Nice," Ronan said.

"You are." Ronan's arm slid around Katie's shoulder.

"Do you really have to start all of this," Ronan asked.

"You did start it," Kian said. Ronan shook his head as Katie looked up at him.

Even in his element, he was still sexy to her. He was wrapped up in the game, smack-talking with his friends and had his arm around her. Somehow, it was like claiming her as his with just that simple move. When she snuggled in closer, he didn't exactly push her away. She started getting more and more comfortable with it and started liking Mia too. When his arm mysteriously slid away from her, she almost wanted to hold onto it. When he got up, she shook her head.

"What," he asked. She noticed her drink empty and after a quick peck to her forehead, he got up and grabbed her a refill. "Food," he asked.

"I guess," Kathryn asked. He ordered something for them to eat and Kian got up and ordered something for himself and

Mia.

"So, how are you two really doing? Honestly, he's never introduced me to anyone he's ever dated. It's been freaking years. I'm glad he finally found someone worthy of sports day at the pub. Someone for me to hang with," Mia said.

"Honestly, I think we're good. We're just getting to know each other. It honestly hasn't been long. I like him even if he is a little much sometimes."

"Who is," Ronan asked as he came and sat down complete with fish and chips for them both in hand.

"You," Mia joked as she stole a few chips from their plates.

"You could've just said you were hungry," Kian said.

"This mean you're feeding me fiancée," Mia asked. Kian kissed her and got up and ordered them each a steak and Guinness pie.

"Yes," Ronan said as he watched his team score. Fact was, Katie was having a lot more fun than being in the house all day with him. She joined in on the fun, cheering their team on. By the time the game was done, they were both a few pints in. When he turned to look at her, Katie shook her head.

"What?"

"I have an idea."

"Which is," Katie asked quietly.

"Go down to the ladies. I'll knock. Let me know if the coast is clear." Katie shook her head.

"No."

"Go."

She shook her head. "Katie."

"Not here." He nodded. He let her out of the booth and watched her walk down to the ladies room. "She okay," Mia asked.

"She's good. Promise," Ronan said.

"You are so bad. Tell me that you aren't doing something stupid," Kian said.

"Just talking. Making sure she's good. That's all," Ronan said.

"That isn't the way to talk. Involves your lips on your face," Kian teased.

"Funny. Excuse me for a minute," Ronan said as he walked back towards the bathrooms and knocked on the ladies bathroom door. She opened it and he slid in, locking the door.

"Are you gonna tell me what all of this is for," Kathryn asked.

He kissed her, devouring her lips until her leg was curling around his. "Making sure you're okay," he said.

"You could've just asked me that," she teased.

"Had something else I wanted to do," he said as he undid the button and zipper of her jeans.

"Not in here."

"Why?"

"Ronan." He kissed her again and his hand slid down the front of her almost naked lace panties and slid into her wetness, teasing. "Shit."

"What was that?"

"Not in here." One finger slid inside her and her nails dug into his shoulder.

"Still say no," he asked.

"Aah."

"That's what I thought."

"Ronan, stop."

"More?"

"Aah." He slid in a second finger and teased until her legs were shaking.

"Sit on the counter," he said.

"Ronan."

"Then bend over the counter." He slid her jeans down and within seconds, she was bent over the counter, and he was sliding deep inside her.

"Ronan." He went hard and fast. He teased with one hand and pounded into her over and over again until he could feel her body throbbing around him. When he went harder, she climaxed around him. "Shit," she said. He kept going until he found his release and her body was spent. When she found her footing again and zipped up her jeans as he zipped up his, she shook her head. "Now I know why you wanted me to wear a skirt."

"And next time you will," he replied as he licked his finger.

"Ronan."

"You having fun yet?"

"I may need you to carry me to your place."

"I'll get the driver to get you home safe."

"So, we're not going..."

He kissed her. "That's up to you. You said something about going home." He washed his hands and headed out, unlocking the door and walked back to the table.

"Katie okay," Mia asked with a smirk.

"Other than dealing with you trying to pry you mean? I heard you Mia. Stop."

"You're so damn private about everything Ronan. Do you blame me? First lass I've seen you with in years. Forgive me for making sure she's a real woman and not just someone you talked into a day of sports at the pub," Mia said sarcastically.

"She's real."

"And where did you meet her then," Mia asked.

"At a bar I went to. Sort of a one-night thing that turned into a few more dates. Stop trying to make it more than it is. It's a few dates."

"And a day watching football and rugby. The one thing that you're determined not to include any ladies in. Last girl you dated was that flaky moron years ago. Is this seriously the first girl you actually gave a damn chance to?"

"Mia."

"It is."

"Love, leave the man alone," Kian said. When Katie came back over, he kissed her and got up, letting her slide into the booth, then sat back down with her.

"And what were you two talking about," Katie asked.

"Nothin," Ronan said glaring at Mia.

"Just talking about how you two really met," Mia said.

"He was at an event, and I was getting a drink. We talked for a bit then hung out a while. What's wrong with that," Katie asked.

"Because she's determined to get all the dirt even when she's been told to stop," Ronan said.

"Had to. I think this one might be able to put you in your

place. I was wondering when that was gonna happen," Mia joked.

"Love, you two can stop any time now. These two have teased each other like brother and sister for years. Just ignore them Katie," Kian said.

"I'll do my best," Katie said.

Ronan's hand slid in hers. "We really should head out. I have to get her home," Ronan said coming up with an excuse.

"Seriously," Mia asked.

"Yeah. Taking your little friend away before you corrupt her," Ronan said as he got up and paid the tab.

"Ronan," Kian said.

"We'll talk tomorrow. Mia, goodnight," Ronan said as he headed out hand in hand with Katie.

"And what was all of that for," Katie asked as they stepped outside.

"I'm not impressed with her prying."

"You've known her for years Ronan. She's just asking. You could've told her to mind her own."

"She doesn't. Even if I said it, she'd ignore me."

"Then why do you hang out with them?" "Because Kian is one of my best mates. She's a pain in my backside and always has been," Ronan said.

"And if I said that she didn't ask anything intrusive?"

"She did. Asking where we met was enough."

"What's wrong with how we met?"

"At least you left out the one-night stand thing." Katie stopped him and kissed him in the middle of the street. He shook his head and walked her to his place.

"What happened to getting rid of me?" He kissed her again, picking her up. "What are you doing?" He walked up to the door, unlocked it, walked inside and locked the door, flipping the alarm on and walked upstairs, pinning her onto the bed.

"What," Kathryn asked.

"You sure you want to go home?"

"No."

"Good answer." He devoured her lips, and her legs slid around his hips.

"Do you want me to stay?"

"What time do you need to be at work?"

"8, but I have to change at home."

"Then you'll leave here at 7. I'll make sure you're awake."

"Ronan, I have to..."

He kissed her again, sliding his fingers through her hair and holding her head in his hand. "Don't leave."

"Ronan."

"Stay."

"We just..." He kissed her again and peeled her jeans off. "Ronan, I have..." He kissed her again, sliding the jeans to the floor. The kisses got deeper, more intense and almost all-encompassing until she was curled up around him.

"I have to go home tonight," she said.

"Stay."

"Ronan."

"Stay tonight." He kissed her again and peeled her sweater off.

"Ronan." He devoured her lips and pinned her onto the bed.

"Stay." She shook her head, and his hand slid down her torso.

"Don't you start. I have to go Ronan."

"Do you have to?"

"We've been inseparable all weekend. You really want me here tonight too?"

"Yes."

"Fine, but I'm leaving early." He nodded and she felt her lacy panties slide off, then the lacy bra. "You're over-dressed," she said.

He kissed her again and slid his arms around her, wrapping her legs around his hips. "I have teasing to do."

"Ronan."

"What?"

"You teased at the pub."

"And now even more."

"Ronan." He kissed her again, devouring her lips. His fingers trailed down her torso and started the rhythmic teasing that had her toes curled in seconds.

"Ronan, aah."

"I take it that means you're staying."

"That means I may pull a Ronan special in the middle of the night so I can actually sleep before work."

"Oh, I can stop that from happening in two seconds flat lass. You really think you can get away with that?"

"I really think that you teasing me until I moan your name isn't gonna keep me in bed all night."

"Then handcuffs will."

"You wouldn't."

"You even think about disappearing in the middle..."

She kissed him and he intensified the teasing. "Shit Ronan."

He kissed down her neck and then down her torso. When he licked and teased, her legs started shaking. "Still think that you're gonna sneak out?"

"Not right now I'm not," she said as two fingers slid deep inside her.

"Good answer," he said as he licked and teased and kept licking and nibbling until he felt her body throb around his fingers. "Much better," he teased as she reached for him.

"Come here."

"Now," he asked. She nodded and he worked his way back up as she slid his arm away from her and wrapped her legs around him. "And what do you want," he asked.

"You out of the jeans, out of the boxers and that sweater. I want you inside me."

"And here I thought you had your fill at the pub."

"Now Ronan." He kissed her and she pulled his sweater and shirt off. He kicked his jeans and boxers to the floor and slid into her. Deep into her.

"This what..." She kissed him and devoured his lips until she felt her hands being pinned to the bed.

"What are you doing," Katie asked as he kept going harder and faster.

"Mine."

"Ronan," she said as her body started to throb and ache for him.

"Say it," he said as he kept going deeper.

"Shit. Ronan, please."

"Say it."

"I'm yours." He exploded into her as her body tightened around him and throbbed.

"Damn," he said as she kissed him.

"Yeah. You aren't leaving lass."

"Walking may be a problem too," Katie joked.

When he went to get up, she stopped him. "What lass?"

"Stay in bed with me."

"Just give me a minute." She shook her head and kissed him. He shook his head and got up.

"What are you doing?"

"Getting a drink." He went and cleaned up a little, slid boxers on and walked downstairs to grab them each a drink. When he came back into the bedroom, she was asleep in his shirt. He shook his head, put the drinks down, put the phones on the charger and slid into bed.

"About time," she said as she curled up to him.

"Drink?"

"Depends on what it is," Kathryn said. He handed her a glass, took a sip of his and she shook her head.

"Burning."

"Tell me you're staying tonight."

"So long as I get home by 7." He nodded and set an alarm on his apple watch.

"Set the alarm for you and everything."

"And how were you planning on waking me up?"

"Lots of ideas lass."

"I'm sure. Still. I have to…"

He kissed her. "You'll be fine. Just don't take off in the middle of the night." She nodded and he finished his drink. "Come here," he said as he slid deeper under the covers and pulled her into his arms.

"What," Katie asked. He kissed her.

"Close your eyes and get some sleep lass." She kissed him and fell asleep in his arms.

The next morning, Ronan woke up at 6 and kissed her neck as somehow during the night she'd become the little spoon. "What," she asked.

"You said to wake you up. I'm waking you," he teased.

"Do I really have to go to work?"

"Sorta," he replied. He got up and flipped the shower on to warm it up for her. When she finally did get up, she came up behind him and wrapped her arms around his waist, kissing his back.

"Katie, shower. No teasing allowed this morning. You said you had to be home."

"But there's something I want before..." He turned to face her, slid his shirt off of her and kicked his boxers off, carrying her into the shower. "Ronan."

"Shampoo." She slid under the water and washed her hair. Ronan kissed her as she rinsed out the shampoo. "Keep going lass." She slid her conditioner in and motioned for him to come closer. "Not falling for that lass. Finish your...." She kissed him and her hand slid down his torso, passed the tattoos to the one thing she wanted.

"Don't start that," he said.

"Don't start what," she teased as her hand slid over him then up and down.

"Katie." When she slid him into her mouth, he shook his head.

"And that's why the handcuffs come in handy with you."

"Mm."

"Shit. Katie, please just stop," he said as he braced himself, leaning his hands against the tile wall behind her.

"Mm."

"Katie, get up." She shook her head and kept going, taking him deeper in her mouth. He pulled her to her feet, freeing himself from her and pinned her against the wall of the shower. "Had to start something."

"What are you gonna do about it?"

He picked her up, wrapped her legs around him and pounded into her having insane morning sex in the shower. Even when he pinned her arms against the cool tile wall, she was moaning. "Had to start," he said.

"If I'm yours, you're mine."

"That's what you think," he teased.

"That's what I know." He kept going until she was shaking in his arms. He exploded into her, and she wriggled her hands free as he set her back on her feet. "That what you wanted lass?"

"Yep."

"Then maybe you should get dressed." He slid under the water, and she slid in with him, rinsing the conditioner from her hair.

"You sure you want me out of the shower?"

"Unless you want to be late to work, yes." She went up on her tiptoes and kissed him then slid out of the shower, wrapping herself in the fluffy towel in the warmer. Ronan finished his shower and stepped out, wrapping himself in

the other towel.

"Ronan."

"Yes lass."

"What are we doing tonight?"

"Sleeping. I have meetings until after 6."

"Ronan."

"You can do what you wish lass. I'll ring you when I get home from work."

"You sure?" He nodded and Kathryn slid into jeans and her sweater. He slid joggers on with a t-shirt and grabbed his phone, walking downstairs to make coffee.

When she made it downstairs, bag in hand, she put it by the door and came into the kitchen to see him making an omelet and toast. "You didn't have to make me breakfast," Katie said.

"I'm doing a workout after you head off. Otherwise, I would've had breakfast with you," he said handing her a mug of coffee.

"Still."

"It's not even time for you to head out. The car is coming in 20."

"I could've called an uber or something."

He shook his head. "Faster and safer with my driver."

"Ronan." He kissed her and flipped her omelet.

"Just go with it lass. A lot easier not to have a fight about it."

"All I'm saying is that I have my own car. I can drive myself."

"Here?"

She shook her head. "Then leave it at home. The driver can handle it," Ronan replied.

"So, that's how it's gonna be?"

He nodded. "You don't have to worry about driving. You can have a drink or two."

"For today then, thank you."

"Most welcome lass. Now, eat while it's hot," Ronan said, plating her breakfast. He grabbed himself a mug of coffee and sat down with her.

"You didn't have to do all of this," she said.

"I know. You had to eat. Better than a bowl of cold porridge or something."

By the time she finished eating, the car was waiting outside. "So, really though, what are you doing tonight?"

"Meeting. Might go to the pub with Kian. I'll ring you when I'm on the way back to the house and let you know."

"Ronan."

"What?"

"You sure you aren't gonna vanish on me?"

"I don't think that Mia would let me," Ronan replied. He put the dishes into the washer and walked her to the door.

"I want to see you tonight Ronan."

"I know lass."

"I'll call you at lunch?" He nodded. He helped her with her coat and slid his hands to her face, cradling it. "What," Katie asked. He kissed her, devouring her lips.

"I'll talk to you tonight." She nodded and with one more kiss, he walked her outside to the waiting car, got her door for her and helped her in. "Tonight," Katie said. He nodded and he closed the door and watched the car head off to take her home.

He came back inside, locked up behind him and went and got a workout in. When he finished, he had a quick breakfast, cleaned up and showered, then got dressed and headed off to work.

"Sir," his assistant said as he came into the office.

"Give me a minute to get to my desk," he said.

"A package showed for you." She grabbed it and handed it to Ronan.

"Thank you."

"It came in at 8 this morning. There's a few messages for you," she said handing him the list of messages. Just as he started to go through them and his assistant headed out, his phone rang.

"Kian."

"So, are you keeping the lass around or what?"

"I'm thinking about it. Why?"

"Because Mia is determined to make Katie her new best friend. We had fun," Kian said.

"I bet you did teasing her."

"Ronan, come on. The first lass that you've had around you at all since what's her name."

"Anna Doyle."

"And that was forever ago."

"She's still texting."

"You dumped her and disappeared. How'd you expect her to react?"

"I dumped her after seeing her with someone else in my house."

"You didn't tell me that."

"Kian."

"You didn't. So, the fact that I saw her at the pub after you two left?"

"Then we're going somewhere else."

"You can't just avoid the lass."

"Yeah, I can. It's been 4 years Kian. I'm not changing my mind on that."

"And if she wanted you back?"

"Because you sat and talked to the cheating bitch?"

"And there's my answer."

"Leave it be Kian. If you see her, tell her to keep her distance. Leave me be. I don't need the reminder. That's why I haven't dated in years."

"So, are you actually dating Katie now?"

"Considering it," Ronan replied as he logged into his email and slid in his AirPods.

"Considering it. I saw you two together Ronan. I know the look."

"Just enjoying each other's company right now Kian. I'm not jumping into anything."

"Was she at your place all weekend?"

"Kian."

"I'll take that as a yes. Like it or not my friend, you're

dating."

"I have work to get done Kian. I don't have time to talk dating or not with you."

"Then we'll meet you at the pub for a pint after work. Bring the lass with you."

"Late day at work."

"Then we'll save you a seat in the booth."

"Goodbye Kian."

"See you tonight."

Ronan got some work done and managed to finish the first meeting of the day then headed to his office and checked over emails. When he saw one from Anna, he shook his head:

> *So that's what you chose? I mean, you could do so much better. Here I thought you'd almost become a monk after we broke up. Good to know you didn't. Miss you. Can we try another round?*

He shook his head and replied:

> *Stay away from me and my friends Anna. Who I date and who I don't is no business of yours. I wouldn't be with you again for all the money in the world. Not worth my time. Leave me be. You come near me or my friends again, I'm seriously telling you off and getting you booted from the pub.*

He blocked her email and phone number and somehow felt like a weight was lifted. He looked at the box and saw Anna's name on the return address label. He opened it and saw a photo in a frame of her with Ronan from when they were together. He opened up the back of the frame and shredded the photo then saw a note:

> I miss you. I have for years. Come meet me at the
> pub tonight.

He shredded the note, put the frame in the box, threw in the shredded photo and note, sealed the box and handed it to his assistant. "Just return it to sender."

"Yes sir," she said as he walked back into his office and heard his phone ring. He looked and saw Kathryn's phone number and answered.

"Hey," she said.

"Hey yourself lass. I guess you made it to work alright," Ronan replied.

"I did. How was your morning?"

"Good. What are you up to?"

"Lunch. Just having some Irish Stew. What about you?"

"Haven't even ordered in yet. Just dealing with some emails."

"Then I get to ask you something."

"Katie."

"Last girlfriend."

"4 years ago."

"And why did you break up?"

"I told you. She was in it for the money."

"The real reason."

"Meaning what?"

"There's more to it than that. Even I know that."

"She cheated in my own damn house."

"Did you move?"

"Yeah. That's why I hadn't gone out to the pub with Kian and Mia in a while."

"Why did you get such a huge house if it's just you?"

"Because I wanted it."

"Ronan."

"What?"

"I saw someone watching us when we were there. That's why I'm asking."

"And if that person does that again, I'm changing pubs."

"She was there."

"Yeah, she was supposedly. I don't want her near either of

us."

"So, are we actually gonna try and date or was that just a test this weekend?"

"I'm thinking about it."

"And what are we doing tonight?"

"I'm going out."

"With who?"

"Kian and Mia."

"Do you want company?"

"Since you're way too dang tempting, I'd say no."

"Tempting?"

"I need sleep tonight."

"And so do I," Kathryn replied.

"Then you're staying home lass."

"Or I could just stay at your place."

"Or you could just stay home."

"Call me after work and we can talk."

"I mean it Katie."

"Fine. Call me anyway."

"I will."

"And Ronan, don't forget to eat lunch. You can be all broody and grumpy."

"Meaning what?"

"I like the broody and sexy part. Nobody wants you grumpy in a meeting."

"Funny."

They hung up and his assistant came in with his lunch. "You got Irish Stew?"

"And soda bread. It's gonna be a long afternoon." He smirked and ate while he went through the rest of his emails. He was just finishing the last of the soda bread when a message came in on his phone from Kathryn:

> You done being all grumpy? I'll drive over and meet you and we can go to the pub together.

He shook his head. She was damn persistent. He was the one that chose whether she came or not, not her. He needed a night free of women. He would've been fine if it was just him and Kian:

> As I already said, no.

He cleaned up, finished his drink and finished going through emails when his phone dinged:

> I see you're still grumpy. I want to see you. Tell me when.

He shook his head and ignored the text. He finished his emails, and his assistant knocked. "Yep."

"Meeting in 10." He nodded and grabbed the papers he needed then went into the meeting. As soon as that one was finished, he went into another meeting that went straight until 6. At 5, his phone buzzed:

> *Hope your meeting is going ok. Let me know if you want me to meet you.*

He ignored it and finished the meeting, then went into his office and got his desk organized then walked down to the car. He was in a mood. One that meant that she wasn't getting her way.

Ronan headed home and when he pulled in, he was happy to see nobody parked in the drive. He stepped out of the car, locked it and went inside. He walked upstairs and changed into his jeans and sweater and his phone buzzed again:

> *Ronan. Can you talk?*

He took a deep breath and called. "How was work?"

"Long. I need a few pints then I'm headed to bed."

"And," Katie asked.

"Honestly, I'm just having a pint or two, maybe something to eat then I'm going to bed."

"Yes or no?"

"Katie, I know you want to be here, but I'm literally having a pint quickly and going home."

"And he blows me off."

"You were here all weekend. I just need a night of sleep."

"I could...."

"Katie."

"For a drink with you."

"You aren't gonna accept no, are you?"

"Nope."

"Fine."

"I'll drive over. See you in a few." He took a deep breath. She was already too clingy. Was he really that damn addictive?

She showed up 15 minutes later just as he was locking the door. "Good timing," she said as she locked her car and walked over to him.

"You gonna tell me why you're so damn determined to spend every single night with me?"

"Because I want to. It's what people do that are dating Ronan."

"Every night?"

She shook her head. "You really are grumpy."

"I told you lass. Long day. I just..." She kissed him, going on her tiptoes and his arms wrapped around her, pulling her legs around him.

"Stop being grumpy." He kissed her again and sat down on the front steps as she straddled him.

"Trying," he replied.

"Was your day that bad?"

"Long. Really long."

"We could just go back inside."

"I already told Kian I was coming."

She kissed him. "Changed your mind?" He shook his head.

"Not with him. He'd show up at the house and drag me down there."

"Better now that I'm here?"

He kissed her. "Getting there." He got up, slid her to her feet and walked her down to the pub to see Kian and Mia waiting on him.

"And here I thought you weren't coming," Mia said giving Katie a hug.

"She almost didn't. Talked me into coming," Ronan said as he went and got two pints and put one in front of Katie.

"So, how was the day," Kian asked as Ronan shook his head.

"Meetings all day plus a few interesting texts during lunch," Ronan said as Katie smirked.

"Wanted to make sure you were in a good mood. That's all," she teased.

"So, does this mean you two are actually dating now," Mia asked.

"Do you ever mind your own business," Ronan asked.

"With you? No. You're like my brother Ronan. I'd ask the same thing if you were family," Mia said as Katie smirked.

"We're dating. Happy now?"

"I have a million other questions." Just as Mia said it, Ronan spotted Anna going up to the bar to get a drink. When she walked over to them, Ronan was livid and shook his head, getting up. He put her drink down on the table and walked Anna to the back of the pub.

"So, you're dating," Anna said.

"And you're leaving. I guess you didn't read the message. Leave me alone, leave Kian and Mia alone and get out of the pub. You don't even live down here. Just get out."

"I'm on a date Ronan. I can do whatever I want to. You don't want me around, but I know that Mia misses me."

"Like she'd miss the biggest liar in the damn planet. Screw off Anna. Go back to the hole you came from and crawl back in. Better yet, go get a damn lobotomy. Maybe it'll correct your pathetic excuse for a life." Ronan walked off, talked to the bartender and then came and sat back down in the booth with Kian and Mia.

"Everything okay," Katie asked.

"Fine," he said as his jaw clenched.

"She isn't," Kian said.

Ronan nodded. "Mia, I'll be right back," Kian said as he got up.

"I handled it," Ronan said.

"Not when she's still here." Kian walked over to Anna and talked her into leaving. When Ronan saw her leave alone, he calmed himself and Kian came and sat back down.

"Handled," Kian said as he grabbed his beer and took a sip. Ronan was almost growling.

"Something wrong," Katie asked.

"Just some garbage we needed to put out," Kian said giving Ronan a look. Ronan shook his head and took a gulp of his Guinness.

"Are you gonna tell me what's actually going on," Katie asked.

"You don't want to know," Mia said. They relaxed and talked and hung out for a while, got some dinner and they attempted to de-stress. As soon as they were done dinner, Ronan went to get up. Katie followed him.

"Where are you going?"

"Katie, I just need a minute."

"First you get all cranky at the table then you start almost growling then you take off. What's going on?"

"My ex was here. Happy now?"

He walked off and went outside to get some air. She gave him a few minutes than walked outside to him. "Katie." She slid her hand in his.

"Talk Ronan."

"Just go inside."

"Then kiss me."

"Katie."

"Kiss..." He kissed her, devouring her lips and deepening the kiss until he had her pinned against the wall outside the pub.

"No more cranky," she said.

"I need to go back in."

"You done being all cranky?"

He kissed her again. "I just needed to breathe."

"And a distraction." He nodded and slid her to her feet.

"Alright. Come on." He walked her back in and sat down

with her.

"Better," Kian asked.

"Much," Ronan replied. They both finished their pints then Ronan opted to head home.

"Seriously," Kian asked.

"Just need some down time. We'll meet up for sports Sunday," Ronan said.

Mia nodded. "As long as you bring Katie," Mia asked.

"Sure," Katie replied.

"Good. See you this weekend." Katie nodded and Ronan went and paid for the food and drinks. They headed out after a quick hug to Kian and Mia and walked back to his place.

"You sure you aren't still mad," Kathryn asked.

"Something I needed to do."

"Which was?" He devoured her lips and picked her up, wrapping her legs around him and walking to his front door.

"Better," she teased as he sat down on the front step of his house with her wrapped around him.

"Getting there."

"So, you're glad I pestered you to come." He kissed her again. "Do you want me to come in with you," Kathryn asked.

"If you do, you won't be leaving tonight."

"I could..."

"You won't be."

Chapter 6

"That wasn't exactly an answer Ronan." He kissed her.

"Before you get no sleep at all tonight," he said.

"Do you want…"

"That's up to you lass."

"Then let's go inside." He kissed her again and got up as she slid to her feet. They walked inside and he closed and locked the door behind them. "Ronan." He kissed her again. He took her hand and walked her upstairs to the bedroom then pulled her into his arms and kissed her again. She slid her sweater off and he slid her onto the bed, pulling her jeans off as she squirmed to the edge.

"Ronan."

"What?"

"You're too dressed." He slid his shirt and sweater off as she watched his muscles tense. "Damn."

"What," he asked. She shook her head, and he slid on top of her.

"Ronan."

"What," he asked as she felt her bra slide undone.

"Pants." He kissed her and she felt her lacy panties slide off, then heard his jeans sliding off. Before she could say another word, he devoured her lips all over again. Her legs wrapped around him, and she felt his bare backside. He was hers even if he wouldn't say it.

"Ronan."

He kissed her again, holding her face in his hands. "What," he asked as he held her hands over her head and kissed down her neck.

"Hands." He shook his head. "And if I said to let go?"

"Then you're getting handcuffed." She shook his head, and he kissed her. He reached into the drawer and handcuffed her to the edge of the bed. "Shit. Ronan, please." He kissed down her neck and nibbled and licked at each breast until she was moaning. "Mm."

"More?"

"Come here." He shook his head. He kissed his way down her torso, kissing and licking and nibbling as she squirmed in his arms. "You do realize that you aren't playing fair right?"

"And either did you this morning." She shook her head and with one lick, one kiss between her legs, her toes were curling, and her stomach was almost trembling.

"Ronan."

"Mm," he said as his fingers slid inside her.

"Shit."

"All wet and turned on already," he teased as his fingers slid in and out and teased until her legs were shaking.

"And it's all your fault. Ronan, come here."

"Why?"

"Because I need you."

He kept teasing until he heard her breath hitch. "Much better," he teased as he worked his way back up her torso.

"Ronan please. No more..." He kissed her neck.

"No more what," he asked as he slid deep inside her.

"Shit." He kissed her again and pulled her legs tight around his waist.

"Thought you wanted..." She kissed him. He slid in harder, deeper until her body was throbbing then slowly sped up.

"Ronan."

"Mine."

"Aah."

"Say it," he said as he kept going a little harder, then deeper then faster.

"Yours," she replied as he exploded into her and pulled her tight to him, rolling to his side.

"Shit."

"So, all of that because you wanted me to be yours?"

He nodded and kissed her neck. She could feel his response. "Ronan."

"What?"

"Do you want me to go home?"

"You have work, and I need actual sleep tonight."

"You didn't sleep?"

"You mean since you kept me awake until midnight?"

"You were kinda part of that," she teased as she turned to face him.

"Do you want to stay?"

"Yes."

"We need sleep lass."

"And I brought a bag with me."

"Would you be mad if I said you should head home tonight?"

"Ronan."

"I just need to get some sleep."

"Then we get sleep." He shook his head and kissed her.

"Where are your keys?"

"In my purse on the step."

"I'll get your bag." He kissed her and got up, cleaned up, pulled on joggers and a hoodie and walked downstairs. He grabbed her keys, got her bag from the car and locked it, coming back inside. He locked up behind him, got himself a drink and came upstairs.

"I was wondering what was taking you so long," Katie said.

"Bag. Don't ask me what you put in there that makes it that heavy."

"Clothes, toiletries and shoes," she teased.

"Pajamas?"

"Figured your shirt would be more relaxing."

"Katie." She kissed him and tried to pull him into her arms. He slid the bag to the floor and slid into her arms, kissing her and putting his drink on the side table.

"You are so very bad," he teased.

"Get into bed Ronan. You said you needed sleep. We're sleeping."

He kissed her again and peeled her shirt off. "Getting me all naked for a reason?"

"I have a few ideas."

"Such as," she asked.

"You not stealing my rugby shirt."

"Just for…" He kissed her and shook his head.

"Not happening lass. My lucky shirt for Sunday."

"You aren't gonna share it?" He shook his head and kissed her.

"Sleep in your own pajamas lass." She kissed him and he let her up. She grabbed her lacy lingerie from her bag, sliding it on and he smirked.

"You do realize you're gonna be cold in that right?"

"I have a big teddy to curl up with to keep me warm," she said.

"Especially since it'll be on the floor in two seconds flat."

"Ronan. You said you wanted to get sleep."

"I do."

"Then why are you…" He kissed her again, devouring her lips and deepening the kiss until she could feel his hands sliding up her legs.

"Ronan."

He kissed her again. "Sleep."

"You naked first."

"Get some sleep Ronan."

"So, you're just gonna sit here and tease me all night in that lacy thing?"

"That was the intention."

"Remind me to get you back for that."

"Meaning what," she asked.

"Meaning payback is gonna be fun."

"And what might payback be?"

"Blindfold. Handcuffs and something that will make you so turned on you'll beg me to stop it."

"I have one of those," she teased.

"And so do I lass. One that does things you can only wish I'd do."

"Ronan."

"Don't even tempt me or I'll do it when you're sleeping in that sexy thing."

She shook her head and curled up with him. "Sleep. You're the one that said you needed to get actual sleep. Just come get some rest."

He kissed her again and leaned to his back. She curled up against him and tried to get sleep, but his hands had other ideas. "You do realize this would look a whole lot better on the floor right?"

"And I also know that sleeping doesn't involve trying to get me naked."

"Then wearing something that's all lace is probably a bad idea. I can't see how that's comfortable."

"I was more comfortable in your t-shirt, but you didn't want to share it."

Ronan shook his head. "Katie."

"Then the lacy stuff is staying on."

"Just don't be surprised when it's on the floor in the morning."

"And what happens if I pull a Ronan and take off in the middle of the night?"

"You won't."

"And why won't I?"

"Because you won't be. Guaranteed I'll be waking you up in the morning."

"I brought clothes for work tomorrow."

"Meaning you're leaving at 8:30?" She nodded. "Good. Then we have time tomorrow."

"For what Ronan?" He kissed her and flipped the light off, making sure the phones were on the charger. "Ronan."

He kissed her. "Goodnight Katie."

Ronan woke up the next morning at 6 and did his workout. When he finished, he flipped the stereo off and looked up to see Kathryn leaning against the door frame. "Shouldn't you be showering or getting ready for work," Ronan asked.

"I have time. I wanted to come see what you were doing," Katie said as he walked over and kissed her.

"Hungry?"

"For that too."

"Katie."

"Are you gonna let me help you cook?"

"You can make the coffee," he teased.

"Okay then," she said as he noticed she was in a different one of his t-shirts.

"I see you found another t-shirt."

"And I hung up your rugby one."

"And stole another one."

"What about it handsome?"

"You're intentionally teasing."

"Taunting. Very different thing."

He shook his head. "Just make the coffee," he teased as they walked into the kitchen. He put the breakfast on, making something they could share instead of omelets.

"Ronan."

"Yes lass."

"You do realize that I like stealing your shirts right."

"Anything other than that sexy thing you wore last night."

"The one that you threatened to drop on the floor?"

"That one," he teased.

"Did you really think that I wouldn't end up in your t-shirt?"

"Was hoping for once that you wouldn't. Also thought that if I managed to sneak back upstairs before you woke up, you wouldn't need my t-shirt."

"I'd still steal one."

"Remind me to grab you t-shirts so you have something when you're here."

"You do realize you have a million t-shirts right," Katie asked.

"Just leave my rugby shirts alone."

"Jerseys?"

"Especially those," he replied.

"Ronan."

"Yes lass."

"What are you doing tonight?"

"Dinner with my folks." He plated breakfast and she brought the coffee over to the table while he grabbed the cream and sugar.

He got breakfast on the table, and they made their coffees. "What are you gonna do tonight," he asked.

"Girl night maybe. Might just stay home and relax. Something tells me I'm not gonna sleep as well as I do when you're with me."

"I just can't tonight."

"I know. It's fine."

"Remember that thing you hid in your bag?"

"What about it?"

"Is it the app one?"

She nodded as she had a mouthful of her coffee. "Send me the link to it and we can have a little fun when I get back from dinner."

"More like you taunting until I beg you to stop."

"Part of the fun lass."

"And if I say no?"

"Then you aren't gonna have any fun at all lass. I can't do anything tomorrow either."

"And what's on tomorrow?"

"Late meeting at work. Won't be home until after 7."

"Doesn't mean that..."

"Katie."

"We have a work meeting Friday."

"I know."

"Are you gonna say something to them about us being together?"

"That's sort of up to you. If you want me to, I can."

"Did you decide if you can handle having a girlfriend or not?"

"Katie."

"Is that a yes or no Ronan," she asked as she had her breakfast.

"I never promised that we would date."

"I dared you to try and date. Sorta means getting to know each other and talking and..."

"What we're doing upstairs after breakfast."

"That too," she replied.

"Do you really want to date me of all people?"

"What's wrong with you?"

"Just saying that I think you could do better."

"And if I said I liked what we were doing?"

He took a deep breath and had his coffee. "Still think you could do better."

"You trying to run me off now Ronan?"

"Trying to make sure you know what you're getting yourself into. I'm bossy, I'm controlling, and I'll make sure you don't walk all night. You sure that's what you want?"

"If it means us hanging out together, yes."

"I know that Kian and Mia like you."

"And what about you?"

"Getting used to having you around."

"Does that mean we're actually gonna try the dating thing?"

"That means we see how it goes. When you change your mind, say the word and we're done."

"Could be a while Ronan."

"Oh, I know lass. Trust me. You'll get sick of me."

"I somehow don't see that happening."

"Just so you know. Next week I have to fly out for a 2-day meeting."

"Where to?"

"Just outside of London."

"Then what?"

"Then I'm back before the big meeting at work that I'll be in all day when I get back."

"Not the end of the world Ronan. I do have a job and a life of my own."

"Just making sure you know."

"Maybe next time I'll come with you for company."

"You really want to sit around and wait for me to get out of the meetings?"

"Maybe."

"We can talk about that next time if you're still around."

"You're just convinced that you'll get me to change my mind so you can go back to your pointless, meaningless flings."

"I just know that's how it's gonna end up turning out. That's all, lass."

"And if I say it isn't?"

"Meaning?"

"If I say that I'm not gonna get sick of this? That you aren't gonna scare me into walking away? That scare you?"

"When it's barely been a week or two? You saying that so dang early in this? Sorta. Yes."

"I know better Ronan. Did she really do that much of a number on you?"

"I'm not talking about that Katie."

"Then stop thinking that I'm like whoever she is. I'm not. I don't cheat, I definitely don't lie, and I don't walk away from anything without a fight. I've been that way most of my life."

"At least that's something," he said sarcastically as he finished his breakfast.

"What scares you the most about this?" "You destroying any chance of me ever having a relationship. Me making a mess of things and you never letting me forget it."

"Would you ever cheat?"

"I can't…"

"Ronan."

"I'm not having this conversation."

"At least tell me that much. That you wouldn't cheat when you're not here."

"I have female friends Katie."

"Ones that come with extra naked benefits?"

"One or two."

"Then stay away from them while you're away."

"And if I don't?" She took a deep breath, getting the hint that it was a test that she was about to miserably fail.

"If you don't, when you get back, your manhood would end up in a specimen jar."

"I can't promise that I won't."

"Ronan."

"What?"

"Just don't bother testing me alright?"

"It wasn't."

"Yeah, it was. I'm not gonna sleep with someone else, and you're not either. Just accept that. I don't want to. If you want to, then there's no point."

"I'm just saying if I did."

"If you did, I'd kick your backside until you couldn't move then handcuff you to the bed and leave you there."

"Nice try."

"Did you really think that I was kidding?"

"You do realize that I get hit on continuously, right?"

"And dating means you do nothing about it unless it's me

hitting on you."

"You sure you really want to do this?"

"Stop trying to convince me otherwise. The answer is yes."

"You do realize we aren't really not dating anyone else right? It's not like it's a committed relationship."

"Then consider it one. I'm not gonna be with anyone else. Just don't bother testing me Ronan. I want you. Nothing else."

"And you're sure that I can't..."

"Quit it."

"Then you should probably leave a change of clothes here for when you stay."

"Oh really?"

"I can get your shampoo and stuff and have it here if you need it."

"Changing the topic?"

"You're not up for that fight. I can see it," he said as he finished cleaning up the dishes and she slid up onto the counter beside him.

"What?"

"What are you so scared of Ronan?"

"You changing your mind and messing around on me."

"After you just talked about you messing around on me?"

"It's instinct."

"And so is me slapping you for bringing it up." He pulled her legs around him and slid his arms around her waist.

"All I know is that every time I think I want to try dating again, it blows up in my face. I tried more than once, and it ended up with them running off with the good guy. Two dates and I scare them off."

"They aren't me."

He kissed her, deepening the kiss until he was peeling the t-shirt off. "Ronan."

"Here."

"But..." He kissed her again, devouring her lips until she felt him hard against her.

"Say yes."

"To what," Kathryn asked.

"Yes or no?"

She nodded and within what felt like seconds, they were having sex with her on that countertop.

"Shit." He slid in and out of her, harder, deeper until she could feel her body tense around him. "Ronan." He kept going faster and harder until her body was throbbing, and he exploded inside her.

"So, fighting with you about things turns you on."

"One phrase."

"What," she asked.

"They aren't you."

She calmed her racing heart, and he picked her up and carried her up the steps to the bedroom and leaned her onto the bed. "Ronan."

"What?"

"What are you up to?"

"It's only 7."

"Meaning what," she teased. He kissed her again, curling back up in the bed with her.

"Meaning you get me all to yourself for another hour before we have to shower and get ready."

"Then come shower."

"Why," he asked pulling her tighter to him and leaned onto his back.

"Because that way we have more time for the other fun," she teased.

"And just what were you planning," he teased.

"You coming with me," Kathryn asked.

"You sure you don't want to stay in bed a while longer?" She kissed him and got up, walking into the bathroom. She flipped the hot water on, and he got up, following her into the hot shower, throwing towels on the warmer before he hopped in.

"And just what was your plan," he teased as he slid under the hot water.

"Depends on whether you're gonna let me..." He shook his head and kissed her.

"No."

"And why is that," she said, sliding her body up against his and slid her hand between them, putting her hand on him and sliding it up and down. His breath hitched.

"Katie, stop."

"Why?"

"Katie." She shook her head, and he kissed her, trying to pull her away from what she was doing.

"Ronan."

"Don't start something you can't finish lass." She pulled away and went back to working him up and down then went to kneel when he stopped her.

"Don't start."

"Don't start what Ronan?"

"You know what. You do realize what you're starting right now."

"What I'm starting and definitely finishing," she teased.

"Oh really?" She kissed him as her hand slid up and down, getting him even more turned on.

"Katie."

"What?" He grabbed her hand, pinned it above her head and picked her up, wrapping her legs around him as he slid deep inside her.

"Shit." He kissed her, devouring her lips and had her pinned against the wall as he slid in and out, deeper, harder and faster until she was moaning between kisses.

"This what you want," he asked.

"Hell yes," she replied. He kept going until he could feel her body tightening around him from the inside out. He pounded into her even harder, and she reached her climax with him right after.

"Ronan."

"What?"

"That's what I meant by fun." He shook his head and pinned her hands to the wall.

"That fun will have to wait a couple days."

"Such a party pooper."

"It hasn't even been a week and already you're determined to get me all to yourself."

"A week and a half, and hell yes," Katie replied.

"And if I said that I didn't want to?"

"Then let me down."

"Katie."

"You don't want to?"

"I think we need to have a breather."

"You're getting your way this week Ronan. Let go."

"Katie."

"Let me go." She slid to her feet and washed her hair, not even looking at him. The tears forming in her eyes weren't something she wanted him to see.

"That's not what I meant."

"And what did you mean Ronan? You didn't want to see me for a while? That you're making an excuse intentionally so you can go have fun?"

"That every night together, while we do have way too much fun with it, is too much. Not that I don't love having you in my bed with me, but we can't rush this."

"Sorta already did," she said as she rinsed out the conditioner and stepped out of the shower, wrapping herself in a warm towel.

"Katie." He looked and she was gone from the bathroom. He wrapped a towel around him and walked into the bedroom, seeing her getting dressed with shaky hands.

"I didn't mean to leave right now," he said.

"You want space, you'll have space. Have all the damn space you want Ronan."

She finished getting dressed and got up. Ronan grabbed her hand. "What," she asked.

"Come here."

"What?"

"Woman, you're giving me a hard time. Are you telling me that you want to be here all the time?"

"I wouldn't have shown up if I didn't."

"And you don't think that we're really rushing all of this?"

"Ronan, we rushed it when we slept together before we even had our first date. We did everything backwards. We slept together twice before we even had a first date. I met your friends already. You really want to slow everything down, you're doing it the wrong dang way unless you really want me gone."

"I never said I did. I just said maybe not every night together in bed. That's all."

"And if I said that I wanted to be here because I sleep a whole lot better?"

"Still gonna be tricky the rest of this week."

"Then we're getting together on Friday. I'm not taking no for an answer," Katie said.

"Then we're spending the weekend here. We're good. I just can't do anything for a couple days."

"Fine."

"Katie."

"It's fine. I just wanted to be with you. That's all I want. Even if I have to take off a dang day at work and show up at your office."

"Since I'm in meetings, probably not a great idea." She kissed him.

"Just don't ghost me Ronan. That's all I ask. I don't want to lose whatever this is. It feels good."

"About that."

"What?"

"Since I'm not gonna be able to see you for a few days..."

"Ronan." He went into his drawer and grabbed a little bag, handing it to her.

"What's this?"

"Open it tonight when you get home. When you do, call me."

"And what happened to being home late?"

"I'll be around. It may be late, but I'll be here."

"And if I want to come over and open it with you here?"

"Then it's gonna be late. After 7. If I don't hear from you, I'll call you when I get home."

"And what am I supposed to do with whatever this is?"

"Charge it, set it up on your phone and send me the link."

"What is it?"

"You'll see when you open it later. Don't open it until you're home."

She nodded and kissed him. "I still want to open it now."

"Trust me. Wait until you get home tonight."

"Ronan."

"Leave it at it's being turned on tonight and we're having fun even if I'm not there with you."

"Toy."

"You'll find out tonight lass. Behave. I mean, if you want a hint, you'd end up being late to work."

"Hint away."

"This mean that you're gonna stop being all mad at me?"

"Just don't keep pushing me away alright?"

"Friday we can get together. Hoping it's not at the pub, but Friday. That work?"

"You know there's a meeting on Friday night, right?"

"What do you mean a meeting?"

"7pm. Meeting at the hospital in the boardroom." He looked at her.

"I guess that means we're waiting until after the meeting then."

"Or we meet up before the meeting."

"Katie."

"What?"

He shook his head and kissed her. "Try to behave."

"Are you gonna stay at a hotel or come home after the meeting," she asked.

"You tell me."

"And if I said you come to my place after the meeting?"

"Flatmate?"

"Forgot about that."

"Then you can come back over here."

"I can get her to go out or something so we can be alone." He shook his head.

"We're good lass. Come over here."

"You sure," she asked.

He nodded and kissed her. "I'm sure lass. I'd rather have you here instead of being interrupted by the flatmate."

"Most of the time she isn't even home. She works nights."

"Still."

"Ronan."

He kissed her. "What are we gonna do about showing up to the meeting together?"

"You actually going to admit that we're dating?"

"That's not exactly up to just me lass."

"And what would you say about telling people that we're dating?"

"If we did tell people, what would you tell them about how we met?"

"We were both at a bar and ended up talking for a while. Sorta went from there and started dating."

"So, you're planning on leaving out the one-night stand?"

"I'm planning on ignoring that part. We sorta grew up since then since we're dating now."

"Think so do you?"

"Ronan."

"Lass, there's nothing wrong with how we met and nothing wrong with a one-night thing."

"There is when I want respect Ronan. I don't want them thinking that we got together because we slept together. That's not..."

He kissed her. "That's what's known as the truth lass. We got together because after we did sleep together, I couldn't stop thinking about you."

"And?"

"And nothing lass. You want to be honest then tell them the actual truth."

"I'm not telling them that."

"And if my friends ask?"

"Then I'll tell them the same thing Ronan. We met in a bar and ended up dating."

"And the truth was so bad?"

"Do I wish we'd met in a different way, yes. Would I change it, not right now. I'd rather have you."

"Good answer lass," he said as he finished getting changed.

"Then what do you want me to tell people when they ask?"

"Tell them that we met at a bar and ended up enjoying our time together. That I didn't realize that we'd be working together. When we did, we ended up dating."

"That's your big idea is it?"

He nodded and kissed her then walked downstairs with her. "That's what you really want to tell people when we see them?"

"It's the truth, at least from my side."

"And if I'd said no to meeting up that night," she asked.

"Then you wouldn't be all mad about me being too busy to meet up for a few days like I know you are," he teased as he helped her with her coat and walked her out to her car.

"So, where was this thing that you said you were sending over that I needed to charge," Kathryn asked.

"You'll see later lass. If I'm home early, I'll give you a call."

"You'd better. I might just have to go have fun without you."

"Trust me lass. You aren't gonna want to go out after that thing shows up. You might not be walking."

"What did you send?"

"You'll see tonight," he teased as he kissed her and got her door for her.

"Call you tonight." He nodded. She hopped in and headed off to work and he went and got in his car and headed his way into his office.

"Sir," his assistant said as he walked in.

"What can I do for you," Ronan asked.

"There were a few messages for you after you headed out." She handed Ronan the messages then his phone buzzed in his pocket. He grabbed it and answered.

"Don't you have something else to do today other than bug me so early," Ronan asked as he chatted with Kian.

"The woman wanted to know when she gets to hang out with Katie again. Are you coming tonight for dinner?"

"If I can get out of the meeting early enough, sure. I have a late meeting at 4. Should be fine, but I have other plans for Katie tonight."

"What are you doing to the poor lass," Kian asked.

"Taunting her. Making sure that she knows who the boss is," Ronan said as his assistant closed the door and left Ronan to finish his conversation in private.

"Ronan, how did you two really meet," Kian asked.

"I met her at a hotel lounge when I had a foundation meeting. We went and talked for a while. That's about it, Kian. I don't know why you two are so damn concerned with how I met her. Mia wanted me to actually date so I'm trying. Nothing wrong with that."

"Except you scaring the lass off with your crazy stuff. What are you up to really?"

"She wanted this. She started it, and I'm finishing it. If it doesn't work, it doesn't."

"So, in other words, you're doing the disappearing act to see if she still calls and shows up."

"I'm busy with work the next few days. Late meetings. If we don't meet up, the plan is to meet up Friday so you and Mia can hang out with her."

"And it's not like you want to see her or anything."

"Don't you have work to do?"

"You do realize that the disappearing act thing didn't work on girls in school and it doesn't work on lasses like her."

"Then stop complaining that I'm not dating. I'm fine being single and I always have been. I don't need to date Kian. I'm perfectly fine doing things my way."

"Except that you like this one. I mean, picking a fight with Anna at the pub wasn't exactly a great idea if you did want to keep her around."

"I want Anna gone. I have since she decided to ruin everything. Since she cheated in my own damn house. I'm not dealing with her, and I'm not letting her near Katie. End of discussion."

"So, you do like Miss Katie."

"She wouldn't have met you two if I didn't. I just need to know that she's not around for anything other than me. That if Anna does make a damn move and talks to her, that she doesn't scare Katie off. I need to know that she actually wants me Kian."

"Sorta like when she showed on pub night while we were watching the game."

"Not like that was planned."

"You do realize that she wants you around. She was practically drooling on you at the table."

"That was partially because I had a little plan that I was putting together."

"I don't need to know all the crazy things you two are doing. All I'm saying is that she's a good girl and Mia likes her. Bring her on game day."

"Maybe."

"Fine. I'm going into a meeting. Try and behave. See you tonight."

"Maybe. I can't promise," Ronan said.

"Right. See you at the pub. First round on me."

"Then I'll be there." They hung up a few minutes later and Ronan's assistant came in with his morning coffee.

"The first meeting starts in 20 minutes. I ordered the Irish stew you wanted for lunch, so you have a little time to relax between meetings."

"That package that I ordered. I need it delivered to her at her office. Shoot me a message when it's delivered."

"Yes sir," his assistant said.

"And thank you. I was in the mood for that stew."

"I had a feeling sir. I'll let you know about 5 minutes before the meeting."

"Thank you." Ronan went through emails and saw one from Katie:

> *To Mr. Bossy.*
>
> *What are you really doing tonight? Your meeting can't be going until 7. Whatever this little surprise is, I have a feeling you'd rather have fun with it when we're together. If you're home late, call me and we can have fun with whatever it is. Thank you for breakfast by the way. I still want to see you tonight.*
>
> *K*

He shook his head. That idea he had about seeing how long she could go without seeing him was working. Another day or two and she'd be pouncing. That's just how he wanted it. He was getting the upper hand like he always did. That's how he wanted things to be. He laughed and got a buzz from his assistant a few minutes later that everyone was heading into the meeting. He grabbed his papers and cell phone and headed down the hall to the meeting, walking into it and sitting down at the head of the table. The rest of the day, he had meeting after meeting and only took a break for an hour at lunch to enjoy his favorite stew. When he went through his emails again, he saw yet another one from Katie:

> So, a little box just showed up with two things in it. Haven't opened them yet, but something tells me that you're up to something very dirty. How are your meetings going? Any chance that we can open these little boxes up together?
>
> K

He laughed and replied:

> My suggestion is to open them when you get home tonight and charge them both. One of them is for playing tonight. The other is for tomorrow since we can't meet up. Hoping that you have a little fun with the bigger one on your own, but give me the link to it. You'll know what I mean when you see it. The smaller one is definitely for tomorrow since I have another late night meeting. Truly, I'm lucky if I make it home before 8. We'll definitely get together Friday. Mia and Kian are looking forward to seeing you again. Just remember to wear the skirt when I say skirt.
>
> R

He took a deep breath and sent the email, finishing up his stew. When his phone buzzed with a call from her, he smirked and answered.

"What do you mean they're looking forward to seeing me?"

"Mia likes you. That's all."

"I bet that's all. You telling me that you had time to talk to Kian already with all those meetings?"

"He caught me as I was coming into the office this morning. He was asking about you."

"And what was he asking about?"

"How we were doing. How we really met. All the good stuff."

"And did you tell them about the packages?"

"Nope."

"Ronan."

"Yes lass."

"What are you really up to? All the disappearing stuff. Did you think that I was gonna go and run off with someone else while you were busy?"

"I wouldn't be surprised if you did." Fine. It was a blatant lie, but he hoped she wasn't.

"Do you want me to?"

"That's your choice lass. I can't promise that I'm gonna be around every night to hang out with you. This week is insane with meetings and I'm going out of town for meetings a few days next week."

"You know, I could just take some time off and go with you."

"I don't want you getting in trouble at work lass. It's only a couple days."

"And if I said I still wanted to come?"

"You'll be coming alright."

"Tease."

He smirked. "Lass, I have to get into another meeting. We can talk tonight."

"Ronan."

"What," he asked.

"We're meeting up even if it's late."

"We'll see lass. Get back to work."

"Have a good afternoon handsome."

"I will." They hung up, he finished the last of his stew and headed off for the next meeting.

By the time Ronan made it out of the meetings, it was almost 7 and he had a missed call from Katie and from Kian. "What can I do for you," Ronan asked.

"You on your way over? Your pint is calling," Kian joked.

"Going home to change then I'll head over."

"You'd better. Mia's getting hangry."

"Get the girl some food and I'll head over. Just have to go home."

"Will do." He hung up with Kian, grabbed his things and hopped into his car to head home. Just as he did, his phone rang and he answered on speakerphone.

"Katie."

"So, you're heading home?"

"Just got in the car. Did you plug them in?"

"All I have to say is that whatever you're planning is gonna be something crazy. Had to go buy them both?"

"Did you send me the links to them?"

"I almost didn't," she teased.

"And why is that lass?"

"Because I have a feeling that I know exactly what you're planning to do."

"Especially with the big rabbit one."

"Ronan."

"What?"

"Do you want me to come meet you at the house?"

"Honestly, I'm going home and eating and getting some actual sleep tonight. Someone kept me up last night."

"And that thing you bought is only gonna make that worse for me. I still want to see you tonight."

"I'll be home in 20 minutes. Honestly, I'm having dinner and that's it."

"And I want…"

"I know. We can get together tomorrow if I'm home early enough."

"Ronan."

"One night without me won't kill you lass. We can play with that thing you're charging up."

"Fine, but we're getting together tomorrow."

"Alright lass."

He made his way back to his place, got changed and went down to the pub, seeing Kian and Mia waiting on him. "You two look so dang impatient. Did you really think that I wasn't gonna show up," Ronan asked.

"And where is she," Mia asked.

"At home. We're not getting together tonight."

"What did you do to her," Mia asked.

"Nothing. I just told her that I was gonna be home late and we could get together another night. That's all."

"So, you're pulling the disappearing act."

"What is with you two? It's not an act. I just started dating her. I'm not gonna be out with her every single night when we just got together."

"And here I thought you liked her."

"Mia, I do, but I don't need to be with her 24-7. Not yet. I need to do this my way even if you don't agree."

"Then stop giving the girl a hard time. She's a good one Ronan. She has a thing for you even if you're being a stubborn mule about letting her in."

"I let her in Mia. I swear, if this is the only reason why you two wanted me to come over here, then I'm going home."

"Then eat. I know you haven't had dinner. How was the meeting," Kian asked.

He gave Mia a look. "It was a long one. At least we got everything finished so I don't have to go through a part two tomorrow."

"This mean that you're actually gonna bring her with you tomorrow?"

"Mia, I love you like a sister but leave my life alone. You want her to be here, then ask her yourself. I don't need to bump into you know who while we're here. You want to, fine," Ronan said.

"And you think I liked Anna?"

"Just leave it. All I'm doing is trying to avoid that specific problem."

"Then stop keeping that girl at an arms length. She has a thing for you and you know it."

"And I like her. I'm just taking my time with it. That's all," Ronan replied.

"Whatever you say," Mia said.

"I swear, you are picking a fight right now..."

"You two, enough. Mia just doesn't want you losing the chance to be with Katie. I get it. Just don't screw it up and tick her off."

"Not planning on it Kian." The bartender came over a few minutes later with Ronan's fish and chips. He ate, finished his pint and Kian looked at him.

"Can you get her over here," Mia asked.

"Not tonight Mia. I'm having a night with my so-called friends."

"Tomorrow?" He nodded and the bartender looked up, motioning for a refill. Ronan shook his head.

"No refill," Mia asked.

"I'm gonna head home and get some sleep. I have a call to make anyway."

"Tell her we said hi at least," Mia said.

"You can say hi to her tomorrow."

"You sure," Mia asked. Ronan nodded, paid for his food and pint, said a quick goodbye and headed back to his place.

Chapter 7

Just as Ronan walked back into the house, he saw the alert on his phone that she'd added him to the links to the items he'd sent and he felt his phone buzz. "Katie."

"So, what did you want to do with these?"

"Cleaned and charged?"

"Yes. What next," she teased. He walked into the house and sat down on his sofa.

"Next, go and get comfortable."

"I'm curled up in bed."

"Naked?"

"Seeing those two things? Hot. Very hot."

"And?"

"Ronan."

"Take the big one."

"Had to go start with that."

"And if I didn't?"

"Ronan, tell me something. Why are you really keeping me at arms' length?"

"Because I said we didn't need to see each other every day and night lass. We're taking our time and enjoying ourselves. That alright with you?"

"Depends on how long you're gonna make me wait." He got up and locked up the house then walked upstairs.

"What are you doing," she asked.

"Going upstairs to the bedroom."

"Ronan."

"Slide it in."

"Please."

"Tell me what you want lass."

"I want you."

"I'm not there."

"Then come here. My flatmate is gone for the rest of the week. Come over here."

"Katie."

"Please Ronan."

"One night. Do what I asked."

"You feel better than this."

"Is it turned on?"

"Yes." He logged into the app that controlled the toy and clicked it.

"Ronan."

"What?"

"Tell me what you're doing."

"Sliding my jeans off."

"Mm." He slid his finger over the toy functions and intentionally had her at a simmer in minutes.

"Ronan."

"Teasing."

"Mm." She moaned.

"And that's just the beginning."

"Please."

He slid his finger over the thrusting part and started it slowly. "Shit."

"Katie."

"Aah."

"Talk to me."

"More."

"Harder?"

"More." He bumped up the thrusting until he could hear her moaning even more and it got him turned on.

"Ronan." He slid his hand over him and started turning himself on even more.

"Aah."

 "Harder," she begged. He flipped his finger over the screen, and she was getting more and more turned on.

"Ronan." When he exploded into his release, he shook his head.

"Stop," she said as he turned the toy down to a slow tease.

"I'm liking this little game," Ronan said.

"Aah. Stop. Please." He turned it back up and could almost feel her body throbbing.

"More," he teased.

"Stop." He flipped it off and could feel her breath slowing down and her heart racing, pounding in time with his.

"Shit. Okay, that one was fun," Katie joked.

"The other one is for tomorrow while you're at work."

"Oh hell no. I have to be in a meeting."

"Then tell me what time the meeting is, and I'll give you a break."

"You're hilarious," Katie said.

"Who said I was joking?"

"Ronan, I'm not doing that. I work in the hospital admin. Please."

"Still think it's a good idea. I'll only do it on high when you're alone at lunch."

"Ronan."

"Mine."

"Meaning what," Katie asked.

"Meaning lunch is mine." She laughed with a giggle then realized he was telling the truth. He meant it.

"Ronan."

"And you can't touch it all day. Only I get to remove it when I say that you've had enough. How does that sound," he asked with a grin as he got up and cleaned up a bit.

"Sounds like you're already making my toes curl."

"And?"

"Okay, but I mean it. I can't be all distracted at work."

"You won't be lass. You'll have curled toes in those boots you always wear. Tomorrow night we're going to the pub. Bring a skirt."

"Ronan."

"Are you gonna do it?"

"On one condition."

"Katie."

"I'm staying tomorrow night."

"I need sleep lass."

"Then be in bed with me."

"This isn't a game, Katie. You're going home to your own bed."

"And if I say that I'm staying and making you breakfast instead of you cooking for me?"

"Katie."

"Well?"

"We'll discuss it tomorrow night."

"Ronan."

"Tomorrow. Get some sleep lass. You'll need it."

"Ronan, just say yes."

"Maybe. Just wear the skirt."

"Then I'm bringing an overnight bag."

"Skirt."

"Okay," Kathryn replied as she smirked, thinking that she'd somehow managed the upper hand with something.

"Just know that if you're that determined to stay tomorrow,

you may be sleeping in the guest room."

"What?"

"Goodnight Katie."

"What do you mean guest room?" When she heard the phone click, she had a quizzical look on her face. "What in the hell," she said to herself aloud.

Ronan changed for bed, slid under the sheets and went through the personal emails that he'd ignored most of the day. He got down to one from an email he didn't recognize and opened it:

> *I know you miss me. Say the word and I'll come over. Seeing you the other night got me reminiscing about us. Just give us another chance Ronan. Fine. I shouldn't have cheated. I made a mistake doing that, but I still love you. – Anna*

He shook his head and re-read it more than once then blocked the email and deleted it. It was history for a reason. One that made him regret letting anyone that close. He took a deep breath and went through the rest of the emails, seeing one or two from his Mom, and his sister with funny jokes or funny photos. When he saw one from his Dad, he opened it and read through it, seeing that his Dad was proud of him. That he'd heard about the new lass from Mia and couldn't wait to hear all about her. Mia always had been nosey and more than willing to share things that had nothing to do with her to anyone that would listen. She'd always been that way, but to his Dad? Just as he was about to put his phone on the charger, his Dad called.

"And how's my Dad doing," Ronan asked.

"Good. Tell me about her."

"You do realize that asking Mia for information isn't exactly fair right?"

"Just spill it. How did you two meet?"

"Dad, I'm not a broody teenager where I have to divulge that information."

"Just tell me. I know she's pretty. Tell me before your mother pesters me for information too."

"We met when I was at a foundation dinner. I went out to the bar to get away from the stuffiness for a while and we ended up talking. Been talking and hanging out since then."

"And what does she do?"

"She works in Admin at the hospital and for the foundation too. She's a good girl," Ronan said thinking back to what he'd just done to her.

"Dark hair?"

"Short dark hair and emerald, green eyes."

"Those Irish Eyes will get you every time."

"She's a sweet lass. I kinda enjoy her company."

"Since you haven't been dating, it's kind of nice to hear

about one that stuck around for a few days."

"Dad, I love you and Mom, but I am perfectly capable of finding a lass of my own. You know that right?"

"And I also know that Anna did a number on you that you never got over. Just give this one a running chance. From what Mia says, she puts you in your place and likes you. Two good points."

"Very funny. I'm just about to clean up and get some sleep. Can we talk later?"

"Was she the lass you brought to church?"

"Dad."

"She was pretty. Almost too pretty for you."

"Goodnight Dad."

"Night son." He hung up with him, shaking his head and almost laughed. He'd forgotten completely that his parents, Mia and Kian were all there that day, albeit a few dozen rows ahead of them.

Ronan shook his head again and curled up in the bed. Just as he was sliding his phone to the charger, his phone buzzed in his hand:

> *You sure I can't talk you into coming over tonight?*
> *– K*

He shook his head and replied:

I'm already in bed lass. Thinking about what I'm gonna do tomorrow night. You should probably sleep. You'll need it – R

When he got another text with a photo a few seconds later, he shook his head and picked the phone up and called.

"Are you attempting to tease your way into round two tonight lass?"

"Determined to get your attention. You sure I can't talk you into coming over here?"

"You're getting your way tomorrow. That not enough now," he asked.

"I want you to come here."

"I'm in bed lass."

"Ronan."

"You're sleeping alone in that big bed tonight lass."

"Did you see the photo?"

"If you're trying to tease me into coming there, you aren't succeeding. While I like the picture, I'd rather see you in person."

"Then I'll come over."

"Tomorrow."

"Ronan."

"You do realize that the more you complain, the worse it's gonna be right? Still not sold on you staying tomorrow night."

"And if I said more?"

"Which part of more?"

"You know what."

"Isn't that what the toy was for?"

"Not the same without you." He shook his head and took a deep breath.

"Then turn it on."

"Ronan."

"Turn it on lass." She turned it on, and he saw it pop up on his screen.

"That's what you're starting with. I thought you'd had enough," he said.

"If it were you instead, I'd be happy."

"Katie."

"You're better."

He shook his head. "Katie."

"Mm."

"Are you still turned on?"

"Still want you if that's what you're asking."

"And if I ignore you when you say stop?"

"Ronan." He almost laughed.

"I'm turning it on."

"Ronan." He turned it up, adding vibration into the thrusting intentionally.

"Shit."

"What," Ronan asked.

"Ronan," she moaned.

"Not enough?"

"Shit. Too much." He flicked his finger across the screen with another function of the toy and heard her breath hitch.

"And now lass?"

"I miss you."

"Why's that?"

"Because you feel better than this." He flicked his finger across the screen again and she moaned.

"Much better."

"Mm. Ronan, please."

"More? That can be done lass. Don't tempt me."

"Harder." He turned the intensity up and could almost hear her heart racing.

"Aah. Aah, Ronan. Ah."

"More?"

"I can't." He ran his finger over the intensity of the rabbit portion, and he could tell she was close.

"Beginning to get the hang of this little thing."

"Ronan."

"Not yet lass."

"I can't."

"Tell me what you want."

"You."

"Tell me what you want me to do."

"Aah."

"Say it lass."

"Against the wall."

"Then what?"

"Over the bed."

"Handcuffs?"

"Aah...yes."

"Then what?"

"I'll do whatever you want. Aah."

"Good girl," he said as he flipped it completely off.

"Ronan."

"What?"

"Shit. I can't even move."

"Clean up and get some sleep. I may just have to use that tomorrow too. Bring it with you."

"I want you instead."

"And call me in the morning. The other one starts tomorrow."

"Goodnight," Katie said as he could hear her heart pounding and her slowly catching her breath.

"Good girl," he teased as he hung up.

Ronan woke up early, did a workout and was just making himself breakfast when his phone buzzed with a photo of the other toy he'd sent her. He called as he drank his protein shake. "Good morning lass."

"I can barely even walk."

"Good. Now, turn the other one on."

"Can I shower first?"

"Nope."

"Ronan."

"Fine. Go shower and message me when you have it turned on."

"I made sure it was charged."

"Good."

"Ronan."

"Yes lass."

"What time do you want me to come meet you?"

"7. I should be home by then."

"And if you're home early?"

"Then you'll know."

"Do I really need to wear a skirt?"

"Or a sweater dress."

"Okay."

"You do realize you can say no right?"

He almost thought that she knew she had that option.

"I know. It's kind of fun."

"Which part?"

He could tell she had a grin ear to ear. "All of it. Being with you."

"Lass, if you don't…"

"I'm good Ronan. Just a little concerned with walking into work."

"You did start it last night. You could've stopped. You have a way to turn it off when it's too much."

"I was enjoying it."

"I have a better idea. I'll send the car to come get you tonight."

"I have my car. It's fine."

"If you're gonna end up telling people we're together anyway, then when you come to my place, I'll pick you up or get a car to come get you."

"I guess so," she replied as he heard her drink the last of her morning coffee.

"Now. Slide the bigger part in and leave it there. Turn it on and let me know."

"I will. Have a good day Ronan."

"Oh, I intend to lass."

He hung up with her a little while later, had his breakfast

and went and showered and got ready for his day. Fine. He had to admit that he almost missed having her there in the morning to taunt him while he showered or to talk to while he had breakfast. She was growing on him. He got dressed, put her favorite cologne on and made his way down to the car when he got a text that it was on and she was on her way to work. He smirked and went into the app turning it on a low buzz to start. It was barely even on from his point of view. He got to work and saw a text that begged him to turn it off. He put it down lower and got another text that she was pulled into a work meeting. He turned it off so it wouldn't buzz and smirked. He liked the upper hand. The control of it. The fun of it was completely in his hands.

He walked into the office, walked past his assistant and went into his office.

"Sir."

"And how are you this morning," he asked.

"Good. And you?"

"Good. What do you have for me," he asked.

"Two messages and the meeting for late today was moved up to 3. Should be over by 5."

"Why the change?"

"Something along the lines of a cancelled meeting that would've delayed this one."

"Good. I have plans tonight."

"Your first meeting starts in 45 minutes. Is there anything you need?"

"Coffee would be great if you can," Ronan said somehow in a much better mood.

"What did you want me to get you for lunch," his assistant asked knowing he wasn't leaving the office.

"Surprise me," he replied as she handed him the messages and smirked, heading out. Ronan went through his emails and saw one from Katie:

> *I swear you're attempting to make me not move. Nice. You realize you had my toes curling.*

He replied:

> *And how was your meeting? Stimulating?*

He nudged the phone intentionally hinting to her that she had an email. Just as he did, his phone buzzed with a text:

> *Don't you start that. I'm getting actual work done. How's your day looking?*

He replied:

> *Looks like I'm done early. Meeting got moved up. And how's your day lass?*

Within a matter of a few seconds, he had a reply:

> *My boss is around. Looking forward to tonight even more now.*

He smirked.

> *Good. Did you pack the skirt? You knew I was going to ask.*

Kathryn: *Yes. Sweater dress. I miss you.*

Ronan: *Good girl. See you tonight. Get back to work.*

He went through the rest of his emails as his assistant brought his coffee in for him. "Thank you," he said.

"Most welcome," his assistant said. She headed out and Ronan got his paperwork together for the meeting. He kept going until he'd made it through his emails and his assistant knocked.

"Yep."

"Meeting in 5."

"Thank you." Ronan grabbed his papers and his phone and walked down the hall and into the meeting as everyone was getting settled.

Halfway through the meeting, Ronan got a text that he tried to ignore:

> *So, where are you going next week? My boss told me I could get the time off if I wanted it.*

He replied:

> *I told you no lass. I won't be gone that long. You can catch up on your sleep.*

He tried to concentrate on the meeting and got another text:

>   *I'm taking next week off regardless. Can we talk about it tonight?*

He replied:

>   *Answer is still gonna be no, but by all means try and change my mind. You have your ways.*

He finished his meeting and went down to his office to see another text:

>   *Curled up together in a big bed in London or wherever. I thought that'd be fun.*

He shook his head and called her. "Ronan."

"You do realize that I said no to coming with me, right?"

"Ronan, if I'm off work anyway, I can come with you. You won't have to go alone."

"Still don't think that's a good plan lass. We can talk about it later."

"You do realize you don't have to go on your own."

"I know I don't. it's gonna be all work, Katie. I have to be there for a day or two then I'm back home. Probably only a day and a half. There's no reason for you to come."

"And if I want to anyway?"

"Then we're gonna have a very long discussion."

"Meaning what?"

"Meaning when I say no, I mean no. It's work. It's not like I'm going to play golf or something."

"And when you get back from meetings, we can go do dinner together."

"Katie."

"Fine. We can talk about it later."

"I'll consider it. How's that," he asked.

"Good."

He smirked. "Lass, don't you have work to do?"

"Meeting's finished. I just get to harass you now." He clicked the link to the toy and bumped his finger against it.

"Um."

"You really want to start when I have this?"

"Mm."

"Is that a yes?"

"Ronan." He flicked his finger on the screen and made it more intense.

"Stop."

"This mean you give up?"

"Later."

"Not the answer I was expecting."

"Please." He stopped it and heard her breathe a sigh of relief.

"What," he teased.

"Thank you."

"If you're so determined to come with me, you can try convincing me tonight."

"Okay."

"Get some work done lass. I have to head into another meeting in the next 10 minutes."

"Call me at lunch?"

"Just make sure you're somewhere alone."

Ronan got his papers together for the next meeting, checked over emails again and saw one from Anna:

> *I was thinking. What if we just went out and talked just us. We could go get dinner somewhere. We owe each other that much. I know you miss me Ronan. I miss you too. It's been too long already. Please?*

He shook his head. "I know I blocked her damn email

address." He blocked it again, took a deep breath, and headed into his next meeting. By the time he got out an hour and a half later, he was ravenous. He walked into his office and saw the Irish stew and soda bread from the local pub waiting for him. He smirked and sat down to eat when his phone buzzed.

"Yes lass."

"How's your lunch," Katie asked.

"Irish stew and soda bread. Kind of needed this today. It's gonna be a long afternoon."

"And I brought bean chili. It's actually pretty good. So, what's the plan for tonight handsome?"

"I'll meet you at the house and we can go over to the pub and have a pint with Kian and Mia."

"Ronan."

"Yes lass."

"Are you letting me stay?"

"Depends on how tired I am when I get home."

"You weren't being honest when you said the guest room were you?"

"If I need sleep, yes."

"Can't sleep beside me?"

"I know better. I'd never get sleep."

"And why is that?"

"Because you'd be naked in my bed and leaning against me trying to taunt me all night like you do."

"Remind me to do that later."

"Katie."

"What?" He opened the app and ran his finger across the screen. "Shit."

"Liking that little thing?"

"Mm."

"Where are you?"

"Walking somewhere we can talk privately."

"Good." He ran his finger over the screen in circles and heard her almost moan.

"Um."

"Knees shaky."

"Yes."

"How about this," he said as he did it again and again.

"Shit."

"How turned on are you?"

"I want you here."

"At your work?"

"I don't care where."

"So the whole thing about you leaving that in place at the pub?"

"Please," she said as he ran his finger over the screen again. He intensified it and she begged him to stop.

"Too much," she said.

"Really?"

"Ronan, please."

"What are you wearing?"

"My sweater dress. No more teasing."

"Too much?"

"My toes are permanently curled thanks to you. They were still curled from last night."

"You do realize you could've said stop last night."

"I didn't want to," she said.

"Next time tell me to stop if it's too much."

"I want you. That's all I want. Everything else is just fun."

"And if I said that tonight is blindfold and tie night?"

"Mm. I think that I'm gonna end up staying in your bed."

"We'll see lass."

They hung up a few minutes later and Ronan got ready for his meeting.

"Sir," his assistant said.

"What's up," Ronan asked.

"There was a call for you. I took a message, but they refused and wanted to wait to talk to you."

"And who was it?"

"Her name is Anna."

"Tell her that I left the office and have requested that she not call back."

"Sir."

"Long story. Just get rid of her."

"Sir, she's been waiting all the way through your lunch."

"Fine. Next time she calls, tell her not to call back." His assistant nodded and headed back to her desk and Ronan answered.

"What do you want Anna?"

"You blocked my email and blocked me from calling or messaging. I had no other option."

"Yeah, you did. I want nothing to do with you or your stupid ideas. I said we were done when I walked in on you with whoever he was. I was done when you tried to get into my bed after messing with him. Go away and leave me and my friends and my family alone Anna. I'm dating someone. I'd rather take that seriously than your childish crap. Goodbye," Ronan said as he texted IT to get them to block her phone number, email address and any other contact. When he got a reply back with a yes sir, he put his papers together and walked down to the meeting room to wait for everyone else to arrive for the first of two meetings that afternoon.

By the end of the day, Ronan got his things together and headed out. He got to his place not long later and was about to head in and get changed when he saw Katie pull in behind him.

"Good timing lass," he teased as she stepped out of her car, and he took her bag.

"And how was the rest of your day?"

"Interesting. This thing that you were taunting me with all day was relentless. You do realize that right?"

"That was part of my plan."

"Can we please take it out?"

He shook his head. "Not yet." He walked her inside, closing and locking the door behind them.

"What time are we..."

She hadn't even got the words out when he kissed her. He devoured her lips, picking her up and wrapping her legs around his hips. "I missed you too," she said as they momentarily came up for air. He carried her up the steps to the main bedroom and leaned her onto the bed. "What happened to not taking…"

He kissed her again, sliding the hem of her dress up her legs. "Came up with another plan," he teased.

"Which is?" He slid it out and she went to undo his dress pants, but he stopped her.

"What," Kathryn asked. He kissed her, sliding his tie off and tying her hands.

"Ronan."

"What?"

"What are you doing?"

"Exactly what I said I was going to."

"I kinda thought that was after." He kissed her again, devouring her lips and her legs wrapped around him.

"You sure that you can handle it," he teased.

"Untie them." He shook his head and undid his shirt. "Ronan."

"What?"

"Untie them," she asked again. He slid his shirt off, throwing it into the laundry bin and leaned into her arms.

"Tell me what else you want."

"You inside me. Licking and teasing until I beg."

"Creative answer. Two points," he joked. He kissed her again and untied her hands.

"Pants off."

"Or?"

He slid the lacy panties off and smirked. "What?"

"They're mine," he said.

"Ronan."

"I'll get changed and we can go."

"Ronan, don't start. Just come here." He kissed her and got up. He slid out of his work clothes and walked into the bathroom to have a quick shower before they left.

He stepped under the stream of hot water and closed his eyes then felt an arm wrap around his torso. "Katie."

"What?"

"Couldn't just stay in bed."

"Not when you're in here and I can enjoy myself after you teasing me all day." He shook his head and washed his hair. Katie slid in front of him, and he stopped her. "I'm showering and we're leaving. Period." He rinsed his hair, washed up and she kissed him.

"But we have time Ronan."

"Katie."

"Why?"

"Because Mia has already texted twice that we're late." He went to step out and she stopped him.

"Ronan." He shook his head and kissed her.

"Get dressed."

"But..." He kissed her again and stepped out, wrapping a towel around him and handing the other to her as she stepped out behind him.

"Ronan, you realize how unfair today was right?"

"I also know that you aren't gonna be complaining when you're in my bed tonight."

"What?"

"You heard me Katie." She looked at him as he blew his hair dry.

"You are just all bossiness today."

"Another reason why you like me," he teased as he finished blowing his hair dry and walked out of the bathroom. She followed, getting re-dressed.

"Katie."

"What?"

"Leave the lacy panties at home."

"You don't let me play, you don't get to play." She got dressed and he slid into his jeans and sweater. "You ready," he asked.

"You get me all over-heated then you just walk off."

"You'll be over-heated again in no time."

"Meaning what?"

"Meaning we're having dinner and a pint or two and then coming back here for that fun that you're complaining about. You wanted a blindfold and handcuffs, you'll get it lass."

"And if I said I wanted toe-curling and leg shaking?"

"That'll start at the pub. Good thing you wore the skirt." Kathryn looked at him.

"Meaning what?"

"Meaning let's go." He kissed her and took her hand, walking her downstairs.

"Ronan, meaning what?"

"You'll find out," he teased.

They headed out, locking up behind them and made their way to the pub. When they walked in, he saw Anna with her next victim, as he called it, and headed over to the table with Mia and Kian.

"About time you two showed," Mia said.

"You can stop anytime Mia," Ronan said.

"And how was your day," Kian asked as Katie shook her head.

"Busy. And yours," Katie asked.

"Other than harassing my friend here, good."

"Honestly, you two are seriously driving me nuts. Do you want a refill," Ronan asked.

Kian nodded and Ronan got up and ordered drinks for each of them. The bartender brought them over, handing Katie an espresso martini and she shook her head.

"Pie or fish," the bartender asked.

"Pie. Katie?"

"Same please," she replied. He looked over at Kian and shook his head.

"What," Kian asked.

"So, you two are all determined to cause a problem. Go ahead," Ronan said.

"Didn't say a word," Kian said.

"You wanted Katie here." She shook her head. "Is that the

only reason you allowed me to come," Katie asked.

"No. Just why I decided to get the pub stuff done before we have our actual date."

"And just what did you have planned," Katie asked.

"A few things that you tried to start earlier." She smirked.

"Did you see your little friend when you came in," Mia asked.

Ronan nodded. "Can we not just ban her from the pub?"

"Unfortunately, unless your buying the pub, no," the bartender said as he brought the second espresso martini over.

"Two," Katie asked. "Everyone else has a pint. Catch up lass," the bartender joked.

She smirked and took a sip of her drink. "Do you want me to go handle it," Kian asked.

"She saw me. She knows better than to come anywhere near me. Honestly, if she knew what was good for her, she'd leave with her victim now."

"You really hate her that much," Katie asked.

"I really don't want her anywhere near me ever again. Leave it at that lass."

"Long time no see Ronan," Anna said as she stood over at the bar getting a drink.

"Ah. They let the devil out of hell tonight. How nice."

"You know that you miss me Ronan. Trying to replace me with that?"

"Be gone devil," Ronan replied.

"Nice," Kian said.

"I don't need her causing crap already. I'm just here for a pint or two and some visit time with you two and Katie. I don't need her crap." When his phone buzzed a few minutes later, he shook his head and looked:

Package arrived. In secure location.

Ronan smirked. "Have to love technology," Ronan said.

"Why," Kathryn asked.

"A package was just dropped off. Good timing."

"You have that delivery lockbox don't you," Kian asked.

"Best thing I ever got. Super handy." Katie looked at him, shaking her head.

"Present," Mia asked.

"Mum's birthday coming up. I found the perfect thing for her." Mia chatted with Katie and Ronan saw them exchange numbers.

"Now you two can hang out," Ronan joked.

"Funny. More like someone to talk to when you go back to

being your miserable self," Mia replied.

"You do realize that we're perfectly fine right?"

Mia nodded. "Just making sure that Katie knows what she's getting into," Mia said.

"I swear, you have a problem then tell me," Ronan said.

"I don't. I like Katie. She's a good person. Don't ask me how she ended up with a guy like you of all people," Mia said.

Ronan shook his head, and the bartender brought over the pies. "Because I liked him the minute we met," Katie said determined to get a word in.

"Then you have some crazy taste lass," Kian said.

"Not you too," Ronan said.

"Just saying. You have your moments my friend. We've been friends this long for a reason."

"And what reason is that," Ronan asked.

"Because I know that you're a good guy. You just got a brutal hand with the devil lady," Kian said.

"Thanks for the reminder." Kian smirked and Katie finished one of her two drinks.

"Did you need another lass," Ronan asked.

Katie shook her head. "I think I'm good. Two is my max," she said. Ronan kissed her.

"So, what else are you two doing tonight," Mia asked.

"Watching a film over at my place. A relaxing night," Ronan said.

"Just don't turn on anything that's all romantic," Mia teased.

"And why's that Mia? Jealous," Ronan asked.

"Just saying."

"Do you really have that much of an issue with me right now?"

"Calling the woman a devil isn't exactly fair," Mia said.

Ronan looked at Mia. "After the crap that she did, I can't react now? You tell me that I never date. Now I am and you're trying to…"

Kian kicked him under the table. "Mia, come here. We're talking until you get this out of your system," Ronan said as Katie shook her head. "Pat, can I borrow your office for a quick minute," Ronan asked. Pat handed him the office key and he walked back there with Mia.

"What," Mia asked.

"You complain that I never give anyone a chance and now you try and scare Katie off so she runs for the damn hills? Try being on my damn side for once. You complained that she wasn't coming. Now she is. What the hell do you want from me," Ronan asked.

"I don't want you to hurt her. For one. Anna cheated for a damn reason."

"She couldn't manage to stop hitting on people whether I was in the room or not. She screwed someone else in my damn house when I was at work Mia. I didn't disrespect her. I didn't screw her around. She cheated on me."

"Then stop holding Katie at arms length and let her see the real you. The whole disappearing thing is juvenile. You know it is."

"I need to know why she wants me around. I like her, but I can't just jump in with both feet or I could drown and go down the bad side again. I could lose the damn chance. I'm doing it my way. It's kind of my choice when she's my girlfriend."

"Just don't do something stupid Ronan. Don't hurt her because you haven't got over the Anna crap."

"I told her about Anna. Happy now?" Ronan walked out of the office, handed the key back to the bartender and sat down with Katie.

"Everything okay," she asked. Ronan nodded and kissed her. Mia came and sat back down with Kian and everything calmed. They talked through dinner, finally respectfully, and as soon as they finished their drinks, Ronan was determined to leave. He didn't want to be anywhere near Anna, especially when she was only there to taunt him.

"Can we go somewhere else tomorrow," Ronan asked.

"And why's that," Kian joked.

"Not funny."

"What if we go to Donahue's tomorrow," Kian asked.

"Thank you." Ronan got up and paid for the drinks and dinner and Pat pulled him aside.

"What's up," Ronan asked.

"She left you a note. If you want me to ask her to leave, tell me. She's not family. You are."

"I appreciate that. Honestly, I needed an excuse to get out of here before I'm 3 more pints in tonight. I'll pop by Sunday for sports day."

"And your table will be reserved. If she shows, I'll ask her to leave," Pat said. He handed him the note.

"Thank you," Ronan replied as he shook his hand and slid his other hand in Katie's and walked her outside.

They walked back hand in hand, and she asked him the one thing he was dreading.

"He handed you a note?"

"Honestly, it's going in the garbage. My ex was trying to mess with us. It's fine," Ronan said.

"Then why are you all uneasy," Katie asked.

"I didn't expect her to start anything with you there. I'm

sorry if that upset you."

"Just feels more and more like Dublin's a lot smaller than both of us realized."

"Feels like the smallest town ever," Ronan said.

"Calling her the devil was a little much."

"I told you what happened didn't I?"

"Maybe she isn't over you Ronan."

"Then she better get goin on that. I'm taken."

"I kinda like that."

They got to the house, went inside and he walked her into the tv room. "What," Kathryn asked. He kissed her, sliding the note in his jeans pocket and wrapping his arms around her as he leaned her onto the sofa.

"Mm."

"Now where were we earlier?"

"Bed." His hand slid up her leg and she got goosebumps. When his hand slid over her wetness, her leg curled around his.

"Ronan."

"Yes lass," he said as he leaned in and kissed her.

"Are we staying down here?"

He kissed her again, teasing her with his fingers. "For a little while until you start ripping my clothes off."

He slid her dress off, knocking it to the floor and saw her in nothing but her boots and her lace bra. He slid the boots off and saw her already curling toes.

Chapter 8

"Shit Ronan." His two fingers slid deep inside her and he could feel how wet and turned on that she was.

"Tell me what you want."

"Sweater and jeans off." He kept teasing until he knew her toes were curling.

"Not quite yet lass."

"Meaning what," she asked as he leaned in and kissed her again. She went to reach for the button of his jeans and he shook his head.

"Hands."

"I want you." He kissed her again and kept teasing until he heard her breath hitch. "Ronan, please." He smirked and kissed her. He got up, picked her up, made sure the front door was locked and walked her upstairs to the bedroom, leaning her onto the bed.

"Jeans off." He slid his sweater off and she slid her hands across his tattoos, tracing one with her fingers.

"What," he asked.

"I like," she said.

"Good thing." She smirked and he kissed her, devouring her lips when he felt her hands going for the button of his jeans.

"Bra off," he teased.

"Jeans first." He undid her bra, sliding it off and she heard a click. "What was that?" She tried to slide her hands down, but couldn't move them.

"What are you doing?"

"Teasing you until you're begging."

"Meaning what?"

"Blindfold." He grabbed it and slid it over her eyes.

"Ronan."

"Be back in a second."

"You are not leaving me in here like this."

"Two seconds." He went downstairs, and when he came back up, he had a drink for each of them in one hand, and a glass of ice in the other.

"Ronan."

"Yes lass."

"What are you doing?" He slid his jeans and boxers off, slid his socks off and kissed his way up her leg, stopping between her legs and licking and teasing. He licked then his fingers slid inside her all over again as he kissed his way up her torso. He nibbled at each of her breasts, teasing and licking and teasing until she was moaning.

"Something you wanted lass?"

"Kiss me." He leaned his body against her, still teasing as his fingers slid in and out of her and teased until she was throbbing. "Ronan." He kissed her, devouring her lips. "Please," she asked as she slid her legs around him.

"How badly do you want it," he whispered as she got goosebumps again.

"Now."

"How much," he asked.

"Ronan." He smirked.

"Yes lass."

"I need you. I want you. I wanted you all night. All day." He slid deep inside her as she moaned again.

"That what you wanted?"

"Ronan." He kissed her, devouring her lips as he slowly started sliding in and out, in and out until her body was throbbing around him all over again.

He started going harder, faster until she was moaning his name and begging him to undo the handcuffs. "Please." He kissed her and her body exploded around him as he kept going deeper and harder. "Shit Ronan." He kissed her again and let her hands free as he exploded into her, finding his release.

"Aah." She pulled the blindfold off and wrapped her arms

around his neck, pulling him to her as he leaned in and devoured her lips all over again. "Ronan."

"Yes lass," he replied as he kissed her again.

"If I said I wanted to stay in here with you?" He shook his head.

"You have no choice lass. You're not moving even if I have to tie you to the bed so you won't."

"Good. The guest room doesn't sound like it's as much fun," she teased. He kissed her again and got up to clean up a little bit. When he walked back into the bedroom, she was asleep in the bed. He slid his boxers on and took a gulp of his drink, seeing the note from his jeans. He opened it and read:

> *The devil? Really? I know you miss me even if you're determined to avoid me. I miss you. I screwed up then. You've been pushing me away for years Ronan. Just come on one date with me. Please? – A*

He threw the note away, put their phones on the charger and took a gulp of his drink, then slid into bed with Katie. As he was about to flip off the light, she curled up to him and fell asleep on his shoulder. He wrapped his arm around her and snuggled her in close. "I love you," he heard as she said it in a silent whisper. He shook his head and kissed the top of her head, nodding off with her.

When he woke up the next morning, he went downstairs and did his workout and when he walked back upstairs, she was just waking up. "Where did you go," Katie asked as he sat down on the side of the bed with her. "Workout. You hungry?"

"What time is it?"

"Half 6. Why?"

"Why are you up so early?"

He kissed her. "Come back to bed."

He kissed her again and leaned into her arms. "Breakfast?"

"You."

"Katie."

"Don't want to get out of bed."

"I'll bring it up for you."

"Ronan, get back in bed with me." He shook his head and kissed her again as she unzipped his hoodie and slid it off of him then went for his joggers.

"Still getting up. Give me 15 and I'll be back up here with you."

"No. Now." He kissed her again and got up. He went downstairs and made breakfast and within a matter of 15 minutes, he was back upstairs with breakfast for both of them in bed.

"Such a party pooper," Katie said.

"And why is that," he asked as he had his eggs.

"Because we could've had fun before work."

"It's quarter to 7 Katie."

"Why do I get the feeling that you're acting weird."

"Did you know that sometimes you talk in your sleep?"

"Meaning what Ronan?"

"You kind of said something last night."

"Meaning what?"

"Before you take a sip of that coffee, you said you loved me." She looked up at him.

"Seriously," she asked.

He kissed her. "Stunned?"

"Just kinda a little much to say isn't it," she asked.

"That how you actually feel?"

"Sort of."

"That's not exactly the answer that I was looking for."

"What about you," Katie asked.

"We're talking about you lass."

"I do love being with you."

"And the fact that you said those words when you were falling asleep?"

"Ronan." He shook his head with a smirk.

"I was teasing lass."

"And if it's true?" He shook his head and finished eating.

"You're allowed to feel whatever you feel lass. I'm not about to tell you that you can't."

"How do you feel?"

"I enjoy spending time with you."

"And?"

"And nothing Katie."

"You don't love me too?"

"I take my time with things. I don't jump in with both feet."

"But."

"But nothing. I care about you, but I'm not there yet."

"That's fine," she said as he noticed her go oddly quiet.

"Katie."

"It's fine. You're not there yet. I'm okay with that."

"Then why are you so oddly quiet all of a sudden?"

"I just thought that now that we're telling people, that you kinda felt more."

"Katie, breathe. It's just something I don't want to rush into.

You'll know when I'm ready lass."

"Oh." She finished her breakfast, and he shook his head.

"If you're upset just say it."

"So, you don't feel the same..."

He kissed her. "Stop. I still want to spend time with you. I still want to be with you. That hasn't changed."

"And if I walked away because you don't?"

"You wouldn't get that far. You'd barely make it to the top of the staircase."

"Ronan, you seriously don't feel it?" He kissed her, took the tray away and put it on the counter then walked back over to her and slid into her arms, kissing her until the worry passed.

She pulled at his joggers, and he kicked them off then pulled her legs around him. "Ronan."

He shook his head and kissed her. "What?"

"Nothing is gonna change right?" He kissed her again and slid deep inside her as he heard her almost moan and her breath hitch.

"Hands." She shook her head. "You still have me all to yourself lass."

"I just..." He kissed her again, sliding his hands in hers and sliding deep into her over and over again until he had her hands pinned.

"Aah," she said.

"Mine," he said.

"But..." He kissed her again, slowly speeding up his pace until she was moaning, and her heart was racing along with his.

"More," he teased.

"Mm." He kissed her again and kept going harder, faster until her body was throbbing around him, and she was almost gasping for breath between moans. When he finally climaxed, he let go of her hands and kissed her again. "Shit," Katie said.

"Do you need to hear the words, or is that enough to tell you how I feel?"

"Words."

He shook his head and got up. "Where are you going?"

"Shower."

He walked into the bathroom and flipped the water on in the shower, freshening up. He walked into the shower and just let the water fall down his body. He wasn't telling her that he loved her when he wasn't ready to. He wasn't about to do something he could never take back. He felt her slide in as he washed his hair. "Ronan."

He rinsed it out and looked at her. "What?"

"Are we okay?"

"Katie, we both have to get to work. Not the time for that conversation."

"Are we or not?"

"We're fine according to me. According to you, we aren't."

He washed up and rinsed off. "Ronan."

"Shower. I'm gonna get dressed."

"Ronan, come on."

"You want me to say something I can't say yet. Yet Katie. Shower," he said as he stepped out. He grabbed a towel from the warmer and wrapped it around him, drying off.

"Ronan, please."

"Finish your shower." He walked into the bedroom and heard his phone buzz.

One look and he saw the mountain of emails that he had on his phone. Only one text:

> *She left something else at the pub for you. I suggested that she stay away for a while.*

Ronan shook his head and replied:

> *If you see her again, tell her that I asked her to stay away. That what's done is done. We're over and we are staying that way.*

Ronan walked into his closet and found something to wear, putting on his black suit with his black shirt.

"Ronan," Katie said as he saw her step into his closet with wet hair and a towel wrapped around her.

"What?"

"Why are you in all black?"

"Because I am."

"Ronan."

"What Katie?"

"Talk to me."

"About what? You're not happy that I don't feel what you do? I get it. You love me. I care about you too. Period. No more stupid discussion about it. When I get beyond just caring, you'll know. You don't think that's enough, fine." He finished buttoning his shirt and she shook her head.

"What?"

"Can't just be with me."

"You want more than I have right now. If that means you don't want to be here, fine. If that means you're walking out, fine. I can handle it."

"So, you're just gonna be mad at me."

"Don't push Katie. I care about you. If I didn't, you wouldn't be here right now. You'd be alone at home." He went to leave the closet, and she stopped him.

"Be honest then. Tell me what you want. Do you want me to leave?"

"I want you to stop pushing. I want you here or you never would've been here at all. I care about you, but I'm not saying that I love you until I'm damn good and ready to. You want to say it, fine. Just don't expect it back when I'm not ready to."

"I just..."

"What?"

"We slept together a million times Ronan. I want more than just messing around and teasing each other. I want an actual real relationship."

"And what makes it a real relationship for you?"

"You coming to my place. Going on dates that aren't just the pub or here so we can have mind-blowing sex over and over again."

"I took you on a date."

"One."

"What do you want Katie? Fancy restaurants? Hotels? Trips? Just say it."

"I want to come to London with you." He shook his head.

"I'm there for work lass. Work. Late meetings. Dinner meetings. Lunch meetings. Breakfast meetings for three damn days. Three where you could be sleeping in your own bed instead of me tossing and turning and disappearing every morning before you even wake up. I wish I could be in my own damn bed and not have to go, but I own the company."

"Then let me come."

"No."

He went again to try and leave the closet, and she stopped him. "What?"

"Let me come with you. I don't care if you aren't around that much. I just want to be there with you."

"Katie, no. It's three days of constant meetings. You have..."

She went up on her tiptoes and kissed him. "I'm coming with you Ronan. I already took the week off."

He shook his head. "I meant no."

"And I say yes."

"Katie, I love being with you, but you're not coming on a business trip."

"Why?"

"Because I don't want to have to explain to people why you're there when it's not a personal trip."

"Can't just say that I'm your girlfriend?"

"Unprofessional."

"Ronan."

"I said no. You want to hang out here while I'm gone, fine. You're not coming with me. Wait and take the vacation time later."

"Later when Ronan? I have to use it before the end of this month. I'm coming."

He shook his head. "I said no Katie. I meant no. Take the time and hang out with your friends or something."

"Why are you intentionally pushing me away right now?"

"Because I can't do this. I can't. You have work to get to and so do I. I have a meeting in an hour. I told you. I'm busy all this week and busy all three days that I'm gone next week. I can't Katie. I can't fight with you because you want me to say I love you with all the damn emotion behind it. When I do, you'll know alright?"

"That's not what I was trying to do."

"Katie, I have work. It means traveling. If I have to go somewhere hours away, fine. I'll invite you. It's three days in the UK. Three. Meeting-filled, long days. I'll invite you next time I travel somewhere worth the trip."

"Meaning where," Katie asked.

"Spain. The USA. Italy. Somewhere worth going to."

"And you see all of that?"

He nodded. "I have to get ready for work lass. Get dressed and I'll walk you out."

"I still want to go." He took a deep breath. We can talk about it later."

She looked at him. "What?" She went up on her tiptoes, sliding her arms around his neck and kissed him.

The kiss deepened and he picked her up, putting her on the counter in his closet.

"Katie, you can't fight me on everything. You know that right?"

She nodded and kissed him again, sliding her legs around his hips.

"Katie, work."

"It can wait another half hour."

He shook his head. "It's almost 8."

"Like I said, we can wait."

He shook his head. "I have to be at work at 9."

"So do I." He shook his head and kissed her.

"Get dressed. We can pick this up later."

"I told Mia I'd come meet up with her."

"Then we're making up for last night."

"Meaning what?"

"I had plans that got distracted when the psycho showed up to ruin them."

She kissed him. "What was the note?"

He shook his head. "She's the one woman I'd never give another chance to. She's why I don't say I love you as easily as you do. Why I hold off. She ruined it. She started crap intentionally."

Katie kissed him. "Ronan." He looked at her. "What did the note say?"

"That she wanted another chance."

She shook her head. "Thank you."

"For what?"

"Being honest. Telling me."

He kissed her. "Now, come get dressed lass. We both have work."

"Am I coming over tonight?"

"That's kinda up to you. I just don't want anymore stress okay?"

She kissed him again and he slid her off the counter. She went and got dressed, did her hair and he sat down on the edge of the bed, going through his emails as he waited.

When he looked up 15 minutes later, she was dressed and ready to go, in yet another sweater dress.

"Intentionally teasing. Nice," he teased.

"Anything else that I need before I leave?"

"Not torturing you today lass. He walked her downstairs, she put her other bra into her bag with the dress, slid her boots on and he walked her outside.

"You have everything?"

She nodded. "Thank you for telling me about the note."

"She broke me Katie. In a major way. I promised myself I'd never let anyone else in that would hurt me like that until I was ready. Just give it a little time."

She nodded and kissed him as he got her car door for her. "Let me know when you get to work?" She nodded and he kissed her again. She got in the car and headed off. Ronan went and locked up the house, flipped the alarm on and went and got into his car and headed to work.

When he showed, his assistant had a mountain of messages and his coffee waiting for him. "Tell me all of those messages are work-related," he said as he walked into his office and sat down, pulling out his laptop.

"Two aren't. Your mom called. Something about not being able to reach you last night. She called first thing this morning."

"Anything else urgent?"

"Your 10am meeting was changed to 9:30. Beyond that, nothing important that you need to do before the meeting. Your coffee."

"Thank you again for that. I'll need it."

"Is there anything you need me to do," she asked.

"I don't even know why I'm saying this, but when I'm away next week. Do I have dinner meetings?"

"One, but it's with Devin Pierce. I think the two of you were old friends. He asked if he could bring a date."

"Then make the reservation for 4."

"Sir."

"And what hotel did we book the suite in?"

"Mandarin Oriental in London. The biggest suite they had."

"Terrace?" She nodded.

"I'm bringing Katie with me. Just book her a massage or something one of the days."

"Yes sir." He got his paperwork, shuffled through the messages, prioritizing them and went down to the meeting, messaging Kathryn:

> *Fancy suite in London. I have 2 dinner meetings,*
> *but one I can bring you to since he's an old friend.*

> *Just don't get all excited about going away alright?*
> *It's for work.*

Not two minutes later, he got a reply:

> *About time. I thought I'd have to convince you with*
> *some really sexy naked lingerie tonight.*

Ronan: *The lingerie would be an added bonus. I won't have a lot of time to spend with you while I'm there, but I'll try.*

Kathryn: *Don't worry. I have a credit card begging me to shop with it.*

Ronan: *So long as you show me what you got. Talk tonight. Going into meeting.*

Kathryn: *Have a good meeting.*

He sat down in his seat and while he was waiting for everyone to come in, he went through emails. He had it knocked down to 150 emails from almost 500 by the time the meeting started.

By the time he was done the first meeting, it was almost noon. He had a quick lunch then went back into two more meetings back-to-back when he realized what time it was. "Are we done," Ronan asked.

"Yes sir," one of the other men at the meeting said.

"Alright. We do a follow-up in a month and see where things stand. Hopefully we can get this going," Ronan said as he grabbed his papers and laptop and shook a few hands as he left and went back to his office. He went and organized his paperwork for the next day and headed home, noticing that it was almost 5:30.

He headed home and when he got there, Anna was sitting on his front steps. "The part where I said to you to go away and leave me alone meant nothing?"

"Why can't you just give me another chance?"

"Because I don't tend to date women who screwed around with my friend in my house. We broke it off for a reason. Go away Anna. Go back to whatever hole you crawled out of and leave me alone. Don't harass me at the bar, don't follow me to another pub. Just go away. Leave me and my friends alone."

"Who's the new girl?"

"None of your business. Go away Anna before I charge you with trespassing." Ronan walked inside and locked the door behind him, making sure that she left.

He walked upstairs and had a quick shower, getting changed to go down to the pub when he heard a car pull into the driveway. He looked out the window and saw Katie stepping out of her car with her bag in hand. He went downstairs and opened the door for her.

"I was wondering when you were coming."

"Why do you look like you're all stressed," Katie asked.

"Long story. Just glad that you're here."

"Ronan, tell me what's wrong."

"My ex showed and decided to be a psycho. Beyond that, nothing. I told her to leave, or I'd call the authorities."

"It didn't really get that bad, did it?" Ronan nodded and took her bag upstairs. She followed him, closing and locking the door behind her.

"Ronan."

"Yes lass," he said walking into his main bedroom.

"Are you letting me stay tonight?"

"As long as world war three about me not saying it doesn't happen again, you can stay."

"Good," Katie said as she kissed him. He picked her up and wrapped her legs around his hips as he leaned her onto the bed. He kissed her, devouring her lips.

"I thought we were supposed to go meet Mia and Kian."

"They can wait." He went to peel off her sweater dress and his phone rang.

"Ronan."

"They're waiting." He kissed her again and slid the dress off, revealing black lace lingerie.

"Ronan, don't..."

He kissed her. "Don't what?"

"The phone." He grabbed it and saw two missed calls from

Kian. When the phone rang again, he answered.

"Kian, kinda busy."

"Waiting on you two. Hurry up," Kian joked as he laughed.

"Working on it. Gimme 20."

He hung up and Ronan peeled the lace panties off and slid them in his jeans pocket. "Ronan, what are…"

He kissed her again and Katie shook her head. "Much better," he teased.

"Meaning what," she asked.

"They're staying off."

"Ronan."

"Don't tempt me or I'm taking this lacy bra off too." She shook her head, and he kissed her again.

"Take your jeans off."

He shook his head. "I'm getting you all warmed up."

"Meaning what?" He kissed her then his kisses moved lower as he nibbled at each of her breasts through the lace bra.

"Aah." He smirked and moved lower. He kissed, licked and nibbled his way down her torso until he got to her hip, then her inner thigh. "Ronan." He licked at the wetness between her legs, and he knew her toes were curling in her boots.

"Yes lass," he said as he kept going and teasing.

"Ahh."

"Want me to stop."

"Hell no." He kept going then his finger slid inside her and teased until her body was throbbing for him.

"I want you," she said.

"How badly," he asked.

"Now Ronan. Please." Two fingers slid inside her, continuing to turn her on.

"Ronan." He shook his head, and she reached for him. "Please."

"And if I say no," he asked.

"Mm. Please." He licked even more, teasing until he knew she was about to explode. "Ronan." He kissed his way back up her torso and she reached for the button of his jeans.

"Later." She shook her head.

"Now." She undid his jeans, and he shook his head. "I'm not done," he teased.

"I need you inside me." He kissed her and he felt her hand on him.

"Katie."

"Now." He was past turned on and had been since the

second she'd walked into the house. He slid up to her and she wrapped her arms around her almost positioning herself so he could slide deep inside her.

"Katie, not..." She pulled his body to her with her legs, and he was deep inside her. "Mine," she replied.

"This what you want right now," he asked. Katie nodded and he slowly started sliding inside her and out, harder and deeper and slowly increased his pace as her body throbbed around him. "Shit Ronan." He kept going, harder then faster. When her body tightened around him, he exploded into her as she found her release.

"That what you wanted," he teased as he kissed her.

"I missed you all day," Katie said.

"Then you should probably get dressed."

"Then give me the lace panties you stole."

He shook his head. "Those are mine for tonight."

"Ronan, not at the pub with them."

"Never know." He kissed her, unwrapped her legs from around him and got up, walking into the bathroom to clean up a little then she came in behind him.

"What," he asked.

"You are intentionally teasing."

"Warming you up for later."

"Ronan."

He kissed her. "I'll meet you downstairs lass." She kissed him and nodded, and he went downstairs, grabbing his phone on the way.

Just as Kathryn reached the bottom step, his phone buzzed with a text:

> *Back at our pub. Anna showed at the other one.*
> *Ordering you a pint. Get over here. Mia thinks you*
> *have her tied up in the house.*

Ronan replied:

> *Had her tied up in a way. Be there in 5.*

"And what embarrassing excuse did you make?"

"Told them we were busy for a little bit. They're waiting at the pub."

"Then we should probably go," Kathryn said as he nodded and got up. He opened the door for her, locked up behind them and they made their way over to the pub.

"Odd question, but why do we always go to the pub when there's a million restaurants we can go to?"

"Sort of like my second home. Pete is almost family," Ronan said. The bartender welcomed them the minute they walked through the doors and brought over a pint for Ronan and an espresso martini for Katie.

"Thank you," Ronan said.

"And I got rid of the riff-raff for you. Thought you deserved a night to relax. I even put on the fish for you."

"Thank you," Katie said.

"Most welcome lass. Enjoy your drinks."

"I take it that means fish and chips," Katie asked.

"Kinda had a craving for them," Ronan replied.

"So, what took you so long," Mia teased.

"Am I not allowed to have alone time with my date?"

"Ronan, she's my friend. Try not to distract her," Mia teased.

"Well your friend is my girlfriend Mia. Try not to get too jealous about it," Ronan teased.

"And how did the meetings go," Kian asked.

"Long. We're not meeting you Friday night. We have a foundation thing," Ronan said.

"Well aren't you two just special," Mia teased.

"It's a cocktail party thing. Not exactly my favorite part of the foundation stuff."

"Ronan, you're Mr. Popular. You even were in high school. If it's a fundraising thing, you can do it and you know it."

"Not my favorite. I'd rather not."

"Our first event as a couple," Katie said.

"Another reason why. I don't need everyone in our business."

"It's not really that bad Ronan. It's a big step," Kian teased.

"Funny," Ronan replied. He took a gulp of his pint, and the fish and chips showed.

"Thank you Pete," Katie said. "Most welcome Miss Katie. Enjoy." He brought two more over for Mia and Kian and they all sat and ate and visited. As soon as they all finished eating, Pete came over with refills.

"So, what are you two up to tomorrow," Katie asked determined to make more small talk.

"We actually have to go pick up the keys tomorrow," Mia said.

"You bought the house," Ronan asked.

"We're already engaged. Might as well get a place we can grow into now right," Kian said.

"At least you'll be able to walk home from the pub now," Ronan teased.

"You won't believe who the last owner was," Mia said.

"No," Ronan replied.

"Still can't quite believe it myself," Kian said.

"At least she won't be around here. I don't need to see her in here," Ronan replied.

"She's still gonna come in here. You and I both know that," Mia said.

"Let's just hope she goes away. I don't want to see her in here or at my place," Ronan said.

"She showed up at your house," Kian asked.

"I got her to leave." Katie took a deep breath. At that moment she knew why he was in such a mood when she showed up.

"So, what are you gonna wear to the foundation thing," Mia asked determined to change the topic.

"It's a cocktail party Mia. One I wish I didn't have to attend to be honest," Ronan said.

"And why is that," Katie asked as he looked at her.

"Because I would rather do anything else except another stupid cocktail party," Ronan said.

"And just what does anything else entail," Katie asked.

"A few things," he teased as his hand slid to her leg and very gently slid its way up to the apex of her thighs as his fingers grazed her and she almost jumped in the seat. She looked at him and he kept teasing, intentionally blocking anyone from seeing anything.

"You two. Seriously. So, boss man said something about working with you on a project," Kian said.

"He's putting something together that is a sort of singles

event. Travel around Ireland, Scotland and England. We were looking at hotel suggestions since we have a hotel in the list of companies I own."

"So, he took my idea and ran with it," Kian said.

"How did I know that's what you'd come up with?"

"Because we've both been trying to set you up for years and you wouldn't let us," Mia chimed in. He continued to tease Katie and when she grabbed his hand under the table, he smirked.

"I didn't let you because you suck at setting people up. The girls you tried to talk me into dating?"

"And how bad were they," Katie asked as she managed to catch her breath.

"They weren't my type at all. I mean, you remember that girl Janie," Ronan said.

"Fine. Mia chose that one, but they weren't all bad," Kian said.

"Most of them were," Ronan replied.

"I suck at setting people up. I get it," Mia said.

"Just bad choice in people, but we don't exactly count in that," Ronan teased.

"I totally would've set you up with Katie," Mia said.

"If you'd ever met her," Ronan said.

"You two realize that I'm right here right," Katie said.

When Ronan's hand slid up her leg again, she stopped him. He brushed her hand away and kept going. She looked at him and shook her head. "So, what time are you two heading to the party on Friday," Kian asked.

"I think we have to be there at 6 or something don't we," Katie asked.

"Meaning no we aren't coming to the pub on Friday night," Ronan said.

"And are you two coming for Sunday," Mia asked.

"Honestly, I think I'll stay home," Ronan teased.

"You haven't missed a Sunday in years. Come on Ronan," Kian said.

"I'll talk him into it," Katie said as he started teasing again. He got up and excused himself and went over to talk to Pete. Katie went down to the ladies to try and regain her composure. She looked and the room was empty except for her. When there was a knock, she opened the door and let him in as he locked the door behind him and kissed her, pinning her against the door.

"You have to stop teasing."

"Says who," Ronan asked. He picked her up and sat her on the counter.

"Ronan."

"What?"

"Not here." He kissed her again and undid the zipper of his jeans.

"Ronan."

"Why not here?"

"Because..." He kissed her, devouring her lips and she felt him slide deep inside her.

"Aah."

"Complaining?"

"Shit Ronan." He kept going and teasing and pounding into her over and over until he could feel her body throbbing.

"Now you know why I said skirt."

"Shit."

"Harder?"

She nodded and he pinned her hands to the counter and kept going, harder and faster until she exploded around him once, then twice. When he finally reached his climax, her legs were shaking around him.

"Now what were you saying?"

"Not fair."

"Not fair would be sliding my fingers inside you at the table and not expecting you to explode," he whispered. He slid out of her and zipped his jeans up.

"You don't play fair Ronan."

He kissed her. "And you love that I don't."

"I think we need to go."

"And why is that?"

"Because this isn't enough."

"Tell me what you want."

"Kinda miss the tie."

"Then come up with a good excuse." He kissed her again and headed out of the ladies room.

Katie cleaned up a little bit, fixed her lip gloss and walked back to the table as Ronan let her into the corner. When Ronan swore he saw Anna show up, he shook his head and got up.

"What are you doing," Kian asked.

"We're gonna head out and have our alone time," Ronan said.

"You sure about that," Mia teased.

"Positive." He paid the tab and gave Kian and Mia a quick hug goodbye, as did Katie, and they headed out, avoiding any sight of Anna whatsoever. He took Katie's hand and walked her back to his place.

"Are we really gonna take off every time she shows up?"

He nodded. "She showed up here before you came and started crap. I told her to back off and stay away, but she's determined to start a war. I'm not playing her game Katie."
"You're playing mine instead," Katie teased.

"If yours includes bed and you moaning my name, I'll accept that," he teased.

"Why do you always go there," she teased.

"Because that's where we're going lass."

He kissed her the minute they were at the front door and walked her inside. "That whole bathroom thing wasn't fair." He pinned her against the back of the front door and kissed her.

"And?"

"Either was what you did at the table." He kissed her again and went to slide the sweater dress off when she stopped him.

"What?"

"No more teasing." His hand slid to her leg and inched the sweater dress up little by little. "Ronan."

"What," he asked as he felt her warmth against his hand and started teasing all over again.

"Mm."

"More?"

"Sofa." He picked her up and walked to the sofa, leaning her onto it and kept teasing, then peeled her sweater dress off. "Ronan, stop."

"What?"

"Teasing."

"But I'm good at it," he said as he kissed her then kissed down her torso.

"You're more than...ahh...good at it."

"Was that a compliment," he asked as he licked at her inner thigh then nibbled.

"Shit."

"What," he teased.

"Definitely more than good." One lick and her body was already reacting. He slid her boots off and saw her toes curling.

"Katie."

"What?"

"You sure good is enough?"

"Mm." He nibbled and licked and teased then his fingers slid inside her.

"Ronan."

"Want something?"

"Now."

"Upstairs."

She shook her head. "Here." He picked her up and carried her up the stairs to the bedroom and leaned her onto the bed.

Chapter 9

He leaned into her arms and kissed her, devouring her lips and she felt something slide around her hands as her hands felt immobilized. "What did..." He kissed her again then kissed back down her torso, getting back to what he'd started downstairs. "Aah."

"All turned on already lass."

"Ronan."

"More?"

"Please Ronan," she moaned.

"Please what?"

"Clothes off."

"You sure that you don't want more of this," he said as his fingers slid in and out and teased even more.

"Ronan," she moaned.

"More?"

"You."

"Again?" She nodded trying to wriggle her hands out of his tie.

"You're not gonna get your hands out of there lass. It's a double knot intentionally."

"Ronan, please." He slid his sweater off and Katie just

watched. He undid her bra and slid it off and the straps undone, knocking it to the floor.

"Ronan." He kicked his jeans off and kissed her.

"What?"

"I want to taste you." He shook his head.

"Oh really," Ronan asked.

"Mine," she said.

"If you start that, you best bet I'll be finishing it. You know that right?" She nodded and he slid his boxers off. "You sure," he asked.

When her mouth opened, he took a deep breath and let her hands go. She slid her mouth onto him and he sucked in a breath. "Mm," she said as she slid her mouth deeper onto him, back and forth, over and over until he was shaking his head.

"What," she asked as she stopped. He slid back and tied her hands again.

"Ronan." He slid onto the bed and pulled her legs around him.

He slid into her until her breath hitched.

"Tell me what you want," he asked as he wrapped her legs around his waist.

"You."

"More."

"I want you inside me. Deep. Hard."

"That I can do sexy lass of mine." He kissed her, devouring her lips and slid deeper inside her then kept sliding in and out, harder and deeper until he could feel her body throbbing.

"More," he asked.

"Mm." He kept going and going until he couldn't hold himself back. "Ronan."

"Mine," he replied as he exploded into her and collapsed into her arms, untying her hands. Her arms wrapped around him and it was almost like it was what he somehow needed. He rolled to his back and curled her to him.

"Why do you feel like you just sighed," Katie asked.

"Just a crapload of stuff on my mind," Ronan said.

"Such as?"

"You know that she showed earlier."

"Ronan, we don't have to talk about it. You know that right?"

"She showed up and tried to talk me into taking her back."

"And," Katie asked almost hesitant.

"I'm not going backwards if that's what you're wondering."

"Ronan, is she the real reason why you haven't dated in so long?"

He nodded. "Second, I never met anyone I wanted to see more than once until I met you and your daring attitude."

"Meaning what," Katie asked.

"I didn't even want to date until I met you."

"Even when Mia and Kian set you up?"

"I just never connected to anyone else. That's all," he said.

"But why me?"

"You're the only one who got my attention somehow. I couldn't stop thinking about you. That's why I called, Katie. Then the second time. Then the third. Then you daring me to go on a real date with you."

"Because I teased you."

"Because you made me look up and think about what I was doing. You're the first girl I even gave a chance to for a reason. She screwed me up badly. Seeing someone do that messed me up."

"Ronan."

"What?"

"I'm a one guy person. You know that. I wouldn't go along with all of the stuff that you're doing if I didn't want it too."

"Katie."

"What?"

"You realize you can say no."

"No need to Ronan."

He kissed her. "And if I tried something that was too much for you?"

"You'd know. I already know what you're suggesting Ronan."

"And?"

"Not tonight."

"Wasn't planning on talking you into that tonight. That's much more of a weekend thing," he teased.

"Oh really? Before or after church?"

"Before. Something to confess to." Kathryn shook her head and laughed. "Who said I was joking Katie?"

"Since I know you aren't you mean?"

"Not even a little bit lass."

"That's not happening this weekend Ronan."

"You sure about that?"

"I'm sure." He nodded with a smirk. "Ronan."

"Next weekend."

"Ronan, cut it out. I know exactly what you're up to and I'm saying no."

"And if I talk you into it?"

"Unless I'm 5 or 6 espresso martinis in, no."

"That could be arranged lass. Sports Sunday with Mia and Kian."

"Still no."

"Could just do that whole counter thing again."

"Or we could just go and enjoy being out with friends."

"Or not."

"I could even wear your jersey."

"Katie."

"Or I could just talk you into staying here," she teased.

"I'd never live that one down. Missing a Sunday," Ronan said with a laugh.

"And if I said I wanted you here in bed on Sunday instead of going?"

"We'd still end up there even if it was only for a drink with them."

"Are they the only two friends you have?"

"Longest two."

"Think we can have a just us date night?"

"Friday." She shook her head and kissed him. "Other than a foundation event."

"And where did you want to go?"

"Anywhere but here and the pub."

"I can come up with something," Ronan said.

"Just warn me so I know what to wear."

"Leave it at a sexy dress or something." She shook her head with a smirk ear to ear.

"And would you start with what you did at the pub tonight?"

"Maybe," he teased.

She smirked. "I'll say it. It was hot."

"That was kind of the idea I was running with. Teasing you until you can barely walk is one of my new favorite things lass."

Katie smirked and kissed him and he leaned her to her back and devoured her lips. "I bet."

He kissed her again and her legs wrapped around his. "What," she asked.

"Promise me something."

"Ronan."

"Seriously. Promise me something."

"Anything."

"Promise me that if somewhere down the road you change your mind about us. Promise me that you won't walk away with someone else."

"Ronan, I don't think I ever could not be honest with you."

"Meaning what?"

"Walk away. Cheat. I couldn't."

"Have you ever?"

"Never. I promise you that. When I decide what I want, I don't walk away from that until we both choose too. Even then I kinda fight until it's not worth fighting for anymore."

"Katie."

"What," she asked as she slid her hand along the side of his head and almost cradled his face in her hand.

"I don't think I could give you up."

"Good. I like it that way." He kissed her again, devouring her lips as he deepened the kiss and his hands slid to her backside, pulling her tight to him.

"Tell me what you want Ronan."

He kissed her. "Just you."

Somehow, those words were enough to make him rethink

what he was doing. He kissed her again and they were curled up together making out for what felt like hours. He leaned onto his back and she curled up to him.

"Ronan."

"Yes lass," he replied.

"Tell me what you really want. Tell me what you want from me."

"Honesty, a little faith in me, trust. I want you to feel like you can say or do anything. Tell me anything. If what I do is too much, tell me. If it's too hard to handle, say something. If I'm pushing you too far, say something. That's all I ask."

"Ronan."

"What?"

"What put you into mush level 2.0," she teased.

"Honestly, you fighting until we fight it out. Nobody gives up until we're both ready to."

"I don't give up Ronan. Anyone that does is pointless," Katie replied.

"I always did give up before. After one date, I walked away instead of getting hurt all over again."

"So what did it? Me daring you to really date me?"

"Partially," he replied.

"What else," Katie asked.

"You. Just you."

"Ronan, be honest."

"I am. The first night we met. I left and I couldn't stop thinking about you. The second time, I didn't want to leave."

"But you did."

"We did."

"Ronan."

"Now, I don't want to let go."

"Ronan, seriously."

"I don't." He kissed her again and curled up in the blankets with her.

"Sleep lass."

"Promise me that you won't break my heart," she asked.

"As long as you never break mine."

"And here I thought that the big tough sexy man didn't have one."

He shook his head. "Just has a few million walls around it."

"You gonna tell me why you were trying to keep me at arms length this week?"

"Because I needed to know that you wanted me and not just all the bonuses that come with me."

"And would those bonuses be what you did tonight that still has my legs shaking?"

"Both times."

"Ronan, come on."

"The money and the restaurants and the trips and everything else. I just needed to know that you were here for more than just that."

"I'm happy with a picnic in the park," Katie said.

"And you're gonna get that picnic when I know it's not going to rain."

"Saturday." He smirked.

"What if we went somewhere alone?"

"Like where? London?"

"Still cruising to go with me aren't you," he asked.

"Yes. I still want to go with you."

"Katie, it's a business trip."

"One where you can bring me."

"Did you really ask for the time off?"

She nodded. "All week."

"You really want to go even if I'm in meetings the entire time we're there."

"I want to be there with you. Be with you when you're done work. Tease you with lingerie pictures when you're in a tough meeting. All of it," she replied.

"Now when you say teasing..."

She kissed him. "Ronan."

"Seriously though. What kind of lingerie are we talking about?"

"The kind that your dirty mind would love."

"You really want to go," he asked as Katie curled up to him.

"I haven't been to London in years Ronan. I just want to go with you. When you're done meetings, we can go to dinner or go walk around together. I know you want company."

"Are you saying it because you're worried that I'll have someone else to keep me company in my bed?"

"Honestly, partially a little worried about that."

"You mean since you don't trust that I won't."

"I honestly don't think you would do that. I just don't want to worry that it happens."

"Then you don't trust me."

"I do. I just want..."

He kissed her again. "You don't."

"Ronan." He kissed her again, devouring her lips.

"If we're together, I'm not with someone else. Nobody else lass."

"What if someone makes a move," Katie asked.

"Lass, we're together. Nobody is making a move and getting anywhere with it. If that's the only reason..."

She shook her head and kissed him. "It isn't."

"Then we're fine. If you really want to come, I'll see if I can take Monday off and we'll go Monday so we have a day to hang out a bit."

"How are we getting there," Katie asked.

"Well, we're taking the company plane over since it's a short trip. You have a passport, yes?"

She nodded.

"Then we'll go Monday."

"You sure?"

"You already took the week off anyway," Ronan replied.

"You sure you're okay with me coming?"

"Gives me a day to take you on a picnic while we're there."

"You don't have to. You know that right?"

"Still doing it. We can get some stuff while we're there and go down to a park somewhere. I mean, unless you really want to go shopping when we get there."

"I think trying out the big bed sounded better." He kissed her and pulled her legs around him again.

"And just what did you want to do in that big bed at the hotel in London?"

"I had a few ideas."

"Any that would make your toes permanently curl?"

His hand slid up her legs. "Ronan."

"What?"

"I know what you're doing."

"Good thing," he said as his fingers started to tease her all over again.

"Mm."

"Katie."

"Yes," she replied.

"I have an idea."

"What?" He kissed her, devouring her lips and slid his fingers inside her.

"Shit."

"All turned on all over again."

"Ronan."

"Say it lass," he said as he kissed her neck then down to her breasts.

"I want you."

"Isn't that just convenient that I happen to be here," he teased.

"Ronan." Her legs wrapped tighter around him, almost coiling like a snake around him. When he felt her hand slide around him, he shook his head.

"Don't make me tie your hands."

"Warming you up like you're doing to me," she said almost breathless. He grabbed her hand, pinning it to the bed and moved his hand, sliding deep inside her.

"Aah."

"You were saying?"

"Ronan."

"What?"

"Shit." He took his time, teasing and going hard and deep but slowly, then sped up a little. He wanted it to last a lot longer. He wanted to feel her throbbing around him all damn night if he could've. When he managed to let her up for air, she was throbbing. He started going a little faster and devoured her lips.

"Ronan, ahh. I…"

"What," he teased as he kept going.

"Mm." She moaned and her body was throbbing all over again.

"Katie."

"What," she said breathlessly.

"You're coming to London."

"Good," she replied as she moaned again. When he finally exploded into her, he kissed her again.

"Don't ever leave."

"Ronan."

"Just don't. Promise me."

She kissed him. "Ronan, I'm not going anywhere. I promise you." He devoured her lips again and leaned onto his back, pulling her to him.

"What," Katie asked.

"You sure?"

"About what?"

"That you want this. That you want me and you no matter how crazy things get?"

"Ronan, I know what you want. I also know that you're scared that it's gonna blow up in your face. I'm not going anywhere. I'm not walking away. I told you. I fight for things until the fight is over. Until you don't want to fight anymore," she said.

"I'm never not gonna fight."

"For what you want?" He nodded. "Ronan, are you really this worried?"

"When I broke it off with Anna, it killed me. It broke me in ways I didn't know were possible. That's why I stayed with one-night stands instead. It was easier to not have any dang strings. Now, I don't care about strings. I just want you and me."

"And who would've thought that one dare would do all of this," she teased.

"That dare was enough to make me realize what I had in front of me Katie."

"And?"

"I'm not letting go."

"You'd better not."

He kissed her again. When he went to get up, she pulled him back to bed. "Two minutes." She nodded and he went into the bathroom and cleaned up a little. When he walked back in, she was sliding on one of his white t-shirts.

"What are you up to?"

"Stealing something other than your rugby shirts," she teased.

"I see that," he said as he grabbed a pair of boxers and slid them on, sliding back under the covers with her.

"Ronan."

'What lass?"

"I want you to come to my place tomorrow night."

"Flatmate."

"She's gone to Belfast for the weekend with her boyfriend. Just come to my place. Please?"

"What if I come over and pick you up and we can go do dinner alone."

"Then we're going back to my place after."

"Katie."

"One night, then we can do whatever you want."

"Whatever I want meaning what," he teased.

"You are so bad."

"What was the answer to that?"

"Meaning we can come back here on Saturday night if that's what..."

"We have the foundation thing on Friday."

"Saturday then you can stay at my place."

"Could be interesting, but I still think we should just come..."

"Ronan."

"One night. I just don't want to be there when your flatmate is in town. We need privacy," he said as he curled her to him.

"And just how much privacy did you need," she asked as she slid into his lap.

"So we can do whatever we want wherever we want to even if it's on the stairs."

"And what were you gonna do on the stairs?"

"A few things. Peeling your clothes off, bending you over the steps and taking full advantage."

"Or we end up having fun on the sofa instead of bed."

"Or I sit you on the kitchen counter and lick every inch of you."

"You have a point."

"Good answer sexy."

"And are you ready for that or am I freaking you out?"

"Depends on where we're staying Friday night after the party."

"Hotel."

"Why?"

"Because I want somewhere we can be alone as close to that stupid party as possible. I may not even make it to the room with you."

"Promises, promises," Katie said as he slid her onto her back and pulled her legs back around him.

"And what do you want?"

"I have plans for you."

"Tonight?"

"Friday. I got the presidential suite."

"Ronan."

"And it involves handcuffs."

"And what else?"

"Blindfold."

"Ronan."

"And you all naked in my arms."

"And what else," Katie teased.

"That'll be a surprise."

"You're teasing intentionally."

"Peeling every inch of that sexy dress off. Getting you naked and tying you to the bed."

"Ronan, you do realize you could just not right?"

"Why? It getting you all turned on?"

"A little, but still."

"I like the control."

"And so do I. I like taking advantage of you when you least expect it."

"Katie."

"And I know you like it."

"I was stunned at the beginning, but I'll admit it. I do like."

"Good. So do I."

"Naughty lass. Very..."

She kissed him and he deepened the kiss, devouring her lips.

"We need to get sleep. No more teasing." "Back at ya handsome." He leaned back onto his back and curled her to him. She leaned onto his chest and curled up with him, wrapping her leg around his.

When he woke up the next morning, she was still curled up to him. He kissed her forehead and managed to get up, then went downstairs and did a workout. When he looked up 45 minutes later, she was watching him from the doorway.

"And good morning to you too," Ronan said with a smirk.

"I was wondering where you vanished to," Katie said.

"Wanted to get a quick workout in before we both head into work."

"And what else," she teased.

"My girl," he said.

"Do I know her?"

"Not funny Katie." He pulled her to him and leaned her against the wall by the door.

"What," she asked.

He kissed her, devouring her lips and wrapped her legs around his hips. "Where are we going," she asked.

"Two choices. Bed or here?"

"Ronan." He kissed her again and carried her to the workout bench. "What are you up to," Katie asked.

"Making up for not being in bed when you woke up."

"Ronan." He kissed her and peeled her shirt off.

"Here?"

He kicked his joggers off and pulled her on top of him.

"Aah."

"That what you wanted?"

She smirked and nodded. "Part of it," she teased as he slid deep inside her and her breath hitched.

"And now," he asked.

"Mm." He leaned her onto her back and kissed down her torso. "Ronan." They had sex and it was more intense than ever. He kept going until she crashed around him more than once. He didn't know the words he needed to say, and he didn't know how or when he'd let himself admit it, but he was falling hard for her.

They came up for air and he pulled her back tight to him. "Shit."

"What," he asked.

"I'm still shaking," Katie said as he smirked.

"Good."

"What do you mean good," she asked. He kissed her, stood up, pulled his joggers on and picked her up, carrying her back to the bedroom and leaned her onto the bed.

"What are you up to," Katie asked.

"Curling up with my girl. I'm gonna make you breakfast in bed."

"That's the plan is it handsome?"

"That is. You wanted me back in bed, which was sorta where I was headed after I finished doing the workout."

"Oh really."

"I was gonna wake you up in the best way."

"And how was that," she mewed.

"Oh I have my ways."

"Give me a hint." He kissed her then kissed down her torso.

"Ronan."

"Then this," he said as he kissed her inner thigh, then the apex of her thighs as her toes almost instinctively curled.

"That's what you were gonna do?"

He nodded and kept teasing. "The start of it."

"Ronan."

"Yes lass."

"I know what you're doing."

"Good. I'd hate to have to explain it to you," he said as he continued to tease.

"Mm."

"Much better."

"Aah. Ronan."

He kept going. "More?"

"Mm." His fingers took over the teasing and she wriggled, attempting to slide away from him.

"And where are you going lass?"

"Aah."

"That's what I thought," he said as she brushed his hand away and reached for the waistline of his joggers.

"Tell me what you want Katie."

"You."

"Which part?"

"All of you." He kissed her and felt her hand slide under the waist of his joggers. He grabbed her hands and pinned them over her head.

"I know what you're up to lass."

"Then take them off." He kicked his joggers off and she slid her legs around him.

"More," he asked.

She nodded. "Katie."

"What?"

"You sure?"

She nodded. "Then roll over." She shook her head. He

turned her to face the bed and slid inside her. Deep inside her to the point that her breath hitched, and he pulled her up, so her back was against his chest.

"Aah."

"This what you wanted," he asked as he slid in and out, harder, faster until she was shaking in his arms. "Tell me," he said as he kept going.

"Aah. You. More." He kept going then let his hand slide down to between her legs and teased as he kept going.

"Ronan."

"What lass?"

"Ahh." She was trembling in his arms and it had him even more turned on. Her arm wrapped around his, and he linked their fingers and bent her over and kept going until he was completely spent.

"Shit," she said as he collapsed onto the bed and leaned to his side.

"That's what you would've done," Katie asked.

"Yes," he teased, kissing the back of her neck and pulling her tight to him.

"I think I'll fake being asleep tomorrow," Katie joked.

"And what makes you think that's the only thing I'll do," he teased as he kissed her shoulder.

"Ronan."

"Yes lass."

"What are you doing tonight?"

"Other than making your legs shake and your toes curl?"

"Good."

"Tomorrow night is the foundation thing."

"How often do they have stuff," Katie asked.

"Luckily, we have a few weeks before the next one after Friday."

"Ronan."

"Yes."

"Do we have to go to work?"

"Unfortunately, yes. We have time though. It's not even 8."

"What time is it?"

"Quarter to 7."

She went to turn and face him and he smirked. "Katie, behave."

"Or what," she asked as she kissed him. He shook his head, sliding his hand to her face and brushing a stray hair behind her ear.

"We're getting up." She shook her head. "Shower lass."

He kissed her and got up, walked into the bathroom and flipped the water on to warm it up for the shower. He freshened up a little then went and slid under the hot water. He washed his hair and just as he was rinsing out the shampoo, he heard her stepping in, then felt her arms wrap around him. He turned her so she was under the water and kissed her.

"You are such a party pooper," Katie said.

"I know exactly what you were up to lass."

"Like you aren't tempted to tease."

"Like this," he asked as he kissed down her neck then to her breasts as she rinsed her hair.

"Ronan."

"That's exactly what I'd be doing if I was teasing you, but I'm not going to," he joked as she shook her head.

"You aren't playing fair."

"Do I ever lass?"

He kissed her, rinsed off and stepped out, drying off with a warm towel. He wrapped it around his waist and walked into his closet, grabbing his dress shirt and pants and boxers, putting them on the bed.

Katie finished her shower, turned the water off and wrapped herself in the other warm towel from the heater.

She freshened up a little and stepped into the bedroom, seeing him in boxers and dress pants. "I say you leave the shirt here," Katie joked.

"Funny. What did you want for breakfast?"

"Anything you want to make."

"And if I wanted you for breakfast?"

"Funny," she said as she kissed him.

"What?"

"Food. The stuff that you cook." He kissed her and she smirked. "I'll be down in a minute. I'm gonna attempt to get dressed."

He nodded and made his way downstairs and put on breakfast. When Katie came down in her dress pants and fancy blouse, he smirked and kissed her, then went and flipped the omelet and bacon.

"Looking fetching today lass."

"And you're flipping bacon shirtless intentionally?"

"I'm good. Promise. The coffee is almost ready."

"Ronan, are you gonna let me cook for you instead of you always cooking for me?"

"Do you want to take over the omelet," he teased.

"I'm cooking tomorrow." He nodded.

"Done."

He plated the breakfast and brought it over as she made their coffees and brought them to the table for them.

"And what's this," Katie asked.

"Omelet. One big one that I halved for us."

"Yum," she said as she took the first bite.

"Your turn tomorrow," he teased.

"Would you be okay with me leaving a few things here so I don't have to drag them back and forth?"

"If that's what you want. Makes sense since you're always coming over here."

"And you love it."

He smirked and kissed her. "Getting used to you being around. That's all it is," he said.

"You sure," Katie asked with a suggestive smirk ear to ear.

"I'm sure. What else were you thinking it was?"

"Maybe that you love me or something like that."

Divulging that wasn't an option, at least not yet. "I told you before lass. When I'm ready to say it, you'll know."

"And just how will I know," Katie asked.

He kissed her. "Trust me. You'll know. Big sign."

He smirked and finished eating. "Ronan."

"What lass?"

"What do you mean by a big sign?"

"Red roses or something."

Katie smirked. "I like that plan," Katie said.

"Might be something else." He got up, kissed her and went and did the dishes, cleaning up.

"So, where are we going tonight?"

"You want to go somewhere nice, we can. Tomorrow is that cocktail party thing."

"I know that you seriously hate the parties, but it's not that bad is it?"

"I've had to go to them for years. Just not a fan. I'd rather just stay away and donate, but since they put me in a higher up position, I have to go to the damn events."

"And that's why you avoid the party and go up to your suite."

He nodded. "Are you gonna stay with me?"

"Since it's 15 minutes from here?"

"Yes or no lass?"

"Okay." He smirked.

"Good answer."

She came and helped him finish the dishes then he picked her up and sat her on the counter. "Ronan."

"What," he asked as he wrapped her legs around him.

"Teasing intentionally."

"Making a very strong point."

"Which is," she asked. He kissed her, devouring her lips and deepening the kiss until her nails were digging into his back.

"Upstairs or are you behaving?"

She kissed him again and he picked her up and carried her upstairs.

"What time is it," she asked.

"Half seven." Katie kissed him again and he leaned her onto the bed.

"Tell me what you want." She slid off her dress pants.

"Mm."

"Words," he replied as he slid his dress pants off and his boxers.

"You. Every damn inch of you." He slid off the sexy panties and kissed up her leg.

"Ronan." He leaned between her legs and kissed and licked and teased until she was reaching for him.

"Come here," Katie begged. He kissed his way up her torso and devoured her lips as her legs wrapped tight around him. He slid deep inside her and her breath hitched.

"That what you wanted?"

She nodded and he kissed her. "Good. You're mine lass. Every sexy inch of you is mine. Don't ever forget it," he teased as he slid deep inside her over and over, faster and faster until her body started throbbing around him.

"Aah."

"Good," he teased as he went harder and faster. He kissed her again and kept going. When her body tightened around him, he couldn't hold himself back. He exploded into her and kissed her.

"Shit," Ronan said.

"What?"

"You're addictive."

"Oh really?"

He nodded. "I'm beginning to think I may have to keep you around after all."

"And why is that," Katie asked as her breathing started to slow along with her racing heart.

"Good way to start the morning," he teased.

"Ronan."

"What?"

"Really good way to start the morning." He kissed her and got up.

"We have to be out of here in 15," he said.

They both cleaned up a little, got re-dressed and headed downstairs to head off. "Phone," he asked.

"In your jacket pocket," Katie said.

"Thank you." She slid hers in her purse and he walked her out, locking up and flipping the alarm on behind him. He walked her to her car, got her door for her and after one last kiss, she headed off and he hopped in his car and went off to the office.

He walked in and saw a package on his desk. "Just showed up this morning for you. Were you waiting on anything, his assistant asked.

"Not exactly," he replied.

"Was it scanned?" "Just. Security gave it the clearance." Ronan opened it and saw an award.

"What's this," he asked as he pulled it out. He read the small plaque on it:

Foundation Chairman – Ronan P Kelly – Longest Standing Board Member

He shook his head. "At least they didn't decide to pull this at the damn event this weekend."

"Did you want me to put it anywhere or did you want to find space in the office," his assistant asked.

"I have one spot on the table for it, but honestly, it almost feels ridiculous. An award they didn't need to do."

"It is nice that they gave it to you though."

"A little much if you ask me. Anything else going on that I missed," he asked.

"No messages. Just that one meeting today. It's a pretty quiet day," his assistant replied.

"Thank you for that. Can you do me a favor and book that fancy restaurant for me? For two," Ronan said.

"Will do. 6pm?" Ronan nodded. She nodded and left his office, and he sent a quick message off to Katie:

> *Dinner tonight. Somewhere nice. Dress or a skirt. You know what I want.*

He smirked and put his phone down, getting a call all of 5 minutes later. "And what do you want," Ronan asked almost laughing as he saw Kian's name on the call display.

"Boss wants to make a donation at that thing tomorrow. He's coming with the wife supposedly. Wanted to warn you so you don't run off before he gets there," Kian teased.

"Then tell him to get there early. Katie's coming with me."

"Go figure."

"She's the admin for the foundation. She kind of has to be there."

"Are you two coming out on Saturday?"

"Not sure. She's determined to get me to stay at her place."

"Are you gonna tell her or what," Kian asked.

"Tell her what?"

"That you like her. You know exactly what I'm talking about."

"You are never gonna stop interfering are you?"

"She likes you. We all see it. You're just blind to it my friend."

"She told me that she loved me."

"Shit. I take it that you feel the same but you aren't gonna tell her as per Ronan usual."

"Not there yet. That's all. I am getting used to her being around. I kind of like it."

"Go figure. It took the one girl who challenges you on everything to make you stop being a dick."

"Kian."

"What?"

"Screw off."

"At least she's a good lass. I mean, if she were anything like Anna, I'd have to kick your butt to get you to snap out of it. I like her."

"And so does Mia. I know."

"Then we'll see you Saturday."

"Or Sunday instead."

"Just let me know."

"Will do. Get back to work Kian."

"Back at ya boss man." They hung up and Ronan's phone buzzed.

"Katie."

"How dressy?"

"Sexy dress for me."

"I know what you meant with that other thing, but still. Why?"

"Because I fully intend on taunting you all the way through dinner, and all the way back to the house."

"Don't you have work to do instead of working that dirty mind of yours," Katie asked.

"I do. Just wanted to make you squirm a little while you were at work."

"You succeeded. What time are you heading home?"

"Probably 4. I'm done my meeting early today."

"Then I'll meet you at 5. I have a few things to grab from the house."

"Alright lass. I'll see you tonight."

"Ronan."

"Yes."

"Thank you."

"For what?"

"Giving me a smile when I needed it."

"Welcome lass. You'll have a bigger one later."

"I bet. See you tonight." They hung up and Ronan went through the mass amount of emails.

By the time he headed home at the end of the day, he was actually relaxed and in a good mood. He stopped and got her some flowers, avoiding red roses, and got them delivered to her place. He got to his place, got his mail, flipping through it, went inside and paid a few bills online, then went upstairs to shower before he took her to dinner. When he stepped out of the shower, he heard his phone buzz:

On my way handsome. See you soon.

He went and changed, put on some cologne that he knew she liked, and went downstairs. Just as he was about to sit and double check emails, she pulled into the driveway. He got up, went outside and helped her with her bag, walking her inside.

"About time you showed," he teased as he kissed her and closed the door.

"So, are you gonna tell me where we're going?"

"Somewhere you haven't been. I'm getting a car to take us," Ronan said.

"Why?"

"So we can both have a drink." He took her bag upstairs and she followed in the sexy black dress.

"You do realize that dress is almost too sexy right," he asked.

"And why is that? You said to wear something sexy."

"And what lacy thing did you put under it," he teased.

"I guess you'll find out later," she said.

"Or not."

"Meaning what?" He pulled her to him and his hands slid to her backside.

"Minimal."

"Ronan."

"Take them off." She shook her head. "Katie."

"No." He kissed her and slid them off himself.

"Ronan, why?"

"Because we're having a little fun on the way there."

"Such as what," Katie asked. His hand slid to the apex of her thighs and started teasing. "Ronan," she said as her breath hitched. "Aah."

"A little of this now, a little while we're in the car, and more when we're at the restaurant." She shook her head, and he kissed her and slid two fingers deep inside her.

"Aah."

"Still want me to stop?"

"No." He leaned her onto the bed and kept going then kissed down her torso and then licked between her thighs sliding the hem of the dress up.

"Shit."

"All turned on and nothing I can do to fix it," he teased. He licked then nibbled and her legs tightened.

"Ronan."

"What," he asked as he kept going with his fingers.

"Aah."

"Do you want me to stop?"

"No." His phone buzzed and he grabbed it.

"Car is here to pick us up," he teased.

"Not yet."

"Come on lass. Let's go before we're late." She shook her head.

"Ronan."

"I'll finish that tonight." He slid to her feet, helping her up and they walked downstairs as she slid her dress back down. He got the door for her, helped her with her coat and they headed off in the waiting car.

"You do realize that wasn't exactly fair right," Katie asked quietly as his hand rested on her knee in the car.

"Yeah I do lass. That was just the start."

"Meaning?"

"That was just the beginning."

"And just what were you planning to do," she said quietly. He kissed her.

"Make you squirm here and at the table. Then I'll take you home and make you explode over and over all night if I have to. My plan was to spend all night in bed together."

"So, you're planning for me to not be able to walk tomorrow night?"

"My plan is for you to beg for more tomorrow night."

"Or you could just not do an all-night thing tonight."

"Or I could just take you straight to the hotel tomorrow night."

"Or we could just go to the event and sneak out early."

He smirked and kissed her. "Ronan, we're there to talk people into donating. We can't sneak out early."

"We can if they don't know where we are." They pulled up to the restaurant and he hopped out and came around to get her door, helping her out.

"Wow," Katie said noticing the restaurant.

"You wanted somewhere nice, we go somewhere nice." The hostess took them to their table and he slid into the booth beside her.

"Can I get you a drink," the hostess asked.

"Red wine. The Shiraz," Ronan said.

"Yes sir," the hostess said as she headed off. "Thank you...Now where was I," Ronan asked as his hand slid to her thigh under the table.

"Ronan."

"Yes lass."

"I know what you're doing." The waitress came over with the wine, poured them each a glass and took their dinner orders.

Chapter 10

When his hand slid up the skirt of her dress, she shook her head. "Ronan, stop teasing." "But that was part of the fun tonight," he joked.

"Ronan."

"What?"

"What are you really up to?"

"Teasing you until you beg me to get out of here."

"You keep doing what you're doing and we won't even make it to dinner."

"Tempting you too much?"

She looked at him with a smirk. "Something like that," she teased.

"Then would this make it worse," he said as his fingers grazed between her legs and kept teasing. Her nails dug into his arm.

"Ronan."

"Yes."

"You realize people are probably looking."

"Unless you start moaning my name, I think we're fine," he teased. He took a sip of his wine and Katie shook her head.

"Please." He kept teasing, faster and faster until she

grabbed his arm. "Please what?"

"Stop."

"I haven't even warmed up yet." When the waitress came back with their dinner a little while later, he gave her a break.

"Thank you," Katie said.

"Thank you what," he teased.

"For stopping long enough to eat," she teased. He licked his fingers and smirked.

"Now I'm hungry," he teased.

"For?"

"Other than the steak."

She shook her head and blushed. "You do realize that we're in public right?" He nodded and had his steak.

"Tempting you," he teased.

"More than tempting." They both had their food, and he eyed her the entire way through dinner like she was his dessert.

"Stop staring at me like that."

"I'm not," he teased as he took a sip of his wine.

"Ronan."

"What?" She shook her head with a smirk ear to ear and it just turned him on more. As soon as they finished their dinner, and the wine, he paid for dinner and they headed out.

"Where are we going," Katie asked. He kissed her the minute they were outside. "My place." The car showed a few minutes later and he helped her in, sliding in right beside her.

"What," Katie asked seeing the look on his face. He took her hand.

"Do you want to know what you did," he whispered.

"Oh, I know. I was tempted to drop my napkin and fix that little problem."

He shook his head and she slid her legs across his lap. "Don't start something you aren't gonna finish," Ronan said.

"Oh I fully intend on finishing my dessert." He shook his head and kissed her, devouring her lips and deepening the kiss until she had goosebumps. They were making out all the way back to his place. When the car stopped, he slid out then helped her out and walked her up to the house, waving as a thank you to the driver. They walked inside, he slid his jacket and hers off, locked the door and picked her up, wrapping her legs around him and pinning her against the back of the front door as he hiked up the hem of her dress.

"What?"

"Teasing me has consequences Katie."

"I'll accept the consequences then Ronan." He devoured her lips and carried her upstairs to the bedroom, pinning her onto the bed.

"Give it to me," she said.

He shook his head. "Don't move."

"Ronan." He slid her heels off then got up and grabbed a tie from his closet, tying her hands to the bed.

"I want it."

"Which part are we talking about Katie?"

"You know what part. Untie me." He slid his dress pants off and his boxers could barely contain him.

"This," he asked running his hand across his length.

"Mine." He slid his boxers off and stood behind her head as she pulled herself closer to him and slid him into her mouth. "Mm." Hell. It was past just being hot. It was turning him on even more. The warmth of her mouth, and those sexy lips wrapped around him as she took him deep into her mouth. "Aah." His breath hitched and she tried to wriggle her hands free. He leaned over her and untied her dress, pulling it open. Only a lace, sheer bra was under it. One that should've been illegal. "Had to try and get me all turned on." "Mm." That's all she could say. He slid in and out, going deeper as she accepted and took him deeper into her mouth. When she felt her tongue glide over him, he knew he had to stop her. He backed up as she shook her head.

"Ronan."

"I can't take it anymore."

"Can't take what," Katie asked. He walked around the bed and kissed up her leg. "That's not fair," she said. "You started this lass." When he got to the apex of her thighs, he licked and teased and his fingers slid deep inside her, teasing her until her body was throbbing around his fingers.

"This is what you do to me," he said.

"Aah. Please."

"What?"

"I want you inside me."

"Hard or fast?"

"Both," Katie said confidently. He kissed his way up her torso as his fingers kept teasing. He untied her hands, slid her bra and dress off, dropping them both to the floor, then re-tied her hands. "Ronan, why are you always tying my hands?" He kissed her to silence her as her body started throbbing harder.

He removed his fingers and slid deep inside her. "Aah." Her breath hitched and he kept going. Harder, deeper then faster.

"You feel so good."

"You're damn near addictive Katie." It got more intense then, he stopped and flipped her to her stomach.

"What," Katie asked as he pulled her back towards him, so her backside was in the air. He slid deep inside her again and heard her gasp for air.

"Mine and don't you forget it," he said as he teased her with one thumb in just the right unexpected spot and pounded into her over and over again, making it more intense as his thumb grazed the one spot that nobody had touched on her. The one spot that would make any orgasm even more intense. "Aah."

"Still want this," he asked.

"Oh my god." He went harder, slamming his body into hers until he exploded into her, and she collapsed under him. "Much better," he teased.

"Ronan," she said as he slid to his side.

"What?"

"That was almost too much."

"There's one other thing I could've done to make it even more intense."

"Which was?"

"Then we're doing it next time."

"Doing what?"

"You'll find out lass."

"Ronan."

"Yes or no?"

"To what?"

"What I teased you with."

"Ronan."

"Up to you lass."

He undid the tie, and she curled up to him. "That isn't happening Ronan. It's one thing to tease, but it's another to do that."

"You realize it's not that bad right?"

"For you." He shook his head.

"If you don't want to it's fine lass." She kissed him and slid into his arms. "What," he asked.

"I liked that. I think you're kind of stuck with me Ronan."

"We'll see what happens tomorrow night at the stupid cocktail party."

"I still don't get why you're even part of the foundation if you really don't like going to the events."

"The truth? My sister was in that hospital and if it hadn't been for the doctors in the pediatric department, she might not have survived. I felt like I had to do something to thank them, so this is what I did. 5 years this year."

"Why did you wait this long to do it?"

"Because before that I was too busy with that idiot woman I dated. She took up all the time I had. That's why I didn't have relationships after that. One-night things were enough at the time."

"And what about now," Katie asked as she curled up to him.

"Now, I'm all distracted by this sexy lady I met. She was so dang determined to get me to date her that I forgot about the other distractions."

"There's more than one woman you're talking to?"

"Nope. Just you. Not that I couldn't go and do something stupid, but I'm not going to."

"That's a very strategic answer Ronan."

"So, are you talking to someone else or no?"

"Just you lass."

"And that answer isn't gonna change right?"

He kissed her. "It's not, unless you changed your mind, Katie."

"I don't see that happening."

"Good answer." He rolled her onto her back and kissed her.

"What," Katie asked.

"Tell me what you really want from me."

"Meaning what Ronan?"

"Tell me what you really want. Me, the money, the trips...what?"

"You. Just you."

"And you're sure?"

She kissed him. "I wouldn't have come over here every night if it wasn't just for you. Ronan, why can't you see that?"

"Because every woman I ever liked was only after the money. I was used to that."

"Ronan, if you haven't figured it out yet, I'm not like those other idiot girls, and I do mean girls."

"I need to say something. If what I'm doing is too much for you to handle, tell me. You don't want to do what I want to, say it."

"And if I said I wanted us to do it without you tying my hands?"

"Control freak tendency."

"Still."

"And the blindfold?"

"I'm not usually a fan, but it was really hot."

"Anything else?"

"The last thing."

"Good answer."

"Almost as hot as that first time we were together."

"Almost?"

She nodded. "Katie."

"What?"

"Almost isn't gonna work for me."

"Tempting," she teased.

"No. Do over."

"When?"

"Tomorrow night."

"We're gonna be at that event though."

"Even better. Hotel suite."

"And?"

"The pink thing," he teased.

"Ronan, not when we're at..." He nodded and kissed her.

"You're really gonna do that in a hotel suite?"

'For you to wear all night without anything else."

"No."

He nodded. "That's the plan lass. I get to tease you all night at the party, then we go upstairs, and you get me."

"That's your little plan, is it?"

"You want what we did tonight, that's the plan," he said. Katie kissed him and he pinned her to the bed. "Is that a yes or a no," he asked.

"That's a yes, but we have to stay until at least 10. I don't want to get in trouble for heading out too early."

"You do realize the only person that could possibly cause a problem would be me, right?"

"Meaning what Ronan?"

"I'm kind of the boss. The entire event is a charity event. You have to show, but it doesn't say how long you have to stay. It's voluntary."

"Meaning we don't have to stay. I get it. I still want to stay for a while tomorrow and at least try and make some money for the foundation. There isn't gonna be another event until mid-month next month."

"Good."

"Ronan."

"It's a meeting next month, meaning I don't have to sit around all night."

"You do know that you could stop going to the foundation events if you didn't want to. Nobody is gonna fault you."

He kissed her. "I don't want to talk about it."

"And what did you want to do then Ronan?"

He kissed her. "I have a few ideas."

"I bet you do." He kissed her again, deepening the kiss until her legs curled around his. "Ronan." He shook his head pressing a finger to her lips. He kissed down her torso and she tried to stop him.

"What?"

"What are you up to?"

"Teasing."

"Ronan, you're taunting."

"And you love it," he said as he kissed and nibbled at her hip.

"Please."

"What?"

"Don't start."

"Don't start what lass?" He got down to her inner thigh and nibbled and licked and kissed until her toes were curled.

"Ronan."

"What?"

"Come here."

"And what do you need?"

"You."

"But I haven't started yet," he teased.

She motioned for him to come closer. "Katie."

She kissed him and wrapped her legs around him, pulling him tight to her.

"Tell me what you want lass."

She kissed him again. "Just you. No more teasing." "And here I thought you liked the teasing."

She went to kiss him, and he pinned her hands to the bed. "Tell me what you want then."

"You."

"Katie."

"I just want us to curl up together."

"So that thing that happened earlier."

"Definitely more than the first time we were together."

"Good answer."

"That what you have planned for tomorrow?"

"More."

"What do you mean more?"

"That little pink thing on high during the party until you're ready to pounce on me."

"Ronan, you know that isn't fair."

"That's the deal tomorrow night. Then you get me all to yourself at your place on Saturday night."

"Ronan."

"What?"

"Do you really want to do that on Saturday?"

"It's up to you. I'm good with you staying here if you want to be here."

"You're really gonna come to my place?"

"That's what you asked. You've been over here. You want me there, that's where I'll be."

"You mean it?"

"Katie, if you want me there, tell me you do. Doesn't mean that you aren't gonna be curled into knots by the time I'm done with you."

"And just what did you have planned?"

"We're doing that thing that we were playing around with."

"Which part? The thing that happened at the beginning was kind of hot."

"The part where..."

"Mm."

"You know that turns me on right?"

"What does?"

"That little noise."

"Mm," she said.

"That's the one."

"And how turned on does it get you," she teased.

"You really want to know?"

She nodded. He took her hand and put it on him, sliding it up and down his length.

"That's what happens when you do that."

"Mine," Katie said.

"Just don't start."

"Don't start what," she asked as she slid out of his arms and slid down between his legs.

"Katie."

She slid him into her mouth and his breath hitched. "Katie,

stop."

"Mm." He shook his head.

"Intentional." She nodded and took him deeper.

"Shit." She looked up at him as her tongue swirled around it.

"Katie, stop." She shook her head and kept going. He shook his head.

"You're teasing Katie." She nodded and he closed his eyes.

"Come here."

"Mm."

"Katie." She looked up at him and he shook his head.

"Come here."

She slid her hand around him and slid it up and down as she got closer to him. "What," she teased. He pinned her to the bed and slid deep into her, hard and fast.

"Aah."

"You started this lass. Now you're mine."

"Ronan." He kissed her and kept going harder and deeper. "Mm."

"Damn," he said as he kissed her again.

"What?"

"Now you're teasing all over again. You know what happens when you tease."

"What," Katie asked as he started going harder until she exploded around him and he followed.

"Damn."

"What," Katie asked catching her breath.

"You keep teasing like that and I swear."

"Mm."

"Katie."

"What? I'm not doing anything."

"You don't stop, I swear to you, you're not gonna be going to that party or work tomorrow."

"So, I can't tease you like you tease me?"

"Not tonight you can't." She smirked. "And don't start with the cuddle thing either."

"So now I can't curl up with you?"

"I'm going to clean up then we're going to sleep. Actual pajamas and no stealing shirts." She kissed him and Ronan got up and slid into a quick shower.

When he came back into the bedroom, she was asleep in something that he knew would look just as good on the floor. He slid boxers on and slid into the bed, making sure the phones were on the charger, and flipped the light off. He slid his arm around her and curled up with her. The one thing that he swore he'd never do again when he broke it off with Anna. He swore he'd never let anyone that close again. That he'd never let anyone in again. That he'd never fall for a girl he barely knew again. Now, Katie had his heart pounding and his mind reeling. She had his heart, even if he was completely petrified to say the words.

The next morning, Ronan woke up to Katie wrapped around him. She was still fast asleep. He smirked, slid out of her arms and got up to get a workout in. When he came back upstairs, she was just waking up.

"What time is it," Katie asked.

"7. Lots of time lass."

"Where were you?"

"Working out. Why?"

"Every morning?"

"Mostly. Have to look good for this sexy lass I know."

"You could just not work out one morning right?"

"When I'm at your place, I can't. Best you can get lass."

"That a promise?"

"How would I get a workout in without my gym stuff?"

"Good. Means you can curl up in bed with me and sleep in."

"You do realize that I never ever sleep in right?"

"You might if I'm coiled around you and won't let you up."

"Or I could find a very creative way to wake you up."

"Oh, I know you have ways Ronan. Probably a million and one. Might just enjoy those ways."

"Good. Part of my plan lass."

"And what else is part of your plan?"

"Breakfast."

"Are you gonna let me cook?"

"At your place. I'm gonna put the food on. I'll meet you downstairs." She kissed him and pulled him closer.

"Katie."

"Come back to bed." He kissed her and smirked.

"Food first." He gave her another quick kiss and got up and headed downstairs to make breakfast.

When Katie came downstairs in his sweater, he shook his head. "You will never learn will you," he asked.

"Meaning what? It's not as warm down here." He kissed her and sat her on the counter, handing her a mug of coffee.

"Thank you." He kissed her, flipped the massive omelet and the bacon and took a gulp of his coffee.

"And how did you sleep," he asked.

"I must've been tired," she teased.

"Someone tire you out?"

"Something like that. I think my legs were still shaking when I went to sleep."

"And who's fault is that?"

"Yours."

"You and that little thing you do. That's who."

"At least I now know just how to get your attention."

"Lass, I hate to break it to you, but you always have my attention."

"And trying to be all cute this morning."

"All I'm saying is that you don't have to try and get my attention. You want something, say it. You want me to strip you naked in a room full of people, that may be a slight problem but if you want it, you get it."

"Oh really. And if I say that I want you to tell everyone that I'm your girlfriend?"

"Already happening. I got an email from one of the foundation members, reminding me about the event. I notified them that you were coming with me and we're dating. She didn't say a word, but I told them."

"And what if I said that I didn't want to do the toy thing?"

"You don't get to say no to that one."

"Ronan." He plated the food and handed her a plate. "You're being serious?"

"That's the deal tomorrow night at your place. If you're going with me, that's the plan for tonight.

"You do realize we could just go to the hotel early and have fun first before we go right?"

"You mean since you have to be there at 5:30?"

"Crap."

"Exactly. No fun until we leave the party. Besides. You're gonna be all dressed up with your hair done. Wouldn't want to mess that up before the party."

"Ronan."

"You're waiting until I can't wait any longer. That's the plan lass."

"And it has to be the hotel."

He looked at her. "It's the biggest suite they have. What could possibly be wrong with that?"

"Just rather come back here."

"Katie."

"I don't..."

He kissed her. "It's a hotel suite. Same as being here except I don't cook breakfast. We can have breakfast delivered to the room and relax."

"And if I want to go back here?"

He shook his head. "Tell me the real reason why."

"How many other women have you met there?"

"Katie."

"How many?"

"Enough. Doesn't change anything. I still want it to be you and me."

"Ronan."

"Katie, you can't just avoid places I might've been with a hookup."

"I just don't want to stay at a hotel. I'm happier here." He finished his breakfast and got up to clean up. "Ronan." He was too quiet. Way too quiet.

She finished her breakfast and got up to walk over to him when he put the dishes in the washer, and she could see him getting irritated. "Talk," Katie said.

"You do realize that a hotel isn't a bad thing right? You want to come to London next week, I'm gonna be in a hotel."

"Ronan."

"Fine. I'll see you at the event then."

"Seriously?"

"I have to get ready for work." He walked off and went upstairs, peeled his clothes off and stepped into the shower. He washed up, washed his hair and just as she was about to step in, he hopped out. He wrapped a towel around him and went and got dressed before she even made it out of the shower. When she did, she wrapped a towel around her and walked into his closet to see him buttoning his shirt.

"So, now you're just avoiding me."

"You don't want to be there with me then don't Katie. Your choice. I have to go to work."

"Ronan."

"Give me the keys and I'll move your car over."

"You're not leaving until we talk."

"About what? Not good enough for you to be in a damn expensive suite? Fine. You can go home."

"That's not what I meant."

"Katie, I'm not playing a damn game with you. You knew I had a past when we met, but now a suite isn't enough? Tell me what the hell you want from me."

"You and me. That's it," Katie said.

"I'll see you when you get there then. No hotel. You can go home."

"Ronan."

"Katie, I have to go. Do whatever you want to do. You don't want to go to the party, don't. You can come by yourself. Leave whenever you want. I'll see you when I see you."

"Ronan." He walked out of the closet, slid his phone in his pocket and walked downstairs.

"Then give me a few minutes and I'll finish getting dressed." Katie sat down on the bed and couldn't help but cry. She fought back the tears, attempting to restrain them as best she could. She got dressed, quickly dried her hair, slid her boots on and packed her things, walking downstairs with her bag.

"Phone."

"Ronan, I get that you're mad, but you can't just blow me off."

"If you aren't going then give me the keys and I'll move my car."

"So, you're just gonna ignore me."

"You don't want to be with me then don't Katie. I have work to do."

"So that's it." His jaw clenched and she could tell that it killed him as much as it was killing her. "I didn't say I didn't want to be with you. I said come back here instead of a hotel where you had a million flings. What's wrong with that?" He got her coat for her and helped her with it. "Ronan." He opened the front door, and she stepped out then he locked up. "Seriously?"

"I have to go Katie."

"That's how you're doing this?"

He got her car door for her, gave her a half-hearted hug and went and got in his car. He had to stay silent. Thankfully he didn't have any meetings that day. He was gonna be in a foul mood. She pulled out of the drive, brushing tears away and Ronan followed, pulling out and heading the opposite way to work.

When he got into the office, he walked right past his assistant and walked into his office, closing the door. He was livid. Beyond livid. When his phone buzzed, he saw Katie's name on the call display. He ignored the call. He was still too mad. When it buzzed a second time, he answered. "We did just talk about this right?"

"Ronan, don't be mad. Tell me what you want."

"Nothing. You don't want to be there with me, go alone. You don't want to stay at the hotel, go home. Period. You get what you want. You don't want to stay in a 5-star hotel then don't. You get what you want. I'll be going home on my own."

"Ronan, that's not what I wanted."

"Don't worry. I'll tell them that we aren't together."

"Ronan."

"Enjoy." He hung up and took a deep breath. When there was a knock at his door, he shook his head. "Yep."

"Just wanted to bring you the messages. Here's your coffee," his assistant said.

"Thank you."

"You do know you could work from home if you needed a little time off."

"I'll be in the office until 2 then I'm gonna head home. I have a function tonight."

"Did you need anything from me?"

Ronan shook his head. "Thank you though." She nodded and walked out. The fact was, if he went home, it was a reminder of Katie. The entire damn house was.

It got to lunch and he got a text from his housekeeper:

> *Just finished cleaning up. Grocery order away and clothes hung in closet. Will see you next week.*

Ronan took a deep breath and packed his things up, sliding his laptop into his bag. He slid it over his shoulder and let his assistant know he was heading home. He'd be working from home all afternoon. He went and got a haircut and headed home. When he pulled in, he got a feeling in the pit of his stomach. He walked inside, locked up behind him and got the urge to go and pack for London. His phone buzzed 10 minutes later. "Yep."

"Sir, the meeting was changed from London to Paris. They wanted to know if it was alright to change the location or if you still wanted it in London."

"Paris is fine. When did they need me there."

"They said they could change the meeting to Monday."

"Just make sure they book me into a suite. Preferably with a meeting table."

"I'll get that booked and update the pilot."

"Thank you." Ronan hung up with her and set his laptop up in his bedroom for while he packed. It'd be the first sports Sunday he'd miss.

Ronan worked the rest of the afternoon after he packed. He finished his emails and got changed into his tux for the event. When his phone buzzed at 5:30, he ignored it. He looked outside and the car was waiting. He cancelled the hotel suite and got in the car.

"I'm heading back here tonight, so if you can be around about 8:30," Ronan asked.

"Yes sir." He got to the hotel and headed inside, walking right past Katie and got himself a drink. When he heard the click of heels getting closer, he walked away from the bar and went to mingle. He chatted away for an hour or so until he felt someone slide something in his pocket. He excused himself and went and got another drink then slid the note out and read it:

Talk to me. Please. I just don't want to feel like another fling Ronan. I need to talk to you.

He crumbled up the note and threw it out, got his drink and went to chat with Declan, his friend.

"So, what's up with the stalker," Declan teased.

"Long story. How's Sophie?"

"She's mingling as usual. She's good. Baby girl is growing up so fast."

"You two picked one heck of a name too."

"She's amazing. I wanted to drop this off to you myself. Sophie and I thought it was kind of important," Declan said.

"It's appreciated. I'll hand it off to the treasurer. We should meet up and do dinner one night," Ronan said.

"Just let me know when. I'll find a place." Declan nodded and excused himself as Katie walked towards him. Ronan handed the check off and grabbed a few appetizers.

"Ronan," Katie said.

"What?"

"Can we talk?"

"No." Ronan walked off and made the rounds then stepped out at 8:30 and vanished from the party, heading home.

He got back to the house, locked up and went upstairs. Just

as he did, his phone rang. When he saw it was Katie, he declined the call. His phone buzzed with a text:

> *Where did you disappear to? Ronan please talk to me. Please?*

He deleted the text and just as he did, his phone rang again. "What did you want Katie?"

"Where are you?"

"Somewhere you aren't. Why?"

"Did you go up to your suite?"

"No."

"So you went home?"

"Packing. I'm leaving tomorrow."

"For where?"

"Work trip."

"I thought I was coming with you?"

"Goodnight Katie." He hung up. He couldn't talk to her. It was ripping his heart out. A half hour later, he was just about to turn the light off when he heard a knock at the door. He shook his head. He wasn't doing this at whatever time it was. He just wanted a decent night of sleep. He ignored it. When she called again, he ignored the call. She called a second time and he answered.

"What do you want?"

"Come downstairs."

"No."

"Ronan, you can't just walk off into the damn sunset. Talk to me."

"No Katie. Go home."

"I'm not leaving until you talk to me."

"Then I'll leave."

"Ronan, please."

"If I come down and let you say whatever, will you leave?"

"If that's what you want." He hung up. He took a deep breath, pulled on jeans and a sweater and walked downstairs and opened the door.

"What do you want?"

"Not even inviting me inside?"

"Katie, just say it."

"You can't keep avoiding me just because we had a fight."

"I'm not. You know my damn past. You want to throw it in my face, fine. I don't have to be there for you to do it. I didn't date for a reason. You demanded that we dated. Dared me. Did you think that was a smart move?"

"And I told you that I loved you Ronan."

"Guess those words don't mean that much."

"Meaning what?"

"I don't say them unless I mean it."

"And you're saying that I didn't."

"I'm saying that you can't have it both ways. The hotel suite isn't good enough. Fine. Cancelled it. No hotel suite will be enough. Got it. You don't have to be in another one ever again. I'm going on the trip alone."

"Ronan, that's not..."

"I'll have the suite to myself."

"I wanted..."

"Go by yourself. Wouldn't want to bother you. Go home Katie. You got what you wanted. You get to sleep in your own bed."

"I want you there with me."

"No."

"Ronan."

"Go home Katie. I'm too tired to deal with any of this tonight."

"That's really what you're gonna do? Push me away?"

"For right now, yes."

"And me saying that I loved you meant nothing to you." He was silent. His jaw clenched and unclenched over and over again. "Let me come inside."

"No. Just go home Katie. I need a night alright?"

"Don't do this."

"I'm not doing anything. I need sleep. Alone."

"Then come over tomorrow."

"I'm leaving in the morning."

"Ronan."

"I'll call you when I get home."

"Call me before you leave." He nodded and she kissed his cheek. "I mean it Ronan." He nodded again and she went and got in her car and left.

Ronan locked the front door, turned the light off and walked back upstairs. He took his jeans and sweater off and laid down on the bed, going through emails. He found the hotel reservation, changed the date for the next day, notified the pilot that they were leaving at 9am, and went through emails, seeing one from Anna:

> *Can we meet up for a drink? Let me properly apologize.*

He deleted and blocked that email too and closed the

laptop, put it on the charger, slid his phone onto the phone charger and curled up in bed, flipping the light off. The pillows didn't smell like her perfume. Either did the sheets where they'd had sex over and over again. There was no trace of her in the bed. Not one.

Ronan tossed and turned all night long. When he woke up at 6, he did his workout, overdoing it to get his frustration out, and went and made a quick breakfast, cleaning up after himself. He walked upstairs and got showered and dressed, grabbed his toiletry bag, sliding it into his suit bag, grabbed his laptop, chargers and phone and slid those into his laptop bag and walked downstairs. He went and put the car in the garage, locked it up and saw the car pull up to take him to the airport. He handed off his bags, slid into the backseat and they left.

They were up in the air by 8:15. By 10:15, they were landing. Ronan hopped off, got into the waiting car, got his bags and they headed off to the hotel. When Ronan turned his phone back on, there were 2 messages from Katie and 3 missed calls:

> *I thought you were supposed to call me.*

> *Ronan, where are you?*

He shook his head, deleted the messages and they pulled into the hotel 20 minutes later. He got his bags, went up to the suite and set his desk up. When his phone rang, he shook his head and answered. "Yep."

"Where are you?"

"Paris."

"Why?"

"Figured this was as good of a place as any. Moved the meeting to here."

"Ronan, I thought you were gonna call me."

"Didn't have time."

"I don't want to fight with you about the stupid hotels."

"Then don't. You have what you wanted. You got to sleep in your own bed."

"I couldn't sleep."

"And now you have a week to catch up on the sleep you missed."

"Ronan, come on."

"What do you want Katie? You don't want to be in a hotel suite with me because I might've been there with someone else. You can't always have your way."

"I just wanted to be with you. I don't care where Ronan. I don't want to fight with you about it."

"Little late for that."

"Can I come there?"

"No. Might be a suite I've been in before."

"You aren't funny."

"I have to go get work done Katie. Have a good weekend." He hung up and the minute he pressed end he had chest pains.

Ronan sat down and went into his emails to get work actually done when his phone rang again. "Yep."

"What hotel are you at?"

"I guess you don't understand the word no."

"I'll fly out and meet you."

"I said no Katie. I'm here for work."

"I want to be there with you."

"Goodbye Katie." He hung up and took a deep breath. What he really needed was a strong coffee and something to eat. He grabbed his wallet, room key and his phone and went off for a walk. He found a café and got his coffee and croissant and sat down outside, watching the people go by. The tourists staring at the Eiffel Tower, the tourists trying to find other tourist spots. Fountains, towers, anything to take photos of with their partners. Fine. Paris would've been a lot more fun with her there, but he couldn't. Not after that. Not after the epic fight where she'd really said how she felt. Just as he got through his coffee, his phone rang again.

"Yep."

"Had to go and piss the lass off," Kian said.

"Meaning what?"

"She's sitting with Mia. Where the hell did you go?"

"Paris."

"Meeting?"

"Went a day or two early."

"You do realize that she's gonna find out where you're staying right?"

"I don't want her here Kian. If I did, she'd be here."

"Even I know what hotel you stay at when you go there."

"Kian, don't interfere."

"She's in tears Ronan. Come on."

"Not a word."

"Fine then you talk to her. Either you tell her, or Mia will. That's the same hotel you sent us to where I damn well proposed to my girl Ronan. I can't keep that a secret."

"I don't want anyone else here."

"The lass is talking to Mia. You know that she's gonna tell her about how I proposed in Paris."

"Not a word Kian."

"Fine."

"I have to go." They hung up and Ronan knew. She'd find a way to get there, and she'd find him.

He relaxed for a while, finished his coffee and wandered around, then headed back to the hotel. He went and checked over emails and saw one from Katie:

> *Just tell me what hotel you're at. I'll fly out and meet you. Please just talk to me Ronan.*

He ignored the email and went through the work emails instead when his phone rang. He knew it was her. He knew deep down that he couldn't say no to her. He'd never been able to. From her asking if she could stay, to her being there almost every night, he couldn't say no.

"Katie."

"Tell me what hotel you're in."

"You said you didn't want to be at a hotel with me. That I'd probably screwed around with too many people here. Why would you want to be here?"

"Ronan just tell me."

"Why?"

"Ronan, please."

"Did you seriously go to Mia and Kian?"

"You vanished on me when I showed up at the house this morning. What else was I supposed to do?"

"Not go talk to my friends. Might've been a good move not to involve them."

"I knew that Kian would know where you were. I was worried."

"Katie, just give it a break. I'll be back Wednesday night. Just leave it."

"Tell me where you are then."

"Paris. Nice hotel. My favorite suite."

"You aren't funny."

"Wouldn't want to be here. I've been in that suite a few times."

"Then tell me what hotel it is."

"No."

"Ronan, please."

"Why?"

"Because I want to come be with you."

"You don't want this, Katie. You just don't."

"Then tell me and we can talk in person."

"No."

"Ronan, stop this. You're mad. Fine. I said something I shouldn't have."

"I'll be back on Wednesday."

"And I'm at the damn airport. Tell me."

"What airport?"

"Dublin."

"Katie, go home."

"No."

"You can't be serious that you're gonna fly here."

"Then tell me what hotel you're in."

"I'll send a car to pick you up."

"Are you gonna talk to me?"

"Depends."

"On what," Katie asked.

"You sure you can handle being in a hotel room with me when I've been here before?"

"We can talk when I get there."

"Fine." Ronan shook his head.

"Please," she said.

"I'll see you when you get here," he replied.

He notified the car service to pick her up from the airport. He got going on the rest of his work emails, determined to distract himself from even thinking about what was coming next. He took a deep breath and tried to relax, but he couldn't. The time flew by and by the time that Katie showed, he was on edge. She called him from the lobby.

"What," he asked.

"Room number please."

"I'll come down." He walked down to the main lobby and saw her with her bag.

"I told you not to," Ronan said.

"We're talking Ronan." He shook his head, and she followed him to the elevator. "Had to just disappear."

His jaw clenched all over again. "Don't start."

"And you ignored me all damn night last night."

"You're the one that didn't want to be at the hotel with me and threw it in my face."

Chapter 11

When they stepped out of the elevator, they walked down to Ronan's suite. "So you aren't gonna talk to me."

"Not in the hallway. I don't even know why you wanted to come. Seems to me you made up your mind about what you wanted and didn't want."

They stepped into the suite and Katie put her bag down. "Ronan, you know that's not what this was about."

"If you had such a damn problem with my past, why did you even dare me to date you?"

"Because I knew you were more than that. That you deserved more than that."

"But not enough to be in a hotel room with me. Well, guess what Katie? You're in a damn suite with me. For someone who said that wasn't what they wanted, seems kind of ridiculous."

"Ronan, I just wanted to go back to your place instead of being at a hotel. That's it."

"And I wanted to stay."

"So instead, you ice me out at the party? You ignore me altogether. You avoid my calls and texts. And that's supposed to be the adult way to handle it?"

"And now you call me a child. Brilliant way to handle it."

"Ronan, you were having a damn fit because I disagreed

with you."

"I opted to handle it quietly. I wasn't gonna have a conversation about it with you in the middle of a donation event. I was still mad, so I left. The meeting got changed to Paris so I opted to leave early and have a little break. You want to go and report that back to my friends, fine."

"Ronan, it was a last resort."

"Not fair Katie."

"You vanished. Literally walked away and thought nothing of it. We've been together every night. Just because I didn't want to stay at the damn hotel with you didn't mean I didn't want to be with you."

"No. The part where you said no because of all the other women was what did it Katie. Fine, I sucked at relationships before we met. I messed around with other people. It doesn't mean that you're one of them. I'm trying here Katie. I am. You saying no to a romantic hotel suite just pisses me off."

"Ronan."

"I don't care about my damn past. You didn't when you decided you wanted to date me. Now you do?"

"Ronan, that hotel specifically."

He shook his head. "Maybe you should be getting your own room."

"Don't do that."

"Meaning what Katie? What else are you gonna throw in my face?"

"Ronan, please. I screwed up alright?"

"You said what you wanted to say Katie. You don't want to be with me because of all the stupid crap in my past, fine. Go home." He sat down and went to grab his laptop when she slid it out of his hand.

"You're not going into the damn laptop and tuning this out. We're talking until it's done."

"It is done Katie. You got what you wanted." She looked at him as her eyes started welling up.

"What I wanted was for you to say that we could just go back to your place instead. I didn't want to have to answer as to why you were avoiding me all day and night. We just told people we were together and you avoided me completely."

"Which part were you mad at?"

"Ronan, we're still together. It's a damn fight. That's all."

"Do you trust me?"

"Yes."

"Then why are you so damn concerned with crap I did in my past? Why say no I'm not staying at that hotel when that was the damn plan all week? Why remind me of my stupid mistakes when you could just go with the plan?"

"I wanted to be with you. I still do. You walking away because I mention you not dating before me isn't fair."

"I walked away before I completely snapped. I don't need the reminder, Katie. I made a million mistakes. I didn't want to date and get screwed over all over again. I give you a chance and you ruin it in a matter of one morning. You ruined it."

"I'm not losing you over a stupid fight."

"What do you want me to do Katie? Sit there and take it? If I'd done that to you, you never would've come back." She sat down on the chair and looked out the window, seeing the Eiffel Tower.

"Ronan, I didn't bring it up to hurt you. I just wanted something special. That's it. If we're staying somewhere, I want it to be somewhere that just you and me were."

"It was." He got up and got himself a drink of water and handed a bottle to her.

"What do you mean it was?"

"I hadn't been in that suite Katie. Only with you."

"Ronan."

"I'm here for work. Period. I needed space from you. From everything."

"Why didn't you say that?"

"What would the point be Katie? You didn't want to go. You

didn't want to be there with me. You just wanted things your way. You wanted me to stay at your place. You could've had what you wanted. Instead, you pick a damn fight. I'm not gonna keep doing this. You want what you want. You want it your way. You got what you wanted. You had me. Now, what's the point?"

"Ronan."

"What?"

"I made a mistake. I don't want to fight about it anymore."

"And then you literally go to my friends for sympathy when you screw up."

"I'm sorry." He shook his head and got up, pacing. He walked into the bedroom and shook his head.

"Ronan."

"Just go home Katie. You don't want to be with me. You never did."

"And that's why I said I loved you right?"

"Game over," he said as he sat down on the bed.

"Ronan, it was a damn fight. The fight is over. I'm not losing you over this."

Ronan shook his head. "Kinda ruined it Katie. You don't get to throw my past up whenever you want. You either accept me mistakes and all, or you walk away. You can't get past the mistakes in my past. Just go home."

"I'm not leaving without you."

"I have work."

"Then I'm staying."

"Then you should probably get yourself a room."

"Ronan, I'm sorry."

"You don't want me Katie. You don't. I know you said what you said, but you don't want me. You want some idea that you had in your head of this guy that you could change into being a damn white knight. I'm not. Never was. I'm not what you want Katie."

"And if I said that you are?"

"Then you're lying to yourself. You stay here. I'll get a different room."

"Ronan, don't leave."

"I can't sit here Katie. I can't. You don't want what I am. I'm not enough. You want more than I can do."

"I don't want to lose you." He shook his head. "Please."

"Do you even trust me?"

"Yeah I do."

"Tell me why Katie."

"Why I trust you?"

"Why you want this."

"I love you. Ronan, I can sit in a room full of people and I keep wondering how many women there were before me. I can't help feeling like that. We met and something clicked. I wanted to see you again. When you told me that you'd had one-night stands before me because you were all screwed up from dating Anna, I knew it was gonna be hard. Just being at a hotel with you after knowing that was hard for me. It doesn't mean that I don't love you, and it doesn't mean that I don't trust you. That I don't want to be with you. It's hard. That's all. I love being with you. I love waking up and seeing you. I just didn't want us to be somewhere you'd been a million times with someone else. That's it. I wanted to curl up in your shirt and fall asleep in your arms at your place."

"You know that we'd already talked about staying there."

"I just wanted us to have a night together. I just wanted you Ronan. Instead, you're mad and ignoring me. You blow me off completely."

"You chose this."

"Are you trying to tell me that I chose for you to walk away and ignore me?"

"You brought it up. I shut down when I get mad Katie. Talking about it when I'm still mad is out. I stepped away from it and went on with my day. I was home at 2 that afternoon because I couldn't concentrate."

"Ronan, please. I shouldn't have done this. I should've just told you that I'd rather curl up in bed with you at home instead. Please just let this fight be over. Let us be okay."

"You don't trust me."

"I do. I promise you that I do."

"I have a past you don't like Katie."

"That's the past."

"I don't want it thrown in my face again."

"I just want you Ronan."

He took a deep breath. "Are you sure?" She nodded and walked over to him. "No more looking through a crowd for people looking at me. No more second-guessing me." She kissed him. "I mean it Katie."

She wrapped her arms around him, and he pulled her onto his lap. "I just want you."

He kissed her. "Tell me what you want, Katie."

"You. Me and you." He kissed her and she straddled him on the bed.

"Tell me what you want Ronan."

"I don't want any more drama. I don't want reminders." She kissed him again. He slid her shirt off then undid her jeans.

"Ronan are we okay," she asked as her shirt slid to the floor. He kissed her again and flipped her onto the bed, pulling her jeans off. He peeled his shirt off and kicked his jeans off.

"Ronan." He kissed her, peeling her lacy panties off and started teasing without a single word. The fact was, he was used to turning off his emotions around women. Hell. He was practically a professional at it. He kicked his boxers off and kept teasing until she was moaning his name. He kept going until she was reaching for him, and he pulled away.

"Ronan."

"What?"

"Come here."

"Which part?"

"Please." He kissed up her torso and she wrapped her legs around his hips. He slid deep inside her without even kissing her. He went hard, fast and deep until her body was throbbing around him. He exploded into her and rolled over intentionally, trying to slide himself away from her. Hell yes, he was still mad. When she went to curl up with him, he got up.

"Ronan." He walked into the bathroom and slid into a shower. When he stepped out, he slid into boxers and pulled his jeans back on. He walked back into the living room area and went into his laptop.

The fact was that it still hurt. He went through his emails, finished delegating what he could, and he leaned back on the sofa and tried to calm himself down. When she came out of the bedroom in his t-shirt, he shook his head.

"Are you gonna tell me why you felt like you were a million miles away?"

"Because I'm still mad."

"So, what was that then?"

"Trying."

"Ronan, what do I need to do?"

"Nothing."

"One-word answers. Really?"

"Katie, I said to give me time and you pushed your way onto the trip. I say go home and you show up here. What do you want me to do right now?"

"I'm here Ronan. I came to be here with you. The fighting is over. Tell me what I have to do to fix this so the coldness is gone."

"Katie."

"You haven't acted like that to me once since the day we met. Tell me."

He took a deep breath and tried to calm himself down. "All I'm saying is that when I tell you I need space, that's what I'd like to have."

"I'm not leaving to go home."

"Just know that when I say I want space, I mean it."

"Meaning I'm okay to be here."

"For now. I still have meetings and work to get done."

"And it''s Saturday. What if we went out to dinner or something?"

"I'm not in the mood for a dinner out Katie. Room service maybe. All of that put me in a mood."

"I see that. Ronan, seriously, tell me what you want. Tell me what I have to do so we're back to the way we were before this."

"It takes time. I just need time to think."

"About what?"

"Katie, just breathe for a minute."

"Tell me what you want me to do so we're okay again."

"Figure out what you want for dinner and I'll order it in. We can talk."

"I don't want to fight anymore Ronan. I just need to know what I need to do to fix this once and for all so we can get past it."

"We can talk tonight. I just need..."

"What? Tell me what I have to do."

"Do you actually trust me," he asked knowing what a fully loaded question that was.

"Of course I do."

"Promise me."

"Ronan, I always have trusted you. I know you wouldn't go disappear with someone else. I know you wouldn't do anything to hurt me either."

"No more talking about my past."

"Fine."

"No more avoiding the stupid hotels."

"Fine. If I'm gonna be honest, I still like being at your place instead."

"Understood."

"Or my place."

"If your flatmate is out."

"Ronan, you realize she doesn't bite right?"

"Unless she has noise cancelling earbuds or something, only when she's out."

"Ronan."

"What?"

"I love you. That's not changing. You know that right?"
Ronan nodded.

"I know. I just need to wrap my head around all of this. Last night wasn't exactly an easy moment."

She sat down with him. "Well, if it's any bonus, we made a good chunk of what they needed for the children's wing," Katie said.

"What time did you leave?"

"An hour after you did. I talked to Declan. He said that you were a hard nut to crack, but a very good friend."

"I told him about you."

"And what part did you tell him," Katie asked.

"The part about you staying with me. He did the same with his wife when they first met. He couldn't go a day without her."

"I kinda know how he feels," Katie replied.

"Katie."

"You know I wanted to come with you. We'd even talked about it Ronan. You just vanished like you were intentionally ghosting me."

"I just needed breathing room. Honestly, it kind of killed me last night. I couldn't sleep, I did a workout and the minute I saw they were moving the meeting to here, I just decided to leave."

"Next time you decide to vanish for a few days, I'm sleeping in your suitcase."

"Next time?"

"You heard me," Katie replied. He shook his head and slid his hand in hers. "Are we okay?" Ronan nodded. "No more cold?"

He shook his head. "I just needed to shut myself off until I dealt with it," he said. She looked at him. "What?"

"You still mad at me?"

"I think we're good."

"Promise?"

"Katie."

"I want us in bed without any fighting. No more cold. Promise?"

He nodded. "I said something I should never have said. I was just wrapped up in that weird feeling."

"Next time, just a suggestion, say a different hotel or that you'd prefer if we curled up by the fire at my place."

"Can we still do that when we're back?"

"We have lots of time for it." She snuggled in close to him and he kissed her.

"What did you want to do for dinner Katie?"

"Anywhere you want."

"Room service?"

She smirked. "First time in Paris."

"Alright then. Put on something nice and we'll go."

"Dressy?"

"Whatever you have lass." He went and slid his dress pants on with a dress shirt and made a reservation at a fancy restaurant near the hotel.

When she came out of the bedroom, she was in a sexy wrap dress and heels.

"Katie."

"What?"

"You are so bad."

"Was part of my plan. Seduce you in a dress you can unwrap like a Christmas package."

"Nice plan." She kissed him and he pulled her into his lap.

"You forgot something."

"Which thing?"

"Underneath."

"Leaving them on. It's not gonna be a booth."

"What makes you think that?"

"Ronan." He kissed her.

"No more fights." She nodded. He kissed her again, devouring her lips.

"What time do we have to be there," Katie asked.

"6."

"It's 5:30." He kissed her again and got up.

"Let's go then lass." He took her hand, slid his wallet, key and phone into his pocket and then walked down to the elevator.

"Ronan."

"What?"

"Where is it," Katie asked. They went to walk down the street and saw the restaurant.

"This one," he said. They walked in and were walked back to the private round booth in the back.

"Had to," Katie teased. He nodded with a smirk. They sat down in the booth and the waitress showed. They ordered wine and Ronan smirked.

"What," Katie asked.

"What do you want to eat?"

"You choose."

"Katie."

"I say steak, but I don't see it on the list." The waitress came back, and Ronan ordered them dinner.

"What do you want to do after dinner?"

"Walk. Show me the Eiffel Tower."

"Dessert?"

"I have you right here. We don't need to get anything."

"Funny." She kissed him and he shook his head.

When the dinner showed, she saw the perfect little steak and smirked. "What," Ronan asked.

"Tiny steak but good," she said.

"How's the wine?"

"So good," Katie said.

"First dinner in Paris."

"Thank you for this," Katie said.

"Which part? Dinner or the wine?"

"All of it," she replied.

"So, you want to go see the Eiffel Tower now?"

She nodded. "I just want to spend time with you. That's all I could ever want."

"Then we'll go for a walk and see the tower then we can go and relax at the hotel."

"Sounds good to me." They finished eating and he paid, then they finished their wine and walked down closer to the Eiffel Tower. She got a picture of them together under the sparkling lights of the tower then walked a little more.

"Ronan."

"Yes lass."

"How many times have you been here?"

"3 or 4 times. I usually was working the entire time. I never really went out to see much."

"Good. Something we're enjoying together. Maybe it's good that I came. Gets you out of the hotel."

He kissed her. "You have a point."

They made their way back to the hotel and when they walked into the hotel suite, roses were there.

"And where did these come from?"

"Warranted after how I acted," Ronan said.

She kissed him. "I'm just glad that I got my man back," Katie said.

He kissed her and pulled her into his arms. "No more talking about it."

She nodded and he sat down on the sofa, pulling her into his lap so she was straddling him. He slid her heels off and pulled her close. Just as he was about to make a move, his phone rang.

"Kian," Ronan said.

"Did she track you down?"

"We just got back from dinner and a walk," Ronan replied.

"This mean that Mia doesn't have to whoop your butt when you two get back?"

"This means that you can get back to wedding planning with the wife. We're good," Ronan said.

"I still can't believe that you bailed on Sunday," Kian said.

"Can I get back to my girl please?"

"Enjoy. I'll let Mia know. By the way, Anna showed up at the pub."

"And?"

"She was asking about you. I told her to leave it alone. That you had your girl."

"Thanks, but I kinda already told her that. Too many times."

"Just go have fun with Katie. We can get her out of here when you're back."

"Goodnight Kian."

Ronan hung up with him and Katie kissed him. "Ronan."

"Yes lass."

"Thank you for the roses." He kissed her and untied the dress.

"Well damn," he said.

"What?"

"Lace?"

"Had to get your attention."

"Hoping that I'd notice?" She nodded and he kissed her. "Still think you're overdressed lass."

"Then undress me." He slid the dress off, putting it on the sofa beside them.

"Ronan." He kissed her again and undid the bra. She unbuttoned his shirt.

"What?"

"You're overdressed." He pulled her to him, feeling her soft and silky skin against him. She slid him out of his dress shirt.

"Tell me what you want," he asked.

"You. Just you." He kissed her and wrapped her legs around him, picked her up and carried her into the bedroom, leaning her onto the bed.

He peeled the lace panties off and kissed up her leg.

"Shit."

"What," Ronan asked with a smirk.

"Making my toes curl already."

"Good."

"Ronan."

"What lass?"

"You're still overdressed."

He slid her leg over his shoulder and undid his dress pants, sliding them off.

"Aah."

"What?"

"Come here."

"And why would I do that," he teased. She motioned for him to come closer. He wrapped her leg around his hip, and she leaned towards him.

"Something I need," she said.

"Oh really."

"Mm."

"Katie."

"Yes."

"Tell me what you want."

"You'd have to come closer."

"Which part?"

"Take them off."

"Katie."

"Fine. I'll take them off." She slid her fingers over the waistband and slid his boxers off just that easily.

"Have what you want now," he asked.

"Almost." When her mouth slid over him, his breath almost hitched.

"Katie."

"Mm." Her tongue slid over him and he shook his head. The deeper she took him, the hotter it was.

"Katie."

"Mm."

"Shit. Please."

"More," she teased. She took him deep again and he shook his head.

"While I love this, and I do mean I love this, I haven't had my dessert yet," he teased as she smirked.

"Waiting for mine," she joked.

"You've had yours lass. Now it's my turn."

She shook her head and wrapped her lips around him all

over again, taking him deep into her mouth. "Shit Katie."
Her hand wrapped around him was enough, but now, she
was intentionally getting him so turned on he wouldn't
have lasted long. He pulled away from her and slid deep
inside her instead, pounding into her over and over, harder
and harder until she was moaning his name.

"Mine," he said.

"Mm."

"Tell me," he said as he kissed her and kept going.

"Mine."

"Tell me what you want."

"More." He kept going, harder, faster until her body was
throbbing around him. When he exploded into her, her
body was holding on. He leaned into her arms and slid to
his side, pulling her to him.

"Hey," he said.

She kissed him. "I missed you."

"Katie."

"I did. Hardest 48 hours ever."

"You do realize we'll be fine right?"

"Better now."

"Katie, just give it time okay? We rushed this. I know it and you know it."

She kissed him. "Do you regret it," she asked as he curled up with her.

"Rushing it, no. That was kind of our thing. We didn't exactly take our time."

"But you don't regret it," she asked.

He shook his head. "Not for a minute."

"I want the truth Ronan."

"We jumped in with both feet. Both of us. We rushed things from the minute we decided to date."

"You mean from the minute I dared you to."

"Do you take it back?"

"I'm glad we did."

"Good answer," he teased.

"Ronan, tell me something. I know that you don't say things until you feel them and you're ready to say them, but I love you. I'm not losing you over that or anything else."

"Do you want me to tell you the truth," he said.

"Just say it. Whatever it is."

"The minute that we were in my house, curled up by the fire and you were just as happy as if we'd been in a fancy suite, I started falling for you. Breakfast in bed. You and me in the gym at the house. All of it made me fall harder."

"Ronan."

"When we spent all that time with my friends, I fell a little more. Dealing with my stupid ex wasn't on my list of fun crap to do, but you handled it."

"I mean, if she'd been with my ex when we showed up, that might not have been what happened."

"Meaning what?"

"Meaning if he'd been there I would've had to warn her that she was with an abuser."

"Katie."

"I wouldn't wish him on my worst enemy."

He kissed her forehead. "Why didn't you tell me?"

"Because my crap shouldn't effect you."

He shook his head. "Come."

He got up. "What?" He walked into the bathroom and noticed the tub. He turned the taps on and drew her a hot bath. "What are you doing?"

He motioned toward the tub. "Ronan."

"Get in the tub." She shook her head and kissed him, wrapping her arms around him. "Only if you get in with me."

He shook his head. "There's no room lass. Just slide in." She slid into the tub, and he went and grabbed one of the roses, taking off the rose petals and put them into the water.

"Ronan."

"What," he asked as he leaned over and kissed her. "Come in here with me." He flipped the water off and slid in with her.

"Better," he asked. She nodded and slid into his arms.

"Why," she asked.

"Why what?"

"The tub." He kissed her neck.

"I didn't know any of that stuff about your past. It's like I don't know anything."

"It went on for 7 months until I walked away. He went after me, but I found my place and got a flatmate, so I felt better and safer."

"So that's why you wanted to be at my place?"

"Because I felt safe there. I could say anything, and you wouldn't throw a punch or hurt me."

"And when I walked away and didn't say anything?"

"I tried to make sense out of it. It wasn't what I was used to. I just didn't want to lose you."

He kissed her neck. "I'm sorry."

"I get why, and I was just wrong with it. I shouldn't have said what I did. I just sort of expected a fist."

"I'm not the hit type. Boxing, yes. Workouts, yes. Raising a hand, no."

"And what happened tonight," she said.

"Before or after dinner?"

"Both."

"What about it, Katie?"

"Walking after dinner and seeing what I wanted. I haven't had that in forever."

"And after?"

"I need more."

"More what?"

"Mm."

Ronan shook his head. "You're relaxing." She turned to face him. "What?"

Her legs slid around him. "I want you."

"Behave."

"No."

"Katie." She kissed him.

"Tell me what you really want," he asked.

"You and me. Bed."

"Still in the mood I see."

"I want to curl up together. No stress, no drama."

"You done relaxing then lass?"

She nodded and kissed him. "It's been a long day," she teased.

He kissed her, devouring her lips.

"Then get up and we'll get some sleep." He got up, wrapped a towel around his waist and wrapped her up in the other, draining the tub. He walked into the bedroom, pulled the curtains and slid boxers on. When he turned around, she was sliding into the bed.

"Teasing me while you sleep, I see." She smirked and he shook his head. He went and locked up, putting the phones on the charger, and slid into the bed with her. He slid his arms around her, pulling her back against his chest.

"Ronan."

"Yes." "That whole thing about falling for me. Does that mean what I think it does?"

"When the time comes, you'll know lass. No rushing things." She turned to face him. "What," he teased. She kissed him and slid her leg around his hip.

"I know what you're doing."

"Good."

"Katie, you need sleep."

"I need you more." He kissed her and slid her to her back and leaned into her arms.

"Katie."

She looked up at him. "What," she asked as he felt her hand slide over the waistband of his boxers.

"Katie, stop."

"Take them off then."

"This is what you want?" She nodded. She went to slide her hand down the front of his boxers, and he grabbed it, pinning her arms to the bed.

"Ronan."

"Don't move your hands or I'm tying them."

"With what?"

"My tie." He kicked his boxers off, knocking them to the floor and kissed her. "How did I know you were gonna be trouble?"

"Because you love having me all to yourself whenever you want." He kissed down her neck. "Ronan."

He smirked and made his way to her breasts, nibbling and licking and teasing until they were hard little peaks.

"Aah."

"Katie."

"What?"

"Very tempting."

"Which part?" He smirked and kissed his way down her torso, kissing her stomach, then her hip, then her inner thigh.

"Ronan."

"What," he asked as he licked at the wetness between her legs.

"Mm."

"Katie."

"What?"

"This what you wanted?" He kept going then his fingers teased.

"Ronan."

"What?"

"Come here."

He shook his head and licked. "Mm."

"What," he teased.

"Come here." He shook his head, and his fingers slid inside her, teasing her from the inside out. "Shit Ronan." He kept going and she started throbbing around his fingers. "I need you," Katie said as he smirked.

"I bet you do lass. Which part did you want first?"

"You." He kissed his way back up her torso and kissed her.

"Tell me," he said. Her legs wrapped around him.

"I want you," she said. His hand slid up her torso and he slid deep inside her.

"Mm."

"That what you wanted," he purred into her ear.

"Mm." He slid in deeper, taking his time to pleasure her with every thrust. He went slow, then sped up and went harder and deeper. "Ronan."

"Damn," he said.

"What?"

"Hottest lass in the damn planet and she's mine." He kept going, harder, deeper, faster until her body was tightening around him.

"Shit Ronan."

"Mine," he teased as he kept going as her body exploded

around him and he followed a matter of seconds later.

"You okay," Ronan asked as he slid to his side, and she curled up to him.

"That's kinda what I was really missing last night."

He kissed her. "Now, you get what you want, and Paris."

"Ronan."

"Yes lass."

"One other thing."

"Do I dare ask?"

"Are you gonna let me stay until your meetings are done?" "I have one Monday, one early Tuesday then I was gonna head back."

"I'll book a flight. Just let me know..."

"You don't have to. Company plane."

"Ronan."

"Did you really think commercial was how I got here so easily?"

"I was kind of wondering that."

"You got a one-way flight, didn't you?" She nodded.

"Fastest booking ever."

"Let's just hope we never go through this again." Katie kissed him. She curled up tight to him and Ronan smirked.

"I know that you want to say something. Just say it lass."

"Promise me that you aren't gonna walk away again."

"And if I have meetings out of the country, you'll be fine at my place. Deal," he asked.

"Still want to go with you."

"You can't take off work every time I have a meeting."

"Since I have 2 months of vacation time to use, I can."

"Still. Most of the meetings are just for the day. You really don't have to."

"Ronan, I just want to be with you."

"I know, but next time I have a day meeting anywhere other than Dublin, I'll go and be back by the time you're done work. Okay?"

"Promise?"

He nodded. "If I go anywhere for more than a day, you'll know."

She kissed him. "Ronan."

"What?"

"No more fights either."

"There are gonna be fights lass. We're human," he teased. She nodded off in his arms and he couldn't have felt better. It was finally a night where he could actually sleep. He nodded off a few minutes later and she was curled up in his arms. Just the way it was supposed to be.

The next morning, Katie woke up to an empty bed and the smell of morning coffee. She smirked and looked over to see a note:

> *At gym. Be back soon with coffee and food. –*
> *Ronan*

When she saw the coffee, she automatically assumed he was back. She got up, slid on her satiny robe that she'd brought with her and walked into the living room area to see him getting the room service.

"You found coffee," Katie said as she walked in.

"Put some by the bed for you. How did you sleep?"

"Good except you weren't in bed when I woke up."

"I had to get a workout in before the meetings tomorrow."

"Ronan."

"Helps. Trust me."

"With what? Teasing me?"

"That too." She shook her head with a smirk and went and got the coffee from her bedside table. She came back in, and he'd set up breakfast at the meeting table in the suite.

They sat down and ate and Katie got a grin ear to ear. "What," he teased.

She shook her head. "Not as good as breakfast at your place," Katie said.

"Homemade is always better than hotel food, but I can't make pastries like these at my place," Ronan replied as he took a bite of his croissant.

They finished breakfast and Katie smirked. "I know that look. What," Ronan asked.

"Since it's Sunday and you aren't going to church, what are we doing?"

"Walking, hanging out and seeing the town. Lunch in the park. Maybe even that picnic we keep talking about."

"Ronan."

"I couldn't get the time to do it when we're home. Since we're here anyway, we can do it here."

"How?"

"I asked the hotel to make something up for us. We can go find a park and do it there."

"Ronan."

"Part of what you wanted right?" She nodded and kissed him.

"What else are you gonna surprise me with," Katie asked.

"Well, long shower, making your legs shake a couple times. Nothing out of the normal," he teased.

"Ronan."

"Did you want to get started on the leg shaking," he joked. She shook her head and laughed.

"Curling back up in bed first. Are you coming with me?" He got up, picked her up out of her chair and carried her to the bed, leaning her onto in and falling into her arms.

"Now, what were you saying?" She kissed him and his arms slid around her, and his hands slid down to her backside.

"We getting back into bed," Katie mewed.

"On bed. Definitely." He pulled her legs around him and undid the belt of the satiny robe. "Much better," he teased.

"Ronan."

"What?"

"You're a little over-dressed."

He kissed her. "Good thing you aren't." He kissed her again, devouring her lips and slid his shirt off.

"Mm."

"Don't you start with that."

"Take them off." He kissed her then kicked his joggers and his boxers to the floor along with his socks and shoes.

"Now what would you like sexy lass of mine?" Her legs tightened around his hips.

"I'll give you a hint if you want," she teased. He kissed her and pinned her arms above her head, leaning himself into her as he slid deep inside her.

"God, you feel good," he said.

"All yours Ronan." He slid deeper into her, slowly getting harder then even more intense.

"Ronan."

"Mm. Yours," he said as he kept going and went harder then faster until he could feel her body start throbbing.

"Mm." He shook his head with a grin ear to ear and pounded into her as she kissed him. When she exploded around him, he followed and collapsed into her arms.

"She always gets her way," Ronan teased.

"Always," she mewed as she pulled him in close for another kiss.

When he leaned to his side, she snuggled up to him and covered them with the blankets. "Good plan to start the day," Ronan teased.

"Very. What do you really want to do today?"

"All of it. We're going home Tuesday."

"Such a party pooper." He kissed her.

"While I love being away with you, I am still here for work. Business meetings."

"Are you telling me that when you go to the meeting tomorrow I'm gonna end up in bed alone?" He kissed her.

"I'll make sure you're awake before I leave."

"You better." He kissed her and went to get up. "Where are you going?"

"Shower." She shook her head, and he flipped the water on to warm up the shower. He freshened up a little, then stepped under the stream of hot water. Fine. It wasn't half as nice as his shower at home, and a little smaller, but still.

Just as he was rinsing his shampoo out, Katie stepped in with him. "Good timing," Ronan said.

"And why is that," Katie asked. He handed her shampoo to her and slid her under the hot water, watching it trail down between her breasts. "Ronan."

"Yes lass."

"Really doing the picnic thing?"

"So long as there's no rain, yes."

"Why?"

"Because every time we think about doing it at home, it rains. It's either that or we have a picnic by the fire at the house."

"Warm picnic. I think I could handle that," Katie said as she rinsed the shampoo from her hair. He kissed her and washed up.

"Still would rather try and do it while we're here. We have nothing else to do today anyway."

"We could go shopping."

"That really what you want to do?"

"No, but we could." He smirked and kissed her then switched spots as he rinsed off.

"If you don't want to do the picnic, we don't have to. There are a million little cafés that we can go to."

"I just thought that maybe we could just do whatever. We don't have to do the picnic if you don't..."

"Katie. I want to."

"Okay," she said.

"We can just sit and relax in the park and have lunch. No stress, no worrying, no drama. No bumping into people we don't want to see."

"Ronan."

"Yes."

"I guess that idea of staying in bed didn't work right?"

"Last day we can really do anything before we leave."

"So that's a no?"

"You really want to stay in bed all day instead of going out and seeing Paris while we're here?"

"A little." He kissed her.

"We'll come back before dinner and have room service instead of going out. How's that sound?" She nodded and kissed him.

"I know it's bad that I don't want to go out to dinner, but I want us time."

"You do realize that I'm not gonna disappear right?"

"You kinda did." He shook his head and gave her a hug.

"Not anymore."

Chapter 12

They stepped out of the shower and dried off. Katie looked him up and down, still stunned that he was hers. All hers. Every muscle rippled. The man was sex on a stick and then some and she knew it.

"Stop staring like I'm dessert Katie."

"But I happen to like dessert," Katie teased.

"I'm sure you do, but we're getting dressed and going out. You and the bed can be separated for a few hours."

"But it's calling my name Ronan. It's saying drag that sexy man back over here and curl back up together."

He kissed her. "Sorry bed, but you can wait until we're back."

He went and slid on boxers and his jeans. "Can't just go out like that," Katie asked.

"Now I'm eye candy too," he teased.

"My eye candy."

"Good answer, but we're still getting dressed."

"Even if I'm your eye candy," she teased.

"I want every single inch of you, but we're still going."

"Which part," she teased.

"Which part what?"

"Do you want?"

"I want it wrapped around me. All of it. If you start something right now, I swear." She walked over to him and grabbed his hand.

"Katie."

She slid it between her legs. "And that's what you do."

"I could make that so much..."

She kissed him. "It's because of you."

"Good thing you brought it."

"Brought what?"

"The pink thing."

"And how did you know..." He kissed her, walked over to her bag and grabbed it. "Ronan." He flipped it on and kissed her as she felt the pressure of the little toy sliding inside her. "Shit."

"Exactly. You start that, I'm making it worse until you're clawing at me."

"Ronan."

"Get dressed lass before I bend you over the damn bed." When she intentionally bent over the bed, he shook his head.

"Get dressed."

He walked into the living room area, pulling his shirt on and grabbed his laptop. He went through emails while she finished getting dressed then slid his phone from his pocket. He pulled up the toy control app and went into the settings for the pink toy that she had. He ran his fingers over the screen making it intense as hell until he heard her breath hitch.

"The longer you take the more intense it's gonna be lass."

"Mm." He shook his head.

"That isn't gonna save you right now lass." He ran his finger over it again.

"Shit." He smirked and went through work emails. When he looked up from his emails, she was walking into the room.

"You ready," he asked.

Katie nodded. "If you don't stop with this thing, I swear." He ran his finger over the screen again.

"Like that?"

"Ronan, you want to leave this room then you have to stop."

"Stop what?"

Katie looked at him. "Are we heading out or are you taking me back to bed? Either way, you're not playing with your toy until after we leave." He smirked, slid his phone in his pocket and ran his finger over the screen again.

"Ronan."

"Bumped it in my pocket. I'm sorry."

"Liar." He kissed her, holding her face in his hands.

"When we get back here, you aren't gonna be able to move and you'll have to beg for mercy," Ronan whispered as he slid his hand in his pocket and bumped the screen again.

"Go ahead and promise that. You can't."

"Did you really want to dare me?"

"Ronan."

"Ties, toys since I know you brought the other one just in case, and napkins to double as a blindfold. I could make every inch of you shake." She gulped. "Exactly," he said as he handed Katie her phone and room key.

"Purse?" He handed it to her and opened the door for her.

"Do you know where we're going," Katie asked. He nodded and went to the front desk.

"Your picnic sir," the front desk attendant said as she handed him the bag.

"We're seriously doing the picnic?"

He nodded. "There's a park near here. No rain either. We can eat on the grass or on the park bench. Up to you." They walked hand in hand and made their way to the park, walking around until they found just the right spot.

"I still can't believe you pulled off a picnic."

"It was either this or a café. This is just as fresh," Ronan said. They sat down and Ronan poured them each a glass of sparkling water.

"This is amazing."

"And we haven't even eaten yet," Ronan replied as he handed Katie a croissant from the bag.

"Thank you for this," Katie said.

"I mean, if we were home, I probably could've got more than pastries."

"Ronan."

"What?"

"This is what I wanted believe it or not," Katie said.

"Cheese," he asked.

"The only way to make this croissant better," Katie said. He kissed her and fed her a piece of the cheese.

"Thank you." He nodded and smirked.

They finished their lunch in the park, packed the rest up and went for a walk for a while. When they stopped to take a few photos, he slid his hand in his pocket, and she shook her head. "I had to grab my phone for the photos. That was unintentional."

"Liar." He snapped a few photos of them together, then intentionally bumped the screen to make her squirm again. "Ronan."

"That was intentional."

She shook her head. "I swear, you are trying to make me..."

"That was the plan."

"Then we should really get back." He shook his head. "You're just gonna do that over and over until I implode?" He nodded and kissed her.

"Why," Katie asked.

"Because it's fun. I get to tease you all day long," he joked.

"Until we get back to the hotel."

"Then you may not be able to think straight."

"Says who? I get my dessert first."

"Nope."

"What do you mean nope?"

"You're mine lass. I'm gonna tease and taunt you until you're begging me to stop, then I'm gonna keep going until you can't move anymore."

"Ronan."

"What?"

"That a promise?"

"Seem pretty sure of yourself." Katie got a mischievous smirk that had him almost turned on.

"I am. I'm also convinced that if I tease you first, you may not be able to tease as much as you say you will."

"And just what did you want to do to me lass?"

"I want to keep teasing you until you think you're spent then keep going."

"If we both get what we want, I'm not gonna make it to that meeting."

"Tomorrow?" He nodded and kissed her, leaning her up against a brick wall nearby.

"Katie."

"What?"

"You do realize that you may not be moving when we get back."

"Like I said, not if I get to you first." He shook his head, and her hand slid to the front of his jeans.

"Katie."

"Turned on already?"

"Have been since I fed you cheese," he replied.

"Want me to do something about that," Katie asked.

"Why do you think we're going back to the hotel?"

"And here I thought we were going for a walk." He shook his head and walked a little faster. He kissed her at the light, and they crossed and made their way back.

"That eager to get back," Katie asked as he got through the doors of the hotel and walked her as fast as he could to the elevator.

"Yes, that eager," Ronan said as he slid his phone in his pocket and intentionally cranked the intensity of the toy.

"Shit."

"Exactly."

"I'll fix that when we get into the room."

"Or you'll crumble to the floor and end up naked and tied to the bed."

"Says who?" He put his finger on the screen of the phone intentionally making that buzzing deeper and harder. "Shit Ronan."

"Says me."

They got to the suite and the minute they were through the door he had her hands pinned behind her back.

"Let go." He shook his head. "Ronan."

"Lay down on the bed."

"Or what?" He shook his head. She walked over to the bed, and he flipped her onto her stomach.

"Not happening," Katie said. He grabbed two ties from his bag and peeled her shirt and bra off. "You're being serious?"

He nodded. "Been thinking about this all-damn afternoon," he said.

"And what do I get to do," Katie asked. He tied her hands to the bedpost.

"Ronan." He peeled her jeans and lacy panties off, throwing them to the floor. He grabbed his phone and pressed on the screen again, taunting her until her toes were curling.

"Stop." She turned over to face him.

"Katie."

"I'm not gonna be at your mercy if that's what you're thinking."

"Tell me what you want then," he asked as he slid his shirt off and put it on the chair.

"Untie my hands."

"No."

"Ronan, come here."

"Why?" "Because I need something. I get dessert first," she said. He looked at her.

"That's what you want?" She nodded. "When I say stop, you stop." She smirked. "Then you stay tied up and at my mercy."

"Fine."

He pulled his jeans off and his boxers could barely contain how turned on he was. "Ronan."

"Yes lass."

"Take the boxers off and come here." He kicked the boxers off and she tried to wriggle her hands free. "Not gonna happen lass."

"For a few minutes," Katie asked. He shook his head. "Ronan." He took a deep breath.

"Fine, but the minute I say stop, they're getting tied." He untied them and within a matter of seconds, her tongue was swirling around him, and he felt the warmth of her mouth all over again. "Katie."

"Mm." She took him deeper in her mouth and he shook his head.

"Katie." His heart was racing.

"What?"

"Aah."

"Mine," she said as she licked and sucked and took him deeper into her warm mouth.

"Katie." She looked up and didn't break eye contact.

"Mm."

"Shit." She kept going as he slid in and out of her mouth, going deeper until he couldn't even think. He intensified the toy and she sucked hard.

"Mm," she said.

"Stop." She shook her head.

"Katie." She kept going, using her hands to tease as she slid up and down his length, still maintaining eye contact. Hell. That just made it hotter.

"Stop."

"No," Katie said as she kept going."

"Katie, stop."

"Mine." He exploded into her mouth and she swallowed.

"Much better."

"Now, you're mine," Ronan said.

"And what are you gonna do Ronan?" He held his finger on the screen of his phone as her toes curled.

"Hands." She let him tie her hands back up and he went to flip her onto her stomach.

"No," Katie said. When she noticed that he was still turned on, she knew. He was about to taunt and tease until she was screaming his name.

He kissed her then kissed down her neck, making his way down her chest, nibbling and sucking and licking at each little peak. "Ronan."

"Look me in the eye," he said.

"Ronan, please."

"Still think that I'm not gonna win?"

"Not fair," Katie said. He nibbled and she looked at him.

"What are you trying to do? Make me actually squirm?" He nodded and kissed down her stomach, nibbling at her hip, then her other hip. He kissed and nibbled at her inner thigh. "Shit Ronan." He licked at the wetness between her legs. When her eyes closed, he stopped.

"What?" "Look me in the eyes. You look away, I stop."

"Ronan, stop being ridiculous."

"Want to tempt me?"

"Ronan, don't start." The toy slid out of her and he flipped it off. "You're teasing."

He nodded and licked and sucked and kissed and nibbled until her toes were almost twisting into knots. "Aah."

"Bad girl," Ronan said.

"Why?"

"Because you just tease and tease and think that you don't have any repercussions." She was looking him in the eyes.

"And what repercussions are we talking about," Katie asked as two fingers slid inside her. "Mm."

"What," Ronan asked as his other hand got him even more turned on than he already was.

"Ronan."

"What?"

"Mm."

"Tell me," he teased.

"I want more."

"How much more," he asked as he kept licking and sucking and nibbling until her legs were over his shoulders and he felt her legs almost trembling.

"I need you inside me."

"You can't handle that right now," he teased as his fingers went faster.

"Shit."

"Still need more?"

"Mm."

"Katie." She looked at him and nodded. "How much more?"

"I need you inside me."

"Not quite yet. I'm not done."

"Aah." Her body throbbed around his fingers.

"Much better."

"Ronan, please."

"Then flip over."

"No." He turned her to her stomach, and she rolled back over.

"I said no."

"Katie."

"Kiss me." He shook his head.

"Do you ever do what you're told?"

"Not that I've noticed. Especially when it's you asking." He looked at her and kissed her, devouring her lips until she got exactly what she wanted. He slid deep inside her, slowly. Almost painstakingly slowly. "Shit," he said.

"You started that with that pink thing all day." He pounded into her and Katie's breath hitched. "Mm."

"What," he asked.

"More."

"Harder?" She nodded. He slid deep into her hard. The

sound was almost like her body was applauding. He started slowly going a little faster. "Aah Ronan. Aah."

"Good. Look me in the eyes Katie." She looked at him and he smirked.

"Good girl."

"Mm." He kept going and when she was starting to throb around him again, he flipped her to her stomach and leaned back into her, harder and faster. "Shit," Katie said.

"Do as I tell you," he said.

"I can't move."

"Good." His hand slid over her hip and teased her while he pounded into her over and over, deeper and deeper until her body was almost humming. When he exploded into her, he leaned against her and continued to tease her until she was throbbing around him again. "Much better," he teased as he untied her hands.

"Shit."

"What," he asked as he slid to his side and she looked at him.

"Fine. You win."

"Which part," Ronan teased as his heart rate calmed along with his breathing.

"My legs are shaking."

"And?"

"The looking in your eyes while you did that was intense as hell," Katie said.

"Good. That's what you're doing from now on."

He kissed her. "Ronan," Katie said.

"Yes lass."

"Can we do that again?"

"Which part?"

"All of it." He smirked.

"I need a few minutes," he teased.

"First the hot stuff then the more hot stuff then that," Katie said.

"Imagine what would've happened if we'd done more than that."

"Meaning?"

"You really want to go there while we're in a hotel?"

"You're not talking about what I think you are."

"It's even hotter."

"For you." He kissed her.

"If you don't want to, just say it."

"I don't."

He kissed her again. "Okay."

"That's it? That's all you're gonna say? Just okay?" He nodded and kissed her forehead.

"You don't want to, I'm not about to talk you into it," he teased.

"Why is everything so damn easy with you? Every time I've ever said no to something, I've got pleading and begging. You just say okay like it's nothing."

"Because it doesn't matter. If we don't, we don't. If you ever decide you want to try it, tell me." She nodded and kissed him, leaned into his arms and snuggled a little closer.

"Ronan."

"Yes lass."

"I don't know that I can move."

"That was part of my plan."

"Not that I don't want seconds on my dessert, but I may have to stay in bed."

He smirked. "Of course. Good thing we're getting room service."

Katie kissed him. "Thank you for a very eventful day," she teased.

"Not done with you yet."

"Meaning what?"

"Not done. We're having a little dinner break then I get round 2."

"Three."

"Four and maybe five."

"Ronan."

"You don't have to do anything tomorrow remember?"

"I may have to be able to get out of bed and walk to the door."

"Says who," Ronan joked.

"Ronan."

"I'll be back at lunch for an hour then I have to go back to the other meeting. What are you gonna do while I'm working?"

"If I can walk, maybe go shopping. If not, I can get some foundation work in. I brought my laptop."

"Katie."

"What? I wanted to come to be with you. If I feel like going for a walk and getting something like a morning coffee, I'll get one."

"Just be safe. They have a café downstairs if you want

something." Katie kissed him and he pulled her into his arms.

"What," Katie asked.

"Who knew that you were coming?"

"You mean other than Kian and Mia?" Ronan smirked.

"Katie."

"My roommate knew. I messaged her to tell her."

"Parents?"

"I told them about you." He looked at her.

"And when do I get to meet them?"

"When we're back in Dublin."

"Pick a day. So long as it isn't sports Sunday, we're good."

"And if I said it was?"

"Katie."

"Saturday." He nodded.

"You do realize that you could just move in if that's what you wanted to do right," Ronan asked.

"Don't you think that's a little soon?"

"Katie, you're at my place every night anyway."

"Yeah, but..."

"Katie."

"You sure," she asked.

"Think about it. When we get back and get going back to real life again, we'll talk about it. When we get back home."

"Ronan."

"What?"

"Yes."

"Yes what?"

"If you want me to move in, I will. Are you sure you want me there?"

"We can talk about it later."

"Ronan, now. Are you sure you want me there with you in your house?" He nodded. He took a gulp, realizing what he'd just offered up. He hadn't had a woman in his house since Anna. He'd vowed to never have another woman in his house. She wasn't just another woman, but still. What the hell had made him think or say that?

"I'm sure lass. If you want to stay with me, we bring your things over. There's more than enough room."

"There's no room in your closet."

"That's why there's another closet. I just have coats in it right now," Ronan said.

"Ronan."

"What?"

"I mean it. Are you sure?"

"You dared me into dating you lass. I dare you to move all your crap into my place."

"You mean my clothes and my sofa."

"That's all?"

She nodded. "The bed was kinda already there. I just got a new mattress on it."

"You can bring it if you want."

"Your bed is more comfortable."

"And if you get stuck in the guest room?"

"That would be you." He smirked and kissed her. He got up and Katie shook her head.

"What are you doing?"

"Cleaning up and ordering dinner."

"Ronan." He kissed her and went and had a quick shower, grabbed boxers and pulled his jeans back on. He went into the living room area and called down to the restaurant ordering dinner and two bottles of wine.

When Katie walked in wearing her blue jeans and his shirt, he smirked.

"Stealing shirts again are you," he teased.

"Just for now. I'll give it back."

"I ordered dinner and wine."

"What did you order?"

"Seafood and wine."

"Ronan."

"Seafood. You'll love it. One of my favorite things, plus fresh salad for an appetizer."

"And the pint drinker goes healthy food."

"Smoothie every morning. Always have been healthy food."

"Ronan, pints and pies or fish and crisps doesn't count as healthy food."

"Katie."

"I can make you healthy food."

"And I can cook it too."

"I guess we have lots of time to figure out the whole cooking thing," Katie said as he sat down on the sofa, and she walked over and slid into his lap.

"And what can I do for you sexy lass of mine?"

"I was thinking about this whole do-over plan you have for after dinner."

"What about it?"

"Can we just curl up in bed together instead?"

"You're the one that said you wanted more dessert I think you called it."

"Ronan."

He kissed her. "Just tell me what you want Katie."

"Honestly?"

He nodded and kissed her. "You sure that all this moving in talk isn't too much?"

"If you want to be there with me, you will be. You want to wait a while, we wait. It's up to you. I'm not pushing you either way." He kissed her and she slid her arms around him.

"Thank you."

"For what? Being nice to you about it? Offering the other half of the bed up?"

"Being you."

"And who would've thought that 24 hours ago you were crying and mad." She kissed him, devouring her lips until she felt him get up and wrap her legs around his hips. He carried her back into the bedroom and leaned her onto the bed.

"Tell me what you want Katie."

"It's crazy."

"Say it. If you could have anything in the world, what would it be?"

"Other than a billion dollars and world peace?"

"Something like that," he teased.

"You. Anywhere in the world, but you."

"Doing what?"

She smirked and kissed him. "This. A little of what happened earlier. A lot of what happened earlier. Then this some more."

Ronan kissed her again, devouring her lips and deepening the kiss until he was peeling the shirt off of her. "Ronan." He kissed her again and the shirt slid to the floor. He kissed down her neck.

"Ronan, the food." He nibbled at each of her breasts all over again, intentionally leaving a little mark or two behind.

"Shit."

"Mine," he said. He undid her jeans and pulled them off.

"Ronan."

"What?"

"I thought…"

He kissed her. "We have time."

"Ronan." He pulled the lace panties off and she wrapped her legs tight around him.

"Ronan, I love you. You know that right?"

He kissed her, devouring her lips and deepening the kiss until she forgot what she was asking entirely. "Take the jeans off."

"No."

"What do you mean no," Katie teased.

"Have to be dressed to get the door."

"And what..." He kissed her and his fingers slid to the wetness that had builded between her legs all over again, teasing and probing until he saw her eyes staring at him.

"Shit."

"Mine."

"Yours."

"And what did you want?"

"You." He kissed her again. His fingers kept teasing as her body throbbed around them over and over again.

"Ronan, naked." He shook his head and kissed her.

"All about you lass."

"Mm." Just as her body imploded around him, there was a knock at the door. He kissed her.

"Don't move."

"Ronan, don't." He kissed her and got up, getting the door. 5 minutes later, he came back in.

"My legs are shaking." He smirked, kissed her and grabbed a robe from the closet.

"What," Katie asked.

"Slide the robe on and I'll carry you to dinner."

She got up and slid the robe on and he walked her into the living room. When she saw the plates and the candles and the wine, she got a grin ear to ear. "Ronan."

"Thought you wanted room service?"

"Candles and the flowers and..."

"Sit lass." He pulled her chair out for her. She sat down and shook her head. "What?"

"And the man who is so known for all those one-night stands is actually the romantic, sexy one."

"And yours."

"Good point. Very good point," Katie teased.

"Now, here's your dinner lass. It's pretty amazing from what I remember," Ronan said.

"What on earth did you order?" He took the lid off the plates and she saw the seafood and pasta and salad.

"You wanted healthy, you get healthy." She smirked and he poured them each a glass of wine to go with dinner.

"Ronan, thank you for this."

"It's dinner."

"And it's just us alone."

"Don't think that I'm done with you lass. I have a lot more planned for you tonight."

"After my dessert," Katie teased.

He shook his head, and they had a quiet, relaxing dinner alone, had their wine, and by the time they were done, Katie had a grin ear to ear. "So, that was the best dinner I've had in a while. Since that last fancy place we went to," Katie said.

"Nice comeback," Ronan joked.

"Only thing that would make it better is if we had dessert."

"You had dessert."

"Second dessert."

Ronan shook his head and smirked. "Katie."

"Or if you were naked."

"Or if you stopped staring at me like I was dessert."

"Oh, but you are." Ronan shook his head, put the dishes back onto the tray and put it into the hallway. When he came back to the table, Katie had refilled their wine glasses and handed his glass to him.

"Come sit with me," Ronan said. Katie got up and walked over to the sofa with him and they sat down together.

"What's wrong," Katie asked.

"Well, I was thinking about something."

"Which was what," Katie asked almost a little worried.

"It's not a bad thing lass."

"Still."

"Did you think that I was gonna call all of this off or something?"

"I just don't want bad news. I'm in a good mood."

"Then stay in the good mood. I was going to say that I was originally thinking about moving to a bigger place. That way you'd have an entire closet, or we could make one."

"I don't have that many clothes Ronan. I don't need a massive closet."

"But it would kinda be a fresh start for both of us. Whole new place to make it whatever we wanted to."

"As long as it still has a fireplace for our picnics, I'm good," Katie teased. He kissed her and Katie slid over onto his lap. He slid her wine glass from her hand, putting it on the table, and devoured her lips, deepening the kiss until her nails were raking through his hair. "Katie."

"Mm." He shook his head, and she kissed him.

"What?"

"You sure you're okay being at that house?"

"I just want the man in it. I could care less about the house."

"Seriously?" She nodded and kissed him again.

"Katie."

"What?"

"You're okay being in that house when I lived there with the psycho ex?"

"Ronan, it's a house. We slept together in that house. We had a picnic by the fire. It's a house. I like the house the way it is, but if you want to find something else, go ahead. I just want the sexy man in it. The guy that I'm attempting to distract into taking me back to bed for dessert."

"Do I know him?"

"Yeah. You see him in the mirror every morning." He kissed her.

"You sure you want this?" She slid the robe off and went to undo his jeans.

"Yes."

"Katie."

She kissed him and he slid a hand around the side of her head, pulling her closer to deepen the kiss. "Bed," Katie managed to say between kisses. He picked her up, wrapped her legs tighter around him and walked into the bedroom, leaning her onto the bed.

"I know exactly what I want. You're way too dressed though." He devoured her lips and Katie pulled at his jeans.

"Take them off."

He smirked. "And if I said no?"

She pulled at them, trying to pull them off. "Katie."

She undid the jeans and slid them off. "What?"

"Stop."

"Nope."

"Katie." She slid her hand over his length. "Shit."

"What," Katie asked.

"You know what." The minute she slid him into her warm, wet mouth, he was done for. She had a way of teasing him and making his entire body want her.

"Katie," he said as the feeling was almost pushing him over the edge. She took him deeper and hummed, making it even more intense.

"Mm."

"Stop." She shook her head and kept going, teasing him as much as he'd teased her before dinner.

"No."

"Katie, let go." She wouldn't let go and he backed away.

"Ronan."

"Not yet," he teased.

"And why not," Katie asked as he felt the wetness between her legs.

"Because I'm not done with you yet."

"Ronan." He pulled her legs around his waist and leaned her onto the bed, sliding deep inside her. "Shit. Ronan."

Her breath hitched and he started pounding into her. "Mine," he said.

"Aah."

"You want to tease until I explode?" She nodded. "Not tonight you aren't." She smirked.

"Says who," Katie replied as he started going a little faster.

"You wouldn't."

"Good way to wake you up when you fall asleep."

"Katie."

"Don't be mad if I do." He shook his head and kissed her.

"Bad girl. Very bad," he teased.

"Just another reason why you love me."

"Shit."

"What," Katie asked as he kissed her again and could feel her throbbing around him. He couldn't hold back. She climaxed at the same time as he did.

"Aah."

"Ronan."

"All mine lass."

"You feel so good." He kissed her again and slid out of her, sliding to his back.

"What," he asked seeing the smirk on her face.

"Nothin."

"Katie."

"I think I kinda like this whole vacation thing. You're a lot more laid back."

Ronan shook his head. "You're in one heck of a mood today."

"Probably something to do with this morning." Ronan shook his head again and laughed.

"I swear, you are in a total mood."

"I'm with the guy I love. Why would I not be in a good mood?"

He kissed her. "Because I still haven't said the one thing you wanted to hear."

"I already know you do. I'm just waiting until you say it." He kissed her, pulling her to him.

"Katie."

"What?"

"You know?"

"Of course I know. You wouldn't have asked me to move in if you didn't."

"Says who lass?"

"So, you asked because it was convenient?" He nodded. "Ronan."

"I asked because you're there every single night. You're never at your place. You're sharing with someone else. Figured you'd rather share with me instead."

"You do make a mean omelet in the morning."

"If you move in, you're cooking breakfast, but you have to get up before I make it down there."

"Or I just find a way to distract you from getting up." He

pulled the blankets up and covered them.

"Thank you."

"Katie, being real now. Are you sure you want to make that big step?"

"Ronan, if you're not sure about that decision, tell me."

"I just want to make sure you're okay with the idea." He snuggled her closer to him and Katie's arm wrapped around him as her head rested on his chest.

"I love waking up beside you. I love curling up in bed with you at night. I love being at your place with you. If you're sure you want me to be there with you and not just visiting, I'll be there. I just want you. Being there with you means you."

He kissed her. "And if you're there, and I have to go to a meeting out of town, are you gonna be okay at the house alone?"

"One night?" He nodded. "Depends on where."

He shook his head. "Katie."

"It depends on where you're going. London, I'd still kinda want to go. Belfast, fine."

"And if I had to come back here for one day and do the meetings then come back home?"

"As long as you woke me up when you got home."

Ronan smirked. The only woman he'd ever known that wanted to be with him that much had stopped acting that way towards him when she started cheating. The fact that Katie wanted to be there with him no matter where he was, made him feel a lot more secure for some odd reason. Part of him still said that the feelings would fade, and she'd do exactly what Anna had done, but he pushed them back down so he wouldn't feel that anymore. He'd gone through it once. It wasn't happening again.

"Katie."

"What?"

"I need you to promise me something." He had to bear his heart.

"Anything."

"Promise me that if you do move in, and things start fizzling out, promise me that you tell me and you don't cheat."

"As long as you promise me that if you end up somewhere overnight, you don't turn back into one-night man."

"I promised you that I wouldn't."

"I mean it Ronan."

"I have what I want lass."

"Are you really that worried that I'm gonna run out and find someone else to mess up what we have?" He nodded, taking a deep breath. "That's what she did?" He nodded again. "Ronan."

"I don't want that happening with us. That's all. If you change your mind about being in this, then we end it. Period."

"And what if you aren't happy?"

"Not gonna be an issue lass. Not with you." She snuggled him and kissed him.

"This why you toss and turn at night? All worried that I'm gonna do that?"

"The thought crossed my mind," he said.

"Is that the real reason why you couldn't tell me that you loved me?"

"Honestly? Partially."

"Ronan, I know that she did a number on you, whatever it was that warranted calling her the Devil, but I don't think in my entire life that I've ever cheated on anyone. I don't think I could. I'm not like that Ronan."

"Is it bad that exact phrase is a sigh of relief?"

Katie kissed him and snuggled him. "I love you means something to me Ronan. It doesn't just turn off."

"And what happens if it does?"

"Then we talk first. We figure out how to fix it and fix it."

"You sure?"

Katie kissed him. "I wouldn't be here if I didn't really want this with us."

He snuggled her to him, and she curled in tight to him. She knew the words would come when he was ready, but she also knew that he did love her. More than he'd probably ever say.

"What," he asked.

"You're still worried?"

He shook his head. "We should go out and do something."

"Like what?"

"Go for a walk. See the lights. Find a café somewhere and have a glass of wine."

"We have wine." He kissed her and got up, getting the wine from the other room. He handed Katie her glass and they looked outside, seeing the sparkle of the stars.

"What do you think," he asked.

"Do we have a balcony?" Ronan nodded.

He got up, pulled his boxers on and grabbed her robe from the living room. He slid it over her shoulders and pulled his jeans on, grabbing a sweater from his suitcase. He walked her over to the door to the balcony and walked her outside. Katie handed Ronan his glass of wine and they looked out at the view. The Eiffel Tower lit up like a twinkling tree, the sky matching the sparkle, the full moon that seemed so much bigger. Ronan went in and grabbed his phone, taking a photo of Katie on the balcony with her wine, looking at the Eiffel Tower.

"Now there's the perfect picture," Ronan said showing it to her.

"What about one of both of us?" He took another picture of the two of them with their wine and the Eiffel Tower.

"I want those on my phone," Katie said.

"What if I frame them instead?"

"Still want them." He kissed her, devouring her lips. "What," Katie asked.

"I love you."

"Ronan."

"Couldn't think of a better time."

"I love you too." He kissed her and wrapped his arms around her. They finished their wine with the million-dollar view, then snuggled a little more.

"I knew," Katie said.

"What? That I did?"

"I don't want you worrying about me messing this up. Nobody is gonna destroy this." He kissed her, sliding his arm around her waist.

"You sure you're gonna be okay while I'm at the meetings

tomorrow?"

"I'm gonna get some work done. I can sit out here and work."

"I'll try and come back and bring lunch for us," Ronan said.

"I could be out buying stuff."

"Such as?"

"Sexy lingerie."

"Katie."

"Something to make you pounce."

"You walking around naked does that," he joked and kissed her.

"That's kinda good to know."

"If you decide to go shopping, just message me where you're headed."

She nodded. "Honestly, I kinda like what we did today, but I know the meeting stuff is kinda why you're here."

"Trust me. I'd rather be here with you."

She kissed him. "Ronan, take me back to bed." He put his glass down, picked Katie up, she grabbed the glasses, and he carried her back inside and leaned her on the bed. He locked the door and drew the curtains.

"Ronan."

"Yes lass."

"What do you think about having kids?"

He took a deep breath and closed his eyes. "It's gonna happen at some point, but if I had my choice we would wait for a while. I don't think either of us are ready for that right now."

"True. Someday though?"

He took a deep breath. "Someday at least a year or two from now." She kissed him and smirked. "What," he asked.

"Nothing. The last guy I dated told me that if I ever even thought about kids..."

"He's not here Katie. It's us."

"I just needed to know." He curled her tighter to him and kissed her head.

"Nobody is hurting you like that ever again, okay?"

Katie nodded and closed her eyes, falling asleep in his arms. Ronan was awake. Wide awake. Every muscle wanted to hunt the guy down and beat him to a pulp. If he ever saw him, the man would be a puddle on the sidewalk. He tried to calm himself, thinking more about the moving her in part instead of being pissed at her ex. The fact was, he was gonna see that fleabag at some point. Instead, he fell asleep eventually, dreaming about their future. Dreaming about wiping away all of her pain from her past and making the future bright.

Chapter 13

The next morning, Ronan got back from his workout and breakfast was just showing up. He hadn't ordered it. He walked in, letting the room service attendant in and saw Katie in her robe. "And here I thought you'd still be in bed."

"You had to go to work early. I wanted to see you before you left."

He walked over and kissed her. "Katie."

"You were tossing and turning last night. I wanted to do something to put you in a good mood before you left."

"You have ways lass."

"Oh, I know. Thought you might be hungry though." He kissed her again and pulled her tight to him.

"We could just get back in bed," Katie joked.

"Food first, then bed, then meeting."

"What time do you have to be there?"

"9:30."

"Good. We have time."

"For what lass? What do you have planned?" She kissed him and went and sat down at the table. When he took the lids off the food, he smirked. Exactly what he would've made for them at home, plus fresh pastries and coffee. "Katie."

"While you're at your meeting, I'm going to get some foundation stuff done, then when you're back for lunch, we can do something together." He smirked.

"Good plan," he teased.

"I thought so. Your fashion show with the new fancy stuff is later."

"Sounds intriguing," he teased.

"What time is your afternoon meeting?"

"1. It's in the hotel, so we're good. I can come upstairs when we're done." They had their breakfast and coffee, and he got a grin ear to ear.

"What," Ronan asked.

"You said the words last night."

"Which words," he teased.

"Funny. Did you mean it," Katie asked.

"I don't say things like that if I don't mean them."

Katie got a smile ear to ear. "I kinda already knew how you felt."

"I know." He finished his breakfast as she had her last piece of bacon.

"Why are you looking at me like that?"

"Just thinking."

"Katie, don't go thinking that we're gonna..." She got up and kissed him, sliding into his lap.

"Gonna what?"

She slid his shirt off. "It's almost 7:30."

"Oh, I know."

He kissed her and got up, wrapping her legs around his waist. "Tell me what you want," Ronan asked.

"You know what."

"My way or yours?"

"Yours." He carried her into the bedroom and slid her robe off, tying her hands with the belt of the robe. "Ronan."

"My way." He kissed her and kicked his shoes, socks and joggers off. He slid his boxers off and leaned down, almost doing a push up as he kissed Katie.

"What," she asked.

"Sexy as hell and all mine." Her legs wrapped tight around his hips. "And you're mine," Katie said as he leaned down and devoured her lips. She tried to move her hands and he shook his head. "You aren't teasing today lass. Later maybe, but now you're mine." "And what are..." He slid his hand down her torso and slid to the warmth between her legs. "Shit."

He teased and kept going until he knew she was hot. Wet and hot. "Ronan." Two fingers slid inside her, continuing to tease until he could see her trying to wriggle her hands free.

"What," he asked as he kissed her.

"You know what I want."

"Tonight I'm all yours lass. I get to tease you this morning."

"Mm."

"Tell me what you want."

"You. Now."

"How badly?" She moved her hip just a little, knocking him off balance so he was flat on top of her.

"That's how badly," Katie said.

"Bad," he teased.

"Says who?"

"You know exactly who lass."

"Mm." He slid deep into her, taking his time and Katie moaned.

"Ronan."

"Yes love."

"More." He slid inside her slowly and intent on making it last, going hard and deep.

"Shit."

"What?"

"Faster," Katie said. He took his time, slowly speeding up a little until her body was throbbing around him, then he went faster until she was moaning all over again.

"Shit," she said as he leaned down and kissed her.

"Ronan, untie them." He smirked and untied her hands, and her nails combed through his hair, pulling him to her.

"Shit," he said.

"What?"

"You want something," he asked as he started speeding up. Her body clenched around him, and he exploded into her.

"Damn woman," he said.

"What?"

"Another thing you do that does it for me."

"Good to know," she teased. Ronan kissed her again, devouring her lips.

"What time is it," Katie asked. He looked over at the clock and shook his head.

"Don't get up."

"Meeting. I have to shower."

"No." He kissed her again and got up.

"Ronan."

"I have to lass." He went and turned the hot water on then freshened up and slid into the shower. He washed his hair and saw her step in with him.

"Katie, don't you start."

She kissed him. "Don't start what?" He rinsed his hair out and shook his head. "What did you think I was gonna do?"

He grabbed the body wash. "You know exactly what I was thinking lass."

"Then move over and quit hogging the water." He kissed her and washed up. Katie washed her hair, and he couldn't help watching the water slide down her silky skin. "Ronan."

"Mm."

"Water." He slid under the water and rinsed off then slid out of the shower.

"Such a party pooper," Katie teased. He kissed her, wrapped a towel around him and went and got dressed, putting his joggers and shirt into his laundry bag. When Katie emerged from the bathroom, he was in his dress pants and his dress shirt.

"Suit," she asked.

He nodded. "The first one anyway." He kissed her and buttoned up, put on a tie and she helped him with his suit jacket.

"You sure you're gonna be okay today," Ronan asked.

"I'm literally going to get some paperwork for the foundation done this morning then after we have lunch, I'm gonna go for a walk and shop a little. That's all. I'll be back before you are."

"Promise," Ronan teased. She nodded and kissed him.

"When you go out, just be careful." Katie kissed him again.

"Go. I'll be fine. How long is your afternoon meeting?"

"An hour maybe."

"Then we'll go shopping together." He nodded.

"Alright lass. I'll see you at lunch?"

Katie smirked. "Go before I drag you back to bed," Katie teased. One more kiss and he headed off to his meeting.

Katie took her time getting dressed and doing her hair, then sat down and went through the foundation emails that she'd avoided for a few days. She got into her email and one from Ronan popped up:

> *Thank you for this morning love. See you soon. PS Save the lingerie store for later this afternoon.*

She smirked and replied:

> *That was the plan. Are you gonna come in the*

change room with me to get your little fashion show?

When she got a reply within a minute, she got a grin ear to ear:

We may get kicked out of the lingerie shop.

She laughed and refilled her coffee. She got through her emails and was about to lean back when she got another email from Ronan:

Meeting finished. The one this afternoon is starting at 1. It's only 10:30. Shopping?

Katie smirked. She went and grabbed her purse, the room key, her phone and a bottle of water and went to leave the room when she saw Ronan. "Good timing lass."

"So, you snuck out of the meeting early?"

"They were more prepared than I thought they'd be. You ready to head out?" Katie nodded and after one heck of a kiss in the hallway, they headed off to go find a fancy lingerie shop.

"Well," Ronan teased as they found one and headed inside. Katie found a few things she liked, then Ronan added in a few that he liked.

"Seriously," Katie asked. Ronan nodded and Katie went to try them on. When she got the first one on, she motioned for him to come.

"Sir," the saleswoman said.

"I just need his help," Katie teased.

He went into the change room and saw her in the one he'd picked. "And?"

He kissed her. "I like."

"I can tell," Katie teased.

"Maybe we should finish up here and go back fast," he teased.

"The saleswoman wasn't impressed," Katie joked. He kissed her again and undid the bra for her.

"Oops."

"Want me to show you the rest?"

"In the hotel suite." Katie nodded and after another quick hot kiss, he stepped out and walked around the shop, finding a few more things and getting them for her before Katie came out.

"And what do you have there," Katie asked when she handed everything to the sales lady.

"Something for later." He got the rest of the lingerie and handed Katie the bags.

"Ronan."

"What?"

"You can't just buy all of those."

"Says who?" He walked out with her hand in hand and made their way to the hotel.

"What time is it," Katie asked. "11:15."

They walked in, went up to the suite and the minute they made it into the elevator, he devoured her lips and had her pinned against the wall of the elevator. "Ronan," she said when they came up for air.

"Taking too long," he replied. The elevator doors opened, and he took her hand, walked her down the hallway, opened the door to the suite and kissed her again, pulling her to him.

"Ronan." He walked her into the bedroom and undid her shirt, then slid her jeans off.

"What," he asked as he leaned her onto the bed, peeling off the lingerie that she had on that was way too sexy to leave on.

"You're overdressed."

"Just getting started," he teased.

"Ronan."

He kissed her and slid his shirt off. "Tell me what you want Katie."

"You, naked." He undid his dress pants, and she reached for him. Ronan shook his head.

"Tell me."

"Take them off."

"Then what?" He slid his dress pants off then slid off his boxers.

"Do I have to say it?"

"Tell me. Say the words."

"I want you. Now."

"To do what?" He was egging her on and she knew it.

"Come here and I'll show you."

"Say the words."

"I want you inside me. Now." He kissed from her ankle all the way up her leg until he leaned in and devoured her lips. Her legs wrapped around his, and he slid into her until her breath hitched.

"Aah."

"What else do you want," he said as he slowly slid in and out.

"I want you to make me make that noise. The one you love." He shook his head and kissed her.

"Mm," he whispered almost purring.

"Ronan."

"That one," he teased as he slowly started speeding up a little.

"Damn."

"Harder?"

"Mm." He went a little harder then a little faster, then deeper.

"Ronan, yes."

"Tell me."

"Harder." He did as she asked and kept going until her body was throbbing around him.

"More," he asked. Katie made the sound he loved. The one sound that turned him on even more.

"Mm. Yes." He kept going until she exploded around him then slowed down and let her body calm for a half second before he kept going all over again until he found his release.

"Baby."

"Shit Ronan."

"Still want me to stay home from the meeting?" She nodded.

"I don't want you out of this bed."

"Still have to get up."

"And if I said no," Katie said wrapping her legs back around him.

"Shower." She shook her head. He kissed her again, devouring her lips.

"Still having a quick shower then we're having lunch and I'm heading down to the meeting."

"And where is it this time?"

"Downstairs in the meeting room."

"Good. What are we doing after the meeting?"

"Dinner. One more meeting tomorrow then we're heading back. If you want to, I can take you home tonight."

"One more night here. I don't want to go home yet." He kissed her with a kiss that was intense, deep and almost rough.

"Shower." He kissed her again, untied her legs from around him and got up, having a quick shower. He came out, got re-dressed and ordered them lunch.

"I still can't believe you're disappearing on me again."

"Lass, I told you. I'm here for work. The fun stuff is while I'm not working."

"Where are we going for lunch?"

"Thought you'd like lunch in."

"Depends on whether I get dessert."

"Katie."

"What?"

"Tonight."

"After lunch."

"Tonight."

"Why?"

"Because the minute you start, you're gonna end up tied up to the bed and begging me to stop. I'm not going to." She got up and slid her satin robe on, tying the belt.

"Is that a promise or a threat," Katie teased as she walked over and kissed him.

"Both." He kissed her and devoured her lips.

"I ordered sandwiches."

"Ronan, are you sure we can't go out?"

"And a fresh fruit plate and wine."

"Or we could stay."

He smirked. "Picnic on the floor."

She nodded and Ronan kissed her. "Then I have to head downstairs. The meeting is at 1."

"Still don't feel like sharing you."

He kissed her again. "I know. That's why I said you wouldn't have much fun if you came. I know you wanted to spend as much time with me as you could. I have to do these last two meetings, then we can head back and get back to normal life. I promise you."

"We can't stay any longer, can we?"

He kissed her. "I would love to be here for another month with you, but we both have work Katie. Vacation is fun, but we have to work."

"I have the rest of the week off." He got a smirk ear to ear.

"Then you have time to figure out the packing stuff if you still want to stay at the house with me."

"You sure you still want me there?"

"That's up to you lass. I want you there. It's your choice. If you want to wait, we can wait. If you want to jump in with both feet, jump and I'll catch you."

"How do you always know what I need to hear?" She kissed him and he snuggled her to him.

"I just want you happy. That's all lass."

"And if I say that I want to move in?"

"Then we move you in. Once you have your stuff packed, you can come and we get you settled and unpacked, then we can have a pub night with Kian and Mia."

"You sure," Katie asked.

"If I wasn't sure, I wouldn't have asked lass."

"Do you want to look for a new place?"

"I sorta built it so I had things the way I wanted in the house. If I don't have to move, I sort of don't really want to. I know that the house has memories, but honestly, other than you there's only been one other woman there other than family."

"Ronan."

"What love?"

"I just want to be there with you. Nothing else matters." He kissed her, deepening the kiss when there was a knock at the door.

"Lunch," he said.

He kissed her, answered the door and they brought the lunch in for them, setting it up at the table. "Merci," Ronan said as they headed out. Katie got a grin ear to ear.

"What?"

"Even talking French is sexy when you do it," Katie said.

"Well thank you, sexy woman of mine." He kissed her and pulled out her chair for her. She sat down and they had a relaxing lunch together.

"What do you think," he asked.

"I think we might be okay. Might take all afternoon to finish this," Katie teased.

"Katie." She smirked and fed him a piece of watermelon.

"Katie, what are you up to?"

"Feeding you." He shook his head and fed her a piece of pineapple.

"Mm."

He shook his head. "I know exactly what you're doing."

"And what is that," she replied.

"Eat the pineapple."

She got a smirk ear to ear. "That was the plan," she teased.

"Katie." She looked at him. "The pineapple."

"You really believe all of that?"

"Leave it at I have proof." She smirked and got up, sliding into his lap.

"Then give me..." He kissed her.

"Before you end up making me late."

"Proof," Katie asked."

"Pineapple. Lots of pineapple." She smirked and kissed him.

"And if I don't?"

He kissed her. "Then you're sleeping in bed alone."

"Party pooper," Katie replied. He kissed her and she got up

and had her lunch.

"Ronan."

"What?"

"Honestly, out of all the women you've met, why me?"

It was a question he knew was coming. She'd asked before and he'd found a way around the answer. "When I realized we were gonna end up seeing each other, I sorta looked into it more. Honestly, after we were together that second time, I didn't want to leave. I didn't want to walk off. I knew we were gonna see each other and I sorta wanted to spend more time together. First time for that in a long time. Then we spent all that time together and I still wanted you. Like I said. Hasn't happened in a long time."

"What was it about me though?"

"Part of it was what we did that first night. Part of it was how we were together."

"Ronan."

"You're beautiful. You're smart, you're sexy and you have me turned on every damn time you do that thing."

"And the pineapple part?"

"My dessert."

"Ronan."

"Dessert then more dessert, then even more."

"You're getting me hot."

"Good."

"Meaning what?" He kissed her, got up and grabbed something from her bag.

"What are you doing?" He grabbed the pink toy and walked back in, sitting down. "Ronan, you aren't serious."

He pulled her chair closer. "It's happening. Nothing else to distract you."

"Ronan."

"It's either that or the big one and you can't turn it off."

"Fine. The pink one." She got up and slid into his lap. He turned it on and slid it inside her.

"Ronan, promise me that you aren't putting it on high." He kissed her.

"Finish your lunch and we can discuss it."

"Ronan, seriously though."

"At least you'll know when I'm heading back up."

"And if I can't move, we can't go out for dinner."

"Then you should probably not let your legs get shaky." Katie smirked and shook her head.

"And if I take it out?"

"I'm on the sofa."

"You wouldn't seriously do that."

"I know I'd get sleep."

"Ronan." He teased with a smirk ear to ear as they finished lunch.

"You are such a party pooper."

"I'm not the one who said they'd take it out before I was done."

"Ronan."

He kissed her. "Finish your lunch. Relax this afternoon. I won't be that long lass."

"Fine, but if you crank the speed on this thing, be prepared for retribution." He smirked.

"Oh, I look forward to it."

"I mean it."

"So do I lass. So do I." He kissed her, freshened up and headed off to the meeting, intentionally running his finger over his screen to begin his teasing. He could almost sense her toes curling.

Katie curled up on the sofa and had her fruit while she went through emails for work. When she saw one from Ronan about a half hour later, she opened it:

Stimulating meeting. How are we doing?

Katie: *Missing you.*

Ronan: *Another hour and I'll be upstairs.*

Katie: *Hurry.*

Ronan: *You sure you want me upstairs?*

Just as she saw the text, the toy buzzed with a deep buzz. One that was there right down to her toes.

Katie: *Mm.*

Ronan: *Good girl. See you in an hour.*

Katie's toes curled and she shook her head. "He had to go and make it worse," Katie said to herself. She went and had a quick shower as he continued to tease. The more he teased with that little toy, the more her knees started to buckle. She stepped out of the hot shower, slid a warm towel around her and went and slid into the sexy lingerie he'd picked and a dress for dinner. She did her hair and makeup, and Katie went and slid on a pair of heels.

When Ronan came back in an hour later, she was looking out at the view from the balcony. "Did you miss me," Ronan asked as he came up behind her and slid his arms around her waist.

"I did. How was your meeting?"

He kissed her neck. "It was a meeting," he said as he kissed down her neck and kissed her shoulder.

"Ronan."

"Yes sexy."

"Where are we going tonight?"

"Fancy restaurant. Somewhere that you'll love. Fancy. Somewhere that you can show off your sexy dress." He kissed her neck again and she slid her fingers in his.

"What time do we have to be there?"

"5. Early dinner so I get three helpings of dessert."

"And what time are you disappearing on me tomorrow?"

"9am meeting. Done before lunch then we head back love."

"Can we stay until after lunch?"

He smirked. "What did you want to do lass?"

"Enjoy the morning."

"Kinda have the rest of the day off tomorrow. We have all the time in the world when we get back."

"And I want to stay here."

"Katie, we do have to go back. Latest we can leave is 11."

"Then we leave at 11. I want us time."

"We have time tonight." She shook her head and leaned back into his arms.

"Come inside."

"No. I want to see the view." He kissed the back of her neck.

"Ronan." He slid his hand in his pocket and buzzed the little toy enough to make her breath hitch.

"Come inside. Lay down on the bed."

"Here." He turned her to face him.

"Not out here."

"Ronan." He picked her up and walked into the hotel room, leaning her onto the bed and pulled the toy out of her, throwing it into his bag.

"I want…" He kissed her again, devouring her lips and deepening the kiss until he had her pinned.

"Ronan." He pulled the lacy panties off and undid his dress pants.

"Don't move."

"I…" He slid his boxers off and slid inside her, hard. It wasn't romance and it wasn't passion. It was carnal need. It wasn't soft and cuddly, it was rough. Hot. Way too much intensity. Her body exploded around his more than once and when he did explode, he kissed her.

"That what you wanted?"

"All damn afternoon," Katie said.

"That's just the warm-up."

"Meaning what," Katie asked.

"You aren't moving unless I say so tonight. Understood?"

"Tie or handcuffs?"

"Don't tempt me."

"Tie?" He kissed her.

"Depends on whether you behave at dinner or not."

"And which part of behaving were you talking about?"

"You know which part."

"And if I taunt you through dinner instead of you taunting me?"

"Then it's handcuffs."

"That a promise," Katie asked as he got up.

"Guarantee." He kissed her and got re-dressed. She smirked and went to grab the lacy panties when he shook his head.

"What," she asked.

"Leave them off."

"You better not do what I think you are."

"Says who lass? Tablecloth."

She shook her head. "Tell me you won't."

"Then the little pink thing is coming back." She shook her head.

He knew exactly what button to push with her. He knew how to turn her on in seconds, and for once he actually loved it. It had been too long. He didn't have to guess anymore. He didn't have to go overboard. All he had to do was tease her the way she craved, give her what she wanted and have mind-blowing sex with her every time.

"Ronan."

"Yes love."

"Should I change?"

He smirked. "Depends. Do you want to go to the restaurant in nothing but the sexy lingerie?"

"You're hilarious."

"And the satin robe."

"Ronan, you are ridiculous."

"Then the dress will do." She smirked and kissed him.

"Where are we going for dinner?"

"Private dinner. Madame Brasserie."

"Where's that?"

"You'll see when we get there."

"Ronan."

"You'll probably need a sweater though. If you need more than that, you can use my jacket."

"Where's the restaurant?"

He kissed her. "You'll see when we get there."

"Ronan."

"And just so you know, there's no booth in the back corner."

"Where on earth is the restaurant?"

"You'll see love."

"Ronan."

"It's a once in a lifetime experience. I had to pull a few strings."

Katie kissed him. "Give me a hint."

"Tall building." Katie looked at him and shook her head.

"I wanted us to have the morning tomorrow so we could go up the Eiffel Tower. I wanted us to see it from up there. Like a postcard."

"We could always go after dinner."

"Ronan."

He kissed her. "I'll find a way lass." He knew the reaction she'd have the moment she saw where they were going. She'd get that photo in a heartbeat.

When he noticed the time, he grabbed her sweater and phone, handed it to her and they headed off. "Why won't you tell me where we're going?"

He smirked. They walked over towards the Eiffel Tower and Katie smirked. "What?"

"Get a photo from down here then we can go up."

"I thought we were going to dinner."

"We are." They found the elevator and Katie looked at him. He pressed the button for the restaurant and Katie looked at him with a grin ear to ear.

"The restaurant is in the tower?" He nodded. "Ronan."

"We can get the photo you wanted and have a nice dinner." Katie got a grin ear to ear.

"How on earth did you find out about this?"

"One of the guys mentioned it would be a great place to take you to dinner."

"This is amazing," Katie said. He kissed her. They sat down at their table and the waiter came over and took the drink orders.

"So, where's the menu," Katie asked.

"Tasting menu. I saw the chef at the hotel for that meeting. We were thinking of opening one in New York with the same idea. We were bouncing around ideas and when they suggested the restaurant, I jumped at the chance. He's an amazing chef."

"This is way too fancy." He kissed her.

"The best for my lass." She smirked.

"Making the best of the last night." He nodded.

Katie snapped a few photos of the view, then got one of them together. "Can we go up after?"

"That was the plan lass." Katie got a grin ear to ear.

"Everything I wanted to do, and we managed it all in a few days. Now all I need is to go to Italy."

"Bucket list?"

Katie nodded. He smirked. "So, now what would you like to do after dinner?"

"Get a picture of us at the top. Kiss you at the top." He smirked.

"Then what?"

"If I said it, you'd laugh."

"We aren't having sex at the top if that's what you're thinking."

"I like the idea though."

"I have a few ideas myself, but there are gonna be other people up there."

"Mm." He shook his head.

"Katie." The first course came, and Ronan got a smirk. By the time they finished all 5 courses, they were both stuffed and Katie was excited to get up to the top. Ronan paid for dinner, and they made their way up, after thanking the chef.

They got up to the top and Katie was in awe. "Ronan."

"I am kinda glad you did come."

"And that you didn't kick me out of the room." He kissed her.

"Now what," Katie asked as she got another few pictures of them and the view.

"So, now that you have the photos and what you wanted from up here, what do you want to do?"

"Bed." He smirked and kissed her.

"Did you want me to get a photo for you," the security guard asked. Ronan nodded and got a few pictures of them kissing with the view.

"Thank you," Katie said. The guard nodded and they made their way back down the tower and walked back to the hotel.

"What do you think love?"

"I wouldn't want to be here with anyone else." He slid his arm around her, and they made their way back.

They got to the room, and she saw the champagne and glasses. "Did you do this?"

He nodded and kissed her. "The last night here. I wanted it to be special."

She slid out of her heels and Ronan opened the champagne. He poured them each a glass, handing one to Katie, and smirked.

"Full of surprises tonight aren't you," she teased.

"Last night here. I wanted you to get to do everything you wanted."

"And what if I said there was something else I wanted to do?"

"Such as?"

She smirked and kissed him. "Involves you and me in bed."

"Katie," he replied.

"That's what I want."

"Could've sworn you got that before we left." She shook her head and reached up to wrap her arms around his neck.

"Oh, I got part of it, but I think we still need to finish dessert."

"Katie."

"What? Change your mind," she teased.

"Champagne. Drink." She kissed him and took his hand.

"What?" She walked him into the bedroom and slid her sweater off.

"And what do you want lass?"

She kissed him. "I want us curled up on the bed." He kissed her.

"You are in a total mood." Katie nodded. She leaned onto the bed and pulled him into her arms.

"Determined."

"I need you."

"Tell me what you want Katie."

"I want you naked."

"Other than that."

"All of you. I want what's in your heart, in your mind. All of it."

"Katie."

"What?"

"Romance. Part of what you wanted."

"Didn't start that way."

"That's what you want? You want what we were like before we started dating?"

She shook her head. "Just the sex part." He kissed her, deepening the kiss.

"You want the dirty part or the part where you fall asleep in my arms?"

"I want us with dessert."

He shook his head and peeled off the dress. "This what you want?"

"Yes." He kissed her again. She went to undo the buttons of his shirt, and he peeled her bra off and tied her hands.

"Ronan."

"What?"

"Untie them." He shook his head.

"I get to do what I want."

"Then take the shirt off."

"Because you want something?"

"My dessert." He shook his head.

"You have to behave first."

"Meaning what," Katie asked.

"Do what I tell you to."

"Ronan."

"What do you want Katie?"

"You know what."

He pulled her legs around him and slid her flat to her back on the bed. "I want you to say the words, Katie."

"Dessert. You in my mouth."

"Good girl." He peeled his shirt off, then his dress pants, then his boxers and his socks and shoes.

"I get my dessert first," he said. He kissed her then kissed down her neck, nibbled and licked and teased each breast until she moaned.

"I haven't even started yet," he teased.

"Ronan." He kissed down her torso and when she got down between her legs, her toes were curling. One lick, one suck, one kiss and her breath hitched.

"Mm," he teased as he kept teasing until she was almost panting. He kept going and slid two fingers deep into her.

"Shit Ronan," she mewed.

"I'm not gonna stop until you beg me to."

"I want you inside me."

"Nope."

"Ronan."

"I'm gonna keep teasing until you can't take anymore."

"But I want you." He kissed and licked some more until she was begging. "Mm."

"Ronan."

"What?"

"Come here." He slid away from her and got up, walking over to her.

"What would you like lass," he teased.

"Mm." She turned to face him and slid her mouth over him, taking his length into her mouth, hot and deep.

"Ahh. Shit Katie," he said.

She slid him deeper into her mouth, sliding him in and out until she could feel him harden in her mouth.

"Mine," she said.

"And what happens if I pull away," he teased.

"No." She went harder, faster, teasing until he was almost reaching his breaking point. She took him deeper, and Ronan shook his head.

"Katie, stop."

"No." She kept going and he pulled away.

"Ronan." He turned her over and pulled her backside towards him. He slid deep into her and leaned against her, pinning her arms above her head. He pounded into her over and over again. It was hard, deep, intense and exactly what she wanted. The more he slid deep into her, the more she moaned his name.

"This what you wanted Katie?"

"Mm. Yes." He kept going until he could feel her getting close.

"Come for me."

"Aah."

"Katie."

"Ronan."

"Harder?"

"Faster." He went faster and she crashed around him with him following a matter of seconds later.

"Shit." Her body tightened around him, and he leaned on top of her back pulling her to her side. "Ronan."

"Yes lass," he said as he caught his breath.

"What would you do if I said more?"

"I'd say you are giving me a minute."

He leaned onto his back, and she kissed him. "Untie them."

"If I untie them, you're still keeping your hands to yourself lass."

"Says who?"

"Then I'm tying them to the bed."

"And here I thought you needed a minute." He kissed her and pinned her back onto the bed, tying her hands to the headboard.

"Ronan."

"Nope. You're staying right where I put you."

"I can't even move."

"That's the point."

"You can't…" He kissed her, devouring her lips.

"Stay where I put you."

"And what are you gonna do Ronan?" He smirked and she shook her head.

"I have ideas lass. A lot of them. Didn't I say earlier that I wanted three helpings of dessert?"

"And I said…"

He kissed her again. "You might get what you want, but you can't touch."

"Ronan, you aren't being fair."

"Fair?" Katie nodded. "You want fair do you?"

Katie looked at him. "I want you. No more tying my hands."

"Nope. You're behaving."

"I can behave without it." He kissed her and Katie smirked.

"What?"

"You know what I want Ronan."

He shook his head. "Not until I get my dessert."

"Then untie them." He shook his head and kissed her then kissed and licked her neck.

"Ronan." He kissed his way down her torso, nibbling, licking and teasing each little peak.

"Ronan, please."

"Please what lass?"

"No more teasing." He smirked and kissed down her torso. "Ronan."

He kept going, making his way to the apex of her thighs.

The feel of his warm breath against her had her toes curling almost instantly.

"Mm." He licked and teased and nibbled until her legs were trembling. "Ronan, please."

He slid two fingers inside her, teasing until she was about to explode. "My girl," he teased.

"Aah."

"That's it love. Come for me." She did and he got a grin ear to ear.

"Ronan."

"Not yet," he teased.

"I can't even move."

"Good. I have a job for you once your legs are too shaky to move."

"Which is what," Katie asked as he kept teasing.

"That dessert you wanted."

"Mm."

"But I have to do one thing first," he teased. "Which is what," she asked as his fingers started teasing all over again.

"Ronan."

"Do it again."

"Shit," she said as he licked and teased and nibbled until her body was throbbing all over again.

"More," he teased.

"Mm."

"I'll take that as a yes."

"Ronan." Her body throbbed and exploded around his

fingers again and she looked at him.

"And what do you want," he teased.

"Come here."

He kissed her. "Yes love."

"Untie my hands."

"And if I said no?"

She smirked. "Untie them."

He untied her hands, and she looked at him.

"What?"

"You know what I want." He kissed her again, devouring her lips and he felt her hand around him.

"Katie."

"Mine."

"Mm."

"I want to taste you." When he felt her warm mouth on him it actually turned him on even more.

"Katie, stop."

"No." She kept going taking him deeper into her mouth over and over again until he stopped her.

"Please love."

"Mine." She kept going and when he finally stopped her, he shook his head.

"Come here."

"Ronan." He pulled her to him, and he slid deep inside her.

"God, you feel so damn good," Ronan said.

"Shit."

"What," he teased.

"I want you so bad," Katie said.

"I'm all yours, baby. All yours," he said as he slid deep into her over and over again, harder then slowly faster until her breath hitched, and she was throbbing around him all over again.

"Ronan."

"Katie, tell me what you want."

"Harder." He did as she asked until she exploded around him not once, but twice.

"Shit."

"Mine."

"Never forget it," Katie said.

"Back at you lass." He exploded into her and collapsed into her arms.

"You never forget it."

"Never have, never will."

Chapter 14

As soon as Ronan's meeting was over the next morning, Ronan came back into the hotel room to see the bags at the door. "Are you ready love?"

She walked into the living room area and nodded. "Still wish we could stay a little longer."

"You don't want to go back?"

She went up on her tiptoes and kissed him. "You sure you don't want to stay one more night?"

He kissed her and picked her up, wrapping her legs around him. "While I would love to, I have work to get back to and you, lass, have packing to do."

She kissed him. "You sure we have to?"

He smirked. "I'm sure. If you want, we can have a night just us at the house tonight. Picnic by the fire. Sound good?"

Katie nodded and kissed him. "Still want to stay though." He slid her to her feet, and they headed out. They made it downstairs, the driver took the bags, and they slid into the waiting SUV.

"Ronan." He slid his arm around her.

"Yes lass."

"You sure it's okay? Me flying back on the company plane with you?"

He kissed her. "It's fine. I'm the one that says yes or no to it. You're fine. You're with me." They got to the private plane area and the driver took the bags onto the plane. Ronan walked her on and they sat down.

"Can I get either of you a drink," the attendant asked.

"I'm good for now. Katie?"

"Just an orange juice please," Katie said. The attendant nodded and brought Katie her drink.

"We should be taking off momentarily," the attendant said.

"Thank you," Ronan said as he got comfortable with Katie.

"This is kind of fancy," Katie said.

"Comfortable. That's all," Ronan said.

"Ronan."

"Yes love."

"You sure you want me to move in?"

He nodded. "You're at my place every single night anyway. This way you don't have to rush home in the morning or bring an overnight bag. I want you at the house with me."

"And you aren't gonna change your mind?"

"Not gonna happen Katie." She sipped her juice, and they took off not long later.

When they landed back in Dublin, Katie got a smirk.

"What?"

"We left and you were mad as hell. We come back and we're back to being good again."

"Just leave Kian and Mia out of it for a while alright? We'll see them on the weekend."

"They're your friends Ronan. You do realize that Mia called me twice while I was there on my own."

"Did you talk to her?"

"We were sort of in the middle of something when she called." He kissed her and pulled her into his lap.

"What," Katie asked.

"We have plans tonight."

"Such as?"

"Getting some of your things from your place and taking them to the house."

"Now?" He nodded.

"My flatmate is home."

"We'll go pick some stuff up. Whatever you need for the next few days."

"You sure?" He nodded.

He kissed her, devouring her lips until the plane stopped. "Ronan," Katie said.

"What?"

"I love you." He kissed her again and wrapped his arms around her.

"You ready to get back to normal life?" She shook her head with a smirk.

"Kinda rather live in vacation mode for a while longer." He kissed her.

"Up. Come on lass. Let's get you home."

They made their way to the waiting SUV, the driver loaded the bags and they went to Katie's flat in town. When they pulled up, Ronan was almost stunned. It really wasn't anything special. She deserved better. She walked with him up the steps to the flat and walked him inside.

"Katie," her flatmate Sara asked.

"Just came to grab some stuff."

"Tell me he didn't ask..." Sara came out from the kitchen and saw Ronan. "Shit. Sorry. I'm Sara," she said.

"Nice to meet you," Ronan said as Katie went into her room and grabbed clothes, throwing them into her bigger suitcase.

"So, you're Ronan," Sara said.

"I am. Not sure if Katie told you or not. She's coming and moving into my place," Ronan said.

"Hold on. Katie, are you seriously moving out," Sara asked walking down to Katie's room.

"I told you I probably was. I've been there every night anyway. It doesn't make sense not to," Katie said as she continued to pack.

"Are you sure this is what you want to do," Sara asked.

"This is what I want. I wouldn't be doing it if it wasn't."

"But it's him. The guy who made you..."

"I'm fine. We talked it all through. This is what I want to do Sara. You know you wanted your boyfriend to move in anyway. Now he can," Katie said as she zipped up her suitcase and went and grabbed her overnight bag for her lingerie.

"You literally have everything in two freaking bags?"

"And my furniture and stuff I'll come and get later this week."

"Can we at least go do dinner or something before you leave?"

"We will. Tomorrow." Sara nodded and gave her a hug.

When Katie walked back into the living area with her bags, Ronan smirked. "Nice to meet you Sara," Ronan said.

"You too I think," Sara said as Ronan took the bags and carried them down the steps as Katie hugged Sara goodbye and followed him down the steps.

"Are you sure they aren't too heavy," Katie asked.

"That's why I workout every morning lass. I'm good. He handed them to the driver and helped Katie into the waiting car. "I take it she didn't like me that much," Ronan said.

"Well, I mean, considering that I was packing all my stuff, I think she took it well."

He shook his head. "It's a good thing that I didn't show up and get you naked."

"Ronan."

"That was an idea in the back of my mind," he teased.

"Then it's a good thing you didn't. She wasn't exactly happy with me dropping the bomb on her."

"You're still good about moving in right?" Katie kissed him.

"As long as you never make me leave."

"Only when we're going to the pub."

Katie smirked. "Or work."

"That too," he teased.

Katie slid into his lap. "Ronan." He kissed her, devouring her lips until the car stopped.

"Yes lass."

"Take me home." He kissed her again and opened the door,

helping her out then slid out. The driver brought the bags in, and Ronan thanked him. "Did you need me to pick you up tomorrow morning?"

"Please," Ronan said. The driver nodded and Ronan walked her into the house.

"Follow me," Ronan said as he locked up behind him and walked up the steps with her bags. He placed them in the other closet in the main bedroom and Katie smirked. "This is a massive closet. We could just share yours Ronan."

"Yours. You deserve your own space." She started hanging clothes up and felt his arms wrap around her.

"You like?" Katie nodded.

"I don't have that much stuff Ronan. Honestly, I'm good with a corner of your closet." He kissed her neck.

"My housekeeper cleaned it up for you. It was literally empty. Waiting for you." Katie turned to face him and kissed him.

"I still don't need all of this space," she said. He kissed her again and picked her up, wrapping her legs around him, walked into the bedroom, and pinned her to the bed.

"Ronan." He kissed her, deepening the kiss and leaned into her arms.

"Mm." He got a smirk and shook his head.

"I don't want to share you tonight." "

Good. I don't think I want to share you either. Ever." He undid her jeans and peeled them off.

"Ronan."

"And take the shirt off." She slid it off and he kissed her again.

"Much better," he teased as he slid her lace panties off.

"You're overdressed Ronan." He kissed her again and she unbuttoned his shirt.

"Katie."

"Take your pants off." He shook his head. "Ronan."

He kissed her then undid the lace bra. "What are..." He nibbled at her breast then licked and teased. Then he moved to the other side. "Shit Ronan."

He kissed down her torso, licking and kissing her hips. "Miss this?"

Katie nodded. When he moved down and licked at her heat, pulling her legs over his shoulders, her breath hitched, and she was moaning. "Ronan."

He smirked and kept teasing. "Something you wanted love?"

She nodded. "Take them off."

He shook his head. His fingers slid inside her and she was moaning again. "Ronan."

"Yes sexy."

"Come here."

"Tell me what you want."

"You naked inside me." He could feel her getting to the breaking point and he kept going.

"Shit Ronan."

"Got you all warmed up," he teased.

"Then come here." He moved back up, letting his fingers continue to tease her.

"What," he asked.

"Naked. Now."

"Nope. Just planned on teasing you until you exploded." She went to undo his dress pants. "Katie."

"I need you inside me."

"Not right now you don't." She nodded and undid his dress pants and slid her hand down his boxers.

"Katie."

"Mine."

"Katie, don't." Her hand slid up and down and she moved closer, sliding him into her mouth as she sucked and licked and teased him as much as he'd been teasing her. "Katie."

"Mm." She slid up and down his length and took him deep into her mouth as his breath hitched.

"Stop." She shook her head.

"Katie."

"Mm." He shook his head and smirked.

"Determined as hell." She nodded and kept going until his dress pants were kicked to the side and he stopped her. "What?"

He pulled her legs around him and slid deep inside her. "Mine."

"Mm."

"Someday lass. You're gonna wish you hadn't started doing what you were doing."

"Meaning what?"

"Meaning me not letting you stop and coming in your mouth."

"Was sorta trying to prove a point," Katie teased as he kept going harder and deeper into her.

"I bet you were lass. Just remember, next time I have handcuffs to stop you."

"Go ahead and tease it Ronan. You just want to..."

He kissed her and pinned her arms and hands to the bed.

"To what?"

"Have all the control. It's yours if you want it."

"Much better," he joked as he kept going as her body throbbed around him.

"Mine."

"For as long as you want me," she replied as he kept going faster, harder and deeper.

"Ronan," she said panting as her body clamped around him.

"Good girl," he replied as he followed. He kissed her and slid to his back.

"Shit," Katie said.

"What?"

"My legs are still shaking," she joked.

"Good. That was part of my devilish plan," he teased.

"Ronan, tell me that what we did never goes away."

"That's just the beginning lass. I have plans for tonight."

"Such as what," Katie teased.

"You, naked, bent over in front of me and letting me do whatever I want to."

"Depends on what you have planned," Katie said as she tried to catch her breath.

"Your legs will be shaking all night."

"That a promise?" Ronan looked at her and devoured her lips.

"It's a guarantee."

"And are you giving me a hint?"

"From behind. Me teasing until every inch of you is shaking."

"I guess that means we aren't going to the pub for dinner." He shook his head. "I'll make something."

"Ronan."

"I'm not going over there to hear Mia and Kian starting a problem. Not happening lass. You're mine tonight. I'm not sharing."

"Ronan."

"Yes love."

"You do know they only do it because they care."

"After the third degree from Mia, I'll pass. I'm staying in a good mood tonight."

Katie shook her head. "We should at least tell them that we're home."

He shook his head and kissed her. "Nope."

"Ronan." He shook his head and kissed her.

"I'm not sharing you today. That's what you wanted when we were still in Paris."

"Still do."

"Then we aren't calling them. Not tonight." Katie kissed him.

"What do you want to do for dinner then?"

"Steaks and potatoes. Sound good?" Katie nodded. She kissed him and curled into his arms.

"What," he asked. Katie smirked.

"You sure you don't want to go to the pub?" He kissed her.

"Not going until tomorrow or Friday. I just want some time to ourselves."

"So, we're curling up by the fire and having dinner?" He nodded.

"Just don't be mad when I'm doing a workout when you get up."

"All things considered; you do know that you don't need to do that every day."

"Kinda do lass. I have a sexy woman to keep up with."

"And you need to kill yourself in the gym every day to keep up with me?"

He kissed her. "Knowing you, yes." Katie shook her head

and snuggled him as he pulled the blankets up and curled her into his arms.

"Why are you so determined to workout all the time when you definitely don't need to really?"

He kissed her, devouring her lips. "Because it makes me feel good. When I don't have the workout, I feel like I'm missing something," he said.

"Sorta like me not waking up with you here."

"Something like that. I'll come up here when I'm done and wake you up."

"That a promise?"

He nodded and kissed her. "I can't promise that if you keep me awake late that I'm gonna be done before you wake up, but I'll try."

"If I keep you up late? Seems to me that you're the one who kept me up."

He kissed her. "While we were away, yes. Here, no."

"And if I intentionally distracted you while you were doing that workout?"

"You wouldn't. You're not up at 5."

Katie kissed him. "I could sneak down there and distract you."

He smirked. "You with a grin ear to ear watching me in

there is a big enough distraction."

"Good to know handsome," Katie replied as he kissed her again.

Ronan shook his head. "I know exactly what's going on in that sexy head of yours. Don't do it."

"I wasn't thinking anything."

"Sneak. Yeah, you were." "You sure you don't want to go to the pub?"

"Sick of us being all alone?"

"Saves you doing dishes."

"Katie, we're staying in."

"Then we order in."

"Now you don't want steak dinner?"

"What if we order something good."

"Pasta or seafood?"

"Part of me says fish and fries." He kissed her.

"Fine, but we're curling up by the fire. No phones." She nodded and kissed him.

Ronan checked the time, ordered delivery for them and pulled on jeans. "Where are you going?"

"Starting the fire and getting the pillows together for

downstairs." He slid his phone in his back pocket and headed down the steps to the TV room area. He started the fire and grabbed blankets and set up the pillows so they could just relax and enjoy the night. Just as he'd finished, his phone rang.

"Of course it's you," Ronan said almost laughing as Katie came downstairs in her jeans and tee.

"So did you two make up or what," Kian asked.

"We're back at my place and no we aren't coming down to the pub tonight. We're relaxing here alone."

"At least you two survived and didn't kill each other wherever you went."

"Funny. You know where I was. Katie is moving in."

"What?"

"You heard me Kian. She's moving in here."

"You left town to avoid her and now she's moving in. Kind of confused," Kian said.

"We talked and decided. That's all."

"You do know that we're gonna talk about this right?"

"Goodnight Kian. Tell Mia we can talk next time we're at the pub."

"She's gonna call Katie she said."

"Not tonight. We're having a night just us without interruptions."

"Fine, we can talk later. Tell Katie that Mia wants to talk to her."

"I will Kian. I have to go."

"Have fun."

"I will. Always," Ronan said as he hung up.

"So, they know that we're back," Katie asked.

Ronan nodded. "They wanted us to come to the pub. Kinda put the brakes on that idea."

"We could still..."

He kissed her and pulled her to him. "We're staying here." She nodded and he sat down, pulling her onto his lap.

"What," Katie asked.

"We're not going to the pub Katie. Second, you didn't have to get dressed."

She smirked. "You're dressed, so am I."

"Just means I get to undress you again," he teased.

"Ronan."

"You are seriously over-dressed."

"We're having dinner."

"Then you should've brought your robe down here."

"Meaning?" He slid her shirt off. "We're eating Ronan."

"And I intend on dessert first." He went to undo the button of her jeans, and she kissed him. "What," he asked as he unzipped them.

"Leave them." He shook his head and stood her up, pulling the jeans right off. "Determined to get you naked," Ronan said.

"And then what?" Just as the words passed her lips, there was a knock at the door.

"Ronan, I swear." He kissed her with a smirk, handed her a blanket and got the food from his driver.

He went in and plated dinner, brought it in and handed Katie a glass of wine. "Thank you, but I still don't see why you wanted me all naked-ish to eat dinner."

"Dessert." He brought the food in, and they had dinner together.

"Stop staring at me then."

"I'm planning dessert." She shook her head and kissed him.

"You're bad."

"And you love it," he teased.

Katie had her dinner, and Ronan ate while he looked her up and down. "Stop staring Ronan."

"Can't help it. You're way too sexy."

"Ronan." He finished his food and Katie shook her head.

"What? I was thinking about that plan," he said.

"The plan where I'm bent over in front of you?" He nodded.

"What about it?"

"Can handcuff you to the table."

"Ronan, I swear, you have a 24-7 dirty mind."

"And? Just another thing you love about me."

"One of the many. Still think you got me all naked intentionally."

"I was actually planning on peeling the lingerie off before dinner showed."

"I bet you were," Katie said adjusting the blanket so she was covered.

"Actually, I kinda planned both of us naked before dinner came."

"Ronan."

"And you bent over the table before we ate." She shook her head and put the plate down.

"And just what else did you have planned," Katie asked as she took a sip of her wine.

"You moaning my name until you begged for me to let you come."

"Ronan."

"What?"

"You're teasing intentionally."

"And you think that's all I was gonna tease you with?"

"What else," Katie asked as she slid onto the sofa beside him."

"You really want me to tell you?" Katie slid his plate to the table and slid into his lap.

"I really want you to show me."

"You're in a mood lass."

"And who's fault is that? Say it."

"That toy you have that makes you explode in seconds. Me and that toy."

"Ronan."

"That thing you said you hadn't done. You bent over the table with that inside you and me in the other end until you're begging."

"And what do I get to do to you," she asked.

"You get your dessert. Until I stay stop."

"Then what?"

"Then you're mine. Every inch of you is gonna be shaking until you can't take anymore."

"Ronan."

"Then we're gonna curl up in the pillows and relax until you can walk again."

"You sure that's what you want to do?"

He nodded. "When I say explosion, I mean it."

"Talking me into things is just a specialty of yours isn't it." He nodded and kissed her as he pulled her tight to him.

"And you love it."

"You have a very dirty mind boyfriend of mine."

"And yet another reason why you love me."

"Probably," she replied with a smirk.

"Mm."

"What," Katie asked.

"Nothing." He undid her bra and Katie shook her head.

"If you're getting me all naked, then take the shirt and the jeans off."

"Dessert."

"Not until you're as naked as I am."

"Katie."

"Shirt off." He shook his head, and she undid it. She threw the shirt to the floor in the pile with her clothes and went to undo his jeans.

"Stop."

"I'm almost naked and you're practically dressed. Not fair." His hand slid between her legs, and she shook her head.

"Don't you start with that."

"Start with what," he asked as two fingers slid deep inside her.

"Shit."

"Leave the jeans alone or you're gonna be starting all of that no moving stuff right now."

"Ahh." Her breath hitched and he kissed her.

"Hands down." She grinded against his hand and fingers and he could see her skin starting to go red from getting all turned on.

"Ronan."

"You want to start now, then we're starting right now lass."

"Shit."

"Exactly," he said as his thumb teased her and his fingers

found the perfect spot to make everything even more intense.

"Ronan."

"What?"

"Stop."

He shook his head. "No."

"Please."

"Tell me what you want then."

"You. Inside me. No more teasing."

"Are you keeping your hands to yourself?"

"What about the handcuffs," she teased.

"Move." She shook her head. "Katie."

"Why?"

"Because I'm grabbing them out of my pocket." He smirked and slid them out of his pocket and almost laughed.

"You still want them?" She slid up against him and he shook his head.

"More," she said as he kissed her and she felt him lock her hands behind her back.

"Ronan." He kissed her and she went to get up.

"And where are you going?"

"Undo the jeans and I'll tell you."

"Nope." He kissed her again, grabbed her hands and pulled her tight to him. "Tell me what you want," he said.

"I want you naked."

"Not enough. She kissed him and he went back to teasing her.

"Ronan."

"I'm gonna keep teasing until you tell me what you really want. You want me to bend you over the table, I will. You want me to do it like this until you can't take anymore, I can. Say it Katie."

"Naked then I want you inside me."

"Katie."

"Over the table then I want you to do the thing with the toy," she said with shaky breath.

"You sure that's what you want?"

Katie nodded and he stood her up, sliding the lacy thong off and throwing it onto the pile of clothes.

He bent her over the table and slid his jeans and boxers off. "Katie."

"What?"

"Are you sure?"

"No, but if you want..."

"Katie, we're not doing it if you don't want to. I'm not that person and you know it."

"I just want you inside me." He kept teasing and then kneeled down and started licking and nibbling and teasing until her legs were shaking. He got a grin ear to ear, and she was almost moaning. "Ronan."

"Yes love."

"Please." She leaned her body against him, and he slid deep inside her, over and over.

"That what you wanted," he teased as he went harder and deeper and started to speed up.

"Mm. Yes."

"Katie." His hand slid to her backside and his thumb slid inside her as she made a deep moan.

"Turning you on even more," he teased.

"Ronan, more." He kept going until he could feel her throbbing. Her body giving into him. He unlocked the handcuffs, and she put her hands down to prop her up.

He kept going, feeling her body tighten around him more than once until she was moaning and he could feel her legs shaking.

"More," Ronan asked.

"My legs." He kept going until he exploded into her and she crumbled beneath him into the pillows.

"I'm not done with you yet," Ronan said.

"What else are you gonna do," she asked as he could hear her trying to catch her breath.

"Tell me you want it."

"Depends on what it is."

"Something that isn't gonna be comfortable at first but will definitely feel good."

"No."

"Katie."

"No. Not now."

"Scared?"

"Determined. No Ronan." He leaned onto the pillows beside her and Katie looked at him.

"What lass?"

"Really is that easy with you isn't it."

"Meaning what," he asked.

"I say no and you don't push me into doing something I don't want to do."

"I'm not about to make you do something you don't want to."

"It's just something that I'm not comfortable with."

"I'm not mad Katie." She looked at him and he could tell there was something she wanted to blurt out but was holding back.

"Tell me what's wrong."

She shook her head. "I can't. It'll just ruin the night."

"About him?"

Katie nodded. "Did he make you do..."

"Ronan."

"He did, didn't he?"

"He pushed me into things that I didn't want." He kissed her and leaned into her arms amongst the pillows.

"I'd never force you into anything. You know that right? I mean I'm a control freak, but I'm not gonna force anything. I never have and I never would."

"Even if it's something that you want?" He shook his head.

"You say no then it's done. Not another thought about it." She kissed him. "Now about this sexy lingerie that you keep teasing me with."

Katie kissed him and he tried not to think about it, but at

that exact moment, he wanted to rip Devlin's face off and beat him into pulp. "Ronan."

"Yes love."

"I'd be willing to try it, but not…"

"If you aren't comfortable with it, it's fine. You don't have to make yourself do something you don't want to."

"Maybe." He nodded and kissed her.

"Anyone ever hurts you or lays a hand on you, I'm dealing with them. Is that understood?" Katie nodded and looked up at him. She could tell he was livid, but it wasn't with her.

"Ronan."

"Yes love."

"I know you're mad."

"I'm not mad at you. I'm pissed at him. You know that right?"

"It's not worth doing anything about Ronan. He's not gonna come around here."

"If I see him, whether we're together or we aren't, I'm kicking his backside to the moon. You do know that right?"

"He's not worth it."

"If he even breathes in your direction." Katie curled up with him.

"That's why I called it off. It's over Ronan."

"Nobody hurts my girl, Katie. Nobody."

"Ronan, I promise you that he's not gonna come near us. We're good just us. Just ignore him." He kissed her, devouring her lips until she forgot all about it...but he didn't.

The next morning, Ronan woke up and carried Katie upstairs to the bed. "Come get in bed," Katie said as he got changed to do a much-needed workout.

"I'll be back up in a little bit."

"Ronan, please." He kissed her and got up, heading into the gym. He slid his earbuds in and warmed up then started on the weights. By the time he was done, he'd punched the crap out of the kickboxing bag and done a long workout that drained him. He walked back upstairs, and she was still curled up in the blankets. "Sexy lass of mine. It's kind of time to get up," he said.

"It's time for you to get back into bed." He smirked and kissed her, and Katie pulled him to her. "Get into bed."

"Love, it's almost 7. I have to be at..."

She kissed him, devouring his lips until she was peeling his shirt and joggers off.

"Now," he asked as Katie got a grin ear to ear.

"Now."

"Katie, we have work remember?"

"I don't." He shook his head.

"I still do." She slid her legs around him, and he shook his head.

"Determined to make me late."

"Determined to get you back in bed." She peeled his joggers off with her feet.

"Please." He shook his head and kissed her.

"Miss me," he asked.

"Yes."

He slid into her arms, kicked his joggers right off and pulled her legs around him. He pinned her hands to the bed and kissed her again. "You sure you want this," he asked. She pulled him closer with her legs.

"I want you. I'd ask you to stay home so we could be in bed all day, but I know you have to work."

He kissed her. "You have me to yourself lass." She kissed him and he smirked. "Tell me what you want love."

"More." He kissed her and felt her hand slide away and slide around him.

"Katie."

"Mine."

"Tell me."

"I want you inside me."

"Then move your hand." He was past being turned on. Way past and when he slid deep inside her and her breath hitched, he smirked. "This what you wanted?" She nodded and he slid inside her all over again. He kept going, harder, faster, deeper until her toes were curling. "Mine," he replied as Katie's body tightened around him.

"Ronan." Her breath sped up and he could feel her heart racing.

"Yes, sexy woman of mine," he teased as he went a little faster until he crashed into her and came. "Had to go and tease didn't you," he joked as he leaned onto his side.

"Stay in bed with me today."

"I have work. Three meetings. I can't."

"Ronan." He kissed her and got up.

"I'm having a shower then I'll make us breakfast," Ronan said as he kissed her.

"Party pooper." He kissed her and got up. He walked into the bathroom, flipped the water on and hopped into the shower. Just as he was rinsing out the shampoo, he felt her hand on him all over again.

"Katie." He felt her warm mouth around him, sucking and licking until he was deep in her mouth.

"Mm."

"Katie, stop." She shook her head and kept licking and sucking. "Katie." She kept going until he had to lean his hands against the wall of the shower so his knees wouldn't give way. When his body gave in and exploded into her mouth, she smirked and swallowed.

"That's what you wanted to do," he asked. Katie nodded and stood up to kiss him.

"Bad girl."

"Yours." He nodded and kissed her, devouring her lips. He slid her under the water and washed her hair for her.

"Ronan."

"What?"

"I kinda need a key if I'm really doing this."

"Downstairs on the kitchen counter."

He rinsed out her shampoo and kissed her, pulling her to him and sliding the conditioner through her hair. He slid under the water and washed up. "Do you mean it," Katie asked.

"It's in a box on the kitchen counter. I was gonna bring it up when I made you breakfast in bed." She kissed him and washed up with a smirk ear to ear.

"When you're done in here, come downstairs." She nodded and after another quick kiss, he stepped out, wrapping a towel around him. He freshened up and went and started getting dressed. He slid his boxers and dress pants on, slid his shirt on and walked downstairs.

By the time Katie walked downstairs, breakfast was ready. He plated it, brought it to the table and handed Katie her coffee. He got his and sat down with her. "You do know at some point, I'm gonna be making you breakfast right," Katie teased.

"If you get up before me."

Katie smirked. "Ronan."

"Yes lass."

"Do you want me to come meet you for lunch?"

"I don't know that you coming to my office is a good lunch plan."

"And why not?"

"Because you can't misbehave at my office. I'm kind of the boss." She smirked.

"Even if I came in that wrap dress that you like to unwrap with the sexy lingerie you love under it?"

"Tempting. We could go out for dinner tonight instead."

"Then I'm moving stuff over today." He nodded.

"Just remember the rule. Leave the panties here."

Katie got a grin ear to ear. It was their normal routine. He teased her until she was practically climbing into his lap then they went home to have mind-blowing sex. Sometimes he'd even pull something out to surprise her with. She loved that feeling. The one that someone loved her regardless of her past. Regardless of the pain she'd gone through. Someone that accepted her just the way she was. It was just another reason why she loved being with Ronan. He had more experience than she did, but he never ever let her feel like she was missing something. The things they'd done would've made a church girl blush tenfold.

"Are you sure I can't talk you into lunch?"

He kissed her, devouring her lips. "While I'd love to sit you on my desk and have my way with you during lunch, I don't know that my assistant would appreciate it."

"She's the party pooper."

He kissed her. As soon as they finished breakfast he cleaned up and poured himself a coffee to go. He handed Katie the key and with one look at the keychain she almost laughed. "What," he teased.

"Handcuff keychain?"

"Thought it was appropriate." Katie smirked and kissed him.

"Question. Should I put my car in the garage?"

He nodded. "I leave before you when we go to work anyway. You have access to a driver now anyway. Anywhere you need to go just call and ask."

"Where's the number?"

"On the side of the fridge. I'll get him to take you to the house."

Katie kissed him. "Thank you handsome." He kissed her forehead.

"Just don't go bringing any guys over alright?" Katie smirked.

"Not even family?" He smirked and shook his head.

"Just warn me on that one."

Ronan headed off and Katie finished getting dressed and headed over to the house to pack up the last of her things. "Are you seriously leaving?"

"You know you wanted the man to move in anyway. I'm barely ever here. It doesn't make sense for me not to move over there."

"I mean, are you sure about him?"

"Never been more sure. He's a good guy."

"Just promise me that if you run off and get married you tell me."

"Who else would I tell Sara? I don't think we've thought that far ahead yet. We're just getting closer. I love him. He told me he loves me too. Why would I not want to be there?"

"Just make sure you take your time Katie. Don't jump in with both feet then expect a life preserver."

"I'm good. Now, about my chair," Katie said as she tried to figure out how she'd get it to Ronan's.

Ronan came back from work to see Katie in a sexy dress and barefoot in the sitting room. "Nice chair," he teased.

"You did tell me to bring whatever I wanted to," Katie said.

"This mean that everything is here?" Katie nodded and he smirked.

"Everything that I went to the house with short of the bed is here."

"We do have an extra room if you wanted to bring it," Ronan said.

"Honestly, it needs a new mattress anyway. Sara said she'd keep it for me since I probably won't need it."

"I'd say you wouldn't," Ronan teased.

"So, where did you decide we're going for dinner?"

"Well, Kian messaged. He wanted us to pop by the pub tonight. Mia wanted to talk to you."

"I thought we were going tomorrow."

"We are."

"Then we get the rest of tonight to be here together. We'll

go to the pub tomorrow." He smirked.

"What?"

"Getting the idea of tonight I see."

"I am a little overdressed for the pub." He kissed her and went to call the driver.

"What are you doing?"

"We're not driving."

They made their way to the restaurant and Ronan had a smirk ear to ear. "What," Katie asked as they sat down at the chef's table like they did on their first real date.

"Ronan."

"You loved it. I had to," he teased as the chef came over.

"Welcome back you two."

"Thank you," Katie said.

"Ronan. How's the world traveler doing," the chef asked.

"Busy as always. Are you coming to the pub on Sunday?"

"For a little bit. I can't stay long. I want to see the game for once," the chef said.

"We'll save you a spot at our table," Ronan replied.

"Thank you. I'll get the wine brought over. Special menu tonight," the chef said as he walked back into the kitchen.

"Had to come back here," Katie said.

"This was our first date. Only seemed fitting to come back now that you're moved in."

"There's so many other restaurants we could've gone to though. Why here?"

"Because the food is good." He kissed her and the wine came.

"Thank you," Ronan said as they had their wine and talked. After another amazing dinner, they headed back to the house to see a car in the roadway.

"Who's that," Katie asked.

"No idea and honestly, I don't care. Come inside lass."

Fact was, whoever was parked outside his place knew that Katie was there. Ronan had never seen the car before, but he had a bad feeling. One that said her past was coming to haunt her. If it was who he thought, he'd wipe the floor with him and eliminate the problem. If it wasn't, he was making whoever it was go away.

They headed inside and the minute they were through the door, Katie was on edge. "What's going on," Ronan asked.

"Nothing. I think I'm just tired from moving everything today."

"Katie."

"I'm okay," she said.

"You aren't okay lass. Talk to me."

"I think it's my ex's car."

"Then I'm going to handle it."

Katie shook her head. "Just leave it. He'll go away."

"If he doesn't, I'm walking out there and dealing with him my way."

"Ronan." He kissed her and walked upstairs.

"You aren't serious." He nodded.

Katie slid the dress off and went and slid into the sexy silky lingerie that he'd picked out. He went and slid his dress pants off, slid his shirt off and slid into bed.

"Ronan, I can see it all over your damn face. You aren't going out there."

"I meant it. He comes near you, I'm kicking his backside."

"So, I take it you are totally not in the mood," Katie teased.

"Just come here." He curled her into his arms and snuggled her to him. He kissed her and devoured her lips.

"What's wrong," Katie asked.

"Just thinking about you."

"What about?" He kissed her again.

"I'm glad you're here."

"Ronan."

"Just come get some rest. Kinda didn't end the way I planned today." Katie kissed him and they curled up together, falling asleep an hour or so later while they talked about everything.

The next night, they went down to the pub as planned. Katie in her jeans and a sweater, and Ronan in his jeans and tee. "You know, you've been on edge ever since that car showed last night."

"Did you recognize it?"

"It could've been anyone Ronan."

"Is it his car?"

"Looked like it but how would he even know that I was living with you? It doesn't make any sense."

"You told me that he wasn't a good guy. If I was a psycho like you say he was, I would want my control back."

"Let's just hope it wasn't him."

They walked into the pub and Ronan saw his ex with a random guy. Nobody important, or so he thought until Katie's nails dug into his arm, and she pulled him close. "Katie."

"Ronan, just come and sit."

"Is it him," Ronan asked.

"Just leave him alone. Hopefully he'll leave." Ronan went and sat down with Kian and Mia and took a deep breath.

"He comes near you and I'm handling him," Ronan said.

"Who's butt are we kicking," Kian asked.

"Her ex is here with the devil."

Kian looked at him. "You get up, I get up," Kian said. When Katie's ex Devlin started walking towards the table, Ronan got up and so did Kian.

"Just sit Ronan. Please," Katie said.

"So, you're the loser that decided to take up with my sloppy seconds," Devlin said.

"Outside," Ronan said.

"Coming to take my girl back," Devlin replied.

"Outside now," Ronan said as he stood between Katie and Devlin.

"Your girl is spoken for Ronan."

"Mine. I highly doubt that since she's living with me," Ronan said.

"She was never worth the effort anyway," Devlin said.

"Outside," Ronan said.

"Why?"

"I said outside," Ronan repeated. Devlin walked outside and the minute that Declan and Kian closed the door, Ronan threw a punch and knocked Devlin to the ground.

"You think beating up on a woman and forcing her into things is how a man should be? You want to hurt someone, go ahead and try to hurt me. You'll end up in emergency. Stay away from here, stay away from Katie and leave Anna alone. She doesn't need scum like you around her."

"Ronan," Anna said.

"Not a good time Anna," Ronan said as he had his foot on Devlin's chest.

"You're fighting for me?"

"I meant it scumbag. Leave Katie alone." When Devlin went to get up, Kian threw a punch and knocked him out completely.

"So you do miss me," Anna said.

"Not even if you were the last woman on earth. I have the lass I want and he's not getting in the way, and either are you," Ronan said as he walked back inside.

To be continued.......